D0983693

ALSO BY VLADIMIR VOINOVICH

———

THE LIFE AND
EXTRAORDINARY ADVENTURES OF
PRIVATE IVAN CHONKIN
(1977)
THE IVANKIAD
(1977)
IN PLAIN RUSSIAN
(1979)

PRETENDER
TO THE THRONE

VLADIMIR VOINOVICH

PRETENDER TO THE THRONE

THE FURTHER ADVENTURES OF PRIVATE IVAN CHONKIN

TRANSLATED BY

RICHARD LOURIE

FARRAR STRAUS GIROUX

NEW YORK

Russian text first published under the title
ПРЕТЕНДЕНТ НА ПРЕСТОЛ

copyright © 1979 by YMCA-Press, Paris
Translation copyright © 1981
by Farrar, Straus and Giroux, Inc.
All rights reserved
Published simultaneously in Canada
by McGraw-Hill Ryerson Ltd., Toronto
Printed in the United States of America
Designed by Cynthia Krupat
First printing, 1981

Library of Congress Cataloging in Publication Data
Voinovich, Vladimir.   /   Pretender to the throne.   /   I. Title.
PG3489.4.I53P713   1981   /   891.73'44   /   81-3137   /   AACR2

AUTHOR'S FOREWORD

The author requests that anyone who takes it upon himself to compare the facts cited herein with those in general knowledge or as described in specialized works should bear in mind that this is not a work of strict scholarship and should be used as historical source material only with some caution. Perhaps what actually occurred was somewhat different or even something else entirely. Much time has passed since the events described here, and if the truth be told, a fair amount has slipped the author's memory.

PART 1

1

To the Director AES.* "Badge of Honor" Prison† No. 1, Com.
Timofeyev, S. P.
For the washing of prisoner Chonkin, I. V., I hereby request
that you order issuance of 20 grams of laundry soap.

Sen. Warder Potapov

To the Warehouse Manager of the MSS,‡ Com. Kudeyarovoi
In accordance with the order of the
CENADMINCORRLABINST§, ‖ VX14–67–31–b "Concerning
certain changes in the provision of food and material supplies
to persons held in prisons and investigational isolation
(INVESOL)," 15 grams of liquid soap are to be issued for
the washing of prisoner Chonkin.

Timofeyev

To the Manager of Bathhouse No. 1., Dolgov District,
Commecon, T. Frukt
I hereby request you provide prisoner Chonkin with sanitary
treatment and for that purpose no less than 8 (eight) tubfuls
of lukewarm water are to be issued.

Dir. AES "Badge of Honor" Prison
Timofeyev

° AES—Administrative Economic Section.
† Prison is prison.
‡ MSS—Material Supply Section.
§ CENADMINCORRLABINST—Central Administration, Corrective Labor Institutions.
‖ The names of institutions, sections, subsections, special services, geographical points,

CERTIFICATE

Chonkin, I. V., has undergone sanitary treatment.

Bathhouse Manager S. Frukt

INVENTORY OF PROPERTY IN CELL NO. 34
"BADGE OF HONOR" PRISON NO. 1

1. Common wooden bunks—3 tiers
2. Common wooden stool—1 unit
3. Wooden sewerage vessel (latrine bucket)—1 unit

Sen. Warder Potapov

N O T E : Persons guilty of premeditated damage or negligent damage or other acts which could cause damage to socialist property will be held responsible under the laws of wartime.

To Troop Unit Commander Field Post No. 249814
Urgent. Secret

Outgoing No. 2–00–44

On September 4 Private Chonkin, I. V., serving in your unit, was arrested in the village of Krasnoye on suspicion of desertion. Upon arrest a Mosin rifle (model 1891/30) and ammunition in the amount of 4 cartridges were confiscated. I hereby request you to inform us immediately when and under what circumstances the accused fled his unit, enclosing as well his personal file.

VRIO Chief of the Institution
Post Office Box 7–BTS No. 86/312
Lt. Special Services Filippov

To VRIO Chief of the Institution, P.O. Box 7–BTS No. 86/312
Lieutenant Filippov
Urgent. Secret. By Special Courier   *Outgoing No. 16*
In response to your inquiry (outgoing No. 2–00–44), I hereby
report that Private Ivan Chonkin was dispatched to the village
of Krasnoye to perform guard duty and protect airplane
No. 634805321, which had suffered damage and completed a
forced landing in the environs of the above-indicated settlement
point. He had in his possession a Mosin rifle model 1891/30
and cartridges in the amount of 20.

As a result of the perfidious attack of Fascist Germany on the
Soviet Union, this unit was assigned to shift its base at once to
a sector where hostilities were occurring. In view of the
impossibility of recalling Private Chonkin in time to his service
post, he was listed among those missing in action. Meanwhile,
an authoritative commission consisting of Lt. Colonel Opalikov,
K. M. (Chairman), Tech Captain Kudlai, Yu. I., and Sen. Motor
Mechanic Sergeant Cheburdanidze, A. G., having studied the
relevant documents, reached the conclusion that the
above-mentioned aviational equipment should be written off in
view of the total incapacitation of its aero- and motor functioning
(report of the in absentia technical analysis is enclosed).

With complete faith in the organs of investigation, the unit
command requests that we be informed of the final decision
in the case of Chonkin, I. V.

> *Commander Military Unit*
> *Field Post No. 249814*
> *Lt. Colonel Pakhomov*

PERSONAL FILE
Private Chonkin, Ivan Vasilyevich, year of birth 1919.
Russian, single, non-Party. Elementary education not completed.
Entered service in military unit No. 249814 in November 1939,
performing duties of driver. During his period of service he
distinguished himself by his lack of discipline, sloppiness, and

careless attitude toward his duties. For frequent infringements of the military code and for failure to observe the Regulations of the Red Army he has been disciplined 14 times (subsequently expunged from his file).

Possessing a poor education and a limited outlook, he manifested passivity during classes in political training, did not keep careful notes, had a poor grasp of current political questions and of the theoretical positions of scientific Communism.

Took no part in social-political work.

Politically solid, morally stable.

> *Commander MUFP No. 249814*
> *Lt. Colonel Pakhomov*
> *Unit Commissar Sen. Pol. Instr. Yartsev*

To the Chief of Administration NKVD of the N Region,
Lt. Colonel S/S Com. Luzhin, R. G.

In response to your inquiry (outgoing No. 014/209), I report that the warrant for the arrest of Chonkin, I. V., accused of desertion, was, on the basis of a statement signed "Resident of Krasnoye," issued by the former chief of our Institution, Captain Milyaga, A. S., and approved by the District Procurator, Com. Evpraksein, P. T.

At the time of arrest, the accused, with the cooperation of his cohabitant, Belyashova, A., showed armed resistance, as a result of which Sergeant Svintsov was seriously wounded.

Arriving at the scene at a later point, Captain Milyaga therewith fled and perished under circumstances as yet unclear.

At the present time, the criminal has been captured and is being held under arrest in cell No. 34 of "Badge of Honor" Prison No. 1, in the city of Dolgov. Request further instructions.

> *Lieutenant S/S Filippov*

2

"Come on, keep going!" the lower bunks called up.

"More?" Chonkin thought a moment.

All cell 34 was eagerly awaiting the continuation of his tale.

It was after lights-out. Chonkin was lying on a middle bunk between a criminal, Vasya Shtikiny, known as the Bayonet, and Pan Kalyuzhny, an elderly man with a drooping mustache.

Chonkin was trying to collect his thoughts, but the other prisoners were rushing him, confusing him, shouting from above and below: "C'mon, dead meat, don't give birth to a calf!"

"All right, then," he said, adjusting the overcoat under him. "So I'm sitting there in the cockpit with the machine gun, Nyura's swinging the tail back and forth, the bottles are flying, and they're shouting: Give up! But how can I surrender? I can't. I'm at my post, I'm not allowed to. Then all of a sudden something flashes and my head starts swimming and everything feels so nice. That's all I remember, because the next thing I'm lying there like a dead man."

The whole cell was hushed as if in homage to Chonkin's memory and Pan Kalyuzhny, who was lying on his back, crossed himself quickly and said softly: "May he rest in peace."

"So then," continued Chonkin after a moment's silence, "I come to again, my belly's rumbling, my head feels like it's somebody else's, I open my eyes and in front of me I see . . ."

"The devil himself," prompted someone from the bunk below, who was shushed at once.

"Not the devil," corrected Chonkin. "A general."

"Ha-ha, a general." Laughter broke out above. "You sure it wasn't a field marshal?"

"Shut your trap!" someone shouted.

"And keep it shut," said Chonkin. "Well, anyway, I didn't believe it at first either and I said, Nyura, that's a general there. So then he says to me, That's right, son, he says, I am a general. So I get up, my brains are buzzing, but I straighten my cap like you're supposed to and I salute." Chonkin raised himself on one elbow, and as if bringing himself to attention in front of an imaginary officer, he bellowed out to the entire cell: "Comrade General, during your absence there were no incidents." Chonkin's tone softened and, imitating the general in a weary, even somewhat elderly voice, he said: " 'Thanks for your service, son.' And then he took off his . . . his . . .'"

"Pants," prompted someone from a lower bunk.

"Fool." Chonkin was offended for his general. "Not his pants but a . . . a round thing . . . a medal, that's it."

Bayonet stirred where he lay, rose a bit, and leaned over Chonkin. "A medal?" he repeated in disbelief.

"A medal," confirmed Chonkin.

"What kind?"

"That . . . that red one . . .'"

"The red banner?"

"That's it, the banner."

Bayonet put his hand, its index finger crooked, up to Chonkin's nose. "Unbend it."

"What's this?" Chonkin said, expecting a dirty trick.

"Go on, unbend it."

"What for?"

"Unbend it. Don't be afraid."

Shrugging his shoulders, Chonkin unbent the finger. Not knowing this simple joke, Chonkin could not understand why everyone laughed when Bayonet farted.

"What a bragger," said Bayonet. "Generals, medals."

"You don't believe me?" said Chonkin, offended. "Here's the little hole it made, right here."

"Got caught on a nail," said Bayonet.

"Bayonet!" they called to him from below. "Can it, will you, stop bothering him. C'mon, Chonkin, don't let him get to you."

"You guys!" said Chonkin, with a wave of his hand.

His feelings hurt, Chonkin fell silent. Getting up on all fours, he took his time fussing with his overcoat, which lay in the narrow space between Bayonet and Pan Kalyuzhny. The other prisoners kept calling to him, promising not to interrupt him anymore; they pleaded, but he wouldn't give in, he remained silent, thinking. He hadn't known that defending your post was anything so special. Now, from the interest and the disbelief of his audience he realized that he had done something special, something even in its own way outstanding. But still some didn't believe him, and there was nobody to back him up.

It was quite a mixed group in the cell. One individual, who for some reason had a woman's name, Manyunya, said to Chonkin: "For desertion you get the max, they shoot you."

"Manyunya!" shouted Solomon the Orientalist (the most remarkable professions were to be found in Dolgov prison), "stop trying to scare him."

"I'm not trying to scare him," objected Manyunya. "I'm saying that if you desert, it's the max. Let's say he went AWOL, or suppose he lagged behind his echelon, well then maybe they'd limit it to a penal battalion. But desertion, and resisting arrest on top of it, no way you don't get the max . . ."

Manyunya stopped talking and thought for a moment, "On the whole, we've got humane firing squads now. Not like it used to be. They used to bring you out to the courtyard, to a rifle squad, a prosecutor, a doctor. They'd read the sentence, blindfold you, then give the order—Squad, ready! Horrible. It's not at all like that now; now it's more humane. Say they're taking you to the bathhouse, and on the way, one bang in the back of the head and that's it. Ooooo," he yawned. "Time for some sleep."

The prisoners were still twisting and turning on their bunks, talking things over, swapping jokes. Cheishvili the Georgian was telling how he had once lived with two women, both singers. Another voice was detailing a long and boring story which had no point other than that it was about a Russian, a Jew, and a Gypsy.

"Whenever I feel bad," said Zinovy Borisovich Tsinubel, a former professor of Marxism-Leninism, "I always read Lenin."

"That makes you feel better?" someone asked.

"Your irony is wasted," responded Tsinubel. "Someday you'll understand that the answers to all questions are to be found in Lenin."

"What are you in for, pop?" Chonkin asked Pan Kalyuzhny.

"Who the hell knows. For some kind of Trotskyism," answered Kalyuzhny lightheartedly.

"Been in long?"

"Since '34. Except before, I was in for theft, swindling, and vagrancy, but now it's for Trotskyism."

"Wish you were free again?" asked Chonkin.

"Free?" said Kalyuzhny in surprise. "No. What's so good about life out there?"

"What?" Chonkin was startled. "What do you mean, what's good about it out there? Out there . . . well . . . the sun's shining, the birds are singing."

"And what do you need birds for, so they can crap on your head?"

Chonkin was at a loss and didn't know what to answer.

"That's what everybody says, freedom, freedom," said Pan Kalyuzhny. "Think about it, nobody needs it. Look, this morning they woke you up and brought you gruel. A lot, a little, the point is, they bring it. And when you're free who brings you stuff? No one, that's who. I don't have a wife, but my sister writes me letters. This one fell in front of a train, that one died from drinking, this one drowned, that one died some other way. And this is peacetime, mind you. Wartime's even worse. There's bombs, bullets all over the place. It's better in jail. Look at the people you've got in here, a whole faculty of professors! All that's left out there is the scum of the earth, I swear to God!"

Pan Kalyuzhny went on for some time, demonstrating to

Chonkin the advantages of prison life, then suddenly broke off in the middle of a word and began snoring.

Chonkin turned over onto his other side, facing Bayonet, brought his knees up to his chin, and covered himself with the free side of his overcoat. He lay still for a while but felt uncomfortable. His back was covered, but his front was not, and there was a draft on his chest. He shifted onto his back and tried to pull both sides of his coat over him, but again there wasn't enough to cover all of him. He moved onto his left side and wrapped his coat around him from the front, but now his back froze. While he was turning back and forth, the bottom of his coat had gotten bunched up and he had to crawl around on all fours again, incurring the displeasure of both Pan Kalyuzhny and Bayonet.

Chonkin had never thought himself the least bit spoiled, but now, to his own surprise, he discovered that the time he had spent with Nyura had made him soft; he had grown accustomed to down pillows, feather beds, quilts. And here it was cold, cramped, and hard.

Prize-winning romantic poets have composed no few lyrics about the Russian soldier's overcoat, as if there could be nothing more wonderful than to sleep wrapped in one. This is best done on snow or, in an extreme case, when it is raining, but the main thing is that the coat be wet, bullet-pierced, and singed in battle. To sleep wrapped in such an overcoat is considered especially romantic. Well, romantic, maybe so; but comfortable, absolutely not.

Chonkin tossed and turned and somehow or other gradually found the right spot; all scrunched up, he was now reconciled to hard reality, knowing that no matter how poor an overcoat was for sleeping, bare boards were worse. Used to it now, he fitted his cheek against his turned-up sleeve and fell asleep all doubled up.

No sooner had he fallen into oblivion than at once—perhaps

not quite at once, perhaps some time did pass—he dreamed that he was not doubled up on a slat bunk wrapped in his army coat but that he was in a feather bed under a quilt with Nyura. Nyura lay beside him, exuding heat like a stove and an appetizing marmalade-like aroma, Chonkin stretched languorously toward Nyura, snuggled up against her, lay his hand on hers, then moved it lower, while his other hand was already fumbling in the same area from the other side. Then, grabbing hold of everything he had hands enough for, Chonkin flared with uncontrollable desire, his breathing grew deeper, faster; he flung himself on Nyura with a snarl and bit her like a spider.

He did not understand why she resisted him, why she kept shoving him away with her hands and knees—she always liked it as much as he did.

Chonkin tried to overcome her resistance, but she grabbed him by the throat; he woke up and saw Bayonet in front of him.

"We got another faggot in here," hissed Bayonet, spitting. "What are you climbing on top of me for, you scum?"

The other prisoners woke up and began stirring on their bunks. From up above someone asked what was going on, and another voice answered lazily: "The new guy tried to screw Bayonet."

"Aha," responded the first voice without any surprise; clearly everyone there was used to everything.

Chonkin shook his head groggily, stared at Bayonet without understanding what was going on, and when he understood he felt ashamed of himself.

"I was dreaming about Nyurka," he explained, and turned on his other side to avoid a repetition of the problem. Bayonet turned his back to Chonkin as well and muttered for quite a while until he fell asleep.

And again, strange as it may seem (but really what's so strange about it?), Chonkin dreamed of the feather bed, the pillow, the quilt, and Nyura. Remembering in his dream that embracing Nyura had just cost him some sort of trouble, this time Chonkin lay without moving for a long while, but the aroma of Nyura's body and the waves of heat coming from her made him drunk and giddy again; he reached out timidly for her, then more boldly; this time she offered no resistance and reached for him. Then their bodies met, they pressed up against each other, his hands ran over her, pressing and kneading her, and her hands did the same to him, and though she seemed somehow bony and rough to him, he threw himself on her, sinking his lips against hers. She kissed him, breathing heavily, passionately whispering to him in Ukrainian for some odd reason: "Do you want me?"

"I want you! I do!" sighed Chonkin.

Wild with desire, he chewed her lips, licked her tongue, and only her mustache hindered and annoyed him.

"Why do you have a mustache?" he asked, puzzled.

"To prickle you with." Nyura giggled in confusion. Chonkin opened his eyes and before him saw the repulsive face of Pan Kalyuzhny, who, kissing him long and hard, was pulling Chonkin's head toward him with one hand while, with the other, he was fumbling at a part of Chonkin Chonkin never let anyone except Nyura touch.

"What are you doing?" mumbled Chonkin, shoving Kalyuzhny's insistent hand away. "You nuts?"

"Shh, quiet," whispered Kalyuzhny fearfully. "You'll wake everyone up."

"Who are you climbing on?" said Chonkin angrily. "For what?"

"Screw you." Now it was Kalyuzhny's turn to be indignant. "Who needs you. First you start with one guy, then you switch to another."

Once again the upper bunks stirred and someone asked what was going on. And once again someone said that the new guy had tried to rape Pan Kalyuzhny.

—13—

"He'll be up here after us soon," conjectured the first voice, though quite without enmity.

Vexed beyond measure, Chonkin climbed down and sat on a stool in the middle of the cell, where he remained until reveille, fidgeting, his head bobbing up and down.

3

After breakfast a sleepy guard entered the cell and poked Chonkin with his finger.

"You!" he said, and then to another prisoner, "You too, out!"

"With our things?" asked the other prisoner, bustling about the cell. He was a small, feeble man with two upper teeth missing.

"Just you and your fleas," said the guard amiably. "When it's you and your stuff, we call you by name."

He led the two of them to the latrine, rather grandiose premises with two dozen holes in its cement floor.

"I'll give you forty minutes to clean it up," said the guard. "Pails, mops, and rags are in the corner."

With these words he left. Chonkin and his co-worker stood facing each other, neither rushing to work. The sharp smell of chlorine and stale urine dizzied them and made their eyes water.

Chonkin's co-worker, as we have already said, was a short man, perhaps even shorter than Chonkin, although Chonkin himself was hardly a giant, as the reader, no doubt, remembers. But his co-worker held himself erect, shoulders back, his narrow chest thrust forward. Though he was short his head was large, with a jutting jaw and intent, unblinking eyes.

His smile was so unexpected it startled Chonkin. Smiling at him, the little man slowly slid his hand into his pocket as if he were going to pull out a pistol; but it was a tarnished metal cigarette case that he withdrew. He pressed a button and the lid clicked open, revealing its contents, Kazbek cigarettes.

"Please," he said, extending the case to Chonkin.

Even more confused, Chonkin reached into the case, fumbled for some time with clumsy fingers, until he finally slipped a cigarette out from under the elastic. He scrutinized it closely, a small miracle—even in his days as a free man he had never seen a cigarette like that up close.

They lit up. Chonkin held the cigarette between his thumb and forefinger, whereas the other man held his like an intellectual, between his index and middle fingers. Inhaling with gusto and exhaling a series of matching smoke rings, he smiled at Chonkin again and said: "Allow me to introduce myself. Zapyataev, Igor Maksimovich, Latin spy."

Chonkin looked curiously at him but said nothing.

"You don't believe it?" The spy grinned. "But I believed you at once. Because my story, which is completely real, sounds much more fantastic than yours. Yes, that's right, don't be surprised. You, for example, how many of them did you wipe out?"

"Them?" repeated Chonkin. "Who's them?"

"I was thinking of Bolsheviks, who else?"

"Bolsheviks?" Chonkin again failed to understand.

"Listen, Chonkin"—Zapyataev grew excited—"I'm not interrogating you, why play dumb with me? Last night you were telling us how you fought an entire regiment. Was that true or not?"

"Why should I lie?" said Chonkin, his pride hurt.

"I'm not saying you lied. I believe you. That's precisely why I am asking how many Bolsheviks you wiped out."

"Not a one."

"Oho," said the spy, gladdened. "That's just what I'm driving at. You had a machine gun, a rifle, a few pistols, you fired— but you didn't kill anyone. Why not?" He looked over at

Chonkin, squinting a little, shaking his head slightly, his face showing that the answer was perfectly clear but that he wanted to hear it from Chonkin. "Why not?"

"I missed," said Chonkin, embarrassed to have been such a dunderhead.

"There, you see!" said Zapyataev with satisfaction. "Not a one. You missed. And what if you hadn't missed, how many could you have killed? One, two, three, a dozen at most. Now me"—he transferred his cigarette from his right hand to his left, bent over abruptly, and then, like a conjurer, withdrew a small object from his pants leg, the stub of an indelible ink pencil.

"There," said Zapyataev triumphantly and shook the stub over his head. "There it is, a contemporary weapon even more terrible than machine guns and artillery shells. I treasure this like a sacred relic. It deserves the place of honor in a museum. With this apparently harmless object I disrupted and annihilated a regiment, a division, maybe even an army."

Chonkin looked carefully at the stub, then at the fragile Zapyataev. A psycho, he thought with a chill.

"You don't believe me, do you?" Zapyataev smiled understandingly.

"I believe you, I believe you," said Chonkin in haste. Taking his last drag, he ground out the butt and walked over to a corner where there were two pails and several mops.

"No, listen to me," clamored Zapyataev, grabbing Chonkin's sleeve.

"Later." Chonkin selected a mop that looked a bit better than the rest, picked up a pail, and walked over to a water tap in another corner.

"Listen, will you!" Zapyataev ran after him. "This will interest you."

"There's no time," said Chonkin. "We've got to work." He set the pail, now filled, down on the floor, dipped in his mop, and began whisking it along the wall.

"All right, have it your way." Zapyataev was offended. He put his pencil away, and then he, too, went for a pail and mop.

For a while they worked in silence. Pushing his mop, Chonkin kept glancing over at Zapyataev cautiously, but not without interest.

With his literal imagination he tried to picture little Zapyataev brandishing his pencil stub at a fully armed regiment.

That's really something. Chonkin chuckled to himself.

"Had you listened," said Zapyataev testily, "you would have agreed that there was nothing incredible whatsoever in my story."

"So, all right, go on, tell me," agreed Chonkin magnanimously. He understood that even though Zapyataev might be crazy, he had to be harmless then and there. Chonkin set his mop in front of him and rested his chin on the handle, ready to listen.

"All right, then," he said triumphantly. "Here, in short, is my background. I come from the Petersburg nobility, not a particularly distinguished family, but a well-to-do one. We had a house with footmen, governesses; we even had our own automobile before the Great War. I was a high-school student, a *cadet*, a second lieutenant in Wrangel's army. When everyone fled I remained behind to continue the battle against the Soviet government, which I hated even more then than I do now. I moved to Moscow and invented a proletarian past for myself. I frequented various circles, seeking kindred spirits, but without success. Of course I did run into all sorts of riffraff, but that was hardly what I was looking for. Some of them wrote abstruse little poems, some smoked hashish, others were attracted to orgies and spiritualism. There were also the type who mimeographed pitiful proclamations and were preparing for a military coup with a couple of rusty pistols. Well, of course, sooner or later, where did they all end up? In the Lubyanka. The poets, the spiritists, and the ones with the pistols, too. I realized in time to stay as far away as possible from that sort. No, I did not yield, I wanted to continue the battle, but with whom, and how? I looked around and I saw the soviets growing stronger year by year. There was no real opposition, secret activity was impossible. Universal vigilance, everybody denouncing each other, the Cheka seeing right through everybody. Completely horrible. For serious battle, confederates and an organization are required, but where were they? You couldn't be open with anyone, no one trusted anyone. I gave a lot of thought to the situation, and I'll tell you frankly, I started to despair. If no battle were possible, then why should I remain? To become like all the rest of them and eat obediently from the same trough? And then I made a discovery which, without any false modesty, can be called one of genius. Yes," said Zapyataev, as he broke into merry laughter. "Genius is what it was. I wouldn't call it anything less. Now you"—he hopped away from Chonkin and poked him with his finger—"now you tell me what you consider the true nature, the chief characteristic of the present government. What would it be?"

"Let me see." Chonkin thought a moment. "Well, all in all I'd say it's pretty good."

"Smart." Zapyataev smiled. "But, jokes aside, I'll tell you a secret." He approached Chonkin and, overwhelming him with the smell of his rotted teeth, lowered his voice to a whisper and said: "Remember this once and for all—the basic, principal, and outstanding feature of this government is its trusting nature. Yes, exactly, its trusting nature," he repeated loudly and hopped back away. "Now you're going to say, What?" He made his eyes bulge and dropped his jaw in imitation of Chonkin's likely surprise. "But that's it, my dear Ivan— what's your patronymic, Vasilyevich?—that's precisely it. You will say, What kind of trust can there be when they suspect everyone of everything, when they grab and destroy their main ideologues and supporters on the slightest suspicion! You'll say to me, Trotsky, you'll say Bukharin and Zinoviev, you'll say

Yakir and Tukhachevsky. Yes, of course, the government is suspicious, it doesn't trust its own, but it trusts people like me. And with what sort of trust? Limitless. Unfortunately, I did not make this discovery at once. I wasn't in Moscow then but out here in the provinces. I was working as a petty employee in a certain important institution. So important that even now I am afraid to say its name. Our chief was a certain Rudolf Matveyevich Galchinsky. You don't remember him? Well, he was a well-known Bolshevik, a Civil War hero, a personal friend of Lenin. So devoted, so trusted that he was always abroad. He procured some sort of military equipment, secrets of some sort, and, if I'm not mistaken, was in charge of general demolition activity, that is, preparing for world revolution. A very harmful man. When I made my discovery I first tried it out on that very Galchinsky. I took a scrap of paper, that same stub of a pencil I showed you (it was a little bit bigger then), put a glove on my left hand, and wrote: *During his stay in England Galchinsky was recruited by British Intelligence.* Then I signed it simply, without any to-do, Eagle Eye. So, how do you like that?"

As he told his story, Zapyataev threw his mop aside, waved his arms, asked himself questions, and answered them himself, laughed, and when he winked, one half of his face would go up and the other down as if it were hinged.

"So there I was"—Zapyataev fell silent and shook his head—"my first test ahead of me. The next day at work, on some pretext I went over to our chief's secretary, that charming plump little pig, Valentina Mikhailovna Zhovtobrukh, and paid her an offhanded compliment—'Valentina Mikhailovna, what a pretty jacket you're wearing.' Though she was an un-believable bitch she was still a woman. She blushed, the color rising through the fat. 'Really, you like it?' 'It's beautiful and it suits you very well.' Then, all flushed, she said: 'Rudolf Matveyevich brought it back from abroad for me.' 'From England?' I asked her. 'No, from Belgium. He's never been to England.' 'What?' I said. 'How about that last time?' 'The last time he went to Belgium and Holland. Before that he was in Germany, France, even Canada, but he's never been to England. Why have you turned so pale? What's the matter with you?'

"You can imagine what my feelings were. I was quite beside myself for several days. Somehow I got through the day at work, but at night it was nothing but nightmares. I'd crawl under the covers and tremble, and not figuratively either. I mean tremble. I imagined all sorts of things. A car stops in the street—they're coming for me. A door bangs—they're coming for me. Footsteps on the stairs—they're coming for me. I'm no coward, Ivan Vasilyevich, but I was mortified to tears that it had all turned out so stupidly and on my very first try. But then one day as I went in to work, I walked up the stairs and couldn't believe my eyes: two lugs in uniform and one civilian were escorting our hero—that is, Rudolf Matveyevich himself, no glasses on and pale, pale. I stepped to the side and I even think I said hello to him. But he didn't notice me, and one of the lugs barked at me, 'Out of our way!' I walked up to the reception room, it looked like there'd been a pogrom—desk drawers upended on the floor, papers strewn everywhere, and, in the corner, by the window, Valentina Mikhailovna weeping. Naturally I went over to her. 'Valentina Mikhailovna, what happened?' Her handkerchief sopping with tears she looked sternly at me and said: 'Rudolf Matveyevich has turned out to be a British spy. I can't forgive myself, I was right there beside him and I didn't notice.' Of course"— Zapyataev winked merrily—"I took pleasure in comforting her, saying 'Don't feel too bad, nothing's been proven, you know, everything may straighten out yet. After all, it seems Rudolf Matveyevich was never in England.' At that point she began to screech, 'What does that mean—seems? What does "was never" mean? Don't you trust our security forces?' I had to answer that I did indeed trust them. Some time passed and then in the newspapers, as you may remember, there was a report on the trial of Enemy of the People Galchinsky. The report said that, overwhelmed by the evidence, the accused had fully admitted that during his stay in England he was, he was what? re-cruit-ed.'"

At that point Zapyataev fell silent and began thinking. Deciding the story was over, Chonkin mumbled something on the order of well, sure, things like that can happen. Chonkin returned to his mopping, but Zapyataev stopped him.

"No, listen to what happened next. Overthrowing Galchinsky encouraged me and I realized that I had taken the right course. I bought several notebooks with lined pages and set to work. As soon as some active Bolshevik caught my eye, I'd send out a signal—'recruited by foreign intelligence.' If I spotted some outstanding commander rising in the Red Army, I'd send out my signal. If I noticed some scientist, some new talent on the verge of inventing some unusual machine or causing an unprecedented increase in the harvest, out went my signal. But, you know, nothing could be simpler than making short work of talented people. A man immersed in his science or art does not notice much around him and inevitably commits some folly. He doesn't attend meetings, or, if asked to speak, he attempts to remain silent, and if he does say anything, it's always the wrong thing. To destroy talented people, Ivan Vasilyevich, is the pleasantest and safest of tasks. There he is with his head in the clouds, and suddenly they bring him back to earth and ask him: So, my good man, what are your thoughts regarding, say, leftist deviation or right-wing opportunism? But he, you see, has never given any of that a second's thought. But how can a person fail to think about such things? Now, when contradictions are sharpening, when the entire world situation is complicated and the capitalists are mounting new attacks. Of course, it doesn't work right away, Ivan Vasilyevich, and it's not every man that they drag away to prison. They play with him a while, the way a cat plays with a mouse;

they tell him to go to the tribunal and acknowledge his political errors. But he makes a stand, he wants them to understand him. 'What are you talking about, comrades, I have no interest whatsoever in politics.' Their response is a shake of the head, a warning finger, and a wink. 'Forget it,' they say. 'You're an intelligent person, so then why take us for idiots. We know that a withdrawal from politics is itself political.' And he'll say: 'What do you mean, I never . . .' Another man may start pretending to be brave: 'What is all this, I'm talented, I'm a genius, you can't replace me with just anybody.' And they tell him—'We'll show you a thing or two about replacing you. We'll take the worst idiot around and give him your job.'" At that point Zapyataev began to chuckle, his body shaking, but then, calming back down, he continued: "Ech, Ivan Vasilyevich, when I think of how many outstanding people passed through my hands I feel like crying. Physicists, botanists, writers, sculptors, actors, Party workers—the elite, the cream of society. I used up two dozen notebooks on them. And with practically no misses either. No, say no more, there is no government more trusting in the world. No matter what nonsense I wrote, they believed it. I reported that one man left the house with tears in his eyes on the first day of Bukharin's trial. I didn't say why his eyes were red from tears. Perhaps it was because his wife had hit him with a rolling pin, and not because he was especially sympathetic to Bukharin, but they picked him up. Of another worthy comrade I reported that in an intimate conversation he had spoken negatively. About what? Our climate. He, too, vanished. And so did the person with whom he had been talking. Sure! Is it really possible to speak negatively of our climate?" Zapyataev winked, was carried away by a fit of chuckles. "So, Ivan Vasilyevich, judge for yourself which, in today's world, is the most terrible weapon—a machine gun, artillery, or this little stub of a pencil."

Suddenly the guard appeared and, seeing that the work was not progressing, began threatening both of them with solitary. But two Kazbek cigarettes, one for now, the other behind his ear for later, proved sufficient to mollify him. He withdrew, and Zapyataev, treating Chonkin to another and lighting one himself, continued his tale: "Any criminal, Ivan Vasilyevich, no matter how cunning and clever, gets caught sooner or later. What causes that? Care-less-ness. No, of course, in the beginning he will be careful and wary, and for that reason he escapes punishment, but that itself gradually and inevitably leads to carelessness. That's how it was with me. At first I wrote my so-called signals with my left hand while wearing a glove. I dropped them in mailboxes a good distance from my home and never used the same one twice. I took other precautionary measures and I never got caught. But with time I grew increasingly careless and imprudent. Either I'd forget to put on my glove or I'd be too lazy to bring the letters to mailboxes far from home. And, naturally, it all ended in complete what? Fail-ure. One evening I was walking down the sidewalk on my way home from work when suddenly—a squeal of brakes and someone says: 'Hey, comrade.' I looked around, and at that moment some force tore me from the ground. I think I even did something like a somersault. I came to in the back seat of an MK, sitting between two lugs with hats pulled down over their eyes. Naturally I attempted to protest—where did they get the right? I said, and so forth, but one of them said: 'Sit still and shut up' and I did. To make a long story short, they took me to a gray building. We drove into a courtyard, got out of the car, and went up a flight of stairs to the office of their superior, Roman Gavrilovich Luzhin himself. If you don't know what Luzhin is like, I'll tell you—a monster. Though he was human in appearance. He was sitting at a large desk, a misshapen creature the size of a dwarf, speaking on the telephone in a low voice; it seemed he was even being courteous, smiling, making jokes, but I knew that he would think nothing of having a thousand men shot in one day.

"I stood there more dead than alive. The creature talked a little more on the telephone, hung up, got out of his chair, glided over to me on his short legs and stared right at me. I realized the game was up and that now the main thing was firmness, calm, self-control. I had done my little bit. But still, you know, no matter how much you prepare yourself for the reckoning, when it comes down to it—how can I put this to you—it's never too pleasant. Then, suddenly I hear him say: 'So this is him, this is the legendary Eagle Eye? You've been hiding from us a long time. A monstrously long time.' That was his favorite word—monstrously. 'Now tell us, were you acting alone all the time?'

"For some reason, when he began talking I came immediately to my senses. I felt that I had myself in hand and I answered definitely, boldly: 'That's right, all alone.'

"Then something I could never have expected occurred. His face broke into a broad grin. 'You see'—he nodded at the men who had brought me there—'what a hero this man is. He acted alone.'

"Then they, too, were smiling benevolently, and I heard Luzhin say, 'You shouldn't have acted alone. You worked hard for us and of course we thank you, but the time of Pinkerton men has passed; let's work together, let's join forces, let's struggle together for our Soviet government.'

"I looked over at him utterly baffled. What did he mean—for? I was against, wasn't that obvious? Was he playing dumb? Laughing at his victim? Then he asked yet another absurd question: why hadn't I joined the Party yet? Not knowing what to answer, I mumbled something; he smiled again and supplied the answer himself: 'You consider yourself unworthy?'

" 'That's right.' I grasped at the straw. 'That's right, unworthy.'

"He was pleased. And so were the others.

" 'Modesty,' he said, 'adorns a person, but self-abasement is worse than pride, you know. So what's there to be modest about here. Join, we'll help you.'

"To be brief, he showered me with kindness and buttered me up. There was only one hitch. He asked me about my economic situation and like a fool I went and blurted that I hadn't done it for money, that my motives were quite unselfish.

"Then, for the first time since the beginning of our conversation, he frowned and looked suspiciously at me. I realized that unselfish people were beyond him. I must tell you that I saved myself by making a quick about-face, saying that I had nothing against accepting money, of course.

" 'Yes, yes.' He nodded happily. 'Of course it isn't the money any of us work for, but we are materialists and we don't hide the fact.'

"He promised to help me materially, as they were fond of saying there. He repeated that same phrase many times—'We will help'—then he showed me to the door, where he shook my hand for quite some time. " 'Go back to your work, Comrade Zapyataev. And remember, we need comrades like you.'

"I went back outside, completely stunned. Just an hour before, when they were bringing me there in the car, I was preparing for anything—prison, torture, death, and then . . . I walked along smiling like a fool, 'We need comrades like you' ringing in my ears. Well, I thought, if you need comrades like that . . ."

Zapyataev doubled up and clutched his stomach, trembling slightly as if having a fit. Chonkin was frightened. He thought something had happened to Zapyataev.

"Hey, hey, you all right?" shouted Chonkin, grabbing him by the shoulder. "Something wrong?"

"No," said Zapyataev, shaking, then straightening back up slowly and wiping away his tears on his sleeve. "To this day when I think of it I can't help laughing. No, just imagine," he repeated, poking his chest with his finger, "they need comrades like me . . ."

His laughter had reached the stage of hiccups and convulsions; he tried to go on with his story, but again he began choking with laughter and writhing, poking himself in the chest and repeating the words "comrades like me." Then, he somehow regained control of himself and continued his tale.

After a few visits to Luzhin his work became significantly easier. He no longer had to resort to such pitiful tricks as wearing a glove while writing with his left hand. Now he openly composed whole lists of people who were, in his view, still capable of some achievement and he no longer ran to distant mailboxes with his lists but went bravely to the Right Place (though he did make use of the rear entrance) to hand in what he had written. Even at work things began gradually improving for him. He joined the Party and began to make an impressive career for himself. All he had to do was rise to the next step on the staircase of officialdom for the step in front of him to soon become vacant, though not without a little help from him. Secret strings were pulled and the other contenders would fall away. Zapyataev rose higher and higher.

But the higher he rose, the more frequently he encountered an unexpected problem. The language he spoke differed sharply from that of the new masters of life.

"You understand," he said, spreading his arms apart, "I am a nobleman, after all. From Petersburg. I was raised by a governess. I didn't know how to speak like those guys . . . see, I still haven't lost the habit yet. Back then I simply could not just switch my way of speaking. It was a bit easier with manners. I quickly stopped kissing ladies' hands. I more or less mastered the art of not helping people on with their coats and of barging through doors ahead of everyone else. If someone reminded me of good manners, I had already acquired the habit of objecting that in our society women were equal comrades and could be shouldered aside because they had the right to do the same to us.

"But language was more of a problem. Elementary words like 'please,' 'thank you,' 'be so kind,' caused bewilderment, people looked at me in surprise and I said to myself, This can't go on any longer. You, I said to myself, can pretend to be one of them all you want, you can make it appear that you share their ideas fully, but if you don't learn to speak their language, they will never trust you completely.

"And so, like an anti-illiteracy worker, I sat down to study. Oh, God, what difficult and exhausting work it was! I always had a flair for languages, you know. I was taught French and English as a child. Then I learned German fairly well, could converse in Spanish, and I could even read a little Finnish. But their language . . . our great and mighty Russian language . . . No, you cannot imagine how difficult it was. Some clever chaps laugh at today's leaders and how they pronounce various words. But you just try to speak as they do. I tried. I know what it entails. And so I set myself the task of achieving perfect mastery of that monstrous language. But how? Where were the courses? Where were the teachers? The textbooks? The dictionaries? There was nothing. And so I attended all sorts of meetings, sessions, Party conferences, listened, watched carefully, and took notes; then, later at home I would bolt my doors, stand in front of the mirror, and repeat their absurd locutions in a whisper. Well, I more or less mastered most of the words and could pronounce them fluently, but some of them still made me break into a sweat, dislocate my tongue, and weep from utter helplessness. But I displayed a diabolical persistence and I performed the greatest of feats. When I had mastered the language, certain comrades began to look fondly upon me. Others even tried to imitate me, but not everyone succeeded. Then, thanks to such comrades and my new language, all roads were open to me. Soon I occupied that very post from which I had knocked, knocked who?

Rudolf Matveyevich, that's who. By that time I had married, and whom had I married? Valentina Mikhailovna Zhovtobrukh. I had acquired two children. I was making a career, but I never forgot my main goal. True, I didn't need my little pencil anymore. I was operating on a grander scale. I delivered all the best engineers and industrial designers to my comrades. I did the best I could to ruin the work I supervised. And do you think I was picked up for that? Not at all, I was awarded a medal. They held me up as an example, someone who conducted cadre politics in exemplary fashion. There were plans to transfer me to Moscow. Oh, what a show I could have put on there! But then . . ." Zapyataev grasped his head with both hands and began shaking it. "Then, Ivan Vasilyevich, I did something so stupid that I am even ashamed to tell you about it. As you recall—what caused my rise? The proper use of language. And what ruined me? Language. You know, I don't feel like talking anymore. It's too hard for me. Let's clean up quickly, otherwise the guard will come and yell at us."

"No, he won't," said Chonkin. "Come on, keep going. I'll do the work myself in two shakes."

"All right, then," agreed Zapyataev. "It's painful but I'll finish the story. So," he continued, trying to stand where Chonkin could see him, "one fine day the First Secretary of the District Committee, Comrade Khudobchenko, came to our office on a tour of inspection. On the simple side in appearance, he wore an embroidered Ukrainian shirt, spoke the same language I did, perhaps without my virtuosity, but still he could hold his own. He was also the vigilant sort, always looking for spies, wreckers, and saboteurs in our area. But he had found only two. I'd done my work too well. Comrade Khudobchenko was quite pleased with me. He called a meeting, praised me, held me up as an example to the others, all of which ended, as usual, in a big drinking bout, at state expense of course.

"There was a good crowd there. We drank, we sang 'Rode a Cossack out to battle' (Khudobchenko's favorite song) and danced the gopak. Everyone spoke the same language I did, everyone was doing the same thing I was, that is, clearly and openly inflicting maximal damage on the work we were in charge of, and at the same time, everyone was proud of his worker or peasant origins. Then, suddenly, like an idiot, or from drinking too much, I had the impression that I was in a close circle of intimate, like-minded people who knew as well as I did what they were doing. Suddenly I had a great desire to expose them all, to say, Let's quit pretending, we're all the same here. And had I said that, it would have been a lesser folly than the one I in fact committed. I rose . . . now here, even if you try to imagine what unbelievable folly I committed, even if you have a vivid imagination, you could ponder for three days, but I assure you, you wouldn't imagine anything even close to the truth. I rose and began . . . my tongue doesn't want to admit it . . . and what did I begin reciting? Ver-gil! Bad enough it was Vergil, but in what language? La-tin! Oh, God! Of course I realized at once that I had made a hideous mistake. I had just begun when I saw their faces fall; they exchanged glances, then looked over questioningly at Khudobchenko. I saw that at first he, too, was scowling, but then he began to smile and beckoned me with his finger, like this. Like a dog. I approached him, wagging my tail.

"Khudobchenko asked quite benevolently: 'I was just wondering what you were spouting there.'

" 'Oh, nothing,' I answered, striking the right tone. 'Just a little, you know, Vergil.'

" 'Who?'

" 'Vergil. You really don't know him?'

" 'No, I don't. And what language was that?'

" 'I'm not all that sure myself,' I said. 'Mighta been Latin.'

" 'Oho!' said Khudobchenko in surprise. 'And do you know many other people like this Vergil?'

"Realizing I was in trouble, I gave him some cock-and-bull story about the teacher in our parish school who knew a little Latin and taught it to us.

" 'That he knew some,' interrupted Khudobchenko, 'that's no surprise. He might have been from the bourgeoisie. But that you remembered it, that's something else again. You guys'— he turned to the others—'any of you speak Latin?'

"No one replied, but each face said, Not me.

" 'I don't speak Latin either. No. Because we're all simple country boys here, we only know how to serve our Party, our Soviet government, and how to fight its enemies. And the only thing we ever learn by heart is Comrade Stalin's historical instructions. But Comrade Zapyataev here, he understands Latin, and maybe a few other things, too.'

"Then all the goodwill vanished from his face in one second and it became cold and hard as a frozen brick. I attempted to repair the situation, I even tried to dance the gopak, but after one look, Khudobchenko remarked casually that even my gopak came out Latin-style.

"That very night they dragged me from my bed. Roman Gavrilovich Luzhin himself interrogated me, he broke my nose, knocked out two teeth, and that's how I came to be a Latin spy."

Zapyataev sighed, took his cigarette case from his pocket, treated Chonkin to another Kazbek, and lit one for himself.

"What can you do," he said. "There's no one to blame but myself. And everything was going so well! So well! If I only could have gotten to Moscow, I could have . . . with wartime conditions, what chaos I could have created. But I missed the mark. Still, I know I'm not alone. There're plenty more people like me, they're everywhere. Night and day, together, sep-arately, they do their work, and they are invincible because none of them can reveal himself under any circumstances. And if a fool like me is caught he should be destroyed quickly and mercilessly. So that no one will ever . . ." Zapyataev threw his cigarette away, made two fists, shook them, and was about to burst into tears when the guard appeared in the doorway and asked: "Which one of you is Chonkin? Move out!" he said, stepping aside to make way for him.

4

The suspect under interrogation, Ivan Chonkin, sat on a small stool by the wall to the right of Lieutenant Filippov but at a good distance from him, close to the door. The distance had been determined in the official instructions, which foresaw the possibility of attacks on interrogators. Above the lieutenant's head hung a portrait of Stalin holding a young girl. The young girl seemed to radiate only profound gratitude to Stalin for her happy childhood. On the opposite wall hung a quotation from a speech by Stalin, mounted to look like a colorful poster.

"We must organize a merciless struggle against everyone . . ." read Chonkin and then, tired of reading, he turned his gaze to the window which was directly in front of him. The lower half of the pane had been painted with blistered oil paint; a single short word, one not unfamiliar to Chonkin, had been scratched in the left-hand corner.

Had the upper half of the window been painted instead of the lower half, or had neither been painted, Chonkin would have seen a small dusty square and Nyura standing in the center of it, twisting her mail pouch in her hand.

Just look at the ridiculous things that happen. Nyura and Chonkin are quite close to each other, all that separates them is a partition of wall and glass painted over with white paint. A gaze piercing millions of light-years of space would still be stopped by that thin, thin layer of paint.

Nyura and Chonkin are near each other; after a while she will go where she wants but he will go only where he is taken. Lieutenant Filippov, who was even nearer Chonkin than Nyura, will also go off where he pleases but, before leaving, he will lock Chonkin in his cell the way he locks his papers in the safe.

A cell's walls are thick, perhaps even thicker than need be. But no matter whether thick or thin, that condensed layer of matter separating him from freedom seems absurd to a person. Unable to reconcile himself to this, a man beats his head against the wall like a fly against window glass, but to what end?

There is yet another barrier, one seemingly finer and more transparent than glass. All Lieutenant Filippov had to do was to open his lips, move his tongue, and say just two words, "Release him!" and the walls would part at once, Chonkin would take a few steps and find himself in Nyura's open arms. However, Lieutenant Filippov will never say any such words, Chonkin will not find himself in Nyura's open arms, though all this would seem so easy, so much within reach. His sense of duty commands the lieutenant to be merciless. His sense of duty does not permit the lieutenant to say the two words which would make two people happy. Time will pass, and perhaps other people, also from a sense of duty, will be merciless to Lieutenant Filippov and ask him those same questions he is now preparing to ask Chonkin.

Meanwhile, Chonkin is sitting on the little stool looking out the window whose lower half had been painted white. Chonkin could not see Nyura standing in the square and Nyura could not see him. Chonkin was, however, seen by a crow which had flown up onto the top of a half-shriveled poplar. The crow sat on a branch and squinted indifferently at Chonkin. The crow could not have cared less at whom or at what it looked—a cow, Chonkin, a post. Then, startled, the crow began to flap its wings and, rising slowly, vanished to the left of the window only to reappear right away and land on the very same branch.

While following the crow, Chonkin began to have thoughts. That's how it is, he thought, so many kinds of different creatures in the world. Crows and dogs and turkeys and bedbugs and people and vipers and fish and all sorts of spiders. And every creature lives for something and wants something, but who knows what that something is?

"Last name?"

Startled, Chonkin tore his eyes from the crow and transferred them to the lieutenant, who, his pen poised above a sheet of paper, was looking expectantly at him.

"Whose?" asked Chonkin in surprise.

"Yours," the lieutenant explained patiently, and dipped his pen in the ink.

"Ours?" Chonkin was even more surprised. He thought, presumptuously perhaps, that his last name was known to the lieutenant.

"Yours," repeated the lieutenant.

"We are the Chonkins," said Ivan modestly, and looked at the lieutenant, apprehensive that his answer might be wrong.

"Chonkin with an 'i' or an 'e'?"

"Chonkin with a 'Ch,' " said Chonkin.

The lieutenant's office was quite cheerfully furnished (no comparison with the cell). A tall pot-bellied iron stove, a pre-revolutionary model with a semicircular inscription: *Kaiserslautern Iron Works*, was crackling with heat. Chonkin began to feel warm and drowsy and the lieutenant's questions seemed unnecessary and even irrelevant.

"Year of birth, education, nationality, social origin . . ."

"What was that?" asked Chonkin.

"Your parents, who were they?"

"People, of course," he answered, failing to grasp the point of the question.

"I know they're not cows. What do they do?"

"They're in their graves."

"That is, they are dead?"

Chonkin looked at the lieutenant amazed. Had he lost his mind or something?

"Not alive!" he said, and made a face expressing the greatest possible bafflement.

"Chonkin!" The lieutenant raised his voice. "Stop playing dumb and answer the questions put to you. If your parents are dead, then you should say, Dead."

"But the thing is . . ." As if seeking support, Chonkin glanced over at the stove, then at the portrait of Stalin. "If you asked me how they were, I would have said dead. But you asked me what they do . . ."

"Chonkin! You're not supposed to disagree with me as if we were playing checkers or something, do you understand?"

"I do," said Chonkin.

"All right, then," said the lieutenant. "We'll move on to something else. Tell me, how did you come to be in the village of Krasnoye?"

"How did I come to be there?"

"That's right."

"In the village of Krasnoye?"

"Yes, yes," repeated the lieutenant, now somewhat irritated. "How did you come to be in the village of Krasnoye?"

"As if you didn't know."

"Chonkin!" The lieutenant banged his fist on the table.

"Chonkin what, what Chonkin!" The prisoner was growing angry. "As if you didn't know how a soldier comes to be any-where. The sergeant sent me."

"Which sergeant?"

"Ha, which sergeant." Chonkin spread his arms wide apart and again looked at the stove, Stalin, and the little girl, as if calling them to witness the lieutenant's utter stupidity. What other sergeant could it possibly be?

"It was what's his name," said Chonkin. "Peskov, that's it."

"So it was Sergeant Peskov," repeated the lieutenant, making a note of the name. "We'll verify that. But maybe there was no sergeant, huh, Chonkin?" Filippov gave Chonkin a sly look and a wink. "Maybe you ran away all by yourself? Maybe you decided, let all those dopes defend the motherland, not me, I'm too smart. I'll crawl in with some woman somewhere. Maybe that's how it was?"

"No," answered Chonkin sullenly. "It wasn't."

"And what was your goal in taking up residence with Nyura Belyashova?"

"With Nyura Belyashova?"

"Yes, yes, Nyura Belyashova. What was your goal in taking up residence with her?"

"My goal was to live with Nyurka," explained Chonkin truthfully.

The lieutenant rose and pushed his chair toward the wall with his foot. The interrogation was taking an idiotic turn. The lieutenant was nervous. That very morning he had returned from the district, where Lieutenant Colonel Luzhin had raked him over the coals all night, acidly questioning him about all the details and particulars of the incident in which a detachment under Filippov's command, at full strength, had been captured by a single, poorly armed Red Army soldier.

"A monstrous story," Luzhin had said. "No, I cannot understand it. Something isn't quite right here. You're hiding something from me. Perhaps you did it on purpose, huh?"

"What for?" asked Filippov.

"If I knew"—Luzhin sighed—"I'd have you shot. The only reason I'm not is that I don't want to attract any attention to this case. That's right. Because then they'd start asking me questions. All right, then, for now you may go, but remember, I can change my mind."

"And what should be done with Chonkin?" asked the lieutenant.

"With Chonkin?" repeated Luzhin. "What should be done? Charge him with desertion, then a tribunal. And I don't want to hear his name again. Never. Ever."

Filippov returned to Dolgov at daybreak, sleepless and in a foul mood. He truly wanted to be done with Chonkin as quickly as possible and, to that end, to obtain the required testimony from him, but Chonkin was openly mocking him and playing dumb.

"Well, all right, then," said the lieutenant, approaching Chonkin. "Everything is clear, more or less. Now the only question is how you, a Soviet man from a simple peasant family, could let things get so out of hand and end up in prison. How are we to understand that, eh, Chonkin?"

Chonkin shrugged his shoulders and was about to say that he didn't understand how it had happened either, but he said nothing, because suddenly he saw the muzzle of a revolver aimed directly at him.

"I'm going to shoot you!" howled the lieutenant.

Chonkin flinched instinctively and the back of his head struck the wall.

It suddenly started to feel rather uncomfortable in the room. The revolver smelled of gun oil and death.

"Right now, you bastard, or I'll empty the whole clip in you!" The lieutenant had turned brutal. "I'll shoot you in the mouth, the nose, the liver . . ."

Here, completely helpless, the author must stop. Fearing to offend the reader's sense of decency, he is unable to depict the lieutenant's further speech except as a series of dots; there is no reason to include the few printable words which happened to occur in it for, taken out of context, they would transmit neither the depth, the vividness, nor even the sense in which given expressions were used.

It would seem, though, that there is nothing so drastic here. A new fashion has caught on these days—if a person wishes to use a certain word in his writing, then he uses that very word, some people even compose entire stories and romances from such words, and in the company of such words a decent word looks as indecent as a man in a black suit and tie in a steam bath. This I note in passing.

Sitting on the stool, Chonkin tried to lean away from the revolver. He jerked his head back, striking it against the wall again. The muzzle loomed before his eyes, the image doubling, tripling, and made the bridge of his nose itch unbearably. Chonkin crinkled his face. Meanwhile, his upper lip began riding up on its own toward his nose, baring his widely spaced teeth, complete strangers to a toothbrush.

Red from excitement, the lieutenant's face bobbed back and forth, blocking, then revealing the portrait of Stalin holding the young girl. Stalin was smiling at the girl and squinting one eye sympathetically at Chonkin, as if to say: "You can see that he's not mentally normal, you better not make him angry, don't refuse, just tell him right away how it all was."

Chonkin was not refusing to speak, he was tongue-tied from fear and could not force a single word out. The lieutenant, however, interpreted the prisoner's silence as unheard-of, impudent resistance. If he were somebody important, and not a lunkhead, and were it not for the circumstances, the lieutenant could do whatever he wanted—put him in jail, shoot him, or even simply let him go off into the forest, to freedom, and let him live in a tree like a monkey.

"Stand up! Sit down!" Filippov began to shout. "Stand up! Sit down! Stand up! Sit down!"

Chonkin stood up, sat down, stood up, sat down, stood up, sat down—a familiar routine.

"You going to talk?"

Chonkin said nothing.

"Hands up! Face the wall! You bastard, you know what this means?" He combed the back of Chonkin's hair with the barrel of the revolver and set his knee against Chonkin's butt.

Chonkin knew what it meant. He felt horrible. He pressed

his nose against the wall. He would have liked to fade into the wall and out the other side. But still he said nothing.

The door opened. Out of the corner of his eye Chonkin saw the secretary, Kapa, enter. Not in the least surprised by what she saw, Kapa called the lieutenant off to one corner and began whispering to him, but Chonkin could not make out what she said. All he heard was the lieutenant asking: "And what does she want?" and missed Kapa's reply.

"You see that," said Filippov in loud dissatisfaction. "They never let you work. This one, that one, they keep coming in and bothering . . ."

Lieutenant Filippov went out on the porch of the Institution and saw Nyura standing beneath the tree on which the crow had perched. A brief conversation then occurred between Nyura and Lieutenant Filippov.

Returning to his office, Filippov found Chonkin as he had left him, facing the wall. But even from the close-cropped back of the prisoner's head it was obvious that during the lieutenant's absence he had managed to think through a good deal.

"Turn around!" the lieutenant ordered amiably on the way to his desk. "Sit down!" He nodded at the stool.

Chonkin sat down, wiping his runny nose with his sleeve.

"Well, then, Chonkin, what will it be, are we going to confess straightaway to the crimes we committed and make a clean breast of it or are we going to clam up, and lie?"

Chonkin swallowed and remained silent.

"Chonkin!" The lieutenant raised his voice. "I'm asking you, do you admit that you're guilty of the crimes you committed?" He drew his revolver again and tapped the handle lightly on his desk.

"I admit it," said Chonkin, barely audible, nodding his head submissively.

"There you go!" The lieutenant came to life and made a

quick note in the report. "And of just precisely what do you admit guilt?"

"Of just precisely everything."

"All right, then, sign your name here."

Chonkin signed. His way. He spent a long time drawing the capital "Ch," dipped the pen in the ink, wrote an "o" then dipped the pen again, wrote the "n," until finally his whole last name stretched across the paper. The lieutenant took the report carefully and spent a good while blowing on the precious signature.

"You're a good man," he said. "Want an apple?"

"Why not," said Chonkin with a wave of his hand.

5

When he returned to his cell, Chonkin was questioned by his fellow prisoners. What kind of a naïve dimwit was he anyway, to fold right away and admit to everything?

"I was real scared," answered our excuse for a hero.

Then they said to him: But how come you acted like that now, when you have performed miracles of heroism?

"It was pure baloney," said Bayonet.

"Who? Me?" Chonkin struck his chest with a fist. "If you . . . Just ask the lieutenant. He knows."

"All right." Bayonet waved his hand in a gesture of dismissal. "It's all clear now. You came in here and handed us some baloney about battling a regiment."

Chonkin was suffering. He did not feel bad because he had signed some sort of paper, he felt bad because they didn't believe him. But how were they to believe him after that? All right, had they used some special measures on him, driven needles under his fingernails, squeezed various parts of his body in the door (even though they were wooden doors) he might not have been able to stand it. But they hadn't used any such tricks on him. Sure, they had stuck a revolver under his nose and no one will argue that that's any fun. But a man could stand up to that.

But Chonkin hadn't. He had signed and admitted that while on guard duty he had violated regulations more than once—he had sung, drunk, eaten, smoked, relieved himself, abandoned his post, cohabited with Nyura Belyashova, moved the object he was guarding, breached military dress code (he appeared among the local population in his underwear), engaged in heavy drinking, led an amoral and even licentious way of life; having learned about the outbreak of war, he took no measures to report to his post, and likewise, he had avoided fulfilling his military duty, which was tantamount to desertion.

Thus was deflated the myth of Chonkin, the legendary hero. The author, himself disillusioned, doubts whether it is worth his while to continue the biography of this person. Why disillusioned? Because the author himself had not expected this. Such things do happen, the well-informed reader will say, recalling a certain imaginary lady who, to her author's surprise, went off and married a general. However, marrying a general and signing a confession are two very different things. The author is at a loss. The hand freezes above the paper, the ink dries, the pen will not write. How to react, what to do? How to answer the severe reader? For he is not only severe but *trusting*. All right then, the reader has resigned himself, so this Chonkin is bowlegged and lop-eared, and, as far as mental capacity goes, no academician, but the author must have had some reason in palming off a hero of this sort, and so shouldn't he, if he's to be called a hero, perform some great exploit?

Yes, he should. But he's scared. The greater the exploit, the greater the fear.

6

Authority, as is well known, is hard to earn and easy to lose. Among the inhabitants of cell 34, Chonkin's authority fell so low that no one took any further interest in his feats: his stories were termed pure crap and he was given the nickname of Crapmaster. When the population of the cell doubled and a fight for living space broke out, Chonkin was thrown out of his plank bed and found himself a place on the floor near the crap bucket, which, naturally, contributed to making his new nickname stick.

7

"Oh, Nyurka, oh poor Nyurka, Nyurka, oi!"

"What's the 'oi' for?"

"I don't even want to talk about it. She's wasting away, her face is all sunken, all she does is cry and cry."

"What's she crying about, what?"

"What do you mean, what? They took her husband."

"Phooey. That wasn't her husband. It wasn't even legal."

Taika was asking the questions, Ninka was answering them. Carrying their yokes, they had run into each other on the narrow path to the river Tyopa; Ninka's pails were empty, Taika's full.

"That's what I'm saying—it's not legal," agreed Ninka.

"And what's she doing?"

"Crying."

Taika looked at Ninka, shrugged her free shoulder, spat, and started up the path, even her back expressing bewilderment at how shameless women had become, to cry about men who were not even their legal husbands.

Holding the yoke with one hand and her stomach with the other (she was in her ninth month), Ninka began carefully descending the path. The rain had just passed, the path was slippery, and she kept losing her footing. Standing on the wooden catwalk, Ninka lowered her pails, took a breath, and then began collecting her water, squatting and leaning to one side. She pulled in one pail, reached for the other, and then, after a moment's thought, replied mentally to Taika: "He may not be her legal man, that's true, of course, but still you feel sorry for her."

8

Every morning Nyura went to the square in front of the Institution and stood beneath the very same tree whose top Chonkin had seen from Lieutenant Filippov's office. There she would stand, twirling her mail pouch in her hands, keeping a close eye on the entry door, hoping for God knows what. She could not bring herself to walk up onto the porch and through that door, but, really, what was the point of just standing there?

The workers of the Institution walked past Nyura in the morning and then disappeared through that mysterious door. Nyura knew a few of them, but there were new faces as well. Nyura nodded to those she knew and shouted from a distance: "Hey, how are you?" Some of them would wince, look puzzled at Nyura, and, having muttered something under their breath, keep moving. Others would pass by without even a quiver, as if vibrations of the atmosphere had no influence at all on their eardrums. Despite herself, Nyura was intimidated and could not bring herself to approach such important persons with such a trifling matter as Chonkin.

After lingering for a while under the tree, she would go to the post office, stuff her bag with letters, return to the tree, wait there a bit, and it would be near evening by the time she'd arrive back in Krasnoye. There she would deliver the mail, feed Borka and her cow, Beauty, who'd been hungry all day, and God only knows whether she herself would eat or not. Then came an endless night, and a pillow wet with tears; then the morning and the familiar route to Dolgov and the pointless standing beneath the tree.

There was a little bundle in her mail pouch which contained two dried-up potato pies, five hard-boiled eggs, and a shag-filled tobacco pouch embroidered with pale stitchery: *To Vanya, greetings from Nyura.*

One time luck was with her. As usual she was standing under the tree when a woman wearing boots and smoking a cigarette walked up to her, asked for whom and for what she was waiting, then said, "One minute," and disappeared through the door to the Institution. It was already time for Nyura to be at the post office, but she couldn't let a chance like this slip by. She waited a bit more and then Lieutenant Filippov appeared in that very doorway, wearing a new uniform and well-shined boots. He walked aimlessly, looked up at the sky, stretched, and then, as he lowered his eyes, he noticed Nyura.

"Hello there," Nyura called to him with a friendly smile.

"You're speaking to me?" asked the lieutenant, regarding Nyura as a stranger.

"Yes, you." Nyura nodded and, growing bolder, walked closer to the lieutenant. "How's he doing in there?"

"Who would that be?" asked the lieutenant complacently.

"Vanka, of course," said Nyura credulously, missing the game.

"Which Vanka is that?"

"Chonkin, of course."

"Chonkin, Chonkin . . ." repeated the lieutenant as if racking his brains. He took a cigarette from his pocket and lit up. "Chonkin," he mumbled, wrinkling his brow. "Sounds familiar. What was his first name again?"

"Ivan," said Nyura sadly. She now realized that the lieutenant was kidding her, but she could not answer in the same spirit.

"Ivan Chonkin!" said the lieutenant sonorously, as if trying out the taste of the name. "Seems we do have him. And just what is your relation to him?"

—**43**—

"You know!" Nyura was beginning to grow angry.

"I don't know." The lieutenant smiled benevolently. "Could he be your husband?"

"My husband." Nyura nodded sullenly.

"You and he registered your marriage?"

"I lived with him," said Nyura boldly.

"All kinds of people live together," the lieutenant observed philosophically. "In our village one man lived with a goat. Do you have a marriage certificate?"

Nyura did not answer. Twisting her pouch back and forth in her hands, she scowled at the lieutenant.

"So, no certificate?" probed the lieutenant. "So, just as I thought. Persons not possessing marriage certificates," he grumbled as if reading a decree, "or other documents confirming familial relations are considered outside parties, and information is not given to outside parties. Is that clear?" He spat out his cigarette, which had gone out, and looked over at Nyura.

"But how . . ." Nyura began.

"I'll show you how!" The lieutenant suddenly turned furious. He ran down from the porch and over to Nyura. "I'll show you how!" he shouted in her face. "There is no Chonkin. None, never was, and never will be. And you better stop coming here and getting under our feet or else we'll pick you up, too, as an accessory. You understand?"

"But I . . ." said Nyura, and burst into tears.

"There's nothing to cry about," said Filippov, changing his tone. "Nobody's done anything to you. We're not picking you up because you're no relation to him, just an outside party. And you should remember that—an out-side par-ty."

With those words he turned, ran up onto the porch, and disappeared inside the building.

9

Chmikhalov, the District Committee instructor, a tall, thin man with a red nose (no doubt from drinking) and a long mournful face, stood in front of Chairman Golubev's desk. He wore a quilted jacket and a long tarpaulin raincoat with the hood back and held a three-tailed lash in one hand, which he knocked against the top of his rubber boot.

Chmikhalov's bay horse, hitched to the porch, was unhappily being drenched by the autumn rain.

The office was quite well heated. Chmikhalov kept wiping away the sweat with his sleeve, sniffling, and asking the chairman why the kolkhoz was not engaged in gathering the harvest.

"Look out the window and you'll see," said the chairman.

"I have no reason to be looking out windows," Chmikhalov whined. "I look into the Party's instructions."

"Ah," said the chairman, and twirled a finger by the side of his head. "Instructions, instructions . . . Instruct the rain to stop. You guys, you sit over there in the District Committee and I don't know what you use to do your thinking. You follow your instructions like sheep."

"Like what?" Chmikhalov was quick to ask.

"Like little lambs." Golubev softened his definition.

"Aha, so now you're going to take it back." Chmikhalov was transformed, his eyes had begun to gleam. "So, in your opinion, the District Committee are a bunch of sheep."

"Keep me out of your politics," said the chairman, rising to his feet. "I'm telling you it's raining, and only idiots and saboteurs would go out and gather the harvest in the rain."

"Now it's all out!" Chmikhalov spread his arms. "So, the District Committee are a bunch of sheep, idiots, and saboteurs. And that means that our entire party . . ."

He was unable to finish his thought. Golubev had sprung out from behind his desk, grabbed Chmikhalov with both hands, one on the nape of his neck, the other on his pants, and, hunched over, had dragged him to the door.

Nyura Belyashova, who had just arrived at the office, saw Chmikhalov suddenly emerge onto the wet porch, his arms and legs flailing wildly. A variety of sufferings were to be read on his long face. Nyura did not even have time to register surprise or to grasp the situation when Chmikhalov, flapping his arms like a bird, tore lose from the porch and began to fly. The flaps of his raincoat spread wide open, the hood swelled like a parachute. It was not to be an especially long flight. Having cleared the steps, Chmikhalov touched down, sprang to his feet, and began running; however, the lower half of his body could not catch up with the upper half, and he came crashing down in the mud, his arms stretched out in front of him as if he were trying to catch a chicken.

He rose slowly to his feet. His arms, stomach, knees, and even one cheek were plastered with mud. Smearing the mud across his cheek with the fist clutching the lash, Chmikhalov walked over to his obediently waiting horse, unhitched it, but it took some time for his hopping foot to find the stirrup. Finally succeeding, he heaved himself up onto the slippery saddle, turned his muddy, woeful face to Golubev, and said, on the verge of tears: "Doesn't matter, I'll show you yet!" He rode a few feet, turned again, and cried more boldly, though rather shrilly: "I'll show you! I'll show you!" and raised the lash menacingly. The horse bolted in fright, Chmikhalov was thrown onto his back, his legs went up in the air, but with one abrupt movement, he returned to a normal position and began rapidly riding away.

The chairman followed him with pensive eyes, which he then turned to Nyura. "You here to see me?"

"With the mail," said Nyura.

"Come in."

In the office she lay the newspapers on the chairman's desk, two magazines, *The Peasant Woman* and *Agitator's Notebook*, four letters, two postcards, and one large package. Golubev grabbed *Pravda* immediately and began reading the Soviet Information Bureau's communiqué about the situation at the front. When he raised his eyes Nyura was still standing in front of him, shifting her weight from one foot to the other. She was holding her mail pouch in one hand and presenting some sort of paper to Golubev with the other.

"What's that?" said Golubev, looking at the paper.

"Sign it, Timofeich, come on."

Volkov, the one-armed bookkeeper, was sitting in the next room, rolling a cigarette with his hand and the aid of his shoulder and chin when some sort of noise reached him from the chairman's office. Volkov wet a piece of newspaper with spit, then stopped moving and listened intently. First he caught the chairman's voice: "You can't be serious!" then Nyura said something, then the chairman again: "I can't, don't even ask, there's no way I can do it. What do you want to do, land me in jail?"

Setting his unfinished cigarette aside, Volkov peeped into the chairman's office. He saw Nyura's tear-stained face, and Golubev looking embarrassed as he said: "You've got to understand, Nyura, I'd like to, but how can I? I'm the chairman. I can't sign papers like that."

Nyura was sobbing, wiping her eyes with the tip of her shawl. The chairman noticed Volkov and beckoned him with a finger. "Come over here. Have a look at what she wants me to sign."

Volkov walked over to the chairman, took the paper offered him, and read slowly, pondering the content:

CERTIFICATE

Presented to Belyashova, N. A. as proof that she truly did live with the serviceman Chonkin, Ivan.

"You wrote this yourself?"

"I did." Nyura glanced up hopefully at Volkov.

"You have to go to the village soviet with this. We're a kolkhoz, we don't issue that type of certificate."

"And they won't sign it there either," said Golubev.

"They probably won't," seconded Volkov, laying the certificate on the desk.

"What do you mean, they won't sign it?" said Nyura. "I'm not making it up . . . I really did live with him."

"True, true, no one's arguing that," said the chairman. "But just think for a second, say today I drank three glasses of tea and then I come and say, Give me a certificate that I drank three glasses of tea. I'll tell you what to do," said Golubev, rising and coming out from behind his desk. "You go right to the District Committee, right to Revkin. Soon as you're in his office, throw your mail pouch on the floor, then throw yourself on the floor, make your eyes bulge out, and holler like crazy . . ." Golubev did, in fact, bulge out his eyes; he turned slightly purple, and then, all of a sudden, to show Nyura how to act, he began screeching, "I'm pregnant!"

"Saints preserve us!" Nyura cowered in fear. "You scared me!"

"Scared you? How about that!" The chairman winked at Volkov, who was observing the scene, his eyes lifeless, without interest. "Revkin will get scared too. Make a scene and holler, I'm pregnant! Give me back my Ivan!"

"You think it'll help?" asked Nyura, interested.

Golubev thought for a moment, then looked over at Volkov.

"Probably won't," he admitted reluctantly.

"So then why holler?"

"Might ease your heart."

Nyura picked up her certificate and said: "All right, goodbye."

She walked to the door, then, her hand on the doorknob, she stopped.

"Timofeich," she said in embarrassment. "You know, I really am . . ."

"What?" Ivan Timofeyevich had not understood.

"Carrying," said Nyura, blushing all over.

10

The rumor that Nyura was carrying Chonkin's child spread through the village that same day, overshadowing all other news. The women, meeting at the general store, at the catwalks by the river where they went to fetch water, or just in the middle of the village, examined the situation from every possible angle, discussed the possible due dates, and predicted consequences. Some had pity for Nyura—how was it going to be for her with a child alone; others were condescending—it happens to everybody. They said that of course she had to have the baby and then live her life for the child. But there were also those with high moral principles, those who rush to condemn anybody suddenly caught in an unexpected difficulty.

For some reason Aphrodite Gladishev was especially worked up. Seemingly a quiet woman who did not meddle in other people's affairs, she now burst into the controversy, coming out of her house carrying her child and hollering to the entire village: "What a shameful end it's all come to. Bad enough she slept with a stranger" (her term for Chonkin), "she had to go and get herself pregnant, too, the tramp!"

Every person wants to be special. And if he is not bold enough to say, "I'm better than everybody else," and if he has no way of showing that "I'm no worse than most folks," then he must have someone of whom he can say, "Well, that one's worse than me."

The women's gossip soon reached Nyura's ears. Ninka Kurzova came running over, offering, out of friendship, to put her in touch with a certain old woman from Old Kliukvino who could give her a quick and painless abortion. Nyura refused categorically.

"You fool," said Ninka. "Use your head. There's a war going on, hard times are coming, what are you going to do all alone with a child?"

"And what are you going to do with that?" Nyura pointed to Ninka's belly.

Ninka scowled, was about to fly off the handle, but she restrained herself. "Nyura, don't be offended. I don't mean you any harm. But how can you compare yourself to me? I've got a husband. Even if he gets killed, phoo, phoo, phoo"—she spat three times over her shoulder—"at least I'll be a widow. But if yours is killed . . ."

"He won't be," said Nyura. "He's not at the front, he's right here near me, in prison."

Taken aback by this, Ninka fell silent. She had not anticipated Nyura's argument. To all appearances Chonkin was in a better position than other men. As if he were protected from the front by the armor of prison walls.

"But he won't come back to you," said Ninka. "Maybe he's had others like you."

"He didn't," interrupted Nyura. "There may have been others, but none like me."

Ninka was at a loss again and did not know how to counter. "You've got to understand, Nyurka," she said, justifying herself. "It's not out of any bad feeling, I only wish you good."

With those words she walked from the hut and did not see Nyura flop down on the bed, bury her face in the pillow, and weep, not only from loneliness, but also because no one, neither the women nor the authorities, would acknowledge her right to Chonkin.

11

For two or three full days, broken only by the nights, Nyura had sat on the bench outside of the reception room belonging to Revkin, First Secretary of the District Committee, who was always either just leaving, summoned by one of the chiefs, or summoning somebody in to see him, or else conducting some conference or other, or preparing for the District Committee Bureau. Although there was a plate on his door indicating which days of the week and which hours he received petitioners, waiting for Revkin was like taking a train which did not run on any schedule, and neither the direction nor the time of arrival was known.

The District Committee had a tense, humdrum life of its own. Secretaries in white blouses and local officials in semimilitary and sometimes even in full military attire, their boxcalf boots squeaking importantly, scurried down the corridors distributing papers for signature. Even Revkin himself would occasionally appear, and then the bench sitters would jerk back their heads and look at him as if he were some higher life form, unable to bring themselves to approach him. And if someone did, the secretary, an elderly woman wearing glasses, would pop out of nowhere, and using physical force, she would shout: "Citizen! Citizen! You can see what a busy man Comrade Revkin is. He will see you all just as soon as he has a free minute."

While she was shouting and pushing the confused citizen out of the way, Comrade Revkin would slip in through his door and vanish. And to force one's way into his office was absolutely out of the question.

On the third or fourth day everyone waiting by the door of the reception room was informed that Comrade Revkin would not be receiving anyone in the course of the next several days because he was preparing for a forthcoming, extremely important, session of the Bureau. Comrade Borisov would take over. Among those waiting, several were disappointed by this news; but Nyura could not tell one official from the other, they all looked the same to her, like Chinese.

How much longer she waited for her turn cannot, at this late date, be determined, but her persistence was rewarded and she at last found herself in an office where Borisov sat at his desk with a bored air, which seemed to say everything human was alien to him.

He looked at Nyura without the slightest interest, as if knowing beforehand that the matter with which she had dared disturb him contained nothing of interest, especially now, when seen against the grandiose background of war. He sat looking silently at her, and she, having met with no questions from him, was forced to say that she had come to petition for her husband.

"Who?" For the first time Borisov's lips parted, proving conclusively that he was not a statue.

"Ivan," said Nyura, and burst into tears.

Borisov stirred slightly, took out his pocket watch, and began looking at it, either to let her know he was a busy man or to time Nyura's tears. Perhaps Nyura cried longer than you were supposed to, for Borisov could no longer restrain himself, and without raising his voice, he said: "Citizen, tears are not believed in here."

Those words, said so simply, produced the desired effect on Nyura; indeed, she immediately lost all desire to weep.

"Now," said Borisov, still looking at his watch, "what happened to him and what is it you want?"

She began by giving Ivan's last name. Borisov came to life, asking quickly: "What was it? What was it?" And she repeated it, "Chonkin."

"Chonkin." He made a note of it on his desk calendar. "And you say he was arrested? So what are you worried about, then?"

"Are you serious?"

"Of course," said Borisov. "Since he was arrested he will be tried. And if this Chonkin of yours is guilty, he will be punished, and if he is not . . ." Here, perhaps, Borisov was about to say, "He'll be acquitted," but after a moment's thought he said, "Then the court will reach a different decision."

"And what about me?" said Nyura.

"What about you?"

Nyura burst into tears, and wiping them away with the end of her shawl, she began a confused explanation. She was considered an outside party, but she really was not an outside party because even though they didn't have a marriage license she had lived with Chonkin, with Ivan.

The first signs that Borisov was losing his patience now appeared. "Citizen," he said, drumming his fingers on the desk top. "What is the point of all this nonsense? What do I care who you lived with? Do you really think that the District Committee has nothing better to do than spend its time on stupidities like this? Leave at once!"

"And go where?" asked Nyura through her tears.

"I don't know. To the public prosecutor or somebody else, but go!"

But Nyura did not leave. She stood and she wept. Borisov sat in his chair, surprised that this stupid woman really could not get it through her head where she was and who she was standing before. Outraged, he came out from behind his desk and began to push Nyura toward the door.

"Now, now, there's nothing to cry about. This isn't like other places. We don't allow anyone to misbehave here. We don't let ourselves be pushed around here."

Yielding to his pressure, Nyura moved back over to the door, and knocking it open with her backside, she jumped through it as if she had been scalded.

12

Leaving Borisov, Nyura somehow came to the conclusion that she had not behaved correctly. Now she resolved to act as Ivan Timofeyevich Golubev had advised her. But deciding on something is one thing and doing it is quite another. When she entered the prosecutor's office and saw the large important man at his large desk beneath the large portrait, for some reason she grew immediately shy and, shifting from one foot to another, even moved backward a little way, but then she returned to the threshold and stopped.

Sober, the prosecutor, Pavel Trofimovich Evpraksein, always knew what he was doing and why. He realized, however, that many people never had any need for such knowledge, and for that reason he was usually not surprised by the oddities of their behavior.

"You here to see me?" asked the prosecutor amiably.

"Yes, I am," said Nyura, so softly she did not even hear her own words herself.

"And what is the problem?"

"I'm pregnant," said Nyura.

Had she followed Golubev's advice to the full, had she begun screeching, thrown her mail pouch and then herself down onto the floor, that might have made the required impression on the prosecutor, but she was too embarrassed; she blushed, and spoke so softly that she was not even sure whether the prosecutor had heard her.

"I don't understand. What?" The prosecutor cupped his hand around his ear.

"Pregnant," murmured Nyura, growing even more embarrassed.

"Louder."

When she pronounced the word for the third time, the prosecutor finally heard it. He smiled and came out from behind his desk.

"Pregnant?" he asked, and taking Nyura lightly by the shoulder, he brought her to the window. "If you're pregnant, this is not the place for you. You need to go over there."

He pointed to the other side of the street to a wood-trimmed building which contained, as its sign indicated, a maternity hospital and consultation clinic.

"No," said Nyura, "I'm not here about that. I'm here about my husband."

"We do not release anyone from front-line service," said the prosecutor abruptly.

"That's not it," said Nyura.

"And if you're here about child support, it's still too early. That's only after the child is born."

"That's not it either." Nyura smiled. In comparison to what the prosecutor thought she wanted, her actual problem now seemed much simpler and more easily settled. "They put my husband in jail."

"Aha," said the prosecutor. "Now I understand. And for what reason?"

"For no reason," said Nyura in all simplicity.

"For no reason?" The prosecutor was surprised. "And in what country do you reside?"

"What do you mean?" said Nyura, failing to understand.

"I want to know where you think you live. England, America, or, perhaps, Fascist Germany?"

"Of course not," explained Nyura. "I live in the village of Krasnoye, seven kilometers from here. Ever hear of it?"

"I've heard a little something about it." The prosecutor nodded. "And is there no Soviet power in the village of Krasnoye?"

"That's right, no Soviet power in Krasnoye," confirmed Nyura.

"What, none at all?"

"None at all," said Nyura. "Our village soviet is across the river in New Kliukvino. All we have is a kolkhoz."

"Now I see, now I see," said the prosecutor. He took a sheet of paper and began sketching. "So, here's the river and here, on the other side, there's Soviet power, we'll just shade that in like so, and on this side here there's no Soviet power whatsoever," he said, gazing with interest at his own sketch. "Then, naturally, that's a completely different matter. Otherwise I would have thought—Soviet power and arrested for no reason, absurd. Personally, as a prosecutor, and, in general, as a Soviet citizen, I have never heard anything so outrageous. No, of course, we do have a few isolated individuals who either from stupidity or purposefully spread malicious rumors like that, and naturally we put such people in prison. For slandering our system, our society, our people, but you can't say that it was for no reason, right?"

"Right," agreed Nyura.

"What is it that you want from me?"

"I'm here about my husband," Nyura reminded him.

"What can I do about it?" Pavel Trofimovich spread his hands wide apart. "I am a Soviet prosecutor. And my power extends only over Soviet territory. And where there is no Soviet power, I am powerless."

Nyura had understood nothing of what the prosecutor had said and continued to sit waiting for the conversation to resume. But the prosecutor apparently had no intention of resuming. He took his glasses from their plastic case, set them on his nose, and opening a folder marked *Case No.* he began to read the documents it contained. Nyura waited patiently. Finally the prosecutor raised his eyes and was surprised to see her still there.

"You're still here?"

"I'm here about . . ."

"Your husband?"

"That's right." Nyura nodded.

"I really didn't explain it well enough? All right, then, I'll try a different tack. Tie a string around your finger if you have to, but remember this." He raised his voice and threatened her with one finger. "Here, in the Soviet Union, we do not put people in jail for no reason at all. And I, as a prosecutor, am warning you in the most severe manner to stop saying that. And there's no hiding behind that pregnancy of yours either. We will not allow anyone, pregnant or otherwise, to do that. Clear?"

"Clear," said Nyura, becoming timid again.

"Well, good, then." The prosecutor softened at once. "We've agreed on the main thing. And, as regards the particulars, well, they can be discussed. If some isolated violations of the law have crept into our treatment of your husband, then we'll suppress them. This I promise you as a prosecutor. What is your husband's last name?"

"Chonkin," said Nyura. "Chonkin, Ivan."

"Chonkin?" The prosecutor remembered that he had once signed a warrant to arrest a Chonkin. And then he had heard that this same Chonkin had turned out to be the leader of a gang which had then been smashed. "Chonkin, Chonkin," mumbled the prosecutor. "So, you say Chonkin. One minute." He smiled politely. "Be so good as to wait out in the corridor. I'll clear everything up and then get right back to you."

Nyura went out into the corridor, where she spent a few minutes. Meanwhile, Prosecutor Evpraksein made a phone call; standing and whispering, covering the receiver with the palm of his hand, he kept glancing over at the door. Then he went out to the corridor himself and invited Nyura back in. He sat down at his desk, she remained standing.

"So, Chonkin, you say?" asked the prosecutor. "And what is your last name?"

"Belyashova," said Nyura, reluctantly realizing there was something behind his question.

"Correct," said the prosecutor. "Belyashova. You and this

Chonkin are not legally married, is that correct? Correct. That is, strictly speaking, you have no relation to this Chonkin, who will, by the way, be punished—very severely."

"What do you mean none," said Nyura. "I'm pregnant."

"All the more reason," said the prosecutor. "Why should you bind your own fate and the fate of your unborn child with that criminal's?"

Then he began talking pure nonsense, speaking as some sort of plural person which was him or of which he was a part. "We," he said, "do not doubt that you are a good worker and a true Soviet person and that your connection with this Chonkin was completely accidental. It is precisely for that reason that we are not holding you responsible. And it is precisely for that reason that you should make a complete break with this Chonkin."

There was no end to the gibberish: a difficult time . . . complicated international situation . . . antagonism of two worlds . . . fence-sitting is not allowed . . . one must choose one side of the barricade . . .

"And for that reason," he said, concluding his thought, "it would be wrong for you to defend Chonkin. On the contrary, you must break with him in the most decisive manner. In your place the appropriate thing is to state in writing that I, So and so, entered into intimate relations with Chonkin by chance and imprudently, not knowing his bestial nature, which I now regret. Well, what do you think, can you write something like that?"

The prosecutor looked over at Nyura and saw that her eyes were full of tears.

"But, sir," said Nyura, sniffling, "the thing is . . . Vanka—he's good."

"Good?" The prosecutor frowned and averted his eyes. "Then I wonder why he was arrested if he's so good."

"For no reason at all," said Nyura.

"For no reason," Evpraksein repeated angrily. "Well then,

Belyashova, I see that you are not just in error, you are persisting in your errors. I see that the time you spent with Chonkin has left its mark. I see that he managed to cultivate you as well."

Thinking the prosecutor had her pregnancy in mind, Nyura nodded and agreed through her tears: "That he did."

13

From what has been written above the reader may reach the conclusion that Prosecutor Evpraksein was a rat and a bastard. That would be perfectly correct were it not perfectly incorrect.

In fact, the prosecutor was a freethinker and a liberal. In his heart he always wanted everything to be good, no one to commit crimes, no one ever to be jailed or shot, and, if they had to be jailed or shot, that it be done simply and without a fuss. But since such tendencies of mind were not, in that period, overly encouraged, the prosecutor concealed his liberal nature so thoroughly and so skillfully that everyone thought him a rat and a bastard. I don't know about you, but to me this contradiction seems easily resolvable. Take a real dyed-in-the-wool rat-bastard, you could come to terms on certain things with him. He might even let you off easy or take a bribe, just because he didn't feel like working. But Prosecutor Evpraksein, fearing that his liberalism might become apparent to all, was unapproachable and incorruptible.

He did have one weakness, though, prevalent even among prosecutors—he loved to drink. And after one too many, Evpraksein bared his soul.

That same day, after his conversation with Nyura, he stopped by the tearoom, ran into someone he knew, drank with him, and it was late at night before he started home. His coat was unbuttoned, his scarf was dangling out one sleeve, and he had left his hat behind in the tearoom.

The prosecutor walked unsteadily, swaying from side to side, stumbling, stopping, waving his arms.

"You're a fool!" he said to an imaginary Nyura. "You say you're pregnant. Well, maybe I'm pregnant, too. And if you are pregnant, what do you want, special treatment? Pregnant! Big miracle, ha-ha, pregnant. So no one will put you in jail. You'll be treated well, with humanism. Renounce him, that's it, and no one will touch you. But, oh, no sir, she says, he's good. And what's so good about him? I might have been better, too, if they had let me. But I can't because what am I? A prosecutor. That's right, a prosecutor." He waved his hand and a band of colors flashed in front of his eyes. "A snake!" decided Pavel Trofimovich. "A snake!" he shouted wildly, and began dashing headlong away. He stumbled, fell, and struck his head on the road. Fortunately, at that time the streets of Dolgov had not yet been paved. Now, however, a good deal has changed, though apparently there are still no paved roads in Dolgov. Anyway, back then, had the roads been paved, the world might have been one prosecutor less. But prosecutors must be protected. You will say, why protect them, there's so many of them? That, of course, is true. But, still, pity is possible even for a prosecutor.

Having struck his head, Prosecutor Evpraksein lay on his back on the road, showing no discernible signs of life.

Then, coming to, he heard someone approach, then bend over his spread-eagled body. The prosecutor began to groan.

"You alive?" asked an unfamiliar male voice sympathetically.

"I don't know." Evpraksein began pushing his hands under him for support, when again he saw some long thing creeping toward him.

"The snake!" he said woefully, and let his head fall back down.

"Snake? What are you talking about, citizen. That's your scarf."

"Scarf?" The prosecutor half-opened one eye and lifted his

arm. The long thing moved with his arm. "Look, it's my scarf. And I thought it was a snake. I don't like snakes. I'm afraid of them. You think I'm not afraid of anything? No, I am afraid because I am a living creature and everything that is alive is afraid."

With the help of the stranger he got to his feet and began swaying, unable to make himself move from the spot.

"Thanks, friend!" he muttered. "Thanks! I don't even know how to show my gratitude. What can I do for you?"

"Got a light on you?" asked the stranger, pulling a cigarette from behind his ear.

"One second." The prosecutor began to hunt for matches. He was filled with gratitude and truly did want to do something for this unknown but indisputably kind man. "One minute." He reached into his left pocket but for some reason to do so he had to make a 360-degree turn to the left. His left pocket proved to contain no matches. Then he reached into his right pocket and again made a complete turn around his own axis. He found a match box in his right pocket, opened it, and began taking out the matches, scattering them on the ground. Finally, he grabbed hold of one match and, brandishing it like a saber, attempted to strike it against the box.

"Give it to me, I'll do it," said the stranger.

"No, no," said the prosecutor. "I want to show my res– res– respec . . ."

His hands shook, the matches kept breaking. Finally one hissed and flared. Evpraksein raised it level to his face. The stranger with the cigarette bent toward the flame, glanced at Evpraksein, then flinched.

"Aren't you the prosecutor?" he asked in agitation.

"I am." Evpraksein nodded.

A light gust of wind blew out the match. By the time the prosecutor took out another and struck it, he saw the stranger retreating rapidly.

"But where are you going?" said Pavel Trofimovich, utterly

perplexed. "Come get your light. Hey, friend, brother! Stop!"

He even ran a few steps after the stranger, but then waved his hand in a gesture of helpless dismissal, stopped, and said with a spit: "Ech, you fool!"

Then he pulled his scarf from his sleeve, wound it around his coat collar and went on his way, arguing with himself.

"You're afraid of the prosecutor, too, you rotten coward. And you're right to be afraid," said Pavel Trofimovich, turning to address a telephone pole that had appeared along the way. "Right! What do you think man is to man? A friend? A comrade? A brother? Ha-ha, what crap! Man is like a wolf to his fellow man. With fangs like these. Yes, of course, I am the prosecutor. I am the prosecutor!" he repeated, and began walking again. "I am a Communist. I am a soldier of the Party. I have no right to be spineless. Now we'll fight the Germans. We'll build Communism and then to each according to his need . . . Then every head will be . . . patted nicely. But now's not the time . . ." He stopped and thought a moment. Yesterday wasn't the time either. He thought a bit more and looked around. And tomorrow won't be the time either. Again he raised his voice. "Doesn't matter! I'm a fighter! I'm a soldier! I'm an executioner!! I'm a murderer!!! I'm a bastard!!!" he howled, beating his fist against his breast.

Azalia Mitrofanovna, or, simply, Aza, the prosecutor's wife, was sitting in front of her mirror rubbing cold cream on her cheeks. It was late. The children, Alenka and Trofimka, had gone to bed a long time ago. The radio speaker was barely vibrating with light classical music. Hearing footsteps by the door, Aza pricked up her ears. The door burst open, revealing Pavel Trofimovich in his muddy, unbuttoned overcoat.

"Oh, Lord, not again!" said Aza in horror.

"Again," nodded Pavel Trofimovich. "And what's all that?" He rubbed under his eyes as if he, too, were applying cold cream. "You want to stay young. Won't help. No. Life puts wrinkles on anybody it wants to, even the prosecutor's wife."

"Pasha!" she said reproachfully.

"Pasha what? Pasha what?" He ran a finger down her dressing gown. "A silk dressing gown . . ."

"Pasha, you bought it for my birthday yourself."

"Of course." He paced the room, making intricate gestures with his hands. "I bought it. For your birthday. And with what dough? The dough they pay me because I"—he brought his red face close to her, then exhaled abruptly—"kill people."

"Pasha!" she cried. "Think what you're saying!"

"Ha-ha," he laughed. "Think. I thought about it a long time ago. But what can I do? I've got a family and all they want to do is stuff their faces!"

"Pasha!" she said reproachfully. "You'll wake the children."

"Ach, the children." He raced into the children's room, and pushing aside his wife, who tried to restrain him, he began shouting: "All right, get up, you parasites! I want to announce that your father is an executioner and a murderer!"

The children were not sleeping. Alenka, a seventh-grader, and Trofimka, a fifth-grader, were each sitting up in bed, huddled against the wall, their blankets pulled up to their chins.

"Alenka! Trofimka!" With outspread arms their mother defended them from their father. "Don't listen to Papa. Papa's drunk."

"Yes, I'm drunk. That's why I'm telling the truth."

He went out into the foyer, where on a sheet of paper torn from Alenka's notebook, he wrote, the pen in his clenched fist spattering ink: *I, Prosecutor Evpraksein, P. T. being of sound and sober* (crossed out) *mind, acknowledge my complicity and announce my resignation from . . . I know what I'm headed for but I have no strength left and my actions are dictated by my civil conscience and*

Here he stopped, using neither a period nor three dots, noting neither the time nor the date, then signed his name. With a lavish gesture he held the paper out to his wife: "Here, take it."

"To whom?"

"To them."

"Fine," she said obediently. "I will. Take off your coat, get a little rest, then I'll take it there."

"You will?" He jumped up. "You want me thrown in jail?" he roared triumphantly. "Give me that paper!" He snatched the paper from her and tore it up. "I knew you were that sort, just waiting to be rid of me. Today a woman came to my office . . . a simple Russian woman . . . not even legally married but ready to . . . And you! . . . You want to see me shot? You bitch! You won't have to wait, I'll . . ."

Then a familiar scene occurred. He took his double-barreled shotgun down from the wall and began shouting, "Outside!"

"Pasha," she said sadly, knowing beforehand that her arguments would have no effect. "For the children's sake at least, you should be ashamed."

At other times the children had thrown themselves on their father, their arms around his legs, crying, "Papa!" Now they sat frightened in their room and watched through the open door.

"Out!" The prosecutor was hurrying her now.

"Wait a minute, let me at least put my boots on."

"Sure, might as well get them dirty, too. Then you'll look pretty."

He brought her out to the communal outhouse, barefoot, submissive, only a dressing gown over her naked body. The night was cold but bright; a full moon sailed out from behind the clouds, indifferently illuminating the spot where an execution was about to be performed.

"In the name of the Russian Soviet Federated . . ." pronounced the prosecutor triumphantly, raising his weapon.

In the past the neighbors had come running out when such scenes had occurred. This time nobody came out. Only one window opened and a woman's voice asked: "What's going on out there?"

And another voice, also a woman's, answered: "The prosecutor has taken Azalia out back to shoot her."

The window banged shut at once. Automatically the prosecutor glanced over at the source of the superfluous sounds, and when he turned back around, Azalia was nowhere to be seen. Just then the moon set and it grew pitch-dark.

"Aza!" the prosecutor shouted into the darkness. "Come out! Don't try to prevent the execution of your sentence."

Azalia did not respond. Pavel Trofimovich walked around the outhouse, peeped into both sides, then stepped in a little pile of excrement in front of the entrance. Cursing, his gun over his shoulder, he started back. But upon his arrival he found the door locked from the inside. The prosecutor banged on the door with his fists and feet, shouting: "Aza! Open up! In the name of the law! I won't do it anymore!" But, receiving no answer, he lay down to sleep on the doormat.

In the morning, as usual, he crawled on his knees before his wife, threw his arms around her legs, begged her forgiveness, and promised to throw his gun out with the trash or sell it.

Then, partially forgiven, fortified with strong tea, he left for work, where he did his duty with a firm hand, as was expected of him.

14

Nyura walked, walked, walked down the long corridors of various institutions, which all merged for her into one endless corridor with dusty floors and benches. On those benches, in postures timid and expectant, sat the petitioners, that is, people who still wanted something from this life, seekers of truth, fighters for justice, intriguers, the insulted and the injured, in ragged quilt jackets, rags, bast sandals, sandals made of rope and tires, some with galoshes on their bare feet and some completely barefooted, old men and old women, peasant women with little children, a young man on crutches, an elderly sailor with a bandaged head, an old Jew wearing a cloth coat covered with flocks of pale fleas, a youth suffering from rickets munching a piece of bread he kept wrapped in a dirty rag bundle.

A pale, unshaven man with a feverish gleam in his eye was telling Nyura how an interrogator had beaten him in the kidneys, ascribing his behavior to the ideological war and the complexity of the international situation.

"They set me free right before the war," said the man, "but now I'm no good for anything."

He showed Nyura a lengthy petition in which he proposed a new classification—invalid of the ideological war—and that he personally be put in category 1 and be given free use of all municipal transportation.

There was a woman who had lost her ration cards. She had been making the rounds of all the departments, saying that she had three children who would die of hunger. She was told, "This is no almshouse. You should have thought about your children earlier. We have no special funds for the negligent."

One citizen, an extremely plain-looking man, had come to fight on the most foolish grounds. At one point, needing to redo his roof, he had requested the director of the sovkhoz to issue him the requisite amount of straw. The director refused on the grounds that the bearer of the request had taken an insufficiently active role in community life, that is, had not attended amateur nights, had not put out a wall-newspaper or attended meetings and, if he had, had not taken the rostrum, and had only participated passively in the general applause.

Instead of simply stealing the straw (as others did) or slipping the director a five (as others did), the straw-petitioner decided to avail himself of legal channels and wrote complaints to everyone, including the highest officials. The replies were turned over to those about whom he had complained and he was beaten twice (once in the director's office at the sovkhoz, once in the police station); he was treated for three months in an insane asylum; however, the treatment had obviously not resulted in a cure.

All the people Nyura encountered in that endless corridor, in front of those endless rows of doors, would sit there for days on end as at a train station. From time to time someone's last name would be called, and removing his hat ahead of time and bowing, he would pass through the long-awaited door, only to dart back out a minute or so later with a troubled expression or perhaps even groaning as if he were leaving a dentist's office.

Important people sat behind those doors. No kid gloves were used. They treated each visitor like a hydra who only wished to snatch something from the peasants' and workers' state. Themselves producing nothing but useless paper, they reproached each caller as if it were he precisely who was living off the state, receiving too much as it was, and now coming in for more.

In that endless corridor lit by a perpetual twilight, always damp and cold as if night never replaced day there, nor one season another, a measured and seemingly otherworldly life took its course.

Nyura went from office to office, one to the other. At times she would forget what it was she wanted; her chief aims had become, first, to get into the office and, then, once in, to get out. The faces of the officials who received her merged into a single face with puffed-out cheeks and unfeeling eyes. The composite Face picked up Prosecutor Evpraksein's idea and began developing it further. And, in one office, the Face said that it was necessary for her not simply to condemn Chonkin's behavior, not enough to disassociate herself from him, but she had to do so publicly, at a meeting of some sort. In another office it was said that better yet not at a meeting but in print. In yet another office it was said, even better, both at a meeting and in print. They proposed that she also condemn her own behavior as politically shortsighted and insufficiently vigilant. The further she went, the more was demanded from her, and nothing was offered in exchange.

Though drowning in tears and despairing, Nyura kept going on and on until, finding herself in the editorial offices of the newspaper *Bolshevik Tempos*, she knocked at a door with a plate that read EDITOR IN CHIEF, COM. ERMOLKIN, B. E.

Boris Evgenevich Ermolkin was, in his way, a remarkable man. He was an old newshound, as he liked to refer to himself, but not one of those hounds who chase after fresh news with their tongues hanging out. No, he always fled in panic from news. If something worthy of interest occurred in the city or the district, that is, something truly newsworthy, Ermolkin did everything to keep it off the pages of his newspaper. Occasionally, reading that even some bourgeois newspapers were unable to conceal something, he would spread his arms in a gesture that said, What kind of editor does this bourgeois paper have if he can't even kill a story.

Outwardly an unremarkable man, Ermolkin possessed one consuming passion—to correct every article or story from beginning to end. From morning till late at night, heedless of rain, sun, time of day, or change of season, knowing the joys of neither love nor alcohol, having forgotten his own family, Ermolkin would spend all his time in the office reading galleys. He was brought the damp gray sheets coarsened by the curved lines of print impressed in them. It would have been repulsive to touch such sheets, but he seized hold of them like a drug fiend; trembling with impatience, he would spread them out on his desk and the sacred ritual would begin.

Aiming his sharp pencil at the galleys, Ermolkin would stare intently at the printed words, swooping down like a hawk if he spotted a mistake among them. All ordinary words seemed to him unworthy of our extraordinary epoch and so he would correct them, changing "house" into "building" or "structure," "Red Army Soldiers" into "warriors of the Red Army." There were no peasants, horses, or camels in his newspaper, but tillers of the fields, steeds, and ships of the desert. The people referred to in his newspaper did not say anything, they declared it; they did not ask, they addressed questions. Ermolkin called German pilots Fascist buzzards, Soviet pilots were Stalin's falcons, and the sky was an aerial arena or the fifth ocean. The word "gold" occupied a special place in his vocabulary. Everything possible was called gold. Coal and oil were black gold. Cotton was white gold, gas was blue gold. They say he once came upon an article about prospectors and gold miners and returned the article to the chief secretary asking just precisely what sort of gold was being referred to. The secretary replied, Ordinary gold. And thus it appeared in the newspaper—miners of ordinary gold.

It was hard to believe that a mere woman had given birth to Ermolkin, had sung him lullabies in Russian, that he had ever heard the voices of the street with his own ears, had ever read Pushkin, Gogol, Dostoevsky. One would think that a Linotype machine had given birth to him and that he had been swaddled in proofs and galleys, and dead, indelible words had been forever impressed in his consciousness, his every cell.

Nyura had ended up in front of this astonishing man. Having knocked at his door and heard a "Come in," she entered and found the work-stunted editor himself, and another man as well, stout but agile and abrupt in his movements. The other man was a certain Konstantin Tsipin, who styled himself a phenologist. This phenologist was rushing from one corner of the office to another, wringing his hands.

"Boris Evgenevich," he appealed to the editor, "I implore you, don't correct my article, it's just a short little piece."

"Now look what he wants," replied the editor, stirring the tea which had gone cold in his glass. "How can I not correct you when you use an expression like 'ladybug'? We no longer have ladies in this society. We have women, women workers; they operate machines, drive tractors and combines, they stand in for their husbands, who have gone off to the front. And to call them ladies is to insult them."

"I didn't call them ladies, I called the bug a ladybug; that's what the common people call them."

"If everything the common people said went into a newspaper . . ." The editor shook his balding head.

"But you can't write women bugs," said the phenologist.

"Why not, women bugs sounds just right."

"Boris Evgenevich," howled the phenologist, "you're murdering me here. Ask anybody, ask your visitor . . . Young woman"—he turned to Nyura—"I can see you are of the common people. What do you call that little brown bug with the black spots?"

"We call them whatever we want to," said Nyura evasively, not wishing to cross the editor.

"There you see," said the editor, livening up. "But we've got a newspaper here. We just can't call anything whatever we like. And what can I do for you?" he asked Nyura benevolently.

"It's about my husband, Chonkin."

Hearing the name Chonkin, the editor pushed his glass of tea off to one side and said, his lips stiff: "I am listening."

The phenologist Tsipin disappeared immediately, as if he had never been there at all.

"I am listening," repeated the editor.

"I'm here to find out what I should do," said Nyura, approaching his desk. "Chonkin is my husband but the prosecutor says I have to renounce him."

"Well, since that's what the prosecutor says, that's what you should do," said Ermolkin.

"But how?" Nyura shook her head. "I'm pregnant."

"Pregnant?" said Ermolkin in surprise. "That changes matters. Wait a moment, I'll have to give this some thought."

He grasped his head with both hands, closed his eyes, and actually seemed to plunge into the depths of thought. Nyura regarded him with a curiosity tinged with both fear and respect. Ermolkin sat, his head gripped in his hands, for what must have been several seconds but seemed more like minutes to Nyura. Suddenly Ermolkin shook his head as if returning to his senses and stared for a long moment at Nyura. He took a fresh sheet of paper from his desk drawer, pushed it over to Nyura, and said softly: "Sign your name down there at the bottom."

"What for?" said Nyura curiously.

"We'll write a notice in the newspaper for you, but we'll need your signature."

"What kind of notice?" said Nyura warily.

"We'll write that as a mother-to-be, you, in your own name and in the name of your child, completely disassociate yourself from this so-called Chonkin and that you promise to raise your son- or daughter-to-be to become a true patriot devoted to the ideals of the party of Lenin and Stalin."

"That's it." Nyura slumped. "The same thing everywhere."

"What is it you don't like?" asked Ermolkin sincerely. "It's all for your own good. You can't really want your future son to bear the name of a criminal, to bear that indelible stain his whole life?"

"All right, I'm leaving," said Nyura, rising.

"Well, suit yourself. People are trying to help you. They want to make the best of it, but you . . . Perhaps you think it's right to be stubborn, perhaps you even want people to view you as some sort of heroine, but, in my opinion, your behavior is dictated by cowardice and cowardice alone. Had you really been sincere you would have said, Yes, I made a mistake. You would have renounced this Chonkin and branded him with eternal shame. I realize that a decision like that is a difficult one, but if you are a real Soviet woman you should make up your mind what is dearest to you—Chonkin or the Soviet government."

Nyura looked over at him with tear-filled eyes. She did not know why she was obliged to choose, why, in a pinch, there wasn't room enough for them both, Chonkin and the Soviet government.

"Yes," said Ermolkin sadly, after a moment's silence, "I can see you are persisting in this matter. To tell the truth, I don't really understand. Perhaps from your point of view I have certain outmoded ideas, but I look at things differently." He rose from behind his desk and paced the room, his hands in his pockets. "I have a son of my own," he continued, a nervous note in his voice. "A little boy. Three and a half, at the most. I like him very much. But if the Party ordered me to cut his throat, I wouldn't ask . . . I . . ." He looked over at Nyura and his eyes seemed to turn to glass. "I . . ."

"Mama!" Nyura wailed wildly and darted from the office. She ran almost the entire way to Krasnoye without once looking back. And almost the whole way she imagined that Editor Ermolkin was chasing her, a knife in his teeth.

15

For some reason his meeting with Nyura had a strange effect on Ermolkin. Perhaps it was because it made him think of his own son, that little towheaded tyke with the large forehead who looked like Lenin as a child. All people take care of their families, are concerned about them, but his sole concern was his work, always his work. In his office day and night, turning yellow from tobacco smoke; he couldn't for the life of him remember the last time he had been home. No, that's it, he said to himself, it's time to give some thought to the family. That day he decided to leave work earlier than usual, that is, not just an hour or two earlier, but to leave at the end of the work day like all normal employees. He formulated his thoughts: Ultimately I am a human being and I have a right to relaxation and a private life.

Nevertheless, before leaving, he took another look at the mock-up of the next day's edition, which had been brought in to him for a final check. He began as usual with the lead editorial. It was never the editorial's theme, content, or, shall we say, its expository style which interested him; all that interested him was that the word "Stalin" be mentioned no less than twelve times. No matter what the subject—the moral makeup of Soviet man, the laying-in of fodder or fish breeding in artificial reservoirs—that word had to be mentioned twelve times, maybe thirteen, maybe fourteen, but never eleven. Why he selected this as the minimum and not some other amount, whether he got it from out of the blue or was following some hint, is difficult to say, but in any case, that was how it was. No instructions from above had been issued on this score, no special orders. However, Ermolkin was not alone in this; probably every editor, whether his was a local paper or one published in Moscow, spent days and nights going blind from proofs gray as dirty tablecloths, hunting for that very word with their little sharpened pencils, their lips moving as they added them up.

Naturally, in all his years in the press, Ermolkin had occasion to meet a variety of people. He had run across desperate madcaps who, either out of youthfulness or from a lack of journalistic sense, would throw tantrums and blasphemously ask why twelve and not eight or even seven. In such cases Ermolkin would only shake his head and grin sadly. "Ach," he would say, "you're young, you're green, you're flying high now, but you'll land low." Some did land low, including prison, though probably not because they mentioned some word less often than they were supposed to but because, having once doubted a rule, a person inevitably increases the scope of his doubts and then it becomes too hard to stop.

Ermolkin began with the editorial. The editorial for the day had been sent down from above and Ermolkin could not correct it except, of course, for grammatical errors. Still, using his pencil as a pointer, he counted up the words and, not so much to his surprise, but, more precisely, to his satisfaction, the requisite word was repeated exactly twelve times; clearly, in literary endeavors, the high-positioned author adhered to the same rule as Ermolkin. The article summoned the people forward to meet the difficult times and to heed with special attention, warm emotion, and even some deeper emotion the instructions of their leader and to use them as a guide in all aspects of their life. Comrade Stalin's instructions, said the article, have become, for all the Soviet peoples, the gilding of wisdom, the most profound understanding of the objective laws of social development. For some reason that phrase arrested Ermolkin's attention. He ran through it a second time with a distracted gaze, tried to read on, but still felt that he was not understanding a thing.

I'm tired, thought Ermolkin aloud, passing his hand across his face. Tired.

In a series of slow movements he removed his frayed over-sleeves, placed them in his desk drawer, and, before leaving the office, looked in on Lifshits, the secretary in chief.

"Here's the thing . . . ah . . . Vilgelm Leopoldovich," he said with a little yawn, "I read through the lead editorial, would you please take care of the rest. Pay a little extra attention, will you? I'm going home."

"Home?" said Lifshits in surprise.

"What, is it too early?" asked Boris Evgenevich.

"No, no, it's not too early but . . ." At first Lifshits himself did not know why he was so surprised, but then, after a moment's thought, he realized that he had never seen Ermolkin leaving for home. "Fine," he said. "Go, Boris Evgenevich, and don't worry, everything will be taken care of."

"But look," warned Ermolkin, "I'm having you take over for me and I just hope that everything will be done right. I trust that your . . . uh, uh . . . weakness won't . . ."

"Come on, come on!" interrupted Lifshits. "You know yourself I've quit for good. It's been a whole month since I've touched a drop."

"All right, all right, I believe you." With those words Boris Evgenevich left his office. The news that he was going home spread like wildfire through the editorial offices. Boris Evgenevich himself did not notice that as he walked down the corridor all the office doors opened and his co-workers watched him leave with long and wondering stares.

Finding himself outside, Boris Evgenevich walked several paces in an unfamiliar direction, then came to a halt. Quite confused, he began turning his head one way, then the other. There were only two addresses he knew well, the District Committee's and the printer's, and now he could not remember the way to his own house. "Where is it that I live?" He began to rack his brain, even seizing his small head and furrowing his brow, but these efforts brought no visible results.

Crammed with official wordmongering, his memory retained the dimly gleaming image of a plank footway across a ditch, a section of wattle fence, a light-blue bench, and that was all. I've completely overworked myself was how Ermolkin explained his state to himself, and he decided to ask a pedestrian for directions.

"Citizen," he addressed the first person he encountered, a woman carrying two bags. "Can you tell me how to get to . . ." He did not complete his sentence and stared at her in a stupor.

"To where?" asked the woman.

"One minute," said Ermolkin. He took his passport from his pocket and began looking for the address at which he was officially registered. "Ah, here it is." He read aloud the name of the street as indicated in the proper column, and the woman, though surprised, explained, with numerous additional details, how he should go and where he should turn.

Ermolkin set off as directed and would have soon been home but, on the way, at the intersection of two streets, he noticed a small group of people milling about on a patch of ground, calling things out as if they were all looking for each other. This was the so-called flea market, which he had known in his youth. Ermolkin was astonished. He had thought that all these flea markets had, once and for all, become a thing of the past; in any case, he had not read anything about them in his own newspaper for a long time. The pages of his newspaper depicted life rather differently. A society of cheerful, rosy-cheeked people whose sole concern was to bring in unprecedented harvests, forge more steel and pig iron, conquer the wilderness, and, while doing all that, sing joyful songs about their fabulously happy life.

The people Ermolkin now saw had lost touch with the beautiful reality depicted in the newspaper. They did not have rosy cheeks and were not singing cheerful songs. Skinny, crippled, ragged, with a hungry, thievish gleam in their eyes, they were buying and selling whatever they could lay their hands on—tobacco, bread, cotton cakes, dogs, cats, old pants, rusty nails, chickens, millet gruel in wooden bowls, and geegaws of every sort. Something akin to curiosity awoke in Ermolkin's soured soul; he entered that circle of people possessed by a passion for profit, and he was spun away in the whirlpool.

A one-armed man wearing a quilted jacket belted with a piece of rope was standing over an open sack of shag, rolling tobacco and shouting at the top of his lungs: "Shag, shag, first-class, two puffs, you're on your ass."

"Home brew, first-class!" said the man behind him, a large teapot in his hand, obviously incapable of thinking of anything original to say himself.

A saucy woman wearing quilted pants was trying to sell two pieces of soap that were black as tar: "Stock up now while it's cheap, all the rest's been grabbed up."

An old townswoman with a haughty face was holding a fox fur with ivory buttons for eyes in her outstretched hands and not shouting anything. The fox was threadbare and moth-eaten, like the old woman herself.

A young man wearing dark glasses was sitting cross-legged in the dust, a placard on his chest: BLIND AND DEAF FROM BIRTH. GIVE WHAT YOU CAN TO MAKE AN UNHAPPY LIFE MORE BEAUTIFUL. "Ta-dum-ta-dum-ta-dum, the devil came riding up on an ox, on a green broom right from the U.S.A.," he sang.

A legless invalid on castors wearing a striped sailor's vest and a sailor's cap spread out three cards on a dusty towel—two aces of spades and one ace of diamonds.

"Step right up, easy to play, easy to win, you watch the cards, you make your bet, the aces fly, keep a sharp eye, or it's rubles goodbye. What are you gawking at?" he said to Ermolkin. "C'mon, try your luck."

"No, no," said Ermolkin, and walked away.

He bought from an old woman two candy roosters and a clay whistle shaped like a rooster for his little son. Then he started elbowing his way out of the crowd.

He was intending to leave the flea market when his attention was caught by an old Jew wearing a long raincoat and a tattered tank helmet. The old man was sitting on a small wooden bench beside a cage containing two black guinea pigs. Nailed to a stick stuck in the ground was a plywood sign crudely lettered in indelible ink: LEARNED GUINEA PIGS WILL TELL YOUR FORTUNE. 1 RUBLE.

"And you," said Boris Evgenevich, approaching the old man, "do you believe in that nonsense?"

"I don't know." The old man shrugged his shoulders. "I'm a shoemaker, not a fortune-teller. When I have a little leather I make shoes no worse than my son Zinovy makes false teeth.

When I don't have any leather, I make my living some other way."

"How can you tell fortunes if you don't believe in them?"

"Who said I didn't? I said that I didn't know, but my wife, Tsila, thinks these little pigs are very smart because they bring us in a little money."

Naturally Ermolkin did not believe in either fortune-telling or predictions, but since it was so cheap . . .

He placed the three roosters, the two made of sugar candy and the one of clay in his pocket, from which he then pulled out a crumpled one-ruble note. Then, after a moment's hesitation, he handed it to the old man. "All right, all right, let's see what those pigs of yours can do," he said.

The old man made no reply. He took the ruble, lifted the box of tickets folded like tooth-powder packets from his lap, and set it in the cage. One of the pigs bestirred himself and began running around the box. Then it started sniffing, looked up at Ermolkin as if trying to determine which ticket would be bad enough to select for him, then thrust its snout decisively into the box and a second later a ticket could be seen flashing between the pig's small teeth.

The old man immediately snatched the ticket and offered it to Ermolkin, who, grinning skeptically, unfolded it and read: *Do not entrust others with what you should do yourself. Another man's error can lead to irreparable consequences. Beware of horses.*

"Just as I said—nonsense." Ermolkin beamed, offering the ticket back to the old man. "What could that mean?"

The old man looked at the paper through his spectacles but did not take it into his hand.

"I don't know," he said. "Maybe it doesn't mean anything and maybe it does."

"Absolute gibberish," said Ermolkin confidently. "I realize that the first half could mean something because it is so general. But what's the horse doing there?"

"I don't know," the old man repeated meekly.

"But didn't you write it yourself?"

"Not me."

"Who, then?"

The old man looked up at Ermolkin, then up to the sky, as if pondering whether or not to ascribe the messages to higher forces, but then he thought better of it and, with a sigh, admitted: "My daughter-in-law, Zinovy's wife, wrote them. Her handwriting's good and she knows your language a little better than me."

For some reason that simple answer disarmed Ermolkin, who was himself perhaps hoping that the messages were otherworldly decrees. He did not resume arguing but only said to the old man that he should be taken away to the Right Place and have his documents checked.

"I wouldn't advise you to do that," objected the old man sadly. "There was one man, a nice man like you; he checked my documents, but he's not around anymore."

The old man was behaving insolently, but Ermolkin decided not to get involved; he just muttered, "Quack" and, regretting the ruble he'd spent in vain, began shoving his way out of the crowd. But getting out proved no easy matter.

A skinny, unshaven man in an overcoat that reached to his heels, reeking of vodka, approached Ermolkin, saying: "Hey, dad, want to buy some stuff?"

"Some stuff?" said Ermolkin in surprise. "What kind of stuff?"

"Stuff like this." The old man opened the flaps of his topcoat and Ermolkin caught sight of a sawed-off antitank gun.

"You're out of your mind!" said Ermolkin, and went on his way. But, as he pushed his way through, other people tried to sell him an Order of the Red Star, a forged passport, and a certificate given the severely wounded.

What's going on here? thought Ermolkin. Where am I?

"Hey, mister, mister." Boris Evgenevich looked around. A

girl with brightly painted lips was tugging at his sleeve. "Hey, mister, let's go in the shed."

"The shed?" repeated Ermolkin, suspecting that this invitation, too, concealed some horror. "And just what for?"

"To get it." The girl smiled.

"It?"

"Sure." She nodded. "I don't want much. Fifty'll do."

"Just what is it you're saying?" hissed Ermolkin, looking around him as if seeking support.

"What is it I'm saying?" Now the girl had taken offense. "They're getting a hundred for a jar of rolling tobacco over there."

"Listen to her now," the tobacco seller butted into the conversation. "What a comparison. You get a hundred smokes from a jar of rolling tobacco, and look what you pay for one shot with her."

"Don't listen to him, mister." She waved her hand at him. "He's stupid, he doesn't understand the difference. Come on, mister, don't be afraid, I'm clean."

"How dare you." Ermolkin raised his voice, his face flushed. "How dare you propose such filth to me. I am a Communist!" he added, striking his sunken chest with his fist.

It is difficult for an outsider to tell what Ermolkin intended by that. Perhaps he was counting on the whole market, upon hearing he was a Communist, to come running over to shake his hand or to anoint his head with oil, or perhaps to use him as an example, fashion their lives on his, and imitate him in all their undertakings.

"Aha, a Communist." The girl made a face. "If you had said it wasn't worth it, that's one thing, but a Communist is a Communist. Communists like you should be strangled," she suddenly began shouting shrilly.

"Ah . . ." said Ermolkin, and began looking around him again. "What's all this?"

He thought that the people in the market, though wallowing in their bourgeois instincts, would still repel this hostile attack, but no one paid the slightest attention and only the one-armed man looked over at Boris Evgenevich with any sympathy. "You better get going or they might really strangle you," he said almost benevolently and then, forgetting Ermolkin, resumed his cry: "Tobacco, strong stuff!"

Finding no other support, Ermolkin seemed to shrivel and contract; he began making his way through the crowd, but the girl spat at his back and with absolutely no fear of the consequences shouted out: "Shit-ass Communist!"

These words made Ermolkin cringe. He thought lightning would strike at once, that thunder would roll, or, at the very least, that a policeman's whistle would split the air. But there was no lightning, no thunder, no policeman's whistle.

16

Free of the crowd, Ermolkin immediately quickened his pace. The girl remained behind. But her shrill voice was still ringing in his ears. "Sh . . . Communist." He could never utter such an unsuitable and even blasphemous epithet before that holy word. What a horror, thought Ermolkin. Where did these people come from? And where were the authorities? And that old man with his idiotic prophecy? Beware of horses . . . what unmitigated nonsense!

Reflecting as he walked, he did not notice either the wooden gangway or the wattle fence or the light-blue bench, but somehow or other he found himself in front of his own house and recognized it at once.

How did I ever find it? marveled Ermolkin, and then answered his own question: Probably like a horse finds his way home. He walks along, he doesn't think about anything, and his legs themselves take him there. Phoo! spat Ermolkin in a fit of temper. Not horses again!

Upon entering his house, he spotted an older, emaciated-looking woman wearing a dark calico dress, sitting at a table covered with a flower-print tablecloth. Setting her cup of tea aside, the woman looked up in surprise and confusion at her guest. This woman resembled Ermolkin's wife, but she was significantly older than he would have expected. He even thought for a minute that it was not his wife at all but that his mother-in-law had come to see them from Siberia. But the woman raced over to him crying "Bóris!" and he remembered that she, his wife, always pronounced his name with the accent on the first syllable. She threw her arms around his neck as mothers-in-law rarely do. Burying her face in his chest, she wept and murmured incoherently, from which he gathered that she was reproaching him for staying away so long.

"Now, now," he calmed her, patting her bony spine, "you know I've had a lot of work lately."

"Lately," she sobbed. "Lately. I could have been dying all that time."

"Why go on like that." He pushed his wife lightly away from him and glanced into the next room, which had been, if his memory served, the child's. But there was nothing childish about the room, no crib, no toys, no child.

Boris Evgenevich turned to his wife. "And where is our . . ." He chewed his lips, trying to remember his son's name. "And where is that little boy of ours?"

His wife wiped away her tears on the collar of her dress, looked over at Boris Evgenevich with a long, questioning glance, then suddenly, having come to some realization, said: "And just how old do you think our little boy is?"

"Three and a half," said Ermolkin, but then was immediately seized by doubt. "Isn't that right?"

"Our little boy," his wife pronounced slowly, "yesterday"—she swallowed—"was taken to the front." Then she burst into tears.

"That's absurd," muttered Ermolkin. "Taking such little children into the army . . ."

He meant to say that taking little children into the army was out of the question, but then he brought himself up short; he began calculating and figured out that his son had been born the year Lenin had died, which was why he had been given the name Lenliv (at home he was affectionately called Lenlivik). So that meant Lenliv was now . . . Ermolkin subtracted twenty-four from forty-one . . . seventeen . . . yes, seventeen years old . . .

But just how did that happen? Unconsciously Ermolkin put his hand in his pocket, where he felt something sticky. He pulled it out. The two sugar-candy roosters he had bought at the market had melted over the clay one. Ermolkin threw them at the stove.

So then how had he gotten the idea Lenliv was three and a half? That was how old he was when they had come to Dolgov and Boris Evgenevich had assumed the position of editor in chief of *Bolshevik Tempos*. At that time he had been the editor, the proofreader, and the typesetter. Then came organizing the printshop, dealing with village correspondents, collectivization, and other interesting events. He had to keep a sharp eye open not to let any political errors slip into print. Ermolkin had begun spending more and more time at his desk, smoking his cheap cigarettes, drinking tea through a lump of sugar held between his teeth, moving his vigilant pencil along the uneven lines, changing camels into ships of the desert and forests into forest tracts of green-gold. In the beginning he would sometimes return home late at night, sometimes even before dawn, with a debauched look, as if he were coming from his mistress, and he would leave home late, when his wife was already at work and his son in kindergarten. But coming home became more and more a symbolic event and he spent the night in his office with increasing frequency, scrunched up on his uncomfortable leather couch, so that in the morning, splashing some water in his eyes, he could again sit down to his job, which gradually turned from a responsibility to an uncontrollable passion. Of course, were he asked, he would say, and quite sincerely, that he was serving his motherland, Stalin, and the Party, but in fact, he was serving his own petty passion for crippling and maiming words until they were unrecognizable and for searching out and divining any possible political error.

Now something had gone haywire in Ermolkin's soul, and perhaps for the first time he began to feel troubled—how had he spent those fourteen years of his life, his one and only life on this earth? No, he said to himself, it can't go on like this, work is work, serving high ideals is also a good thing, but you must set some time aside, even if only a little for yourself . . .

"Here's what, my dear . . ." he said to his wife.

"My name is Katya," she said.

"Yes, of course, I remember," said Ermolkin, pretending to know. "Here's what, Katya, my dear. I think we must change the way we live. I've really overworked myself. Let's do something together today."

"What shall we do?"

"Well, how do people usually spend their free time?"

"How? Well, for example, people go to the movies," she answered readily.

"To the movies?" said Ermolkin, livening up. "All right, let's go to the movies."

It was stuffy in the Railway Workers' House of Culture, which was crowded with soldiers and evacuees. The best film of all time and of any country, *The Battleship Potemkin*, was playing. The print was old; it kept sputtering and breaking. There was only one projector and the lights went on after each reel. After the third reel two ushers appeared and began checking people's tickets. Years of fatigue caught up with him after the fourth reel and Ermolkin fell asleep. From time to time he would wake and stare bug-eyed at the screen, where someone was being thrown overboard. He would fall back asleep, then wake up again, and again someone was being thrown overboard.

Afterward, home in bed, he was still falling off to sleep and waking back up as he listened to his wife's endless story of how she had lived all those years, how she had raised Lenlivik, how he had cut his first teeth, how he had come down with measles and scarlet fever, how he had gone off to first grade and gotten his first marks, how he had joined the Pioneers and the Young Communists. Again dozing off, Ermolkin thought how nice it was to be in his own home and not sleeping alone but with his wife, and not on his bare couch but on a feather bed, on sheets crackling with starch. He thought his wife noble for not having left him during all those years and thought himself noble for coming to his senses in time and returning to her.

But his old habit of sleeping on the office couch had left its mark. Opening his eyes the next morning, Ermolkin needed time to realize where he was and who was lying there beside him. Then he remembered everything and he smiled.

He got up a little later, put on his striped pajamas (set out the night before by his wife, who had hung them on the back of a chair), his slippers, and went to the mailbox. He collected all the newspapers to which he subscribed, including his very own *Bolshevik Tempos*.

As a matter of fact, he was beginning his day as he usually did, as he had in all his fourteen years of newspaper work. But today the principal difference was that he had picked up his own newspaper not as an editor but as an ordinary, happy man who has the habit, before embarking on his own daily duties, of glancing through articles to catch up on the news of the world, while sipping tea in the comfort of his home.

And so his eyes began slipping from line to line. He started with the lead editorial. But he was not able to think of himself as an ordinary reader for very long. Gradually the editor in him overcame the reader. Years of habit made themselves felt, and distracted from his tea, he began scanning the lines with his spoon, automatically noting how many times the word "Stalin" appeared, whether the commas and periods had been properly used, how the article had been type-set, and to check if, all in all, everything was in order, when suddenly . . .

I truly do not wish to write any further, my hand will not move, the pen falls from the hand.

Comrade Stalin's instructions, read Ermolkin, *have become, for all the Soviet peoples, the gelding of wisdom, the most profound understanding of the objective laws of social development.* Understanding nothing, he read it again. And again without understanding. The word "gelding" wasn't quite right. He tossed aside the spoon, took up a pencil, and, making special marks on the margins of the newspaper indicating an insertion, changed "gelding" to "horse of the draught persuasion." He read the new version: *Comrade Stalin's instructions have become, for all the Soviet peoples, the horse of the draught persuasion of wisdom, the most profound understanding of the objective laws of social development.* The sentence had not become any clearer in its new form.

He restored the word "gelding" and read it through again and . . .

Ermolkin's wife, Katya, was in the kitchen ironing her husband's white shirt when she heard an inhuman howl. She ran into the bedroom, where she saw her husband in an unnatural stance. Slipping slowly to the floor, he was twisting his legs, beating his head against the back of the chair, and, his eyes bulging, was shouting as if two dozen scorpions were stinging him all over.

"Bóris!" she cried, rushing to her husband and shaking him by the shoulder. "What's the matter with you?"

Boris howled, still slipping downward. She grabbed him under the arms and pulled him to her, trying to keep him on the chair. Though outwardly frail he proved quite heavy.

Finally she succeeded in returning him to a state of uncertain equilibrium.

"Sit there a minute," she said, pushing him against the back of the chair. "I'll be right back."

She brought him a mug of water. Boris Evgenevich seized the mug eagerly, and his teeth knocking against the rim, spilling the water over his chest, he took a few convulsive sips. Then seeming somewhat calmer, he flung his head against the back of the chair as if he were about to be shaved, opened his mouth, and rolled his eyes.

"Bóris," said Katya tenderly, "tell me what's wrong with you."

"There." With no change in position Ermolkin pointed at the newspaper, his finger crooked. "There . . . Read it yourself . . . the underlined part."

"Comrade Stalin's instructions," read Katya, "have become, for all the Soviet peoples . . ."

Ermolkin was listening, his eyes half closed as if from too bright a light. With trepidation he was waiting for the ill-fated word, hoping Katya would read it the way it should actually be.

". . . the gelding of wisdom, the most profound . . ."

"Enough!" Ermolkin jumped up and began dashing about the room with uncommon energy.

She watched him in utter confusion. "But you asked me . . ."

"I didn't ask for anything!" Continuing to dash about, he now stuck his fingers in his ears. "I don't want to hear even one word of it."

She picked up the newspaper again and moving her lips she slowly read not only what had been underlined but several lines both before and after it. Ermolkin ran over to her and ripped the newspaper from her.

"Bóris!" she cried. "I don't understand, what are you so excited about?"

Ermolkin came to a dead stop.

"You don't?" He turned to the stove. "She doesn't understand." Then he turned to her again and asked, syllable by syllable, "What-don't-you-un-der-stand? You see what's written there. It's complete nonsense. The instructions have been turned into a gelding. A gelding, a gelding, a gelding . . ."

He threw the newspaper to the floor and seized his head.

Katya looked at him with sympathy and confusion. She really did not understand. Making allowances for the shortcomings of her own female mind, she thought that the line which had set up such a storm in her husband was no more nonsensical than any of the rest.

"But Bóris," she said softly, "I think . . ."

"You think!" he shouted. "She thinks! What do you think?"

"I think," she said quietly, trying not to incite his anger, "that maybe it isn't so stupid. You remember in physics the unit for measuring power is horsepower. And perhaps Comrade Stalin's wisdom could be measured by . . ."

"Gelding power?" prompted Ermolkin.

"That's right." She nodded with a smile. "Not one- but two- or three-gelding power."

"Ha-ha-ha-ha." Ermolkin broke into loud laughter. He was laughing as hysterically and uncontrollably as he had just been crying. Suddenly he stopped, his eyes bulging. "Fool!" he said softly.

She recoiled as if from a blow. "What?"

"Fool! Total fool. You've got a hundred-gelding-power stupidity in that bird brain of yours."

"Bóris," she said in reproach, "I waited for you all those years."

"And for nothing," he screeched. "It's all your fault and that overgrown son of yours."

"Bóris!"

"Boris what? Once in all these years I allow myself a little . . . and then . . . No, something must be done."

He pulled off his pajamas, tossing the tops and the bottoms in different directions. He put on his usual suit. And, having called his wife a fool and cursing himself for giving in to weakness and deciding to visit his family, he dashed out of the house.

Bolshevik Tempos was already sold out in the town's single newspaper kiosk. Just to be on the safe side, Ermolkin peeped into the post office, where he learned that all the subscribers had been sent their copies and one, as usual, had gone off to Moscow, to the Lenin Library.

17

Different people tell different stories about what happened next.

According to one version, Ermolkin undertook a desperate and, in its own way, unprecedented attempt to confiscate and destroy the entire edition containing the ill-fated "gelding." To that end he supposedly ran around to all the subscribers living within the city limits of Dolgov and drove out to those who lived outside the city. He also paid a visit to the district library, the office for Party education, all the recreation and reading rooms of the kolkhozes, sovkhozes, and local industrial enterprises. He bought up some copies (sometimes at great expense—in one case the sum of one hundred rubles has been mentioned), some he begged for nothing, others he stole. As a result he succeeded in gathering up the entire edition except, naturally, for the one copy which had been sent off to the Lenin Library. After that, they say, Ermolkin began suffering from nightmares. He would dream of the Lenin Library, the edition being read swiftly and the Right People being informed of it and from There (everything's close in Moscow) it would reach Stalin himself. They also say that apparently Ermolkin had the same dream each and every night: Stalin is brought the edition with the word "gelding" underlined in red pencil.

Stalin reads, Stalin puffs on his pipe, Stalin asks calmly: And who committed this sabotage, this ideological subversion?

One of his closest co-workers points out to Stalin the next page, which has the heading EDITOR IN CHIEF B. ERMOLKIN.

Then Comrade Stalin issues a brief order which descends rapidly through various departments, reaches the local organs, and that night a covered vehicle known as a Black Maria drives out of a gate, stops in front of the entrance to the newspaper office, leather boots come stomping down the corridor.

"Aaaaaa," Ermolkin would scream in his sleep, and wake up from his own scream in a cold sweat.

Another version has it that Ermolkin failed to obtain two copies—besides the one sent to the Lenin Library, there was the one subscribed to by the local Institution, and the order to send out the Black Maria originates not with Stalin but with the Institution itself, that is, not at the top but the bottom.

In version three, Ermolkin did not succeed in collecting even a single copy, the entire issue having been put to use at once—for rolling cigarettes, for wrapping herring (which at that particular time were being issued to ration card holders instead of meat), and for one particular use which was, in fact, why people subscribed to it at all. According to this version, the readers simply never noticed the "gelding" because in Dolgov nobody ever read *Bolshevik Tempos.*

A fourth version maintains that everyone read it, everyone noticed the "gelding," but, like Ermolkin's wife, they decided that it must be the new official position. And only the two Thinkers argued furiously for three days in an attempt to understand what it could mean and constructed the most fantastic conjectures on this account.

And so there were diverse versions, but they all concluded with Ermolkin's nightmares, the arrival of the Black Maria, and the muffled scream, "Aaaaaaaa!"

It is known for certain that, in time, Ermolkin regained his composure. Perhaps he even decided that the whole thing would blow over. And it was then that he received an anonymous story at the paper, entitled "Can a Gelding Become a Human Being?"

The anonymous author answered his own question in the affirmative. He introduced arguments, already familiar to the reader, concerning the horse's unparalleled capacity for work. *And that the horse has no fingers,* he wrote, refuting any possible objections, *only bespeaks its inability to fire a rifle or play musical instruments, but this shortcoming should not be seen as a reflection on its capacity for abstract thought.* The author did not stop there. He made his question even more pointed: what sort of man can the hardworking horse be transformed into, Soviet or non-Soviet? He maintained that if a horse labored under the conditions of the Soviet system, then he would undoubtedly be transformed into a Soviet man.

The author concluded his story with misgivings that his scientifically daring thoughts could be misinterpreted by conservatives and bureaucrats, and he wrote that it was precisely for that reason that he could not, for the moment, reveal his name to the reading public.

The story drove Ermolkin into a fury. He stamped his feet and demanded to know who had dared pass this rubbish on to him. It turned out the culprit was Lifshits, who had just finished a bout of hard drinking. Ermolkin summoned Lifshits, tongue-lashed him, and threatened not only to fire him but to bring him to court for malingering and being late to the job. Later on, he calmed down and began to think, and decided that the note was not simply the ravings of some unknown graphomaniac but an allusion to the fact that he need not wait in lordly fashion for the Black Maria to come to him but that he should go himself and confess everything.

18

Had Chonkin only known how much trouble his mere existence was causing! To all appearances he was just sitting in his cell, not disturbing a soul. If they made him do something, he did it. If they gave him food, he ate. If they didn't, he didn't ask for any. And still he was managing to be a disturbance.

But, as a matter of fact, what's so surprising about that? Just by being where he is every living person causes somebody some trouble. The world is packed with people and every one wants to get ahead.

To be free of Chonkin was not such an easy matter. I tried it myself. I thought, to hell with that damn Chonkin, let other people write about him or nobody at all, for that matter. I'll get myself one of those heroes the newspapers are always praising and publishers pay good money for. I'll get a general . . . Well, doesn't even have to be a general, could be a sergeant who trains his subordinates by his own personal example. Or maybe some worker-hero, merciless in daily life and active in his factory.

Well, and what do you suppose happened? I tried, but nothing came of it. I write general, out comes Chonkin. I write worker-hero, out comes Chonkin again. This is not from any perniciousness on my part and not because I want to denounce or subvert anything, that's just how it keeps coming out.

19

Well, let's turn back to Lieutenant Filippov. He can't rid himself of Chonkin either. He prepared everything in the proper way, drew up the proper papers, sent Chonkin's case to the military tribunal, and then he began waiting for them to take that cursed Chonkin off his hands. But they didn't. And so the lieutenant put in a call to the military tribunal. He was in luck.

"Colonel Dobrenky here," came a voice through the receiver.

The lieutenant was terribly happy because it was precisely Colonel Dobrenky, who was never in, with whom he needed to speak. The colonel was never in because he was the chairman of the traveling three-man commission known as the troika and was always out on assignment. The lieutenant stated the nature of his question concisely. The case against Chonkin was completed and had been given over to the disposal of the military tribunal. So then shouldn't Chonkin himself be transferred to them? While in prison Chonkin was avoiding the punishment he deserved and, what's more, was having a corrupting influence on the local prisoners.

"I understand. I'll explain," rattled the receiver. "We are not taking that Chonkin of yours at the present moment because we have no room here. The garrison guardhouse is full up. Besides, an order has been issued—deserters, soldiers with self-inflicted wounds, panic-mongers, and other such small fry are to be tried publicly, on the spot, which will have enormous educational significance for the entire local population. Understand, Lieutenant?"

"I do," answered Lieutenant Filippov. "And when can we expect you?"

"No need to wait for us. The province is stuffed to the gills with Chonkins and we only have one troika. When it's your turn, we'll be there."

The lieutenant replaced the receiver and thought, Well, all right, doesn't matter. In the end it's not me who's waiting, it's Chonkin. And even without Chonkin I've plenty to do. There's somebody standing over there and he, too, needs something from me. But just who is that and how did he get in here?"

The lieutenant snapped to, shuddered, and looked over at the man who was standing like a petitioner by the door.

"What's your problem?" asked the lieutenant.

"Are you speaking to me?" asked the man, touching his chest with one finger.

"Who else? I don't see anybody here but the two of us."

"True, true," agreed the man sadly, and approached the lieutenant. "I realize you know everything. But I request that the fact that I have come myself be taken into consideration."

"What are you referring to?" asked the lieutenant wearily.

"To a certain gelding . . ."

"Gelding?" The lieutenant pulled over his desk calendar and noted down the word "gelding" with a capital G, thinking it a last name.

"First name and patronymic?" he asked.

"Boris Evgenevich."

"Yes." The lieutenant nodded, jotting it down. "And what has he done?"

"Who?"

"Why that . . ." The lieutenant checked his calendar. "That Boris Evgenevich Gelding."

"You misunderstood me. Boris Evgenevich, that's me." He again tapped his chest with one finger, as if explaining something to a deaf-mute.

"I see," said the lieutenant. "And what is it you want, Citizen Gelding?"

"Excuse me." The visitor smiled. "You have misunderstood me again. Gelding is only a typo. A terrible, awkward, amazingly stupid typo. It should have been 'gilding,' but the typesetter took the wrong letter from his box. An awful mistake. A tragic misunderstanding. You understand, I always looked after everything myself, but that day, as soon as that Chonkin's wife came . . . And the result is that sort of error . . ." Ermolkin grabbed his head and gnashed his teeth.

The lieutenant frowned. From everything his visitor had said he had only understood two words: "Chonkin" and "mistake."

"Citizen Gelding," he said sternly, "stop talking nonsense.

For the first and the last time I advise you to understand, and to remember, that we do not make mistakes."

"I assure you that you are making a mistake," objected Boris Evgenevich animatedly. "I am not a gelding, I . . ."

"I, I, I," mimicked the lieutenant, wrinkling up his face. "I can see you are not a gelding, you're an ass."

Ermolkin changed countenance. "What? What? What did you say? How dare you call me that, me, an old Party member . . . If Dzerzhinsky were alive . . . Even with ideological enemies he did not permit . . ."

"Aha," said Filippov, taking him at his word. "So you are an ideological enemy?"

"What?" Ermolkin paled from the unjust insult. "Me, an ideological enemy? Yes, of course, I do realize that I have made a mistake. But I am a Communist. I have been a Party member since nineteen-twenty—" His lips kept moving but he was unable to remember the exact year. "I understand," he said, flaring up, flapping his arms like wings. "You won't take into consideration that I've turned myself in. But there's no way you can conceal that fact. I will not tolerate . . ."

"*You* will not tolerate?" Completely losing his self-control, Filippov cursed a blue streak at Ermolkin and his mother.

"Snot nose!" cried Ermolkin, forgetting where he was. "The same to you!"

This was beyond toleration. Filippov pressed a button and Sergeant Klim Svintsov appeared on the scene. Svintsov made a few energetic movements and Ermolkin, his collar torn off, found himself at liberty again.

"I won't let this matter rest here," he said, rubbing his bruised knee, and he set off to the district capital in search of justice—that is, to demand that he be placed in jail but that it be noted in his file that he had appeared voluntarily and not been brought in by force.

At this point some readers may well ask: While Ermolkin was so busy seeking justice, did the newspaper *Bolshevik*

Tempos appear or not? And if it did, under whose name? If the truth be told, the author could not be less interested and cannot say anything definite on this subject. As for Ermolkin, it is know that he made his way to the provincial capital, spent the night at the railroad station, and the following morning was the first to call on Roman Gavrilovich Luzhin.

20

___

It is difficult to imagine how he contained it all, but Ermolkin believed, on the one hand, that our special agencies consisted entirely of pristinely pure people (though a bit, perhaps, mysterious), and on the other hand, he pictured the district chief as something of a vampire with a wolf's jaws and enormous hairy paws. Instead, what he saw sitting at the broad desk was not a man but a head: a shaved head with large ears resting its chin on the desk and looking at Ermolkin with little eyes through thick, pinkish glasses. Ermolkin was thrown into confusion and stopped in the middle of the office. The head swung to one side, and suddenly a little man, almost a dwarf, in a military uniform appeared from behind the desk and glided swiftly over to Ermolkin on his castor-like little feet.

"Boris Evgenevich!" exclaimed the little man, grasping Ermolkin's hand in both of his. "Monstrously happy. To see. You. Here," he said, as if putting a period after almost every word. He began to click his teeth, which were large but in no way wolflike.

"You know me?" remarked Ermolkin without surprise.

"Of course, of course," said Luzhin. "It would be strange. If I didn't." He smiled with his entire mouth and clicked his teeth again.

"So, you know everything?"

"Yes. Of course. Everything. Absolutely."

"I thought so." Ermolkin shook his head. "But I ask you to note that I turned myself in."

"Yes," said Luzhin. "Of course. We will. Without fail. Where is your statement?"

"My statement?" said Ermolkin confused. "I actually thought. To do it. Orally." Unconsciously, he had become infected by Luzhin's way of speaking.

"Too bad," said Roman Gavrilovich. "We like everything. To be on paper. And so. Please." He took Ermolkin by the elbow and led him to the door. "There, the secretary. Get a piece of paper. From her. And state everything briefly but in detail. As our great proletarian engineer. Of human souls said. So that the words are close but the thoughts . . . How did that go again?"

"Have room."

"That's right." Luzhin laughed and clicked his teeth. "So they have room. Then drop back in. Meanwhile. Excuse me. Things to do. Monstrously busy." And thrusting the heavy door open in front of Ermolkin, he made a sweep of his little hand, saying, "Please."

Stunned, Ermolkin went out into the reception room. There he almost bumped into a woman he immediately recognized: it was after her visit that all his troubles had begun. "So that's it!" Ermolkin was thunderstruck. "So, it was a put-up job, was it. How clever! How cunning!"

"Hello." Ermolkin smiled at her. "You remember me?"

"I do," said Nyura, frowning.

She realized that it was no accident that the child murderer was there. Obviously he had already warned them of her coming. She was even backing up toward the door when Luzhin peeped out of his office and, seeing Nyura, asked: "Here to see me?"

"Yes," answered Nyura.

"Come in."

Nyura vanished behind Luzhin and the closing door. Ermolkin stared at the door for a good minute, then, remembering what he was about, walked over to the secretary, a buxom woman in uniform with two triangles in her buttonholes and a "Voroshilov Rifleman" badge. Ermolkin asked her for paper, sat down at the visitors' table in the far corner, took his fountain pen from his pocket, shook it until ink spattered on the floor, and then began his sad tale: *The workers of our district have, with a great upsurge of labor, met the* . . . Then Ermolkin stopped. What am I writing? he thought. What upsurge? What workers? And what did they meet?

In his long years of service in the press, he had always begun his articles, notes, editorials, and topical sketches with this sentence, and it had never failed him. That sentence was always appropriate, and led easily into his basic idea, but in this case . . . the old newshound looked at his opening line and gradually realized that he, who could write anything on any given theme—labor initiative, socialist competition, the shearing of sheep, ideological hand-to-hand combat—could not find words to describe an actual event whose witness, accomplice, or, even more precisely, whose culprit he himself happened to be.

Crossing out what he had written, Ermolkin began thinking of a new opening when the clatter of approaching boots sounded in the corridor; three men entered the reception room—two soldiers, and between them a civilian wearing a dark-blue suit.

"Is Roman Gavrilovich in?" one of the military men asked the secretary.

"He's busy," she said.

"We'll wait."

They took chairs by the wall, the civilian in the middle, the soldiers on either side of him. The soldiers sat frozen, with immobile faces, while the citizen, on the contrary, showed the liveliest interest in everything he observed. He examined the reception room, the secretary, and Ermolkin. For his part, Ermolkin stole a quick glance at the civilian. He was a tall, middle-aged man with a look of authority about him. He conducted himself as if wishing to demonstrate that he was there by accident, due to a misunderstanding which would be cleared up immediately, and then those who had brought him here would be severely punished.

21

It should be noted that Nyura and Ermolkin had come to Lieutenant Colonel Luzhin's office at a most inappropriate or perhaps, on the contrary, a most appropriate time. Luzhin was in no mood for them. A dispatch had just arrived from the Center, Moscow, but Luzhin had been unable to fathom its meaning even after it had been decoded.

> Ramzai* [the dispatch read], citing information received from the German Ambassador Otto, reports from Tokyo that, in the district of Dolgov, the personal agent of Admiral Canaris,† code name Hans, formerly preserved,‡ has begun his activity. Judging by indirect indications, he has access to secrets of state importance. More specific data not presently available.
>
> Taking into account Dolgov's strategic position and the damage which could result from the leakage of highly important information, Com. Lavrentev§ has ordered that all necessary measures be taken and that the spy be uncovered and rendered harmless within a period of seven days. Responsibility for fulfilling this order rests directly on you.

---

* Ramzai—code name of the Soviet Intelligence agent Richard Zorge.
† Canaris—Chief of the Abwehr (German Military Intelligence).
‡ Preserved——clearly, a specialized espionage term. It would be difficult to assume that Admiral Canaris's personal agent was preserved in the literal meaning of the word, that is, sealed in some sort of tin can. However, I have heard that certain agents can be extremely accommodating.
§ Com. Lavrentev—code name of Com. Beria, an agent of international imperialism.

Luzhin was dumbfounded.

Spies had been uncovered previously in the territory under his jurisdiction, but they had all either been dreamed up by Luzhin himself or by his subordinates. It was possible that this Hans had been dreamed up there, in the Center, but, naturally, you couldn't just ask whether he was a fiction or a fact. Someone not in the know might think, What's the difference? But the difference is crucial. Because a fictitious Hans could be found in two minutes—grab somebody, call him Hans, lock him up. But if he's real . . . It's harder to work with real ones.

Luzhin reread the decoded dispatch many times, pondered each word, but could not understand a thing. Who was this Ramzai* and why was he reporting from Tokyo? How was it possible to issue such orders without having some approximate information as to who this Hans was? Well, all right, let's suppose that his last name, residence, and place of employment are unknown, but there have to be certain clues. Height, age, hair, and eye color, certain secrets are accessible.

Like any man in his place, like his own subordinates, Luzhin cursed those above him, considering them fools, bureaucrats, and petty tyrants who issued orders without once considering their viability in practice. Still, it would have been difficult to guess from Luzhin's appearance that he was at all preoccupied. He received Nyura just as amicably as he had Ermolkin. He seated her in a comfortable armchair, while he, legs dangling, perched on the other. He crossed his arms over his chest and smiled. "I'm monstrously interested in hearing what you have to say."

Nyura, confused by such an affectionate reception, said, "I'm pregnant."

"What did you say?" Luzhin clapped his hands. "Well done!" Sliding down from his armchair, he ran over to Nyura and

* At that time the name of Richard Zorge was known to a very small circle of people, of which Luzhin, clearly, was not one.

began shaking her hand. "Congratulations. From deep down. As they say." He returned to his chair. "And where do you want to send him?"

"Who?" asked Nyura.

"Him." Luzhin pointed at his stomach. "You've got to find a place for him. Why don't you give him to us? We'll make a man. Out of him. A real one. Of course, I'm only"—Luzhin clicked his teeth—"joking."

Nyura dropped her eyes in embarrassment and smiled.

For a moment neither of them said anything. Luzhin asked Nyura if he could help her in some way. Nyura burst into tears and began to explain that her husband had been put in prison and she was trying to intercede for him; she had been turned down everywhere as an outside party, but she wasn't an outside party because she had lived with him. Luzhin asked her to relate everything in order and she, seeing that he was truly interested, began telling him how the two airplanes had come, how Chonkin had appeared, how they had become acquainted, how they started living together. She told him that Chonkin was dying to go to the front but was not taken, how he was attacked and had to defend his post. And now, just because he had stuck to the regulations, he'd been taken away and she'd been driven from one official to another but could not find any justice anywhere. They would not give her an appointment, would not accept her parcels for him, and always called her an outside party.

Luzhin listened attentively. From time to time he hopped down from his chair, darting in excitement about the room, and then would return to his place and listen again. When Nyura had finished her story he walked over to her, stroked her head, and said sympathetically, "You poor woman!"

Nyura looked over at Luzhin, moved forward, set her head against his shoulder, and began wailing. She had frequent occasion to cry lately but she had never yet sobbed like that. She tried to stop but she couldn't.

Luzhin stroked her hair and murmured, "You poor thing! You've been through so much! It's all right. There, there."

Then Nyura grew calmer and he began darting about the room again, rubbing his hands and clicking his teeth.

"A disgrace!" he exclaimed, and clicked his teeth. "Still so many soulless people in the world. Bureaucrats, formalists. No matter how much we struggle against them, they . . . Well, it's all right. We"—he darted over to Nyura and poked a finger against his chest—"we will help you. Yes. We will help."

He then muttered a few words from which Nyura understood that he, Luzhin, would spare no effort and, if they failed in returning Chonkin to her, "We will choose. Someone else for you. An even better one. We will help. You. But you, too. Will help us. Please. Please!" Luzhin closed his eyes and laid his hand across his heart.

Nyura did not understand how and whom they could select for her in place of Chonkin; she wanted to say that she didn't need anybody better, that Chonkin was perfectly fine for her. But Luzhin's request for her assistance had made her lose her train of thought and she said that, of course, if she could . . .

"You can," interrupted Luzhin. "You live in Krasnoye?"

"I do." Nyura nodded.

"How are things there? What's the prevailing mood?"

Nyura looked over at him questioningly.

"Didn't you understand?" Luzhin smiled. "I speak in my own way. Completely clearly. I'm asking, What kind of mood are the villagers in? Sad?"

Nyura didn't like the question. She shielded her fellow villagers, assuring him that, on the contrary, their mood was extremely good.

"Good?" Luzhin beamed as he hopped away from Nyura.

"Good," confirmed Nyura.

"Monstrously interesting. There's a war. People are dying.

But they feel good. And just why? Perhaps they're waiting. For the Germans?" He winked at Nyura and smiled.

"No!" Nyura was frightened that she had said something wrong. "They're not."

"Who are they waiting for?"

"They're not waiting for anybody."

"So why are they in a good mood?"

Nyura decided to correct the mistake on the spot and said that she had not expressed herself well; sometimes the mood was good but mostly it was bad.

"Bad?" repeated Luzhin. "Depressed? They don't believe we'll win?"

"They do! They do!" Nyura hastened to reply.

"But the mood is bad?"

"It's not bad," said Nyura, realizing that she'd muddled it.

"Then how is it?" asked Luzhin.

"I don't know," said Nyura.

"So there." Luzhin glowered. "You see. I give you my all. I wanted to help. I was sincere. But you weren't. It's good. It's bad. You don't know. Does that mean you don't want to help us?"

"No, why?" said Nyura, frowning.

"I don't know why. But I see you don't want to. Of course, we know everything anyway, but I wanted to hear it from you. What do people believe in? What are they saying? Some people have improper thoughts. We'd like to expose them in time, correct them, retrain them. Later they themselves will say. Thank you. By the way, what does your chairman have to say?"

"Our chairman?" repeated Nyura. "About what?"

"Just in general."

"In general?"

"In general."

"Swears all the time," said Nyura.

"Swears?" Luzhin perked up. "But just how? No. I don't

want you to repeat it. I just want to know, is it political or just plain swearing?"

"Just plain," said Nyura.

"Hm!" Luzhin was clearly dissatisfied with her replies. It seemed that not only did he not believe but he did not want to believe that everything was going so well in the village of Krasnoye.

"All right then." Hands behind his back, he paced the office. "You still don't wish to be sincere with me. All right then. You can't force a person. To be nice. As the saying goes. We will help you. But you won't help us. Yes. By the way, do you happen to know Hans?"

"Hens?" said Nyura, surprised.

"That's right."

"Everybody knows hens." Nyura shrugged her shoulders. "How can you live in a village without hens?"

"You can't?" repeated Luzhin quickly. "Yes. Of course. To live in a village. Without Hans. Impossible. Absolutely." He pulled over his desk calendar and took pen in hand. "Last name?"

"Belyashova," Nyura answered readily.

"Belya . . . No. Not that. I don't need your last name but Hans's. What?" Luzin frowned. "You don't want to tell me that either?"

Nyura looked over at Luzhin, completely baffled. Her lips trembled, tears appeared in her eyes again.

"I don't understand," she said slowly. "How could hens have last names?"

"Hens?" repeated Luzhin. "What? Hens? Ah!" He suddenly understood everything and hopped down to the floor and stamped his feet. "Get out! Get out of here!"

Nyura, too, rose and retreated, looking around her.

"Out!" shouted Luzhin, pushing her in the back. "Out, you miserable woman!"

"But what about Chonkin?" she asked stubbornly.

"Out!" flared Luzhin, shoving her. "Out! I'll show you Chonkin. You want to be his wife, you will! That we can do. That we'll arrange. Without fail."

Having shoved Nyura out, he returned to his desk, wiped his face until his handkerchief was drenched in sweat. Recovering his breath, he rang his bell and the secretary entered.

"The thing is," he said to her, "this Chonkin case has me monstrously confused. Why did this deserter show such stubborn resistance? Something's not right here. And then there's that Hans. Ask Filippov if that Chonkin is connected with anyone by the name of Hans. Send a coded dispatch to Chonkin's former residence. Data should be gathered. Who is he? What did he do before the army? Everything. Who else is here to see me? Send them in!"

22

Ermolkin was still writing his deposition when Nyura, flushed and weeping, came rushing out of Luzhin's office. Ermolkin thought he would be called in immediately and began writing hurriedly. But the bell rang and the secretary, straightening her field shirt, went into Luzhin's office. Upon returning she said to one of the soldiers: "Roman Gavrilovich will see you now."

The soldiers sprang up, lifted the civilian to his feet, and all three of them disappeared into Luzhin's office.

They had been inside only two or three minutes when suddenly an inhuman howl was heard, the door was flung open, and the soldiers led the civilian across the reception room. He no longer bore any resemblance to that self-assured person who had just entered Luzhin's office. His jacket was gone, his shirt was torn at the back, his head hung low, and his half-bent legs staggered underneath him. The soldiers were supporting him from either side so that he wouldn't fall.

Suddenly an unsmiling Luzhin sprang out after them into

the corridor, from where Ermolkin could hear his loud voice: "Take him down below and have a little talk with him there. Try to convince him!"

Luzhin returned, ran to his office, but, having noticed Ermolkin, turned around at the threshold. "How are you doing? All ready?"

"Almost," said Ermolkin, struggling with various feelings. "One minute. Still a little more to go."

"Monstrously sorry." Luzhin smiled. "But there's no time. None. Give me what you've done."

He darted into his office ahead of Ermolkin. With an elegant sweep of his foot he kicked aside the dark-blue suit jacket lying on the floor, sat down at his desk, and his head smiled with all its teeth at Ermolkin.

"Please." His little hand hopped across the desk.

Trembling with terror, Ermolkin handed him what he had written.

"Fine," said Roman Gavrilovich, bringing the paper up close to his eyes. *"With a great upsurge in labor . . .* Is this an article?"

"No." Ermolkin lowered his eyes. "It's my confession."

"Original," said Luzhin encouragingly. "Even very. But somehow. Too much background."

"I'm still a journalist, you know." Ermolkin smiled modestly.

"Ah, well. Yes. Of course. Your own style. Very original. On the whole. People here write more simply. Some begin straightforwardly: I did such and such. But usually. These are not journalists. However. We even get . . . Anyway," he said, opening his desk drawer and inserting Ermolkin's composition in it, "we'll read it. With the greatest pleasure. I anticipate monstrous delight."

He closed the drawer and smiled at Ermolkin.

"But please tell me," asked Ermolkin, now in a state, "what will happen to me for this?"

"For what?" asked Luzhin. He had no idea what Ermolkin meant. "In general we don't determine the punishment. The court does that. However. If we keep in mind the laws of wartime . . ."

"But I'm asking that the fact that I turned myself in be taken into consideration," Ermolkin hastened to interject.

"Oh, yes," recollected Luzhin. "Almost overlooked that. If we take into account that, on the one hand, wartime law is in effect. But on the other, the fact that you came yourself and we did not have to hunt you down, then . . . remember, I'm not deciding for the court . . . this is my personal opinion . . . but I think. Maybe. Oh. Ten years."

"Ten years!" cried Ermolkin in horror. "But I didn't do it on purpose."

"That's just what's going to save you," explained Luzhin. "Had you done it on purpose, we'd have you shot."

Ermolkin's head was spinning. His body slackened. He covered his face with his hands and sat without moving for quite a while. Then he took his hands from his face and again saw before him Luzhin's benevolent face.

"Any further questions?" asked Luzhin obligingly.

"No, no, that's all."

"All right. Then just what are you waiting for?"

"Well, I'm waiting . . . for when . . . for them . . . to take me away," said Ermolkin, finally finding the right words.

"Aha." Luzhin nodded. "I see. I'm monstrously sorry. But right now. We just cannot. So go back home. Continue working. Write about upsurges in labor. And wait. You can depend on us. As soon as you're needed, I'll send someone right away. Meanwhile, all the best. But one minute. Were you ever called Hans? No?"

"Me? Hans?" Ermolkin gnawed his lips. "I've been called a gelding. But Hans . . ."

"No?" asked Luzhin.

"No."

"Too bad." Luzhin smiled. "Give me your pass, please. I'll sign it."

They say that afterward, in the company of friends, Luzhin told the story of the unfortunate editor and laughed wildly. They say that he intended to read what Ermolkin had written when he had time to spare, but either forgot or never got around to it. Later on, when our troops were retreating, parts of the archives were destroyed, including Ermolkin's manuscript. A monstrous pity.

23

To Lieutenant S/S Filippov
EXTREMELY URGENT
Top secret, by special courier
Ramzai, citing information received from the German Ambassador Otto, reports from Tokyo that in the district of Dolgov, the personal agent of Admiral Canaris, code name Hans, formerly preserved, has begun his activity. Judging by indirect indications, he has access to state secrets. More specific data not presently available.

Taking Dolgov's strategic importance into account and the damage which could result from the leakage of highly important information, Com. Lavrentev has ordered that all necessary precautions be taken and that the spy be uncovered and rendered harmless within a period of five days. Responsibility for fulfilling this order rests directly on you.

I am expressing my extreme concern that the Chonkin case has still not been concluded.

Luzhin

24

The boy sent from the kolkhoz office found Gladishev sitting on a bench in front of his house. Ever since the "misfortune," as he put it, Kuzma Matveyevich had been spending all his free time there if the weather was good. Everyone had noticed that Gladishev had changed greatly after Nyura's voracious cow Beauty had gobbled up his experimental garden. Gladishev had grown gloomy, no longer engaged his fellow villagers in scientific conversation, and since the time of the disaster, no one had even seen him once in his garden. Moreover, when Aphrodite took advantage of the incident to throw out of the house all the pots of human excrement that Gladishev had been collecting to use as fertilizer, Gladishev offered no resistance.

At that moment he was sitting on his bench gazing off into empty space beyond the river Tyopa when a headless boy appeared in front of him, the head cut off by Gladishev's hat. Gladishev raised his hat a bit and saw that the boy was Grinka, older son of the bookkeeper Volkov.

"Uncle Kuzma, there's a telephone message for you," said Grinka, handing the breeder a strip of yellow paper.

Gladishev was surprised, they never used to deliver telephone messages to him. Messages were delivered to members of the District Committee, deputies of the local soviets, and sometimes to members of the government and activists. But he was unable to read the text, the letters were tiny and irregular. All he could make out was his last name and the number 10.

"Wait a minute," he said to the boy and went into his house waving the sheet of paper.

Aphrodite was rolling cookie dough on the table with a green bottle. Hercules was sitting on the floor in the middle of the room, sucking the big toe of his right foot. Still waving the paper, Gladishev skirted Hercules and walked past his wife, hoping that she would ask him what the paper was. Aphrodite looked over at him, noticed the paper, but did not ask about it. Gladishev found the sugar bowl, took out a piece of lump sugar, thought for a second, broke it in two, and brought half out to the boy in his yard. Then he went back into the house for his glasses. Nothing had changed there except that Hercules was now sucking on his left foot. Gladishev knew that his glasses should be in the cabinet but began looking for them on the windowsill, hoping to attract more attention that way.

"Now where are those glasses of mine," he said with deliberate annoyance, rummaging with both hands along the windowsill. "I have to read this telephone message and my glasses are gone."

Aphrodite rolled the dough into little cylinders and began cutting it into narrow strips.

"You hear me? I said they brought me a telephone message," repeated Gladishev louder, passing from feigned to genuine irritation. "A special courier just galloped up." Forgetting the little boy, Grinka, he pictured a daring horseman on a lathered horse.

Aphrodite, a stubborn woman, again said nothing and allowed no expression of delight at such an uncommon event. Gladishev had no choice but to find his glasses in their usual place. He sat by the window, fixed his glasses to his nose, read the telephone message, and went cold. He was being summoned, not to the District Committee office, not to a session of the District Soviet, not to a conference for top production people, but somewhere else entirely.

"Aiyayayayai!" howled Gladishev, grabbing his head.

This so surprised Hercules that he took his foot out of his mouth.

Even Aphrodite realized that something bad had happened. She stopped cutting the dough and looked over at her husband questioningly. Gladishev continued howling.

"What's with you?" she asked.

"Don't even ask." Gladishev shook his head. "I'm sunk, completely sunk."

"What are you howling about?" said Aphrodite in a hysterical voice. "Talk sense."

Gladishev stopped howling, removed his glasses, and said softly, "They're summoning me, Aphrodite."

"Summoning you where?" asked Aphrodite, failing to understand.

"Where, where." Gladishev grew angry. "You know where. I wrote to the newspaper about that gelding. And now here's the upshot."

Aphrodite threw her knife down on the table and then she, too, began howling. At first she howled inarticulately, then separate words could be distinguished; Gladishev realized she was lamenting for him as if he were dead. Frightened by all this, Hercules, too, burst into tears. Aphrodite took him in her arms and began wailing even louder.

"Who are you forsaking us for, a little child understanding nothing, a little orphan, your own flesh and blood, and a wretched widow! You, our breadwinner, where are you leaving us for? We'll go begging our way through the world asking alms for Christ's sake! And who will help us, who needs us? Aiyayayai . . ."

Gladishev was moved to tears. Kuzma Matveyevich had always thought he meant nothing to Aphrodite, less than nothing, and now just look at her grieving away. She must really love him! This was so sweet to his soul that he began to look as if he were truly dead. But Aphrodite took her lamentations further, conjuring up for her listener her own and her child's joyless future: "The two of us, with no man to help us, we'll live from hand to mouth, we'll die of hunger; without a roof over our heads we'll be drenched and freeze in an open field . . ."

"Aiyayai," Gladishev began to wail. "But what are you moaning about? I'm leaving you a nice warm hut and a new roof put on last summer. And why are you already burying me, before it's time? I'm not guilty of anything, and if they try to understand they'll see I'm one of them, almost one of the poor and one of the first to join the kolkhoz. They'll see, you hear me, Aphrodite, I'm telling you the truth, they'll see and let me go."

"A-ai!" grieved Aphrodite hopelessly. "Nobody's let go from there."

The gruel in the oven began simmering, then boiled over onto the coals. Steam mixed with smoke poured from the oven.

"You should have been watching your pot instead of burying your husband alive!" shouted Gladishev, and grabbing the oven tongs, he reached into the oven.

Aphrodite continued to howl and lament, accompanied by the childish bass voice of the naked Hercules.

Ninka Kurzova ran into the hut at that moment, alarmed by the crying.

"What's happening here?" she asked, looking around the hut, her eyelids swollen. "Saints preserve us, Kuzma is alive. I thought I heard your Aphrodite lamenting that you'd passed away. The other day you were complaining the weather was making your legs act up, and your face was all pale. Taika even asked me. Why, she says, is Froska grieving? And I says, Kuzma must have passed away."

"Get out of here!" shouted Gladishev, advancing at Ninka with the tongs. "We'll see who's going to pass away!" and he raised the tongs over his head.

"Fooligan!" screamed Ninka, and protecting her stomach with her hands, she opened the door with her backside.

And there, by Gladishev's fence, the whole village had gathered again in curious silence.

"What's going on in there?" The women approached Ninka.

"Ai, women, don't even ask!" said Ninka with a wave of the hand. "Our gardener was teaching his Froska a lesson with the oven tongs and I almost got some too. He's not looking where he hits."

"What a thing," said Taika Gorshkov. "I thought he was really dead, and he's beating her with oven tongs."

"It's his own wife, he can teach her a lesson," Granny Dunya maintained.

"Who doesn't beat his wife," replied Taisiya the storekeeper. Disappointed, they dispersed.

But the next day a fresh piece of news rocked the village—Gladishev had vanished. The field brigade had been issued groats and cabbage, Shikalov went to the warehouse to pick it up, but Gladishev the warehouseman wasn't there. "Probably sleeping," decided Shikalov and turned his horse toward Gladishev's house. There he found Aphrodite in tears. Kuzma Matveyevich had left that night, she said, disappeared nobody knew where, leaving a note behind. Aphrodite showed it to Shikalov:

> Due to certain circumstances [he had written], I am leaving for good; it's not you I'm leaving behind, but my own unhappy life. Don't think badly of me and raise our son so he will become a devoted Bolshevik of the Party of Lenin and Stalin, like Pavel Korchagin and other such heroes. And if he goes into science, perhaps he can finish the work I failed to complete. I remain devoted to you.
>
> Your late and lawful husband
>
> *Gladishev, Kuzma*

The whole village ransacked the neighboring woods, thinking he might have hung himself from a tree, but they couldn't find him. Shikalov went on horseback to the dam (twelve kilometers down the Tyopa) in the hopes that the body had been washed up there, but to no avail. They summoned a commissioner from the district, who did not come right away and only then with great reluctance. He drew up a statement of the case, grumbling that in wartime, when people were perishing by the tens of thousands for the motherland, they were still supposed to bother about suicides. A few more days passed, and new events overshadowed a fact as insignificant as the death of one ordinary kolkhoznik.

25

For Filippov the disappearance of such an important witness was a great annoyance. Nevertheless, he displayed maximal activity, summoning witnesses one after the other. But they conducted themselves very strangely. Zinaida Volkov, upon receiving her summons, climbed up onto the stove, quite beside herself. Zinaida's husband, fearing the consequences, chased her off with the oven tongs, dragged her outside, and then drove her with a switch like a nanny goat all seven kilometers to town.

"Don't be scared," he tried to convince her on the way. "They're people too, they don't mean you any harm. Don't blab on, just tell them what you saw."

"I didn't see anything, I didn't hear anything, I don't know anything."

Volkov passed her on to the duty officer answering the bell. The officer let her in ahead of him, and she started off down the zigzagging corridor, stumbling blindly against the walls.

Volkov waited for her, not knowing what else to do. It would be a shame to lose Zinaida, she was good and healthy and of great use during the harvest. She worked at the kolkhoz and on her own plot and still managed to look after their five children and keep them clean and tidy. Of course, there's lots of women around during wartime, reflected the bookkeeper, but ones like Zinaida are scarce as hen's teeth. And if you do find one like her, she'll know her own worth and wouldn't be likely to marry a man with five children and one arm. And it's one thing if she would marry him and another how the kids would feel about her. No matter how you looked at it, it mattered to children if they were with their own mother or some other woman.

Without noticing it himself, he had begun thinking out loud, and bending down the finger on his one and only hand, he was counting up Zinaida's positive qualities and the undoubtedly negative ones of that unknown woman who was to take her place. But all he had was five fingers and Zinaida had considerably more positive qualities than that, and the unknown woman had even more negative ones.

It was drizzling. Volkov took a small ragged sack from inside his shirt, made it into a hood, which he put over his head, and rose to his feet, intending to leave. Then he spotted Zinaida. She had just walked down from the porch and was standing looking straight ahead, fumbling in the air with her hands as if reaching for some invisible obstacle. Volkov ran over to his wife and stood smiling broadly in front of her. But she pushed him aside and began walking with an uncertain gait across the square, though she should have taken the exact opposite direction. Overtaking Zinaida, Volkov again stood in front of her, but she pushed him aside again and set off as if keeping to a straight path invisible to Volkov.

"Why are you doing this, Zina?" Volkov caught her by the sleeve. "Don't you recognize me? It's me, Konstantin, your husband."

Zinaida stopped, but her face expressed nothing and her eyes looked past him.

"Let's go home," said the bookkeeper firmly, and began dragging her along after him. She went wherever he dragged her and turned wherever he turned. While they were walking through the town, he did not put any questions to her, but when they entered the fields he couldn't hold back. "What happened in there?"

"I didn't see anything, I didn't hear anything, I don't know anything," Zinaida snapped out at tongue-twister pace.

"Get hold of yourself!" Volkov tried to make her see reason. "Who are you talking to, this is me, Kostka."

"I didn't see anything, I didn't hear anything, I don't know anything," Zinaida repeated dully, and it seemed that all other words and ideas had flown out of her head.

They must've tortured her, thought Volkov, wincing.

In fact, this was far from the truth. To the honor of the Right People and of Lieutenant Filippov personally, no one had tortured Zinaida. Lieutenant Filippov had greeted her perfectly politely and proposed that she be seated on a stool in his office.

"I didn't see anything, I didn't hear anything, I don't know anything," said Zinaida.

"We'll clear that up later," promised Filippov. "Meanwhile, be seated."

"I didn't see anything, I didn't hear any—"

"Sit down," said Filippov.

He didn't even raise his voice. He only walked over to Zinaida, placed his hands on her shoulders, and pressed down lightly, causing her to sit. Obediently, she lowered herself onto the stool, where she immediately created a rather embarrassing situation. A stream issued from her, a not uncommon occurrence in there, ran down onto her boots and beyond. A good-sized puddle formed. A Belomor cigarette butt on the floor rose and floated away like a toy boat. The author requests his women readers to forgive him for such naturalism, but most of all, he requests forgiveness from the workers of that punitive department, always so pure when evaluating works of art. It is they who are most often shocked by the depiction of the dark and cruder sides of our life. That's already too much, they usually say in such cases. What good is this? What does this teach? And indeed the incident with Zinaida was not very beautiful. But still it does teach us something. First, it teaches us to rid ourselves of everything superfluous before visiting the Right Place.

Most interestingly, Zinaida did not even notice what she had done. Sitting on the stool, she continued mumbling her incantations. Lieutenant Filippov didn't notice anything at first. But then, hearing a strange sound, he looked down and saw the puddle and the cigarette butt floating by the left leg of his desk. In confusion, the lieutenant stomped his feet at

Zinaida and then ran out of his office, ordering Kapa to take the witness outside and let her go.

Supported on her husband's arm, Zinaida returned home. By evening she had developed a fever. She lay on the stove, her teeth chattering, and to anything said to her, she replied, "I didn't see anything, I didn't hear anything, I don't know anything." First they called the medic from Old Kliukvino, then Granny Dunya came with her herbs and spells. Nothing helped. It even reached the point where Dunya suggested a priest be called. It turned out, however, that there wasn't a priest left in the vicinity, since the anti-religion movement had been particularly successful there. Besides, perhaps it was better that they didn't find one, it would have been a waste of money, especially since after a short while Zinaida managed to recover.

26

They were sorting the latest mail, sitting languidly on the floor in front of a small iron stove: twelve women wearing unbuttoned quilted jackets and shawls worn through at the shoulders; the thirteenth was a man, Dementy, from another kolkhoz, who had not been taken to the front because he was an epileptic.

The stove door was open. The wood was crackling and the reflection of the ruddy flames played on their weather-beaten faces.

Smiling, Liza Gubanov was telling the story of a recent event. Two women from their village went to the forest for mushrooms. They hadn't gone very far when they heard a noise up in a tree. One of them, Shurka, raised her head and then started screaming, "Oi, Mama, it's a wood goblin!" and fainted dead away on the grass. But, the other one, Tonka, she was a bit braver. She looked up at the tree too and said, "Don't be scared, Shurka, that's not a goblin, it's a monkey."

"What was it wearing?" asked Dementy.

"That's just it. It wasn't wearing anything, just all covered with hair, like a billy goat." Well, Shurka came to and started throwing sticks at the monkey. "Come down," she says, "or I'll whack you." And he says, "I won't come down."

"He spoke Russian?" Marusya Zybin was amazed.

"What's he supposed to speak!"

"But the Germans," said Dementy, "speak German."

"They think they're so smart, that's why they speak that German," remarked Liza. Anyway, they both started throwing sticks at him, and he's up there swinging on the branch and laughing. "Don't strain yourselves, girls," he says, "you can't throw that far. Tell me, are the Bolsheviks still in power?" Tonka answers, "We'll go right back to the village and find out if they've gone yet. You wait here." They went back to the village, gathered the people, and brought them back there. Some brought pitchforks. Some brought rifles, but the monkey was gone. He wasn't fool enough to wait. The next day a police inspector came. He took Tonka and Shurka to the district office and tried to threaten them. "There can't be any monkeys in our woods," he says, "and if I hear of any more such backward talk, I'll make monkeys out of you."

Nyura entered the room during this conversation, a few minutes late. Her face was tearstained. She said hello and was about to find a place on the floor beside Dementy, but Marusya Zybin stopped her.

"Nyura, Lyubov Mikhailovna wants you for something."

Puzzled, but not particularly alarmed, Nyura went into the small office no larger than the platform of a railway car.

Her chief, Lyubov Mikhailovna, a large woman around forty with a permanent wave in her blond hair, was squeezed in between the wall and the small table held up by a single pedestal. Katya, the telegraph operator, was standing by the window. She was holding a large book in her hands and reading some sort of numbers from it while Lyubov Mikhailovna was clicking away at an abacus. On the fingers of her right hand were dark-blue tattoos reading L-y-u-b-a.

"Hello," said Nyura.

Both women stopped counting and looked in silence at Nyura.

"You called me?" asked Nyura.

"Ah, yes, yes," said Lyubov Mikhailovna, who, for some reason seemed embarrassed. She tried to pull out her desk drawer, but since there was no room for it, she pushed it right back again. "I wanted to ask you, Nyura, what has happened to you. Just please don't say that nothing's happened. I know everything."

Nyura looked silently at her boss while she looked past Nyura at the wall.

"Unfortunately, Nyura, we have to part ways."

Nyura said nothing, not understanding what Lyubov meant.

Lyubov Mikhailovna raised her eyes to Nyura, but then averted them at once.

"You understand that it's unpleasant for me to say this to you, you're a good person and an honest worker but . . ."

Lyubov Mikhailovna stopped to think, rolled a cigarette, then lit it.

"But you realize, Nyura, that right now we have to be especially vigilant . . ."

Nyura nodded. She was an ignorant woman, but she realized vigilance was necessary.

"You've got to understand, Nyura, I still feel the same way about you. But your husband turned out to be a very bad man. I'm a woman too, Nyura, and I can understand everything, but there are different kinds of women. I was reading about one in the newspaper who went so far as to sleep with a German. Now when the Germans are killing our men, our fathers and brothers, driving our sisters, mothers, and daughters into captivity, to go to bed with a German, you have to have lost all shame, I don't know where it will all end."

"Lyubov, Lyubov," interrupted Katya, who had not said anything till then, "her Vanka's not German, he's Russian."

Lyubov Mikhailovna was taken aback. She had gotten so worked up that she was beginning to believe that Nyura had been sleeping with a German.

"I wasn't talking to you," she said angrily to Katya, then addressed Nyura again. "Anyway, Nyura, as a woman I sympathize with you, but as a Communist I cannot put up with that sort of thing. We have important work here. All sorts of information passes through our hands and we cannot entrust this work to just anyone."

Lyubov fell silent, signaling that the conversation was over. Waiting for Nyura to leave, she ran her spread fingers along the abacus, fanning out the letters L-y-u-b-a.

"Lyuba, Lyuba," Katya butted in again. "Nyura's man, he wasn't her husband at all, she was living with him with no license."

"No license?" repeated Lyubov Mikhailovna, not knowing how to answer this latest objection. "And you," she said angrily, "don't stick your nose where it doesn't belong. Now she's got herself a defender. No certificate. That's even worse. That means she did it for love."

They say that day Nyura Belyashova returned from Dolgov earlier than usual, and ran around the village as if she were half crazy. If she stopped by someone's house or met someone on the road, she showed them her work book and boasted: "They fired me. 'Cause of Chonkin. 'Cause of Ivan. They say I lived with him for love."

27

It should not be thought that Lieutenant Filippov was an evil and bloodthirsty man whose only wish was to send Chonkin to prison or have him shot. He was simply executing orders from above, doing his duty as he understood it. Until that time he had thought that the accused's own confession was sufficient to close the case and so he had obtained Chonkin's confession. He had been ordered to complete the inquiry and he had done that too.

And although the witnesses had for the most part proved fearful and stupid, from their confused and contradictory statements the lieutenant had reached the conclusion that Chonkin was not essentially guilty of anything. He had been assigned a post and had remained at it. He had been attacked and had defended himself, displaying a quick wit, self-possession, and heroism. According to regulations, a guard could only recognize the commander of the guard, his assistant, and the corporal of the guard.

People say (though this is hard to believe) that Lieutenant Filippov even planned to write a resolution concerning the outcome of the investigation, suggesting that Chonkin be freed due to the absence of any crime. He even set about composing this document several times, but something hindered him, something wasn't quite right. Somehow the whole thing didn't add up. He simply could not imagine freeing a person who had confessed his own guilt. They say that for several days Filippov suffered the pangs of creativity, went through a stack of paper, tearing up sheet after sheet and tossing them in the wastebasket. From all his efforts, only one sheet remained (it flew under the bookcase, where it remained for quite some time). It read:

I, Lieutenant Filippov, having examined the materials relevant to the interrogation in the case of Chonkin, I. V., and having questioned the witnesses . . .

That was as far as he'd gotten.

While Lieutenant Filippov was agonizing over the writing of his resolution, Roman Gavrilovich Luzhin's investigation of

Chonkin had reached the very place where our hero had lived before being called up to military service.

A worker from the local organs, a likable young man resembling Lieutenant Filippov, took the office motorcycle and drove to the village where Chonkin had been born and raised. (By the way, the village was called Chonkino and contained the Chonkinsky village soviet.)

Upon seeing the red I.D., the chairman of the village soviet grew talkative and without hesitation expressed his readiness to give all assistance necessary. "The trouble is," as the chairman put it, "we got more Chonkins here than dogs. The whole village, up and down, nothing but Chonkins, believe it or not. By the way, I'm a Chonkin myself." The chairman showed the young man his deputy's I.D.

"Yes," said the young man without looking, "but this one's named Ivan."

"We've got plenty of Ivans. For example, I'm called Ivan too," said the chairman, smiling in embarrassment.

"But I think," insisted the likable young man, "there couldn't be that many Ivan Vasilyeviches."

"But I wouldn't say there's that few either," answered the chairman, now even more embarrassed. "Take me. An Ivan, and, you'll forgive me, a Vasilyevich."

The young man was thinking of returning to his motorcycle (he had no intention of killing himself over some Chonkin he didn't know and didn't know who cared about), when the secretary of the village soviet, Ksenia, whose last name, by the way, was Chonkin, appeared.

The chairman told her to find the Chonkin the likable young man needed.

"Why bother?" said Ksenia. "Ivan Vasilyevich? In the army? That's Vanka. The one who used to cart manure with his horse. Don't you remember him? The prince."

"That's it, the prince!" The chairman was delighted by the

discovery. "That's him. Why didn't I think of him right away. The prince."

"Prince?" The young man's brows rose.

"That's what they used to call him," said the chairman lightheartedly. "You know, tongues are always wagging in this village; someone gets an idea, they've got to blab about it."

"What do you mean blab," objected Ksenia. "It might be a village but people here don't live any worse than other people. We don't go in for idle talk. I know his mother Maryanka well; she and I worked together cleaning houses since we were young, and I remember how that prince, Golitsyn was his last name, was billeted at her house. He was real young, with curly hair black as soot, but his face was real white."

"Young, curly-haired," mimicked the chairman, "but you weren't standing there with a candle and you don't know if that young man with the curly hair was sleeping with her or not."

"He was," said Ksenia confidently, though without presenting any proof at all. It was simply that this version, contrasted with the humdrum, everyday life, seemed to her more attractive than any other. She wanted to prove to the likable young man that even though their village looked completely unremarkable and no better than any other, extraordinary events occurred even there.

That version suited the likable young man perfectly. He had not labored in vain or wasted time or government gas. Afterward he gave no thought to how the information he had gathered would affect a person's fate. He did not know who Chonkin was, what he had done, or what he was accused of; he wished Chonkin neither well nor ill, but the version put forward by the secretary of the village soviet seemed more interesting to him than any other possibility, and returning to his office, he tapped out a coded telegram with a sense of pleasure: CHECK-UP DONE AT YOUR REQUEST HAS DETERMINED

THAT CHONKIN, IVAN VASILYEVICH, BORN IN 1919, NATIVE OF THE
VILLAGE OF CHONKIN, IS DESCENDED FROM THE PRINCES GOLITSYN.

28

Lieutenant Colonel Luzhin was not to be numbered among
those unable to control themselves, but when this communiqué
had been deciphered and placed on his desk he said, "Oho!"
and began fidgeting in his chair. Then he darted about his
office, rubbing his hands, murmuring: "A monstrous success!"
He resumed his darting about the office, again experiencing
amazement, joy, delight; that is, what a fisherman would feel
when casting for a gudgeon and reeling in a shark.

"A monstrous piece of luck," he repeated. "A monstrous
piece of luck. And to find it just like that!"

But it hadn't been all that easy. No, he had been working,
thinking; he might not have bothered sending out any inquiries
but he had, which meant that he had sensed some missing
link in the Chonkin case, perhaps even an important one.
That meant his intuition had prompted him to start doing
what the person conducting the case, that is, Filippov, could
himself have done. And not only could have but should have.
And why hadn't he done so? Youth? Inexperience? But no
special wisdom was required here, it was an elementary rule
of investigation that one must make inquiries at the criminal's
former residence. No, no matter what anyone says, said Luzhin
to himself, this Filippov is acting oddly, monstrously oddly.
First he allows a lone man to take an entire detachment
prisoner, then he does a thoroughly poor and unprofessional
job of conducting the investigation, allowing the criminal to
pass himself off as an ordinary deserter, though if in fact he
is a deserter, he is not such an ordinary one.

Once again intuition whispered something to Luzhin, and he
was pondering its vague mutterings when a new dispatch was
brought to him and placed on his desk.

HIGHLY URGENT. TOP SECRET.

To Lt. Colonel Luzhin

Last night in the district of Dolgov, signal service radio intercept fixed on the broadcasting of an unidentified transmitter operating at a frequency of 4,750 kilocycles. The beginning of the transmission was missed, but the remainder was taken down and deciphered. Included is the complete text received as a result of decoding: ". . . echelons with military equipment passed by twice under cover. Judging by their outlines—tanks and medium-caliber guns. The silhouettes of four of them clearly correspond to the description I received from Colonel Peckenbrock of the Russian top-secret weapon, the so-called Katyushas.

"Rain has been falling incessantly in the district, which, according to my observations, is extremely disturbing to the local Party leaders. The delays in gathering the harvest threaten them with problems which could result in their being sent to the front.

"The weather conditions could turn out to be unfavorable for us as well, insofar as the local roads which are unpaved could become nearly impassable for our modernized units.

"Via some Japanese from Tokyo, the Russians have picked up my trail, but their information concerning me is still too vague. I think there is still no cause for special alarm; the security organs here have been corrupted by working on fictitious material and display extreme helplessness and incompetence when dealing with reality. Ours are much more efficient. Nevertheless, I shall try to operate with utmost discretion.

Hans"

Luzhin looked at the dispatch, reread the text, and could not believe his own good luck himself. Sometimes a person just gets lucky. But for strokes of luck to come in one after the other, and such strokes . . .

A monstrous fool, thought Luzhin of Hans. Russians display

"extreme helplessness and incompetence . . ." You're the incompetent, you idiot! Who would ever reveal himself like that right off the bat? After all, only one person in Dolgov knew of the report from Tokyo and to figure out who that was isn't too complicated, even for an incompetent like me.

Luzhin called in the head of the investigation section and ordered that the suspected Hans be put under round-the-clock surveillance.

Then he sent a coded message to Moscow: *The agent mentioned by Ramzai has been uncovered and will be arrested shortly.*

In reply he received an uncoded telegram reading GOOD MAN.

29

Shortly after Chairman Golubev threw Chmikhalov out of his office, Chmikhalov filed a memorandum and a personal case was brought against the chairman. Golubev was accused of interfering with the grain harvest, underestimating the guiding role of the Party, and taking violent action against one of its representatives.

On the day before the announced session of the District Committee Bureau, Golubev went to Dolgov and forced his way in to see Borisov.

"And why did you call us a bunch of sheep?" asked Borisov curiously.

"What else are you if not a bunch of sheep?" flared Golubev.

"So there you see." Borisov spread his arms to depict the magnitude of the insult.

"No, you tell me, have you ever seen what happens when, let's say, the worst peasant harvests grain in the rain? It's just stupidity!"

"Stupidity?" repeated Borisov, then suddenly agreed. "Possibly. I come from peasant stock and I know as well as you do that gathering the grain wet and putting it through the thresher can ruin the harvest. Right?"

"Right." Golubev nodded.

"Times are rough and we really need this harvest, right?"

"Right."

"But what we need even more is that every person carries out any and all Party directives unquestioningly and to the letter, without deviating either to the right"—Borisov struck the heel of his hand against his desk—"or to the left"—and he struck the desk again. "And in striving for this we will not take any losses into account. Now go, you still have time before tomorrow, so think it over."

The chairman said nothing and left. He was extremely upset and, climbing up on his two-wheeled cart, he lashed the horse angrily with his whip. Unused to such treatment, the horse froze for a second and even seemed to cower, but then started up with a jerk and darted off, almost overturning the cart.

"Hey!" cried the chairman, and struck the horse with the reins again. A bunch of sheep themselves and they want to turn other people into sheep. "Hey!" He struck the horse again.

The horse was so agitated that for what probably was the first time in its life it raced past the tearoom. The chairman returned to his senses on the way out of Dolgov, regained his calm, and, swinging the horse around, rode back to the tearoom at a walking pace.

"There, there." Hitching the horse to the fence, he tapped its head as if in apology. "There, there."

With a heavy step he walked up onto the porch and opened the door. His nose was struck by the odor of soured beer and sweaty foot cloths. Ragged layers of smoke and steam floated like jellyfish in the air, and the light from the lamp on the ceiling was dim and diffuse.

Standing in the center of the tearoom Golubev sniffed and squinted.

"Hey, Ivan" came a call from one corner.

Golubev squinted even harder, and through the fog he spotted Prosecutor Evpraksein waving his hand, calling him over. Ivan Timofeyevich set off toward the prosecutor. The floor was strewn with a thick layer of cigarette butts. The customers swayed in silhouette at the little tables, their voices hollow and blurred as in a bathhouse.

Everywhere were heard snatches of those special conversations in which Russian drinkers engage, the themes of which vary greatly but are, more often than not, exalted in nature— the mysteries of the universe, the dark powers, the scientific means of predicting earthquakes, and how to have sex with a hen. Quite often highly original and profound thoughts are expressed in such conversations, and if somebody blurts out an obvious stupidity, people still hear him out with respect, understanding that sometimes even a stupid person must have his say.

Ivan Timofeyevich made his way among the little tables where these conversations were going on: one man was beating his breast to prove a point, another was trying to sing, some failed actor, striking a pose, was reciting Mayakovsky's poem "It's Good" with genuine emotion.

Around midway he was stopped and taken by the elbow. "Careful, there's a comrade on the floor, don't step on him." He looked down at his feet and saw a man there—no doubt a traveler. He was lying on his back and sleeping peacefully, having covered his face with a crumpled gray hat. Stepping politely over the sleeper, Golubev walked over to the prosecutor.

"Have a seat, Ivan!" invited Pavel Trofimovich, pulling a chair out from under the table with his foot. "Will you have a drink?"

"I guess that's why I'm here," admitted Golubev.

"So, take a seat. Anyuta!" The prosecutor snapped his fingers and Anyuta appeared out of the fog. "Bring us another bottle."

"Maybe you've had enough, eh, Pavel Trofimovich?" said Anyuta with concern.

"What?" thundered the prosecutor. "Resisting the authorities? I'll put you in prison! Have you shot! In the name of the federated . . ."

He was joking, of course, and Anyuta knew that he was joking, but she also understood there were certain limits on joking with prosecutors.

A bottle appeared on the table, followed by a second glass, two mugs of beer, macaroni navy-style w/m (that is, without meat, though it did come with a cucumber, which, however, was so flat it looked like it had been run over by a train).

They drank. Soon, relaxed and flushed, Golubev began telling the prosecutor about his mishaps and complaining about his foolish character, as he put it.

"Ach, what a fool!" the chairman kept saying, striking his fist against his forehead.

"That's true, you are a fool," the prosecutor agreed. "But never regret what you've done. That's smart."

"I wouldn't," sighed Golubev, "but they're going to punish me."

"That they will," confirmed the prosecutor. "We couldn't get along without punishments. It is even a certainty that they will punish you. How could they do otherwise. Only you're thinking that they'll punish you because you refused to harvest wet grain or called them a bunch of sheep. No, brother, that's not it at all. It's just that you've attained a position where sooner or later you'll turn out to be guilty. Of what? The guilt'll be found. War, drought, loss of livestock, they'll look for the guilty party and there you are. Or it could have been me. It's inevitable. But that's good too. Inevitability is our strength."

"Our strength?" The chairman was surprised.

"Our strength!" confirmed the prosecutor. "What is it that keeps us from living like human beings? Hope. Hope, that bitch, keeps us from living. Hoping to escape punishment we twist and turn, we connive, we try to grab somebody else by the throat, we behave like loyal dogs. And if only this gave us pleasure. But no. We are people, after all, and not dogs; we suffer, we become drunkards, we go out of our minds, we die from terror, thinking we might have done someone in and that we'll be punished for that. And when they drag you off to settle accounts and you howl—for what? I was a loyal dog! Act like a human being. A human being, I tell you, and not a dog. Abandon hope, it'll deceive you anyway. Live the way you want to. You want to do a good deed, do it. You want to cut somebody's face, do it. You want to say something, don't deny yourself, say it. Have a good time. Tomorrow you'll be punished, one way or the other you'll be punished, but today you will know that you lived like a human being."

Golubev liked what Evpraksein was saying. He had flirted with this thought at times, though it had seemed to him insane because it was so obvious. The majority of the people he knew thought differently, which confused him; now he was glad that he had met a like-minded soul.

They drank, they nibbled on the cucumber, they smoked.

"Look, Ivan"—Evpraksein bent close to Golubev—"look what we've come to. Fear has turned us into complete fools. Just take me. I'm afraid of those above me, I'm afraid of those below me, but I'm not afraid of my conscience. Aren't we materialists, and conscience, what is it? You can't touch it and that means it doesn't exist. So then what's that gnawing away at me? Huh? They tell me there is no conscience, it was invented by bourgeois idealists, the world is material, and here's what matters for you—an office, a chair, a buzzer, a telephone, here's your apartment, here's your rations, gobble them down, you'll get fat, fat is also material, but conscience is nothing. Then what the hell is gnawing away at me, huh, Ivan?"

"Let's drink," said Ivan.

They drank and took a few chews of the cucumber. Again

the prosecutor bent close to the chairman. "This woman comes to me trying to intercede for her husband. All right, I can't help her, but still I could sympathize with her. But no, I glare at her like a crocodile. But you know, Ivan, I was once a good boy." The prosecutor smeared the tears across his cheek. "I loved nature and animals. Sometimes I'd be bringing home a piece of my bread rations and some dog'd be trailing along behind me. Hungry, shabby, but with eyes like that woman, Ivan. I'd get angry at it, stamp my feet. I was hungry myself but I knew—someone would take pity on me but no one would take any pity on that dog. I'd pinch off a piece and give . . ."

The prosecutor waved his hand, shook his head, and choked with sobs. Taken aback, Golubev grabbed the prosecutor by the shoulder.

"Pasha," he said, "what's this for! Forget it. If, like you say, we'll all be punished one way or the other, then what's there for us to be afraid of? The worst they can do is kill you, and you can't escape death anyway. They can kill us, but they can't make us immortal, and that's their weakness."

"Right." The prosecutor nodded. "That is their weakness."

It was almost closing time. The old cleaning woman was wiping off the empty tables, then setting the chairs upside down on them. Anyuta was chucking out one of the customers; he broke free of her, waved his hands in the air, and recited emotionally:

Smokestack.
Save the air,
Puff, puff, puff,
go the factories.

Golubev and Evpraksein were the last to leave the tearoom. The entire area had been deserted for quite a while, but they were still marking time in the middle of the road beneath a streetlight, unable to say goodbye.

"Ivan!" cried the prosecutor, grabbing the chairman by the shirt front, "Don't be afraid of anything. I'll go to the Bureau myself tomorrow. When they start in on you and ask, Who is for it and who's against? I'll stand up and say, I'm against it! I don't know about you, but I personally, Prosecutor Evpraksein, I personally, in the name of the Sovunion, am against it. You can kill Ivan, I'll say, you can kill me in the name of the Sovunion, but still we are going to perish like human beings while you"—he released the chairman and held up one long finger in front of him—"you will live like worms and die like worms."

It took them still more time to say their goodbyes. They shook hands, pounded each other's back, walked away, and then walked back to each other again. Finally, the chairman managed to tear himself loose and climb up onto his two-wheeled cart. The prosecutor walked alongside, holding on to the cart with one hand, still trying to convince Golubev not to be afraid of anything. Then he fell behind and, shouting words of encouragement, disappeared into the darkness.

Driving out of Dolgov, the chairman let go of the reins, stuck his hands in his sleeves, and curled up, pressing himself against the back of the seat. The horse knew the way. Looking forward to his rest in the warm stable and an armful of fresh hay, the horse ran easily and quickly. The cart rocked gently, Golubev felt fine and cozy. Recalling with pleasure his conversation with the prosecutor, he thought, Yes, Pasha's right, no need to be afraid of anything.

He thought the same thought when, having turned in the horse, he walked home from the stable, and later on as well when, knees tucked up close to his chin, he sank into sleep under the warm quilt.

30

Golubev woke up at nine o'clock and immediately remembered that the Bureau was meeting at two to examine his case and the best he could get was a stretch in jail and the worst . . .

Sitting up in bed, he smiled, stretched, glanced out the window, and noticed a saddle horse hitched to the fence. Who could that be? he asked himself.

There was a noise outside his door; the door opened and his wife appeared in the doorway. "Ivan, someone to see you."

The prosecutor peeped out from behind her back, his face rumpled and pale.

"Pasha?" said Golubev, surprised. "Did something happen?"

The prosecutor looked first at the chairman, then at his wife.

"Leave us," Golubev said to her.

She left, closing the door behind her.

"Here's the thing, Ivan," Evpraksein began indecisively, shifting his feet. "Yesterday . . . we were talking . . . I was drunk . . . Anyhow, I was drunk, understand?"

"And you came galloping five miles here in the morning to tell me that?"

"Yes, that's right. I mean no . . . That is, I mean . . . sometimes when I'm drunk I say the wrong thing. On the whole, that's not how I think. On the whole I . . ."

"I understand everything," said Golubev softly, and blushed in embarrassment himself.

"You do. That's good . . ." The prosecutor started backing toward the door, but then stopped. "No, you shouldn't think . . . I'm not out for myself . . . I'm for you . . . if the Party says you're wrong, you should admit you're wrong."

"Oi, oi!" The Chairman frowned and waved his arms. "Why are you saying that? Get out of here, get out."

Now the prosecutor turned red and grasped the doorknob.

"Pasha!" Golubev stopped him. The prosecutor turned around. "Pasha!" repeated the chairman, excited now, lowering his legs from the bed. "Everything you said yesterday was right. But was it only because you were drunk?"

"Only because I was drunk," said the prosecutor firmly, looking down fixedly at his right foot.

"That's a shame," said Golubev. "And you spoke so well, you were so skillful at finding the right theoretical basis."

"Theoretical, theoretical," mimicked the prosecutor. "What does that have to do with anything? Maybe it's theoretically right, but on the practical level . . . on the practical level I'm scared!" he cried, and dashed out of the room.

31

It was an overcast day; suspended in the air, the hoarfrost settled on the cheeks and made the hands unpleasantly cold. The maples along the fences were still green but were already showing red splotches.

Hands in his pockets, Lieutenant Filippov walked straight across the square. He walked with the unhurried pace of a man burdened with affairs of state, a man who knew his own worth. Not that long ago he would have been running, a young man ready to fulfill any order from his superiors. But now, having replaced the prematurely departed Milyaga, Filippov seemed to have matured all at once; he stood up straight, his shoulders were squared; he seemed a completely changed man, and this change was most apparent in the way he walked. His gait had acquired that special slowness of a man aware that, even moving slowly, he will always arrive at his destination on time.

He walked, staring pensively ahead, as if not noticing anything, whereas in fact he took note of everything. There was a rather long line pressed up against the walls near the district store. People were waiting for millet, the store was out, but a delivery was expected any moment. By the bathhouse, which had been turned into a delousing station, there was a long line of women evacuees wearing smart but threadbare clothes which set them off from the locals. Taking a right past the bathhouse, the lieutenant walked half a block down past the post office and came out at the building which housed the two District Committees, the Party's and the Komsomol's, as well as the Executive District Committee. A policeman stood at the entrance, sternly asking those who entered who they were going to see and why. Naturally, he did not ask Filippov anything but only stiffened and saluted. The Secretary of the District Committee's office, located on the second floor, was reached by a broad staircase with a carpet running down the center (the Assembly of Nobles used to convene in this building). On the top landing stood two large plaster-of-Paris busts, of Lenin and Stalin, on plywood pedestals wrapped with red cloth. The lieutenant, scraping the soles of his boots a couple of times against the worn marble floor, set out decisively on the carpet, while an old woman wearing a quilted jacket, felt boots, and galoshes, carrying a sack on her back, came down the stairs toward him, though not on the carpet but off to the side of it. Passing through the large reception room, the lieutenant exchanged greetings with Anna Martinovna, Revkin's secretary. There were quite a few people in the reception room besides Anna Martinovna. For the most part, these were solid-looking people, men and women (the majority were men in spite of its being wartime) who were sitting along the wall on crudely made chairs. These were the chairmen of kolkhozes, directors of sovkhozes, officials, and section heads, that is, the very people who are referred to as the captains of production. Not being members of the Bureau, they did not have the right to participate in its sessions, but they had been summoned there, some on business, some just in case there was a sudden need for any information concerning the work done by the enterprises they headed.

Filippov exchanged greetings only with Anna Martinovna, then slammed the black-upholstered door decisively behind him as if entering his own office. Striding through the small lobby, he opened a second door and then found himself in the First Secretary's office.

The office was thick with tobacco smoke. The members of the Bureau—there were more than twenty of them—wore either semi-military clothing or long civilian jackets, and were seated at the long table or on the leather couch by the wall; a few were standing by the far window, extending their lips like pipes and blowing smoke through the casement windows.

Before the lieutenant entered, the room had been as loud as a bathhouse, but it grew silent as soon as he appeared. Only one person on the leather couch who had not caught sight of Filippov continued to talk, saying that dog fat was the best remedy for tuberculosis. Somebody nudged him in the side, he looked around, then he, too, fell silent and jumped to his feet as had those beside him. Chairs scraped, and those at the table were now standing as well. The lieutenant did not understand why they were in such a hurry to rise (he still was not entirely used to his new position), and he looked around, thinking someone else was entering behind him. But nobody was there. Revkin was the only one not to rise immediately, waiting until Filippov had approached him. After offering Filippov his hand, he sat right back down. The others continued to stand, though several pretended that they had only risen to stretch their legs and that they would sit back down when they felt like it. The lieutenant walked around to everybody, shaking hands with each person. He still did not know them all and several told him their last names, but he did not say his own in return, for he realized that everyone knew it. Among those present were three men in uniform, a military commissar, the chief of police, and the commander of the military garrison temporarily billeted in the area. Filippov was not a member of the Bureau, but he had been invited, since problems of extreme importance were to be decided.

While the members of the Bureau were arriving, Andrei Eremeyevich Revkin, First Secretary of the District Committee, paying no attention to the general hubbub, had been preparing for the upcoming session. He was reading through the drafts of the resolutions prepared on various questions and, where necessary, making corrections. From time to time, without looking and without himself rising, he would thrust his hand out to the latest arrival and then plunge back into his papers. Sometimes he would press his buzzer and Anna Martinovna would appear silently and immediately. A tall, elderly woman with glasses on her impassive face, she could miraculously divine her boss's slightest wish even at a distance. Revkin had only to reach out to one side for the very paper he needed to appear in his hand. At that moment he was handing Anna Martinovna another paper in which something had to be re-typed, giving her brief, whispered instructions, and at the same time observing who had arrived and calculating if there were enough to begin.

As a group, the people present in Revkin's office represented the ruling elite of the district and belonged to the so-called nomenclature. What set these people apart was that they had been appointed to direct, and without a twinge of doubt they had undertaken to direct firmly and decisively whatever it was they had been appointed to direct—vegetable growing, hog breeding, any industry, any art, any science. And if by chance it so happened that someone displayed skill or knowledge in some area of human endeavor, he would immediately be booted to another field until, by degrees, he was brought to that field where he did not know his ass from his elbow, where he swam as in a boundless sea with no points of reference before him except for that lodestar known as the Daily Directive. The imaginary line connecting the swimmer with that star was known as the Party line, to which absolute adherence was required.

It seemed that everyone had already arrived, but the session had not begun. They were still waiting for someone. Now they had begun talking about their illnesses, the weather, the harmfulness of tobacco, the value of vitamins, all sorts of subjects which no one there found the least disturbing, while they said nothing at all about what was truly disturbing them—the situation at the front, ration cards, the rumors that certain posts might lose their military deferments, people's usual concerns. Suddenly Anna Martinovna appeared in the doorway.

"Andrei Eremeyevich!" she said excitedly.

As Andrei Eremeyevich went to the door, the others pressed against the windows. They all saw a luxurious Zis–101, polished to a gleam, roll gently up to the main entrance of the District Committee building. The car looked like an ocean liner mooring at a dock on some insignificant little river. Running up just in time, Revkin flung open the front door. Climbing out toward him with a friendly smile was a portly man in a gray gabardine raincoat and a soft hat with its brim turned slightly up. They kissed three times, long and hard for some reason; the newcomer pounded Revkin's back while Revkin, though he considered himself the man's close friend, did not pound his in return. Instead he made a gesture of invitation and the newcomer began walking leisurely up the stairs. The members of the Bureau instantly recoiled from the windows and resumed their places; smiles appeared on their faces now turned toward the door as if they were expecting a famous movie star or simply some beautiful woman to walk in. But it was not a woman who entered, it was the man who had driven up in the Zis–101, the Secretary of the Regional Committee, Comrade Khudobchenko, Piotr Terentevich. The smiles in the room were directed at him, not because he enjoyed their respect for his merits (little was known about them), it was the position he occupied which demanded the respect. And had this position been occupied by a turkey or a crocodile, they would have smiled at it exactly as they were now smiling at Khudobchenko.

As soon as Khudobchenko appeared in the doorway, everyone rose to his feet. But Piotr Terentevich lifted a hand courteously. "Sit down, comrades," he said in his native half-Ukrainian language.

He then removed his gabardine raincoat and hat and handed them to Revkin, who hung them both on his personal peg. Khudobchenko was dressed in semi-military attire and boxcalf boots. The top button of his field jacket, with its patch pockets, was open, revealing the collar of his Ukrainian shirt.

"Well," he said, smoothing down his sparse hair, "looks like I'm a little late."

"The authorities are never late, they are detained," said Revkin, offering a little joke.

Khudobchenko had expected this jesting reply, and, as always, it was met with Khudobchenko's benevolent smile and the approving laughter of all. It happened every time Khudobchenko was late, and he was always late.

He wasn't late because he had so much to do (though he did have quite a bit to do), and not because he was disorganized and could not find the time; he was late intentionally, assuming that the longer subordinates waited, the more respect they would show him.

"Please, Piotr Terentevich." Revkin offered him his own seat at the table.

"No, no." Khudobchenko raised his hand. "You're in charge here, you sit down. I'm a guest, I'll go sit in that little corner over there."

He sat down in that "little corner" by the window on a soft leather armchair which had been placed there especially for him.

Pshenichnikov, his general assistant, a young man around thirty with a painfully pale face, settled himself down beside

Khudobchenko in a chair. It was said of this Pshenichnikov
that he knew six languages, had a profound understanding of
physics, mathematics, economics, and knew something of all
the other sciences. It was also said that he not only knew *Das
Kapital* and *Anti-Dühring* but also had a good grasp of local
problems, knew by heart all the figures for the indices concerning industrial and agricultural production, from the amount of
steel smelted in each province to the laying-hen population of
every kolkhoz. People called him a walking encyclopedia and
said that with talents like his he should join the circus, but
everyone knew such a career was closed to him, for, with all
his knowledge, he had become indispensable.

33

"Well, then, comrades," said Revkin with a glance that took
in everyone, "I guess we should begin."

They closed the doors and disconnected all the telephones.
A closed meeting began—that is, one kept secret from others,
or, to put it another way, an underground session. Why closed,
why underground, I will not take it upon myself to explain, it
must just be a tradition. The Party held underground sessions
before the Revolution and therefore held them after it as well.

The first item on the agenda was Borisov's report on the
progress of the grain harvest.

Although everyone knew that due to the rain there had been
absolutely no progress in recent days, Borisov read his report
with the most serious of expressions and everyone listened to
it with the most serious of expressions. The great successes
achieved by the village toilers were noted, but certain individual shortcomings were noted as well. Here everyone understood that the shortcomings were not at all individual ones but
were, one might even say, rife and rampant, but even this part
of the report was heard with careful attention. Borisov severely
criticized a certain kolkhoz chairman who was guilty of carry-

ing out decisions obediently—he had sowed too early in the spring and the frosts had killed the shoots. (Others who had only reported that they were carrying out the decisions—as they were now again during the harvest—and had in fact not carried them out were currently in favor.) Among those lagging behind, Borisov mentioned the name of Ivan Timofeyevich Golubev, but at once announced that Golubev's case would be taken up later that day.

Several rather stupid resolutions concerning the progress of the harvest were adopted, not because the people at the meeting were all fools and had no understanding of such matters, but because to speak out substantively required courage, whereas stupid statements were encouraged.

They passed from the progress of the harvest to the question of preparing for the wintering of the livestock. The question was resolved in a most original manner—of all the possible alternatives they selected the worst. But what precisely it was has, unfortunately, slipped my mind.

At that point Revkin rose again and announced that Comrade Filippov would now make his report.

Comrade Filippov rose, straightening his field shirt. He was a bit nervous. It was the first time in his career that he had ever spoken in front of such an important audience. He had heard that experienced speakers, to make their speeches smooth and convincing, choose one person from out of the mass of listeners to address in particular. Filippov decided this was good advice. He began by saying that they were all Communists and so there was no need to beat around the bush. It was war and war was hard. Taking advantage of having struck the first blow, the enemy had seized important territories and was still on the move. The Red Army was fighting with extraordinary fortitude but at times had been forced to retreat before the onslaught of the enemy's superior forces. In such conditions the strength of the rear had become more important than ever before. Only if the rear were strong could our troops hold the enemy on the ground already taken and then, that accomplished, switch to a decisive counterattack. Speaking about one part of the home front in general, the limited territory of their own district, Lieutenant Filippov characterized their position as, on the whole, satisfactory. The workers of the district were accomplishing miracles of heroic labor behind the slogan "Everything for the front, everything for victory." Warm socks were knitted for the front, scrap metal collected, large sums of money donated. The lieutenant told the meeting of a certain heroic kolkhoznik who had built a heavy bomber at his own expense.

At that point the Bureau members began shifting their chairs, stirring, and coughing. None of them could help but think, What kind of a kolkhoznik was that and where did he get so much money? If someone had told them that the kolkhoznik had earned that money from daily farm work, then all the members of the Bureau would have convulsed in silent laughter. But Lieutenant Filippov himself knew that it was too much to come from daily work and offered no details as to where the heroic kolkhoznik got his money, the important thing being that he had donated it when he could have kept it in a cash box or a sock.

As he spoke, Filippov kept looking at Boris Evgenevich Ermolkin, who thought that perhaps Filippov suspected that he, Ermolkin, instead of building a bomber or a biplane, was hoarding his money in the larder. Ermolkin immediately reached into his pocket, raked out everything it contained, which, all told, was four rubles and change. Ermolkin held the money out on his palm as if to say that he did not have one kopeck more but, if with this four rubles and change even a small bomber could be built, then he, Ermolkin, would be more than happy.

Lieutenant Filippov cited other examples of selfless heroism but, at the same time, noted (again looking directly at Ermolkin) that among the workers in the rear, and in particular among the population of their district, definite negative signs had begun to appear. Among the more backward elements, said Filippov, the most absurd rumors were circulating, possibly incited and spread by covert, hostile elements (another glance at Ermolkin).

The rumors about Chonkin and his so-called gang were among those rumors.

The lieutenant confirmed that such a gang had, in fact, existed but it had been fully uncovered and rendered harmless. Chonkin himself was in prison awaiting a stern trial and justice.

"But Chonkin is not the point," explained the lieutenant. "I think we are all Communists here and know how to keep our mouths shut. This I am telling you in secret—an enemy even more dangerous than Chonkin is at work in our district, a certain Hans, the personal agent of the German Chief of Intelligence, Admiral Canaris."

Ermolkin cringed at the mention of the word "Hans." He had at once recalled that Lieutenant Colonel Luzhin had asked him about this Hans not too long ago. Ermolkin fixed his honest eyes on Filippov, his entire expression demonstrating that he had no connection whatsoever to the Hans just mentioned. But, in turn, Lieutenant Filippov fixed his eyes on Ermolkin, which Ermolkin could not endure, and giving himself away completely, he averted his eyes and looked over at Military Commissar Kurdyumov. Kurdyumov, deciding that Ermolkin suspected him, looked over at Neuzhelev the lecturer; a chain reaction of terror spread through everyone there, each of whom had no belief in the actual existence of any Hans, but neither did anyone possess any proof that he and Hans were not one and the same person.

However, it seemed that Lieutenant Filippov still did not suspect anyone in particular. He explained that one spy could inflict more damage on the country than a regiment or even a division, and asked all present to show utmost vigilance, not to divulge state and military secrets, to keep a close eye on those around them, and if even the slightest doubt or suspicion arose, to inform the Right People at once.

34

Chairman Golubev was among those waiting in the reception room. He was sitting by Revkin's door with a school notebook on his lap, working out his upcoming answers to all the possible accusations.

The poet who will someday undertake to sing and celebrate Soviet life will not be able to avoid the theme of the Personal Case.

A personal case is when a large human group closes ranks in the course of an interspecific struggle, to suffocate one of its members, out of sheer foolishness, out of malice, or for no reason at all.

A personal case is like an avalanche—if one falls on you, you can explain all you want, you're dead either way.

Golubev knew all that full well when it concerned other people. But now he was making the same error thousands before him had made and thousands after him would make. He was preparing answers to the questions which would be asked him; that is, he was hoping that, in the specific case at hand, his arguments and the considerations of common sense would prevail.

A few personal cases had been scheduled for that day. An elderly teacher from the local school, Shevchuk, a small man with red sclerotic veins on his cheeks, was sitting beside Golubev. He wore glasses, quilted felt boots, galoshes, and a patched quilt jacket tied with a thin belt.

On his knee there was an old Budenny hat missing one of its earlaps. Golubev knew Shevchuk casually, they'd met once in the tearoom. Shevchuk's face looked frightened, he kept crumpling his hat in his hands and mumbling to himself: "I'll repent . . . I'll confess. What do you think?" he said, turning to Golubev.

Golubev shrugged his shoulders.

"What to do?" Shevchuk continued to mumble. "I have four little children. I married off my daughter but the others are like this." With his hand he indicated the approximate heights of his remaining children.

"What are you here for?" asked Golubev.

"For my tongue," said Shevchuk, sticking out his tongue, pointing a finger at it to drive the point home. Golubev thought the teacher would tell him just what trouble his tongue had caused but, staring off into space, he said no more.

There were two other people there for personal cases. One, Konyaev, was the Party organizer from the XVII Party Congress Kolkhoz; the other man was a stranger to Golubev. The former was accused of squandering Party funds and the latter of rape. Both their faces were tense and aloof, and neither of them spoke to anyone.

Konyaev was called in first. He had not been inside long when he came back into the reception room, crossing himself.

"What happened?" asked Golubev.

"A reprimand."

"Did they give you a tongue-lashing?" asked Shevchuk.

Konyaev took his measure, then answered through his teeth: "I don't answer enemies of the people."

Shevchuk flinched in confusion and fell silent. The rapist came out next. He was a bit more talkative.

"Don't be afraid," he said to Shevchuk, slipping his Party card in the pocket of his field shirt. "They're not animals in there, they're people too."

The secretary peeped out of the room. "Shevchuk, you're next."

"Oi, heaven help me," said Shevchuk, crossing himself.

He hopped to his feet and dropped his glasses. As he bent

over to pick them up, he lost his balance and stepped on them. Completely confused, he began picking up the pieces.

"Comrade Shevchuk," said the secretary, "leave it there, it'll be cleaned up. And you, Comrade Golubev, may come in as well."

Golubev followed Shevchuk into the smoke-filled office. He said hello, but no one answered him. Only Prosecutor Evpraksein gave an indefinite nod of the head, then flushed and turned away. First Shevchuk, then Golubev took seats on one of the empty chairs against the wall.

35

"And so, comrades," said Revkin, "it remains for us to hear the two personal cases of Comrades Shevchuk and Golubev. Is Comrade Shevchuk here?"

"Here!" cried Shevchuk, hopping up.

"For this case our speaker will be . . . Comrade Babtsova?"

"Correct," said Babtsova, a stout woman in a dark-blue jacket. She was the secretary of the Party organization in the school where Shevchuk taught. She came forward to Revkin's desk and, standing beside him, began reciting the tale of Shevchuk's crime.

On June 22, celebrating at his daughter's wedding and learning of the attack by Fascist Germany on our country, Shevchuk had made a politically naïve statement. The comrades from the school's Party organization, taking into account Comrade Shevchuk's conscientious work in the past, proposed to him that he write an explanatory note and condemn his own remarks. Thus, the comrades showed sensitivity and tolerance toward a member of their own Party organization. Shevchuk, however, spurned the hand offered him and refused to write any explanation. The comrades were thus forced to suspect that Shevchuk's statement was not the result of political naïveté but was, rather, a considered position. However, displaying humanity and acting in the spirit of comradeship, his colleagues, at the next Party meeting, asked Shevchuk to realize his error and to acknowledge that, although his statement was perhaps not of a deliberately provocative nature, it did, objectively, provide grist for the mills of our enemies. It must be said that under pressure from his comrades Shevchuk did soften his position somewhat. But, fundamentally, he continued to persist in his errors, considering that, as he put it, he had not said anything so terrible. The Party organization of the school drew the conclusion that Comrade Shevchuk had not surrendered to the will of the Party and thus could no longer bear the noble name of Communist. The meeting passed a resolution to expel Comrade Shevchuk from the ranks of the VKP, and now requested the District Committee to confirm this resolution.

"Is that it?" asked Revkin.

"It is," said the speaker, folding up her glasses.

No one said anything. The secretary's pen could be heard scratching out the minutes. Revkin waited until she had finished writing and then turned to the accused. "Shevchuk, do you wish to explain, or add anything?"

"I do . . ." said Shevchuk, his lips numb, barely moving. "I . . . strictly speaking . . . while completely admitting the error I made, nevertheless I want to draw the comrades' attention to the fact that my statement contained no hostile intent."

"Contained none?" Borisov jumped up. "What then, perhaps the collective of this organization is in error?"

"But what did he say?" rang out a voice.

"What did he say?" repeated a second voice.

"Yes, what did he say?" insisted a third.

"Let him repeat it!"

"As a matter of fact, I didn't say anything so special . . ."

"What does that mean? Come on, repeat what you said!"

"Comrades, when I heard that we had been attacked by Germany . . ."

"Fascist Germany," he was corrected from the floor.

"Yes, yes, of course. Fascist Germany. When I heard about it I said, 'Now we'll be locking the barn door after the horse has been stolen.' That's all."

"Nothing much." Neuzhelev the lecturer shook his head.

"I'll say," agreed Military Commissar Kurdyumov, who was sitting beside him.

"So you think you didn't say enough?" asked Borisov. "You should have said a little more, huh?" He winked slyly at Shevchuk.

"What are you saying!" Shevchuk lay his hand across his heart. "I didn't mean it like that."

"No, not like that," said Borisov disbelievingly. "What do you think we are, a bunch of kindergarteners here? No, brother, we're old birds and you won't catch us with that chaff. Everyone here understands full well just what you meant by those words. You meant that our country was going to war unprepared, you wanted to cast aspersions on the political wisdom of our Party and belittle the personal merits of Comrade Stalin. And now, you're going to hand us some cock-and-bull story about what you meant and didn't mean."

"Comrades, I am asking each of you in order, what other opinions are there here?" Revkin interjected.

"May I speak?" Prosecutor Evpraksein rose and began slowly, directing his gaze off into the distance. "Comrades, it is universally known that ours is the most humane social system in the world. But our humanism has a militant, aggressive character. There now stands before you a miserable, blithering man and it would be a natural and human impulse of the heart to pity him, sympathize with him. But, after all, he had no pity for us. He had no pity for his native land. Comrades, I ask you to note that his words, which my tongue refuses to repeat, were not just spoken at any old time, not on the twenty-first of June and not on the twenty-third but, precisely, on the twenty-second, in that very hour when, with a profound sense of outrage, our people first heard of Fascist Germany's attack on our country. This can hardly be considered a casual coincidence. No! This was a carefully calculated blow at a time carefully calculated so that blow could inflict maximum damage on us." The prosecutor fell silent, thought for a moment, then continued sadly. "Well, comrades, this isn't the first time we've had to repulse surprise attacks from our enemies. We defeated the White army, we won out in an uneven battle against the Entente, we liquidated the Kulaks, we smashed the Trotskyite gang, and determined, we will win this battle with Fascism. And so then, are we not able to deal with Shevchuk?"

A sound arose and rolled through the audience, signifying yes, no matter how hard it will be, we will deal with him.

While the prosecutor was delivering his speech, Ermolkin was twitching and fidgeting in his chair. It seemed to him that everyone including Khudobchenko, Revkin, and Filippov was, from time to time, glancing over at him to check how he was reacting to everything and if he was sympathizing with Shevchuk as a possible confederate.

No sooner had the prosecutor taken his seat than Ermolkin sprang to his feet—no one had given him the floor, but he had already begun speaking. No doubt he, too, wished to deliver some worthy speech, so that everyone there could evaluate the correctness and firmness of his world view.

"With a great upsurge the workers of our district," he began, but grew muddled immediately, no doubt due to his agitation; having lost his train of thought, he grew hysterical and began yelling something about a little three-and-a-half-year-old boy whom apparently Shevchuk wanted to murder, whose throat he wanted to cut, but he did not finish what he was saying; his twitching grew more severe and he began shouting "Low life" and "Bastard." He was now thrashing convulsively, sputtering saliva.

"Boris Evgenevich, what's the matter with you?" asked Revkin uneasily from the floor.

"Low life!" Boris Evgenevich continued thrashing. "Bastard! My son . . . is three and a half . . ."

"Borya! Borya!" Neuzhelev ran over to him. "Please, get hold of yourself. Drink some water. I understand, you find it insulting. We all do. The holiest . . . What we fought for . . . What we're all shedding our blood for today on all fronts . . . But I promise you, Borya, we will not allow Soviet power to be insulted by any of these Shevchuks."

Water was brought him. They waited for Ermolkin to regain his composure.

"Let us continue, comrades," said Revkin, returning to the matter at hand. "Perhaps Boris Evgenevich has just spoken with excessive fervor, yet, in essence, he is correct. And, in my opinion, everything is clear in this case."

"Couldn't be clearer," seconded Borisov.

"Not to me, it isn't."

Noisily pushing back his chair, Veniamin Petrovich Parnishchev, the director of the grain elevator, rose to his feet in the far corner of the room. He was an enormously tall man with broad shoulders and curly hair tumbling onto his forehead.

"And why isn't it?" said Borisov, startled. Surprise, and anxiety that things might take an unexpected turn, could be heard in his voice, as well as the threat that if things were not clear enough for someone, they would clear things up for him but good.

"Not to me, it isn't!" repeated Parnishchev, sweeping the threat aside. "Perhaps Comrade Borisov is the smart one here, he understands everything in one minute, but me, I'm stupid. I don't understand things in a minute. This is what I have to say—I see there're some nervous people here, they're in too much of a hurry, they get all hysterical, all worked up. But, what we are talking about here is nothing less than the fate of a human being. A hu-man be-ing!" repeated Parnishchev, syllable by syllable, shaking his index finger above his head. "And we don't have the right to decide that fate without going into everything properly. So, comrades, I am not acquainted with this person . . . What was your name?"

"Shevchuk," the teacher was quick to remind him.

"Yes, right, I am not personally acquainted with this Shevchuk. We might have seen each other somewhere, in the street or at the movies, I don't recall. So, up until today, I couldn't have, as they say, given a good goddamn whether there was any such Shevchuk alive anywhere. But now I've heard the entire case and there's something I can't fathom. Are you then," he addressed Shevchuk, "a Soviet man?"

"Yes, I am a Soviet man," Shevchuk hastened to agree.

"And a Communist?"

"And a Communist," confirmed Shevchuk.

"Then how could you have done it?" thundered Parnishchev.

"What should I do?" asked Shevchuk timidly, clearly confused. He had thought that Parnishchev was trying to defend him in some cunning way and Shevchuk wanted to play along with Parnishchev, but he didn't quite know how.

"Shevchuk, here's what to do, stop pretending to be a virgin, if you'll pardon the expression. We are your comrades, and we all are anxious about your fate. Take a look around, practically all the leaders of the district are here. Even Comrade Khudobchenko has put in a personal appearance. They tore themselves away from more important matters in order to listen to you and you, you . . ."

Parnishchev flushed red and his eyes bulged as he sang on as inspired as a nightingale.

"But I—" began Shevchuk. Parnishchev cut him off with a wave of the hand.

"Hold those 'But I's.' Enough I, I, I. All right, let's say you don't want to be a Communist, you don't want to be a Soviet man . . ."

"But I do!" said Shevchuk passionately, laying his hand across his heart.

"But now," continued Parnishchev, paying him no attention,

"at such a serious time for our country you could at least remember that you are a Russian. Comrades"—Parnishchev now switched to an elegaic tone—"I read an article in the newspaper about a certain count or prince, one of the White Guards we didn't get to polish off, who is now living in Paris. And this man, who hated Soviet power with a passion, has now categorically refused to cooperate with the Germans. 'Now,' he says, 'when a dark cloud hangs over our motherland, I am not a count, not an anti-Bolshevik, now, first and foremost, I am a Russian!' "

Everyone applauded. It was clear to all that Shevchuk's position was considerably lower than the count's.

"Here's what, Shevchuk," continued Parnishchev. "You committed a low and filthy act. Now at least have the courage to admit it and I'll be the first to embrace you like a brother." Spreading his arms, Parnishchev even took a step toward Shevchuk, but then he took that step back and sat down. "That's all I have to say, comrades," he said softly.

No one said a word. Everyone looked over at Shevchuk, who was shifting from one foot to the other, rumpling his well-traveled hat with its missing earlap.

"Well, then, comrades," said Revkin. "We have given Shevchuk the chance to speak his mind. You heard what he said here yourselves. He does not want to admit the error of his statements . . ."

"I want to! I do!" cried Shevchuk, almost sobbing.

"So you do?" said Revkin in surprise. "All right, comrades, let's listen then."

Shevchuk rose, walked up to the table, and grabbed hold of the tablecloth.

"So!" said Revkin to encourage him.

"Comrades!" began Shevchuk, his voice unexpectedly clear. "I committed an act disgraceful for a Communist. On the first day of the war, hearing news I found shocking, I showed a lack of spirit and a well-known Russian saying came flying out of my mouth. This was a mistaken, and politically naïve, remark. I understand that in those circumstances it might even have seemed hostile to certain comrades . . ."

"What do you mean, 'might have seemed'?" interrupted the military commissar.

"That is, I meant that objectively my statement might appear hostile but I didn't want . . ."

"He didn't want." Neuzhelev shook his head in disbelief.

"What next," said Kurdyumov.

"Now, here's what, Shevchuk," said Borisov with apparent benevolence. "Since you've started owning up, don't hedge with us. We're all comrades here and we've heard a lot, so just stick to the facts. You wanted, you didn't want, everybody wants something. Maybe I want to be doing somersaults with a woman on a feather bed right now, but I've got to be wasting my time in here with you. So don't give me want and don't want. We've got a line waiting for you to finish and you're in here fogging up our brains. You've started, so finish— Your statement was politically immature, slanderous, and objectively directed against Party policy, right?"

"Right," Shevchuk confirmed barely audibly.

"All right, then." Borisov turned to the other members of the Bureau. "As you see, Comrade Shevchuk has admitted everything. But there's a few, kind, tenderhearted souls here who want things limited to a reprimand. But how can there be a reprimand here, comrades, when this case smells of a hostile attack and political provocation. It isn't we who should be dealing with Shevchuk but, to put it bluntly, Lieutenant Filippov over there."

Borisov sat down. Shevchuk continued to stand, pale as a sheet. He glanced around at Parnishchev, who was not rushing to embrace him like a brother.

"All right, then," said Revkin softly, having exchanged glances with Khudobchenko. "For the moment we will not decide the question of who should be handed over to Filippov.

For now we will punish Shevchuk under our own authority. I think that after everything that's been said, the right course would be to confirm the decision made at the meeting of the school's Communists to expel Shevchuk from the Party."

"Confirm the decision?" Raisa Semenovna Gurvich, the physician in chief at the hospital, spoke up. "May I be allowed a few words?" she asked, rising.

She was given the floor.

"Comrades," she said in agitation, "I am simply horrified by what I've heard here today. My hair is literally standing on end. I don't understand anything. My daughter Svetlana is in the seventh grade in the very school where this comrade, or citizen, I don't know what to call him, teaches. My husband and I have always raised Svetochka in the spirit of our ideas, always inculcated her with love for the motherland, the Party, and Comrade Stalin. We believed that our pedagogues were teaching our daughter the same things. But now I see who's been teaching her. Comrades, I don't understand. Can we entrust the education of our children to a man like that? With views like his, how did he slip into a Soviet school? And who helped him slip his way in? After all, if he could say such a thing"—she began shouting now—"on the day when all Soviet people . . . then what was he saying before? No, comrades, to expel Shevchuk isn't difficult of course, but it is not enough! We must check up on the entire pedagogical collective, the school administration, and find out how such unhealthy circumstances came about where this Shevchuk could operate with impunity. Comrades, I think we must send a Party commission to the school. And all the unhealthy elements must be brought to light. Otherwise, I personally, as a mother, simply will not be able to allow my daughter inside that school. Better she receives no education at all than she receives . . . than she receives . . . than she receives . . . I'm sorry, I can't go on . . ." Raisa Semenovna began to cry and sat down, covering her face in her hands.

Raisa Semenovna's speech had made an impression, everyone was buzzing. Revkin rapped his pencil against the pitcher.

"Raisa Semenovna is absolutely right," said Revkin. "Apparently some highly unseemly situations have arisen in the school where Shevchuk taught. This must disturb us. For it is precisely the school which is called upon to educate our replacements. It is precisely the school which lays the moral foundation of the new man. And we cannot be indifferent to the laying of that foundation. We will return to this in a moment. Meanwhile, comrades, let us not be distracted and conclude this case hastily. So, there is a motion to confirm Shevchuk's expulsion from the Party. Are there any other opinions? No? Let's vote, then. Only members of the Bureau will vote. Who is for? Against? No abstentions? Passed unanimously. Comrade Shevchuk, do you have your Party card with you?"

Shevchuk said nothing, grasping the tablecloth and staring straight ahead.

"Shevchuk, I'm talking to you!" Revkin raised his voice. "Lay your card on the table."

Suddenly Shevchuk's eyes began to bulge, he rose on tiptoe, inhaling with a strange sound, a whistling, a rumbling; he started backing away, dragging the tablecloth and with it all the pitchers, glasses, ashtrays and inkwells.

"Comrade Shevchuk!" cried Revkin. "What are you doing? Stop!"

But an aloof and malicious expression had appeared on Shevchuk's face. He continued backing away, farther and farther, a froth of pinkish bubbles foaming on his lips. Someone sprang to his feet. Someone else, sitting on the other side of the table, grabbed hold of the tablecloth, trying to counteract Shevchuk. The tablecloth ripped. A pitcher fell, followed by the sound of breaking glass. Suddenly Shevchuk, with a scrap of cloth in his hands, toppled backward stiff as a post, his knees not bending. The back of his head made a loud cracking sound.

The members of the Bureau sprang to their feet, and craning their necks, they stared at the pitiful body spread out on the floor. Shevchuk was still holding a scrap of cloth and his hat out in front of him, as if offering them up for sale.

"Is there a medic here?" asked Revkin in confusion. "Raisa Semenovna!"

Raisa Semenovna bent over the body, and those standing behind her could see her stout thighs straining her light-blue knitted breeches.

"There's no pulse," said Raisa Semenovna, straightening back up with some effort.

36

They took a break and called an ambulance, which delivered Shevchuk to the morgue at the local hospital. Revkin invited Khudobchenko to lunch, but after a glance at his watch, Khudobchenko said he didn't have the time and then, accompanied by his advisor, and without saying goodbye to anyone, he set off for his car.

Revkin caught up with him in the corridor. "Piotr Terentevich," he said, mincing beside Khudobchenko. "I'm very sorry about what happened."

"Forget it." Khudobchenko waved him away. "Nobody knew he had such a weak heart."

"So then maybe you'll still have lunch with us?"

"No, no, I can't, my friend. Work to do," refused Khudobchenko decisively. "Go back. Continue the meeting. You don't need to see me out."

He shook Revkin's hand, but without his usual friendliness, then continued on his way. It was obvious that he wanted to separate himself from the incident. His eyes following Khudobchenko, Revkin paused on the staircase, then, starting to walk back up, he almost collided with Borisov, who was holding some papers in one hand.

"And where are you going?" Revkin asked him.

"I, uh, just, uh." Borisov was confused and averted his eyes. "Piotr Terentevich forgot these," he said, finally getting hold of himself, and then he rushed past Revkin down the stairs.

Quickly returning to his office, Revkin looked through his window and saw Borisov standing coatless in the cold wind, handing the papers to Khudobchenko, who was already inside his car. It was obvious from the way Khudobchenko accepted the papers that he had not only not forgotten them but had never seen them before.

He's written something against me, the snake, thought Revkin of Borisov.

Later it was learned that on the morning before the meeting of the Bureau Borisov had said farewell to his wife and daughter, then added to his wife while leaving, "Well, Manka, I've got something terrible to do. I'll either win a medal or lose my head."

Borisov returned to the office. Revkin looked searchingly at him, but again Borisov averted his eyes.

"Well, all right, then," said Revkin with a sigh, "we ran into a little trouble here, but I hope it will remain our secret. I wouldn't want to try to scare anybody, but I'm warning you— anyone who takes it into his head to talk about what happened here will be held responsible to the Party. And now let's continue. Next we have the personal case of Comrade Golubev. Comrade Chmikhalov will address this question. Come on, Chmikhalov, just keep it short, we're late as it is," he said with a look at his watch.

Chmikhalov rose. A bit perturbed by the incident, he glanced frequently at his notes while muttering the accusations against Golubev. All in all, they came down to the fact that for some time Golubev had been ignoring the decisions of the Party organs, had been overly sensitive to comradely criticism, and now had gone as far as to frustrate the time plan for the harvest as projected by the District Committee. When this was pointed out to him, Golubev had replied coarsely, and, in the presence of non-Party kolkhozniks, had made certain caustic remarks, thereby discrediting the Party's role as leader in the eyes of the masses.

Golubev's thoughts had drifted off. The previous year he had been in a large city. A car had struck a pedestrian. Traffic had stopped. A crowd had gathered, the police and an ambulance arrived. The victim was taken away. Something was measured with a tape measure. They sprinkled sand on the blood, then swept it up. The traffic policeman waved his baton and the traffic started its viscous flow through the streets again. Pedestrians began hurrying again, as if nothing had happened. Golubev was thinking of Shevchuk. He had been lying by the table as if he'd been knocked down by a car. Good God! thought Golubev. And now I'm going to drop dead from fear in front of them . . .

"Golubev!" His name reached him. "You gone deaf or what?"

Golubev raised his head and saw that everyone's eyes were on him.

"Comrade Golubev," repeated Revkin, "I'm asking you for the third time, do you wish to say anything?"

"What is there to say?" said Golubev.

"What do you mean by that? Did you hear Chmikhalov's report? Do you wish to object to anything that was said?"

"Possibly," said Golubev, after a moment's thought.

"Just make it short," interjected Borisov.

"No problem," agreed Golubev.

Neuzhelev jumped up. "Comrades, I propose we set a time limit."

"What kind of time limit are you proposing?" asked Revkin.

"Five minutes."

"Five's a lot," observed Borisov. "Three's enough."

"Comrade Golubev"—Revkin turned to him—"are three minutes enough for you?"

"More than enough." Golubev rose and walked slowly over to the First Secretary. "Here, take it," he said, laying his Party card on the table in front of Revkin and then starting for the door.

"Comrade Golubev! Comrade Golubev!" Revkin and Borisov shouted in unison.

Golubev waved his hand in a gesture dismissing them all, and walked out the door. The Bureau members exchanged confused glances, not knowing how to respond to such an astonishing move.

"It's a provocation!" Neuzhelev suddenly howled out in an inhuman voice. "We should stop him at once!"

Without waiting for things to go any further, Borisov dashed out after Golubev. He caught up with him outside, where Golubev, having unhitched his horse from the fence, was climbing up onto his cart.

"Ivan Timofeyevich!" Coatless and hatless, Borisov was shivering. "Ivan Timofeyevich, what are you doing this for?"

Ivan Timofeyevich hoisted himself up onto the cart and sorted out the reins. The horse started up at once, but Golubev reined it in and looked expectantly at Borisov.

"Come back!" said Borisov, a note of invitation in his voice.

Golubev continued looking at him without saying a word.

"Come back, Timofeyevich," asked Borisov. "Nobody wants your blood. We'll scold you a little, you'll confess a little, and that'll be that."

"Confess to what?" asked Golubev.

"Something," Borisov replied quickly. "Just don't try to prove anything about the weather and objective conditions. Just say, I'm guilty, I was drinking."

"So, drunkenness is forgivable?" asked Golubev.

"Drunkenness can be forgiven," said Borisov. "As long as everything else is politically correct."

"Now I see," said Golubev and flicked the horse with the tips of the reins. "Get going!"

"Wait a minute," Borisov ran alongside, holding on to the side of the cart.

"Get lost, you hear me." Golubev brandished his whip.

The horse lurched forward, Borisov lost his grip.

Borisov returned to total confusion. Everyone was discussing what to do. Parnishchev proposed, "Since he laid down his Party card himself, we have no alternative but to accept it."

Neuzhelev sprang to his feet. "No, comrades, that's not the way. That would be a political error. Comrades, we cannot allow Communists to just fling around a document so precious to us all. We must force Golubev to take his Party card back. Then when he does take it back, we'll . . ." Neuzhelev made a rapacious snatching motion with his hand.

"Right!" said Revkin. "Neuzhelev appears to be talking some sense here." Neuzhelev dropped his eyes modestly. "Let's make a rough draft of a resolution: to censure Communist Golubev's unworthy behavior and to point out to him that his negligent treatment of his Party card was intolerable. Second, to oblige Comrade Golubev to accept his Party card back. I entrust this task"—he raised his head and came eye to eye with Borisov—"to Comrade Borisov," he concluded with malicious satisfaction. Borisov bowed his head obediently.

37

It is now high time for us to give you a Soviet version of Gogol's troika—a covered half-ton truck with military numerals stenciled on its sides. As it winds its way down the roads of the military district, the squeal of suckling pigs and the crazed cackling of chickens stream from inside.

The crew of the truck consisted of three men, not counting the driver, and was somehow reminiscent of a concert brigade serving remote areas. The performances given by this brigade did resemble concerts, or, more precisely, short dramatic plays which always had one and the same finale. But this was not a concert brigade, this was the traveling board of the Military Tribunal, this was the troika. In front, beside the driver, sat the chairman, Colonel Dobrenky, a pleasant-looking man with a bluish nose on his fullish face. Nikolai Spiridonovich was a lover of life. He loved to drink vodka, crack jokes, sing songs, and was not indifferent to the opposite sex. "I don't like them skinny," he would say. "I like them so there's something to hold on to." He was fatherly toward accused men, often calling them "son." "What's this now, son, I see that the motherland has reared and raised you and you betrayed it like that Judas for thirty silver kopecks." He handed out only two sentences—the firing squad or a penal brigade—and it would seem that they left no trace on his soul. In the evening, after a day of sentencing, he would, if he found good "soulful" company, eat, drink, and sing with pleasure:

> Oh Galya, Galya so young,
> They deceived her, abandoned her, Galya.

At the same time, he would direct those joining in the song, wink, and frown immediately if someone hit a false note.

In the covered rear of the truck Dobrenky's colleagues, Tselikov and Dubinin, both somber men, sat with their backs to the cab. Sacks were bouncing on the floor, sacks of flour, sacks of peas, sacks of potatoes, as well as sacks containing small animals—suckling pigs, chickens, geese.

The brigade covered the territory of the military command, its assignment the "strategic implementation of socialist law in wartime conditions." The troika tried deserters, those with self-inflicted wounds, and others of military age trying to evade the sacred duty of defending their motherland. It would have been more efficient to shoot them all on the spot with no trial, but then where would the members of the tribunal have gotten their potatoes, flour, sucklings, and so forth? And, for that reason, they had to linger first in one locale, then another. They simply had not found the time for Dolgov yet.

But now, apparently, they were on their way there.

On their way! On their way! Are not you, too, O Russia . . . But didn't somebody else write that already?

Flying toward the half-ton truck, leaving a whirling trail of dust behind it, came the Zis–101 and Dobrenky's fellow Ukrainian, Comrade Khudobchenko, who was busy reading the document presented him in Dolgov by Borisov, which he now kept from the eyes of both his driver and his advisor Pshenichikov, who was sitting beside him.

> . . . as an honest Communist I consider it my duty to inform you that in our region the ideological education of the populace is at a dangerously low level . . . a certain Chonkin aided by Belyashova, the woman he lived with . . . an operational group of seven men under the command of Lieutenant Filippov . . . only with the aid of a military unit did it prove possible . . . the consequences still arouse an unhealthy interest among the backward elements of the district and give rise to various rumors . . . apparently Captain Milyaga . . . All this undoubtedly has a negative effect on the authority of the organs . . . like many Communists in the region I consider it necessary to conduct a careful . . . and to bolster the Party's personnel . . .

Colonel Dobrenky and Comrade Khudobchenko were approaching each other at a speed equal to the sum of the speeds of their vehicles. Then, all at once, the Zis–101 and the half-ton truck were stopped side by side, blocking the entire road. Dobrenky jumped out of the truck as Khudobchenko beckoned him with a finger.

"Where are you bound for, old Cossack?" asked Piotr Terentevich, gazing benevolently at the colonel's face, puffy from booze.

"We're going to try a deserter, Piotr Terentevich," answered Dobrenky respectfully.

"A deserter?" Khudobchenko's brows rose. "Not that Chonkin, is it?"

"Yes, Chonkin." The colonel nodded, surprised that Comrade Khudobchenko had heard of such an insignificant case.

"Aha . . . so . . ." mumbled Khudobchenko, pensively regarding the appearance of his countryman. "Here's what, old Cossack, don't go there just yet. Chonkin's case is being put off. There'll be more important cases soon. So, go back, you understand?"

"Understood!" Dobrenky snapped to attention.

"That's good," said Khudobchenko, and lazily raised his puffy hand as if saluting the colonel, at the same time signaling the driver to drive on.

<h1 style="text-align:center">38</h1>

Ermolkin was the last one to leave the meeting of the Bureau. Depressed, he was on his way back to the editorial office when he saw a staggering sight. Leaning against the wall of the public communal lavoratories stood a thin, barefooted woman, clad only in a slip. The wind lifted the hem of her slip, revealing her knees, bony and blue from the cold. Gazing submissively at the two barrels of the shotgun aimed at her, she was saying timidly but insistently: "Pasha, please hurry up, I'm cold."

"No problem," answered Prosecutor Evpraksein. "You'll warm up in the hereafter. The devils will warm you up good in a frying pan." He shifted the gun to a more comfortable position and pressed his cheek against the stock. "In the name of the Russian Soviet Federated . . ."

"Pavel Trofimovich." Ermolkin touched the prosecutor's sleeve.

Without lowering his weapon Pavel Trofimovich glanced at

Ermolkin and then looked him over from head to toe as if trying to grasp how this obstacle had appeared.

"What do you want?"

"Are you going to shoot her?"

"Any objections?"

"No, no, of course not," Ermolkin was quick to assure him. "Like they say, it's a family affair. I've had some little rows with my own wife. Only . . ."

"Only what?"

"Could you shoot me, too, while you're at it?"

"You?" The prosecutor lowered his gun and peered at Ermolkin, perhaps trying to decide whether such a small fry was worth the powder.

"Yes, me," confirmed Ermolkin. "Because sooner or later, one way or the other . . . And my son, he's three and a half . . . I mean he's at the front now . . ."

"Perfectly clear," interrupted the prosecutor. "Stand against the wall. And you," he said to his wife, "go home. And put on some clothes instead of walking around in just your slip like some sort of slut. Take her place."

Ermolkin took her place and flung his head back, pressing it against the damp wall. He imagined how any second flames would come bursting from both the barrels, and not wishing to see that, he closed his eyes. He did not see the prosecutor raise his shotgun and only heard him recite clearly and distinctly: "In the name of the Russian Soviet Federated Republic . . . you, Ermolkin, Boris . . . uh, what's your patronymic again?"

"Evgenevich," babbled Ermolkin, his lips drained of blood.

"Evgenevich, for being a rat and a bastard, for taking part in the murder of an innocent man . . ."

"Murder?" Ermolkin opened his eyes in surprise. "I never killed anyone. I couldn't kill a chicken."

"Maybe not a chicken, but how about Shevchuk?"

"Ah, Shevchuk." Ermolkin understood now. "Yes. Yes, of course, in a certain way you could say . . ."

". . . to death by a firing squad," continued the prosecutor, not listening to Ermolkin. "Sentence to be executed at once."

He aimed his shotgun at Ermolkin and, pressing his cheek against the stock, closed his left eye.

"Stop! Stop!" shouted Ermolkin. "Stop!" He fell to his knees and, holding his arms out in front of him, began crawling toward Evpraksein.

"What's the matter now?" asked the prosecutor with displeasure, lowering his weapon.

"I'm afraid," admitted Ermolkin, and burst into tears.

"Ach, and a coward to boot. Of course, that's a horse of a different color. In that case . . ." He rolled his eyes and began to mumble in a singsong voice: "In the name of the Russian Soviet Federated . . . having examined in open session and having deliberated on the spot, I have determined that . . . due to newly disclosed circumstances . . . taking the cowardice of the accused into account . . . the previous sentence to be rescinded, no grounds for its leniency . . . Ermolkin, Boris . . . what's your patronymic again?"

"Evgenevich," Ermolkin prompted obligingly.

"Evgenevich, you are hereby sentenced to fear for the rest of your natural life, your work to continue as usual. The form of punishment is to remain exposed to the condition of freedom as a recognized necessity of life. The sentence is final and not subject to appeal. Defendant, is the sentence clear to you?"

"It is," answered Ermolkin dolefully.

"Then go live as you please," said Evpraksein, regarding Ermolkin with disgust.

39

Certain shortsighted people with bias against the Right People make the unsubstantiated claim that they, the iron knights, are beyond the reach of our sufferings or any understanding of them. No, a thousand times no! Nothing is beyond their reach, they understand everything. And if those knights were jabbed in the rear end with a red-hot awl, I think it would be just as unpleasant for them as it would be for you and me. Well, perhaps a bit less.

Evening fell. Returning home from work, Lieutenant Filippov walked at the slow pace of a man burdened with affairs of state.

He walked unhurriedly, moving his precious feet carefully. It seemed to him that the fences and the trees behind them and the pig lying on the road all knew that it was not just any old person walking past them but the head of a serious Institution. He possessed an unspoken awareness that it was somehow due to his presence in the world that the houses stood, the trees grew, and the pigs grew fatter. The lieutenant felt like a wise magician who could bring all this to a halt but did not wish to.

It was warm and humid after the recent rains. Many houses had their windows open, letting the sounds of human life out into the streets—a hammer rapping, a child crying, a samovar whistling, a husband beating his howling wife. A man was sitting on the porch of his tumbledown hut with a hand-rolled cigarette and discoursing confidently in a drunken voice: "I'm telling you, a German's a man same as us, he just doesn't talk like us."

"There he goes again!" came a woman's stern voice from around the corner. "That tongue of yours is going to land you in jail."

Two windows were especially noisy—a gramophone was singing "La Cucaracha" at the top of its lungs and people were dancing. Without meaning to, Lieutenant Filippov came to a halt in front of those windows. He caught glimpses of the local girls in their smart dresses and the uniforms of the artillery officers whose unit was temporarily billeted in the town. Sure, thought Filippov paternally, let them have a good time. Resting his elbows on the sharp tips of the pickets, he looked into those open windows and was suddenly stung by envy for that life which was closed to him.

During the first days of the war, he had met a girl named Natasha in the club. She and her mother were stuck in Dolgov waiting for word from her father, a commander of some sort. Both Natasha and her mother liked the lieutenant for his intellectual qualities. The mother was a schoolteacher and Natasha a future teacher, now in her third year at the pedagogical institute. Filippov had twice been their guest, been served tea sweetened with jam, and had discussed the war with them. Natasha's mother was asking the lieutenant one thing and another when all of a sudden she asked why he was there and not at the front.

"I suppose you're in the reserves?" she had asked.

"Yes, something like that," he had answered a bit disconcerted. Fortunately, she did not seem to know one branch of service from another. He tried to appear a decent young man, did not put his elbows on the table, did not cut his fish with a knife, did not tap his teaspoon against the glass, and drank his tea in small sips.

A few days later, leaving the Institution for his lunch break, he ran into Natasha, who happened to be passing by at that very moment. After hellos, he began walking alongside her and asked her what her plans were for the evening. She did not answer that question but, clearly disturbed, asked him: "Do you work in there?"

"Yes," he said casually. "And so?"

He needn't have asked. He had already noticed more than once how people like Natasha reacted to his colleagues. He suddenly felt uncomfortable about working where he did, but he pretended that he had not understood Natasha's confusion and asked, "And so?" as if in all innocence.

"Nothing," Natasha was quick to reply. "Just asking."

It turned out that she was busy that evening, and the follow-

ing day he had been sent out to arrest Chonkin. When he returned from that protracted operation and had gone to see
Natasha, he learned that she and her mother had left Dolgov
for points unknown.

They changed the record inside the house. A languorous
voice plaintively drew out the words:

> *The weary sun has bade*
> *a tender farewell to the sea.*
> *It was at that hour you confessed*
> *that you no longer loved me.*

The couples swayed to the music. They floated slowly
through the cigarette smoke like fish in an aquarium. The
leather straps on the officers' waists and shoulder belts caught
the sun. Suddenly the lieutenant had a terrible longing to be
like them, straight and open, not to terrify others and not to be
afraid himself, to dance with a bouncy, sweating girl, to kiss
her in the dark passageway, bumping up against yokes and
pails, then to walk out with bitten lips ready even to die for his
country, for Stalin, for Natasha, for that girl, or just for nothing
at all. What am I doing? He reined in his thoughts. Where are
these moods coming from? Yes, they don't like us. Yes, they are
afraid of us. But, after all, someone's got to do it. He attempted
to convince himself though, in the depths of his soul, he suspected that what he did never needed to be done by anybody.

Reluctantly he pried himself away from the picket fence,
from those young strangers and their tipsy cheer, and went on
his way.

40

His sadness turned to anxiety. Suddenly the lieutenant
thought . . . no, not suddenly, but gradually, there arose in him
a mounting sense that he was being followed. No, he did not
hear anyone's footsteps behind him, but the absolutely irre-

futable feeling that someone's piercing gaze was burning into the back of his head kept growing within him. Naturally he realized this was impossible. A gaze was not material, not something that could actually burn. And yet . . .

Pure rot, he said to himself, feeling an irresistible urge to look behind him, an urge to which he did not submit. No one would dare follow him. Still, having gone a few more feet, he could bear it no longer, stopped and turned around. There was no one behind him. The lieutenant continued on his way. Something's wrong with me, he thought. Maybe I'm coming down with something.

Yes, this wasn't the first time that he had thought he was being followed. There was more to it than that. Sometimes, on the contrary, it seemed that everyone liked him very much. Especially after becoming head of the Right Place, the lieutenant encountered demonstrations of popular affection at every step. Strangers bowed to him in the street and sometimes even doffed their caps.

In any room, any place, at any moment, he could sit down without looking behind him, certain that someone would have a chair waiting for him. The local intelligentsia were respectful to the lieutenant. A local artist, Shuteinikov, gave him his painting "The Tractor Driver" as a present and the poet Serafim Butilko sent him a newspaper clipping of his poem "Ballad of the Leader." Kolkhoz chairmen loved Filippov too—to take but one example, Maxim Petrovich Shileiko. It was enough for Filippov to inquire (on his aunt's behalf) if Shileiko's kolkhoz could spare him a suckling pig (of course he would pay for it and everything would be strictly legal) for Shileiko personally to deliver a fifty-pound pig in a sack the very next day and to give him a paper to sign which certified that the lieutenant had paid the value of the animal, one ruble fifty-six kopecks. (The lieutenant was afterward to think that, all in all, our kolkhozniks couldn't be too bad off if they could sell hogs like that at such a low price.)

On the whole, things did not seem to be going badly for the lieutenant. He had bcome a chief, he was praised at the District Committee office, everyone liked him . . .

Everyone, but not everyone. Roman Gavrilovich Luzhin had been openly finding fault with him. First the Chonkin case, then he dreams up that Hans. "I order you . . . in a period of five days . . ." Giving orders was the easiest thing in the world. But where was he to look for him, that Hans, and what were his identifying marks?*

Perhaps these petty troubles had brought on something like a persecution mania in him. Wherever he was—at work, in the street, at home—it always felt as if someone was watching him.

The situation at home had become impossible. Even his own aunt Pelageya Vasilevna, or, for short, Aunt Polya, had begun to notice that something was wrong with him. Sometimes he would suddenly shudder at dinner, raise his head, look at the door, and say uncertainly to his aunt: "Isn't that someone knocking?"

"What's wrong with you?" she would say in surprise. "You're hearing things."

But he wouldn't take her word. He would tiptoe over to the door, listen carefully, then fling the door open. Naturally there wouldn't be anyone there. He would steal up to the window, tear aside the curtain, and his heart would fall into his stomach as he saw some yellowish face pressed against the glass from the outside. It was his own reflection that frightened him. Things had reached a point where sometimes he would even get up in the night and check the bolts on the doors, the locks on the windows, and stand for hours by the stove, trying to determine whether a sufficiently skinny person could climb in through the flue. Aunt Polya noticed all this.

"And just who are you afraid of?" she would ask. "You're the most fearsome person in the whole district."

---

* Filippov was unaware that that very morning the Right Place would receive not less than fourteen denunciations of nineteen alleged Hanses.

Ach, that Aunt Polya! She had raised and reared him. She loved him. But ever since he had begun working at the Right Place, her attitude toward him had changed, and in spite of her proletarian origins, she had turned into a terrible counter-revolutionary. She kept saying that it had been much cheaper to live under the Tsar.

"You're looking backward, Auntie Polya," he would reproach her. "You have to look forward."

"But I see you're doing a lot of looking." His aunt grinned. "You even peep under the bench to make sure there's nobody there."

At other times she would suddenly ask, with an innocent look on her face: "Tell me, how many people murdered in the current quarter?"

"Keep that down!" he would hiss, looking behind him. Then, sighing, he would shake his head in distress. "You don't share our views."

"You can say that again!" she was quick to agree.

Why did he permit such talk in his own home? Why did he try to defend himself?

"You know I only ended up there by chance, Auntie."

"You know how people end up there by chance—like this!" and his aunt eloquently put her hands behind her back.

41

A twig crackled behind him. The lieutenant started and looked back. He thought he saw someone's shadow flash and vanish behind the house he had just passed.

Filippov continued walking. He unsnapped his holster without losing a stride, drew his pistol, and transferred it to his pocket. There was something large and dark up ahead of him. As he approached, the lieutenant realized that it was some sort of agricultural machine—a seeder or a winnower, he didn't know too much about such things. In any case, the object was large enough to hide behind and this the lieutenant did. Peering out after a few seconds, he spotted a dark figure stepping out irresolutely onto the path from behind the house. Now there could no longer be any doubt—he was being followed. Now, having lost him, his shadow looked about in confusion and then, with a quickened pace, began heading down the path toward the farm machine. The lieutenant drew his revolver from his pocket and quietly clicked off the safety catch. Over the pounding of his own heart he heard the careful steps and the intermittent breathing.

"Stop or I'll shoot!" The lieutenant sprang out from behind the machine and stuck his revolver in his shadow's face.

"Oi!" she shrieked and dropped her bundle to the ground.

"Oh, it's you," said Filippov, lowering his revolver. "I almost shot you. What do you want?"

"It's about my Vanka, you see," said Nyura, picking up her bundle. "You say I'm an outside party, but I'm not an outside party; they fired me from work," she said not without pride.

"People aren't fired from work, they are let go," corrected the lieutenant. "But for what?"

"For living with him, with Ivan," explained Nyura and unable to restrain herself boasted. "They said because I lived with him for love."

The lieutenant stood looking at Nyura, unable to make any sense of it all. "What kind of nonsense is this?" he said. "Who let you go?"

"Lyubov Mikhailovna, head of the post office."

"For what?"

"For Vanka. For my relations with an enemy of the people."

"Enemy of the people?" said Filippov, surprised. "And who told her that Chonkin was an enemy of the people? He's just a deserter."

"Maybe not just," objected Nyura.

"Strange," said Filippov, "very strange. Here's what you do: come see me tomorrow at ten and we'll go into all this."

"Tomorrow?" Nyura beamed. That was hardly what she had expected. "And can I bring him a parcel?"

"You may."

42

Leaving Nyura behind, the lieutenant continued on his way and began to think about what was going on. Who allowed the head of the post office to declare an ordinary deserter an enemy of the people? Could she know something he didn't?

At home, in a flurry, his aunt told the lieutenant that people were looking for him. A messenger had come running to the house to say that Lieutenant Colonel Luzhin and a major had arrived and would be awaiting Filippov in Luzhin's office.

The lieutenant found Luzhin seated at his desk. Roman Gavrilovich's head looked more monstrous than usual in the light from his desk lamp.

The major, his hands on his knees, was sitting by the wall. They both looked searchingly at the lieutenant. Then Luzhin rose and slowly approached Filippov. "Well, hello, Hans," he said and, jumping up into the air, slapped Filippov's face so hard it made him fall to the floor.

By the evening of the following day, former Lieutenant Filippov, somewhat paler and sprouting a beard (it is a fact that the beards of corpses and prisoners grow very quickly), had already supplied the necessary testimony.

43

FROM THE TESTIMONY OF
FORMER LIEUTENANT S/S FILIPPOV

". . . fully repenting of the crimes I have committed and wishing to help the investigation, I openly admit that while working as an authorized agent of German military Intelligence, under the code name Hans, I systematically collected information of a

—**173**—

military, political, and economic nature constituting military and state secrets of the U.S.S.R. and transmitted them to Admiral Canaris personally or through the chief of the Section "Abwehr 1," Colonel Peckenbrock.

Acting in the interests of a state at war with the U.S.S.R., I used all means to disorganize production, to damage the economy by means of sabotage and other treacherous acts; I abetted the spreading of panic-producing rumors, I sought out and incited to action the hidden enemies of the Soviet state from among the former kulaks, peasants employed by kulaks, and covert supporters of the so-called Trotskyist-Zinovievist opposition, whose number included persons holding key positions in the district's leadership.

I established a direct connection between the German high command and the henchman of the White Emigré groups, the so-called Chonkin-Golitsyn, who was working in tandem with me in carrying out sabotage in the village of Krasnoye.

Having learned that Chonkin-Golitsyn was threatened with arrest and thus with inevitable exposure, I, heading a group sent to capture him, arranged matters so that we did not capture him but he us, and in so doing, the warrant approved by the prosecutor was intentionally damaged.

After Captain Milyaga was lured into the trap set for him, the activity of the security forces in the district was in fact completely paralyzed, which in turn allowed those forces opposed to the Soviet system to move into action. All this led to the Red Army having to weaken its front line when it threw part of its forces into suppressing the so-called Chonkin-Golitsyn gang. After their defeat I, producing the damaged and thus invalid warrant, took the criminal away from the military authorities and subsequently, temporarily seizing the post of Head of the Institution, 7–BTS, No. 86/312, I purposely led the investigation into a blind alley to save Prince Chonkin-Golitsyn from the punishment he deserved, since the German high command was counting on employing him in the future in the capacity of inspirer and organizer of actions against Soviet authority.

I have given this testimony voluntarily and this recording of what I said is correct.

given to prisoner Filippov, Hans, as proof that he has undergone a medical examination. No lice, venereal, skin, or infectious diseases were found. No counter-indications to his being kept in a common cell.

Military Medic Semenovna

PART 2

1

Chonkin was sleeping on the floor, his cheek resting against the slop pail, when he was shaken awake and pulled up onto his feet. He shook his head and then, fully awake, he met with a surprise. Six guards had squeezed into his cell; at their head was the prison warden himself, Senior Lieutenant Kuryatnikov, a small, thickset man with a womanish, pockmarked face. All of them, Kuryatnikov included, seemed to be very excited about something and were looking curiously but, at the same time, timidly at Chonkin.

The prisoners began stirring on their planks and someone asked what was going on.

"They're taking Crapmaster," said Bayonet with a certain tone of surprise.

"Why so many of them?"

"Who knows?"

Then Manyunya spoke up: "That many people coming for just one man means a firing squad."

"What do you mean, a firing squad?" said Bayonet. "There hasn't been a trial yet."

"No trial needed," argued Manyunya. "Wartime law."

These words made Chonkin flinch, though he could not believe that they would just take him out and shoot him. Besides, the guards looked perfectly harmless. The warden himself picked up Chonkin's overcoat, shook it, and helped Chonkin on with it like a doorman.

"What time is it?" asked Chonkin, fumbling, his hand missing the sleeve.

They didn't answer him. Kuryatnikov, having taken a step back, regarded Chonkin with a critical eye.

"Of course we ought to give him a shave," he said with concern. "But it'll be all right."

"You hear that, Manyunya," shouted Bayonet. "He says they ought to give him a shave. And you're talking about firing squads."

"Sure," responded Manyunya. "How can you shoot an unshaven man? That's not how things are done. If he's sick, you cure him, and if he needs a shave, you give him one."

"Silence!" screamed Kuryatnikov. "If I hear one more word out of you I'll . . ."

At that point Professor Tsinubel rose from behind the slop bucket, walked over to Chonkin, and offered him his hand. "Farewell, Chonkin," he said warmly. "Don't lose heart. Take a lesson from Lenin's self-control. Remember . . ."

Chonkin never heard what it was he should remember, for by then he had been escorted out of the cell.

The dense little crowd walked down the corridor and across a courtyard to a gate where a guard stood by a table, a pistol at his side.

"The car hasn't come?" asked the warden.

"It broke down," answered the guard.

"All right, we'll walk, then."

The warden signed the book lying on the table, and then Chonkin was escorted out past the gate and across the square. It was dark and cold and drizzling.

"What time is it?" asked Chonkin again, and again he received no answer.

They walked up to an unmarked door and rang the bell. The door swung open and they found themselves in what Chonkin knew to be Lieutenant Filippov's reception room.

"Wait a minute," said Kuryatnikov, and knocking timidly, he

stuck his head in through the door. "Request permission to bring the prisoner in."

"Permission granted," came the reply.

2

A lamp was burning brightly in Lieutenant Filippov's office. But instead of Filippov sitting at the desk, there was a major in a new field shirt crisscrossed with gleaming leather straps. Another man Chonkin had never seen before, with a large, shaved head and thick glasses, was sitting on a chair by the wall. His overcoat had a fur collar (Chonkin had never seen a coat like that before) and was unbuttoned, his hands were joined across his stomach, and his feet, which did not reach the floor, were dangling in the air. On the chair beside him lay a service cap onto whose high crown a pair of gloves had been tossed.

With a ceremonial step Kuryatnikov approached the man with the shaved head, saluted him, and shrilled out: "Comrade Colonel, the suspect Chonkin has been brought in according to your orders."

Can't be a colonel, thought Chonkin.

"Wait outside the door," ordered the colonel, without changing position.

Kuryatnikov and the escorts left the room.

From where each sat, the colonel and the major examined Chonkin closely while he stood in the middle of the room, not knowing what to do with his hands.

Suddenly the colonel sprang to his feet and began darting rapidly around Chonkin, leaning to one side like a motorcycle.

"You," muttered the colonel, flashing before Chonkin's eyes, "expected to see Hans and not us. But he's gone. Alas. He's monstrously busy. He's giving testimony. Extremely valuable testimony, by the way. And I recommend. The same to you. Urgently. Especially since we know everything. Everything."

He stopped circling Chonkin just as unexpectedly as he had begun; he returned to his chair, sat down, and assumed his previous posture.

The major began to speak, slowly and without passion: "Here's the thing, my good man. As you have just heard, Hans has been arrested. He's giving testimony and we already know a great deal. But we need to put a fine point on a few matters. We are capable of respecting an enemy. You led us around by the nose for quite some time, playing the role of Ivan the fool. What can we say, your acting was magnificent, but now, as an intelligent man, you have to admit the game is up."

"Well said," approved the colonel, again springing from his chair. "Your card has been beaten, Prince!" he said, as if on a stage, flinging his hand out to one side.

Chonkin was startled. He had not realized that these people knew his old nickname.

"As I said"—the major grinned after exchanging glances with the colonel—"we know everything. So it's best you make a clean breast of it right away."

"Yes, a clean breast, right away." The colonel walked over to Chonkin. "Please, for your own good. And so, who sent you to the village of Krasnoye?"

"To the village of Krasnoye?" repeated Chonkin.

"Yes, yes." The colonel clacked his teeth in impatience. "Who sent you to the village of Krasnoye?"

"Me?" specified Chonkin, touching his chest with a finger.

"Yes, you. Precisely you. Who sent you to Krasnoye?"

"It was that, uh," said Chonkin, hoping that the colonel truly did know everything, "uh, sergeant, uh, Peskov."

"Peskov?" repeated the colonel mistrustfully. "A sergeant? But what did Anton Ivanovich say?"

"Anton?" said Chonkin. "Ivanovich?"

"I'm thinking of Denikin," prompted the colonel.

"Dikin?" Chonkin strained his memory. "Maybe you mean Zhikin, the one who rides around on the little castors?"

"On what? On castors?" repeated the colonel. "Ach, on castors?"

Making a short lunge, he punched Chonkin in the stomach. Chonkin opened his mouth in an attempt to draw breath and even managed to produce a sound like "ah-ah," but he could draw no breath at all. Eyes bulging, Chonkin fell to his knees, and only then did the air start forcing its way in spurts into his lungs.

"Enough?" came a voice from above him. "So then, who sent you to the village of Krasnoye? Who? Who?" screamed the colonel. "Tell me, you bastard, or I'll put a bullet through your squash right this second!"

Chonkin raised his eyes. The muzzle of the revolver, as at his first interrogation, was pointed right at the bridge of his nose. But this time he felt no fear.

"All right, I'll count to three. One! Two! . . . ."

Chonkin said nothing. He realized that no answer he gave would be to their liking.

"There's no point in resisting." The major's soft voice reached him. "You know that one way or the other we will force you to talk. Answer one question and we'll let you go rest in your cell. Who sent you to the village of Krasnoye?"

"That's known by who's supposed to know," said Chonkin, panting.

The next punch hit his chin like a sledgehammer. He flew up in the air, his back and the back of his head cracked against the wall, and he fell to the ground, his ragged boots spread wide apart.

The major and the colonel stood over him. A fly crept across his face, now pale.

"A tough nut," said the colonel pensively, rubbing his bruised hand.

"Yes," agreed the major. "This one'll cost us some work."

They felt neither hatred nor any other strong emotion for the limp body before them. As specialists in their field they were simply evaluating the resistance of the material with which they had to work.

Kuryatnikov was then summoned and ordered to place the prisoner in a cell by himself and to keep him in the strictest isolation. It was no simple matter for Kuryatnikov to execute this order because all three solitary cells were occupied at that time: one housed the brig, Kuryatnikov was keeping his cow in the second, and he was renting the third for fifteen rubles a month to Tukhvatullin, a civilian with a family of six. Naturally, the fifteen rubles didn't matter, the warden could live with that sacrifice, but winter was coming and Tukhvatullin had the right to kick up a fuss if his family was evicted.

Seeing no other solution, Kuryatnikov ordered that a large common cell be cleaned out especially for Chonkin, its temporary residents to be shunted off to various other cells, which were already quite overcrowded. Thus, the information that Chonkin was apparently held in solitary should not be considered absolutely reliable—more precisely put, he was a solitary prisoner in a common cell.

3

Revkin had a lot of trouble during that rainy month. For a week and a half a special commission had been at work in the district and had compiled a secret report: "Concerning Certain Shortcomings in the Work of the Party Organization of the Dolgov District."

The report listed examples of underfulfillment of plans in various branches of agriculture and local industry, but special attention was given to the breakdown of ideological and propaganda activity among the populace, which bespoke political shortsightedness, a dulling of vigilance, and an atmosphere of complacency rife among the district leaders. The report also mentioned the so-called Chonkin gang. The name Golitsyn had as yet to make its first appearance in any official document.

But the very fact that Chonkin and his gang were allotted no less than four pages in this report allows one to suppose that the commission had certain new information at its disposal, although it is also possible that the commission had simply not yet received clear instructions about calling Chonkin Golitsyn.

One way or the other, the commission reached the conclusion that the local situation had reached unhealthy proportions, and it proposed a quick end to all the complacency, bungling, and thoughtlessness, an increase in vigilance, mass political and educational activity, and personnel changes in the leadership of the District Committee.

The personnel changes occurred first in the Right Place. Lieutenant Filippov, as we know, was arrested. However, a few days later a new radio message reporting Filippov's arrest was intercepted from Hans. This radio message was most unfortunate and threatened to ruin everything. The brilliantly executed operation to uncover, expose, and render Hans harmless had been rewarded with promotions (Lieutenant Colonel Luzhin had now become a full colonel), expressions of gratitude, and medals. To admit that the wrong person had been arrested would have also meant canceling all those rewards and promotions . . . No, that was absolutely out of the question. And for that reason the following instructions had been written on the intercepted message: *This is a trick by which the enemy hopes to lead us astray. I hereby order that all radio messages signed "Hans" be ignored and the monitoring of his wavelength cease.*

A highly experienced specialist in his field, Fedot Fedotovich Figurin, arrived to replace Lieutenant Filippov and behaved very oddly right from the start.

Upon assuming his duties, Fedot Fedotovich did not even think to present himself to the First Secretary of the District Committee. That was incredible. Usually the Regional Head and the Secretary of the Regional Committee bring such new leaders (and if not the former, then at least the latter) and present them to the district Party leadership. Moreover, a new chief usually acquaints himself with the local situation in conversation with the Secretary of the District Committee. Fedot Fedotovich was not only not presented by anyone but he himself did not express any desire for a meeting. Such behavior on the part of a new official seemed extremely odd to Revkin, but he was not going to force himself on Figurin. After all, it was not Figurin but he, Revkin, who was still headman in the district.

That was just it—"still."

Some rather vague rumors were making the local rounds to the effect that the new man had launched into furious activity, was summoning in the oddest people, questioning them, and obtaining from each one, without respect to person, a signed statement swearing not to divulge anything at all. In spite of that, Revkin learned that Figurin had already paid calls on many people and had been to see Borisov more than once. It also became known that Editor in Chief Ermolkin had been spending time with Borisov. Neither man divulged the content of these conversations, but Revkin learned that the new chief was interested in his, Revkin's, activities as well. This was evident in the way Revkin's subordinates related to him; they no longer smiled at him so affably and did not race headlong to execute his orders.

One morning, while glancing over the local paper with his tea, Revkin found a special article on page 3 with the large headline: CAPTAIN MILYAGA'S EXPLOITS. Revkin felt giddy. His tea long cold, the First Secretary kept running his eyes down the page and returning to the beginning, because he could make no sense whatsoever of the article. The article related the exploits of the Right People from the very inception of the Soviet Union through the present day, stressing what quiet and inconspicuous people they were. The author of the article expressed his regrets that it was not always possible to speak of such heroes publicly. The author promised that one day all the exploits of these modest men would be made known to the people and that their names would be entered in the golden book of honor. Meanwhile, only heroes who had perished could enjoy such glory, and that was not always the case either. One such hero, according to the author, was Captain Milyaga, the former chief of the Dolgov Institution. The article became vague when dealing with the fact that recently a gang (whose gang was not indicated) had been active in the district. An operational detachment under the command of Captain Milyaga had been hurled into battle to liquidate the gang. Milyaga had perfidiously been taken prisoner. He was tortured, a star was cut into his back, melted lead was poured down his throat, but the enemy never heard what they wanted from this hero. "Long live Stalin!" were the heroic captain's last words. The author of the article did not take the trouble to explain how a person could cry out with a throat full of melted lead.

Revkin could not believe his eyes. He called his wife Aglaya. "This is a total lie!" he said to her.

"And a dangerous one at that," agreed Aglaya.

Revkin phoned Ermolkin, but he was neither at home nor at work. That same day Revkin convoked the Bureau of the District Committee. They found and delivered Ermolkin, who had attempted to hide and whose cheeks were trembling from terror. At the meeting Revkin subjected the article to harsh criticism. He said that such an article should absolutely never have been printed, for everyone was aware that in fact Captain Milyaga had died a coward's death.

"Of course," said Revkin, "our Party press should display events in a way useful to us. But you, Ermolkin, should have taken the time to think whether it was worthwhile to portray a traitor to our motherland as a hero. Your article only discredits our newspaper and our entire press in general. Ask any kolkhoznik on the street and he'll tell you how Captain Milyaga died. So why then did you print such an outright lie? Was it your own idea or did someone put you up to it?"

Ermolkin stood with his hands at his sides, trembling. His teeth could be heard chattering. Seeing his confusion, Revkin decided to continue his attack. "Ermolkin, I am asking you," he said now more specifically, "who assigned you the task of discrediting our press?"

"It was me . . . myself," Ermolkin began babbling barely audibly. "Fedot Fedotovich told me . . ." At that point he held his tongue and looked back over at Borisov.

Revkin realized that it was time to show some muscle to Ermolkin and those behind him. "So now you listen, friend," he said, pronouncing each word distinctly. "I still have not made the personal acquaintance of any Fedot Fedotovich. And *Bolshevik Tempos* is not the organ of Fedot Fedotovich but of the District Committee Party, and I request you to make a mental note of that. Meanwhile, I am suspending you from work and initiating a personal case against you." Revkin's tone of voice was already one that he used not with comrades but with enemies, those beyond the pale.

"Well, well," said Borisov suddenly.

"Do you wish to say something, Comrade Borisov?"

"Yes, I do." Borisov rose and began speaking slowly. "There's something I don't understand here, Comrade Revkin. I had somehow thought that our Bureau was a collective body and you seem to be suspending Comrade Ermolkin from work and initiating a personal case all by yourself. So, what I fail to understand is, why have we been convoked? That's the first thing! And the second thing I don't quite understand is your attitude toward Captain Milyaga. As you know, we are now at war with a deadly enemy. I don't need to tell you that the situation is very serious. Especially since not only our external but our internal enemies are now working full swing. And I mean right here in our own district. You will recall that the Chonkin gang was operating right under our noses. You know as well as I do who this so-called Chonkin turned out to be. And I believe you've heard about the notorious Hans as well. In such circumstances when, one could say, our Party obligation is to combat these gangs with our security forces, I cannot understand why the First Secretary of the District Committee needs to have the workers of our security organs appear as traitors and turncoats in the eyes of the populace."

Revkin knew Borisov well enough to know that he would never go against the opinion of his superior. And if he was doing so now, then it could not have been without someone's approval. Revkin closed the debate and drove home troubled and disturbed. Aglaya was surprised to see him back so early. "Are you feeling sick?"

"No," said Revkin, and went to his room, locking the door from the inside. Her eye to the keyhole, Aglaya watched her husband rapidly pacing the room, his hands crossed behind his back. From time to time he would release his hands to threaten someone with a fist.

"All right," he declared, brandishing a fist, "you've attacked the wrong man! I can bite too! I'll show you yet!"

Then he would again cross his hands behind his back and resume walking quickly back and forth across the room. Suddenly he came bursting out of the room. "Where's the car?"

"At the garage." Aglaya was breaking matches, nervously trying to light a Belomor cigarette.

"Call Motya, get her over here."

"Has something happened?"

"Nothing's happened. Just call her, you hear me!"

"If you're going to speak that way to your own wife you can call her yourself," raged Aglaya.

Revkin stopped and stared at Aglaya. He looked at her with the merciless gaze he reserved for enemies of the people. "Comrade Revkin," he said softly but distinctly, "I am not ordering you to call as your husband but as your Party leader . . ."

Aglaya dashed to the telephone. Motya was not at the garage. They said she had gone to the tearoom. But there was no phone at the tearoom. Aglaya sent their son Vladilen to the tearoom while she paced, smoking, in front of the door to her husband's room.

Finally Vladilen appeared with Motya. The car was waiting by the gate. Aglaya knocked at her husband's door. Revkin sprang out and ran to his car with Motya and Aglaya right behind him. When they caught up with him, Revkin was already fidgeting impatiently in the front seat.

"Move it!" he shouted to Motya.

His anxiety communicated itself to Motya, who could not fit the key into the ignition for quite some time. Aglaya ran around the car to the passenger side and opened the door. "Andrei, tell me, as your wife, where are you going?"

"To the Regional Committee!" he said, snatching the door away from her and slamming it shut.

The car lurched forward and flew off, plopping into puddles and splashing passers-by.

4

It was a long way. The road lulled and calmed Revkin. After half an hour he was sitting in his usual majestic posture and, glancing from side to side, was calmly weighing his chances.

You, Idiot Idiotovich, Revkin mentally addressed Fedot Fedotovich, seem to have made a small error. Pursuing cheap popularity, you chose to fish in some murky waters.

Revkin realized that Milyaga as such did not seriously interest Figurin, who was simply looking for a pretext to replace the leadership of the district with his own people. But Figurin had overestimated his forces. He did not know that Revkin had a powerful friend in the region—Piotr Terentevich Khudobchenko himself, whose ties with Revkin went way back. In 1925 they had studied together at the workers' high school, and then Khudobchenko had recommended him to the Party.

Together they had worked on the implementation of collectivization . . .

"We'll see who holds the winning card," said Revkin aloud.

"What?" asked Motya.

"Nothing. I was talking to myself." Revkin smiled, not because he was in a good mood again, but rather in his usual businesslike frame of mind. He even stopped looking from side to side.

An old woman in bast sandals lugging a sack on her back was walking toward town along the side of the road.

"Hey, stop!" ordered Revkin.

Motya put on the brakes. Revkin flung open his door.

"Where are you headed, old woman?"

"To town, dearies, to town." The old woman smiled trustingly.

"To market?"

"No, not to market. I'm bringing my daughter some peas. Her husband's at the front and she and her two children get so terrible little to eat . . ."

"Very good," said Revkin, and closed his door.

The car continued on its way. Revkin thought about the old woman they had left behind. So you see, he thought, how selfless our people are. That may be all she has, but she'll take it to her daughter. With a people like that, how can we fail to win . . . He was moved to tears. Not so much by love for the people as by his own nobility.

5

Revkin did not find his friend at Regional Committee headquarters. He had just left for home, Revkin was told.

That's even better, thought Revkin, setting off for Khudobchenko's.

Piotr Terentevich's home was not far from the Regional

Committee headquarters. He lived in an old-fashioned private house enclosed by a stone fence and protected by a special police squad. Leaving his car by the green gate, Revkin passed through the checkpoint. He was known there and they let him go right past. Even the doorkeeper guarding the main entrance did not ask for his papers.

"They're eating lunch," he said, smiling at Revkin as a friend of the family.

"Andrushka!" Revkin heard a voice happily calling his name.

He raised his eyes and saw Khudobchenko's wife, a pretty, well-fed little lady who was officially known as Praskovya Nikitovna but who was, in her small circle of friends, just Paraska. She was standing on the top step of the marble staircase.

"Come in, come in," she said, "We were just sitting down to lunch. Take off your mackintosh and join us in the dining room. Your friend's already there, picking his nose."

Waiting until Revkin climbed the stairs, she led him into the room she liked to call the dining nook. It was a large hall with a patterned parquet floor and expensive chandeliers and curtains. Potted fig trees and palms stood by the windows, hunting scenes were hung on the walls, and among them portraits of Lenin and Stalin. The master of the house was seated at an enormous table.

"Oh, who's this!" He beamed. "Paraska, bring out the vodka."

He came out from behind the table and shook Revkin's hand, thumping him on the back and giving it a good rub.

"Sit down, old friend, sit down." Khudobchenko grabbed a walnut chair, dragged it across the parquet, and pushed it over to Revkin. "I was just sitting here thinking, What a nice place! And who used to live here? The bourgeois. And now I'm sitting here, me, Piotr Khudobchenko, a peasant from a family of corn growers. And so I guess the Revolution didn't happen in vain."

He clapped his hands and a girl appeared wearing an apron

and a little cap. "Natusya"—Khudobchenko turned to her—
"set a place for Andrei Eremeyevich. We'll drink some borsch
first off. The real stuff, Ukrainian style, not that cabbage and
water you Russkies eat. This one's got beetroot, red eggplant,
carrots, sour cream . . ."

He then launched into a long and colorful recipe for the
making of borsch, and for dumplings of various sorts, but we
will not repeat all his recipes. Those wishing further information should consult a cookbook.

Only after they had had a few drinks and appetizers did
Revkin decide to confide his troubles. He told Khudobchenko
how Figurin had appeared in Dolgov, how he had summoned
everyone including Borisov, and how the article on Captain
Milyaga had been printed in the newspaper. Khudobchenko
listened sympathetically while Praskovya Nikitovna even shed
a few tears (they always came easily to her).

"And so you understand," said Revkin in conclusion, "now
they're accusing me of discrediting the organs."

"I understand." Khudobchenko pushed the rest of his borsch
aside and lit a cigarette. "It's not a pleasant story you tell. So,
why did you do it?"

"Do what?" asked Revkin.

"What was it . . . discredit the organs?"

"Piotr Terentevich," said Revkin. "I'm in no mood for jokes."

"I'm hardly joking. I'm asking you seriously why you did it."

"Piotr Terentevich," said Revkin, offended, "perhaps you
didn't understand. I'm telling you that this Milyaga . . ."

"What do I care about this Milyaga of yours?" said Khudobchenko. "It's you, Andrushka Revkin, that interests me, not
Milyaga."

"But that's just the point. Milyaga . . ."

"And I'm telling you that I spit on your Milyaga and I rub
it in too." In fact, he did spit on the floor and rub it in.

Revkin tried a different approach. "Piotr Terentevich, do you
know me well?"

"Well, yes, I do," Khudobchenko agreed, but, it seemed to Revkin, without much certainty in his voice. "We've drunk some vodka together, we've gone fishing."

"And that's all?"

"What else is there?"

"But after all, you've known me since 1925."

"All right, I admit I've known you since 1925. But superficially."

"Superficially?" repeated Revkin, hoping that he had not heard him correctly. He even turned to Paraska in search of sympathy, but she lowered her eyes quickly.

"Well, of course, superficially. If you remember what we talked about, not counting work of course, they were the same things everyone talks about when they're off work. That means nothing. The weather, borsch, vodka, and when we went fishing we'd discuss if they were biting or not. You did teach me how to use lures in the winter, but that's all there's been since 1925 to the present. I was never inside your skin, I don't know what's going on in there."

"But didn't you recommend me to the Party?"

"Now that's blackmail!" The words came flying from Praskovya Nikitovna's mouth.

"You keep quiet!" Khudobchenko shushed her. "This is men's talk. I don't know about blackmail, but as for the recommendation, I did, and what of it. I'm human too, I can make mistakes. Maybe Lenin recommended Trotsky, for all I know."

"So now you're comparing me to Trotsky?"

"No, that was just an example. Even now I would say that you were a good worker, efficient . . ."

"Why 'were'?" cried Revkin, almost in horror. "I don't appear to be dead yet."

"Come on," said Khudobchenko, with a flick of his hand. "I see you're still a good demagogue. Were, are, that's not the point, the point is that if the organs are having their doubts about you, then maybe they know you better than I do and maybe they've got grounds."

Revkin rose. He wanted to exit in silence, but it was hard not to have his own say. "So," he said, bitterly, "so that's what you're like in the end, is it? And I thought you were my friend."

Khudobchenko did not reply. He sat, his head in his hands, staring at the table.

"What's a friend?" said Paraska suddenly. "You're mixed up with that Milyaga or whatever his name is, and now Petro is supposed to stick out his neck for you? A friend is a friend, and if you were a real friend, then in a position like yours you wouldn't have set foot inside our house. You know that Petro hasn't been well, that he's not alone, that he has children . . ."

"The children have nothing to do with it," said Petro. "And neither does my being sick. The main thing is that I am a Communist. Of course friendship is sacred, but as a Communist I put the Party first and friendship second."

He flung his head back a bit and brought his eyes up to the ceiling. In those days there were still no concealed telephoto lenses, no supersensitive microphones. But Piotr Terentevich had no doubt that somewhere (perhaps in the ceiling) there was some sort of eye which saw everything and some sort of ear which heard everything. And it was to that Eye and to that Ear Khudobchenko was now saying, Look how principled I am, look how low I am. There is nothing I am incapable of.

"All right, then," said Revkin, rising. "I see there's no point in my remaining here."

Khudobchenko made no reply. He sat puffed up with self-importance, not looking at Revkin, his face red. Paraska was standing in the doorway, her arms crossed over her luxurious breasts.

"Well, I'll be going, then," said Revkin, in the vague hope that they would stop him.

Khudobchenko maintained his silence and Paraska stepped out of the door, clearing the way.

"I'm leaving," said Revkin again.

Again he received no answer. He went down the stairs, grabbed his coat from the doorkeeper, and dashed outside.

6

Khudobchenko remained seated, supporting his head in his hands.

"What's with you!" said Paraska reproachfully. "You're over-reacting."

"Ah!" said Khudobchenko, with a wave of his hand. "What a friend I've lost," he said, and broke into tears.

Paraska walked up behind him and entwined her plump arms around his sinewy neck. "Petro," she said with emotion, "that's your work. People die in war too."

"Yes." He nodded, wiping away his tears. "In war too." He pulled her over to him and sat her on his lap. "Let's sing our favorite song."

Paraska raised her head and, looking off into one corner by the ceiling, struck up the song in her sonorous voice:

> *Rode a Cossack into battle*
> *and he said: Farewell, my love.*

And Piotr Terentevich, languid until that moment, began to tap his hand on the table in time to her song and joined in softly:

> *Farewell, my black-browed beauty,*
> *I'm going to a foreign land.*

The more she sang, the more the veins swelled on Paraska's neck, and the more flushed her face became; at the highest and most piercing note she began the second couplet of the song and it seemed that any moment her voice would catch and break, but it did not. Her husband provided a melancholy accompaniment with his soft and pensive bass. Anyone hearing them might have thought that, in spite of the words and the melody, their song contained something of the underground, something illegal, and that they, locked up in their shell, found the whole world hostile and were themselves hostile to the whole world.

> *Give me your kerchief, girl.*
> *I will die in a field somewhere.*
> *In dark night they will close my eyes*
> *and then lay me in my grave.*

7

Afterward Revkin told Aglaya that he didn't remember leaving Khudobchenko's or getting into his car. Motya also confirmed that Andrei Eremeyevich "didn't seem himself" the whole way back. He seemed oblivious the entire trip, sitting with his eyes closed, though from time to time he would jump up and shout: "I am an honest Communist! I will not allow this!"

But then he would immediately sink back into his torpor. He had visions of the past—a large city, an institution of learning where young Communists were taught how to manage the economy. A simple guy in an embroidered Ukrainian shirt was walking among the other students. He was the first to walk up to everyone, extend his hand, and introduce himself: "Khudobchenko." And then he would laugh loudly, knowing his name sounded odd.

A good, simple guy. No genius, theoretical problems would throw him but instinctively he understood practical matters.

He used to kid himself but perhaps he was serious when he said: "I've got something better than all that theory, I've got this." He would point to his good-sized nose, which did in fact seem to help him get his bearings quite deftly in shifting situations. It cannot be said that he was especially liked, but all the cliques accepted him because he was neither malicious nor touchy, and when quarrels arose about whose turn it was to run out for a half liter, he would end them by saying: "I'll run out and get it."

He always treated everyone equally and benevolently, he knew how to make seemingly offhand pleasant remarks, he remembered everyone's birthday, and was always ready to do small favors—loan someone three rubles till his grant money came or loan his large pocket watch to someone going out on a date. He seemed completely free of both vanity and ambition and was quick to agree with his opponents' arguments in debates, permitting the other man to feel his intellectual superiority.

"When a person argues," he used to say to Revkin, "he doesn't want to prove the truth, he wants to prove he's smarter than you are. So I always agree with them. You want to be smarter? Fine with me. If you feel a need in your soul to spit in my face, go ahead, spit. I'll wipe it off. It doesn't make a bit of difference to me."

There was only one person in the school toward whom Khudobchenko did not conceal his antagonism. This was a professor of mathematics nicknamed "Tell me, my good man." But the antagonism was reciprocal: the teacher despised Khudobchenko for his inability to master math, and he threatened to prevent him from taking the state exams.

"Tell me, my good man," the teacher mocked Khudobchenko, detaining him at the blackboard, "let's say you're transporting sacks of potatoes by ox cart from point A to point B at a speed of X kilometers per hour and a horseman is riding towards you at a speed of X squared. Can you tell me what portion of the distance you each will cover if you meet after a quarter of an hour?"

"Of course, you realize," Khudobchenko would say afterward to Revkin, "he doesn't want me to solve the problem, he wants to put me in my place. Keep me low where I belong. But he's wrong. Maybe he understands his mathematics, but he still hasn't mastered dialectics. He can't imagine that for us the main thing is not to understand X's and Y's but the Party line and its inner meaning. As far as mathematics goes, the ones with a little extra something between their ears can take care of that and we'll just run the country, them included." Saying that, he would nudge Revkin in the belly, wink, and laugh loudly.

"Tell me, my good man" kept his word and did not permit Khudobchenko to take his state exams. But it was he who suffered. The commission investigating Khudobchenko's complaint suspended the teacher from work, and he was forced to repent his outmoded world view in the newspaper—for displaying lordly arrogance toward students and for impeding the instruction of the proletarian cadres. A few years later, when the teacher was arrested, Khudobchenko was already a leading worker.

"So you see," he said to Revkin, with a grin, "how much more valuable dialectics are than mathematics. So now let him calculate how much time you need to get from point A to point B in a prison transport train."

Paraska appeared later. She was preceded by Netochka, whom Khudobchenko intended to marry. One day he came up to Revkin in great excitement. "I've got some big trouble, my friend. Netochka's parents have been dispossessed as kulaks. I just sketched out a statement condemning my connection with her. What do you think, should I turn in the statement or just dump Netochka and be done with it?"

Revkin himself was no saint, but still he was surprised. "Petro," he said, "can you really do that? You love her."

"I love her, Andrei. I love her," said Khudobchenko with feeling. "I love her so much I don't even know how I'll get through all this." Tears appeared in his eyes. "But to tell you the truth, I love myself even more."

8

Threading his way through the dark and bumpy streets of Dolgov, Motya brought the car to a halt by Revkin's house. Andrei Eremeyevich was sitting with his eyes closed, no doubt sleeping.

"We're here, Andrei Eremeyevich," said Motya.

Revkin did not respond.

"Andrei Eremeyevich!" Frightened, Motya seized hold of his shoulder.

"Huh?" Revkin opened his eyes.

"Oh, you had me frightened." Motya sighed with relief. "We're here, I said."

"Good," said Revkin.

Revkin left the car and was on his way to the gate when he wheeled around, resumed his place in the car, and said: "Let's go!"

"Where?" said Motya, taken aback.

"To see Stalin."

Motya looked over at him, said "One minute," and ran in to get Aglaya.

Placing her hand on Revkin's forehead, Aglaya understood at once. She and Motya pulled Revkin carefully from the car.

"Is Comrade Stalin in?" asked Revkin.

"He is," answered Aglaya sternly.

"Announce that Revkin has arrived."

That night he suffered fever and chills. Aglaya applied mustard plasters to him and tried to wrap him up, but he kept uncovering himself, kicking up a row and demanding to see Stalin. But, after a time, he seemed to regain his calm.

Revkin heard someone ask Aglaya: "Where can I wash my hands here?" He realized it was Stalin. He was afraid that Aglaya would want to be present at the conversation and he absolutely had to talk with Comrade Stalin alone. The only solution was to pretend to be sleeping and wait for Aglaya to leave. Revkin lay with his eyes closed until he heard the door squeak shut. Then he opened his eyes and saw Stalin wearing a white smock, sitting on the bed by his feet.

"Comrade Stalin," said Revkin elated, tearing his head from the pillow.

"Lie back, lie back. The most important thing," said Stalin to Aglaya, who had reappeared, "is for him to sweat it out. More liquids—tea, soup, bouillon—and, as much as possible, complete rest."

9

Margarita Agapovna, a stout, white-faced woman, was sitting in the reception room which now belonged to Major Figurin, the new chief of the Right People. She was sitting by the window with two lunch boxes tied together for Major Figurin, her husband.

"You realize, Kapochka," Margarita Agapovna was saying in her whiny voice, "my Fedochka, he never eats in the mess hall. He's terribly afraid of microbes. I tell him, Fedosha, but you're so brave, you're not afraid of any enemies of the people. All he does is smile. What kind of comparison is that? Enemies of the people are big, you can see them a kilometer away, but these parasites are so tiny you can't even see them with a microscope. You'd think that if he was so careful he would spare himself, but, oh no, he doesn't. Other people work any old way, just put in their time, but Fedosha . . . for him, you see, the family is second, work comes first. Work, work, and nothing but work. Sometimes he will wake up at night and lie there tossing and sighing. I ask him, What are you thinking about, Fedosha? Just thinking, he'll say. But I know all he's thinking about is work, work. I'll teach my son my trade, he says. You know what Fedosha's like. As soon as he takes a new job, he immediately uncovers some type of organization, some new kind of conspiracy. It's a terrible life, Kapochka, terrible. Right now people are walking down the street like regular people, but each one's got something on his mind. Just take that Prince Golitsyn. And what was he pretending to be? A simple deserter. Fedosha says that if you didn't know he was a prince you could never tell just by looking. But my eyes, he says, are better than any X ray. And so that's why they keep throwing him into the most important and dangerous sectors. Another man would refuse, but my Fedosha, he's so reliable . . ."

At that point Margarita Agapovna pulled out her handkerchief and began to sob and blow her nose . . .

10

Loving wives at times ascribe virtues and merits to their husbands which an outsider might fail to notice. Some people who, at that time, lived, as it were, side by side with Fedot Fedotovich and knew him quite well maintain that there was nothing exceptional to be observed about him, that he was of average height, spoke in a soft, somewhat nasal voice, parted his black hair on one side, and smeared it with vegetable oil to give it a gleamy look.

His uniform was always spick-and-span, so clean and so well pressed it looked as if it could never wrinkle or wear out. His belt gleamed with lacquer and made a delicate creaking sound. All things considered, he was no different from anybody else. However, all that now remains to us is the testimony of average, common people whose opinion should be treated with great caution. The average person cannot tell a genius from a mere mortal. He thinks that a genius must always possess some distinguishing feature, some unusual fire in his eye perhaps. But we of course know that that isn't so and a genius can look like the most ordinary of men, like you or me. Perceiving no genius in Figurin, many people disliked him, especially his subordinates, who, among themselves, called him Idiot Idiotovich.

By the way, after a certain amount of time had passed and Major Figurin had vanished from the region of Dolgov, a notebook was found with entries made in his own hand, among which were some bold and original thoughts. Here are just a few taken at random:

Everyone is suspect.
He who is doing something suspicious is suspect.
Most suspicious is he who is not seen doing anything suspicious.
Every suspect can become an accused.
Suspicion is sufficient grounds for arrest.
The arrest of a suspect is sufficient and conclusive proof of his guilt.

There can be no doubt that these thoughts belong to a highly uncommon man. However, we lack sufficient proof that they were the fruits of Major Figurin's own reflections and not something he copied down from some other source.

That notebook contained yet another thought, remarkably fresh for its time, though it relates not to jurisprudence but to medicine:

The Soviet system is so objectively good that any person who dislikes it, completely or partially, is insane.

Such striking brevity and clarity is available only to the greatest minds. The fundamental principle of an entire direction in the science of psychiatry had been formulated in a few words.

Certain skeptically minded critics and certain critically minded skeptics may point out that this formula suits only one particular social system existing in a particular place at a particular time, but that is simply not so. Replace the words "Soviet system" with any phrase suitable for a given time and place and you will see that this formula is all-embracing and suits all times and all nations.

Now the name of Major Figurin is forgotten, but this last idea has gained wide acceptance. Fundamental and unique, it has influenced numerous dissertations, textbooks, basic works, whose authors have received academic appointments and wear academic caps, even though the idea which took them thousands of pages had been formulated earlier by Major Figurin, and more succinctly as well. If, I repeat, he did not copy it down from some other source.

11

After Chonkin was discovered to be of high birth, his case was removed from among the ordinary cases, that is, those which could be decided any way one wished. His had become a case of special importance, or, more precisely, a case of special state importance, and it was directed "up top," because even though people down below realized or at least guessed what had to be done with Chonkin they preferred to await official instructions rather than run any risk. Before receiving those instructions, the lower officials displayed a certain indecision which was reflected in the documents and other materials of the investigation, where Chonkin was called simply Chonkin and the "so-called Chonkin" and, in certain cases, even "Chonkin the White." However, by that time, there were occasional glimpses of the dual surnames Chonkin-Golitsyn and Golitsyn-Chonkin.

And so, Chonkin's case was directed up top and went from department to higher department. Meanwhile, Major Figurin,

taking advantage of the lull, decided immediately to rehabili-
tate the reputation of the organs now stalled by the imprudent
(let's leave it at that) death of Captain Milyaga. To that end,
the major managed not only to place the article about the late
captain's exploits in the newspaper but he also decided to take
other and more important political measures—the public burial
of the hero's remains with appropriate honors.

However, a somewhat unusual difficulty arose attendant to
the carrying out of that operation.

Funerals are distinguished from other ceremonies by re-
quiring the presence of no less than one deceased individual.
The snag here was that there was no such deceased individual
to bury. All that was known was that Captain Milyaga had
perished near the village of Krasnoye, but no one knew for
sure whether he had been buried there or was just left lying
around.

To locate the hero's remains the major dispatched a search
party of six men led by Sergeant Svintsov, who was ordered
to conduct the operation in total secrecy and not to attract
the attention of the local populace.

12

It was getting on toward evening. Burly was returning
from Dolgov, where he had gone on business of his own,
when a strange sight greeted his eyes. People were wandering
through a field apparently looking for something. They kept
walking off in different directions, then would come back to
huddle and discuss something, and then would walk off in
different directions again. Drawn by curiosity, Burly started
toward them. When the people wandering about the field
noticed him, they began behaving even more strangely—they
formed a column and began retreating toward the forest,
single file. Burly caught up with them at the edge of the
forest.

"Hey, you guys," said Burly loudly.

No one stopped and no one answered.

"Hey!" Burly touched the sleeve of the last man in line. "Can you spare a light?"

"No," he barked, turning an angry face toward Burly.

"Oho!" said Burly, surprised to recognize Svintsov. "And I was wondering who it could be. Looking for someone?"

Svintsov did not answer, but he did stop walking. The entire party stopped as well. They spread out and began surrounding Burly.

"What are you guys doing?" said Burly, frightened and edging back. "I was just asking. I didn't mean anything," he mumbled, keeping a close eye on Svintsov, who had opened his raincoat, put his hand in his pocket, and was now slowly pulling it back out.

Svintsov moved his hand abruptly, startling Burly.

"All right, here's a light," said Svintsov, handing him the matches.

"Och, you scared me!" admitted Burly. "The thing is, I don't have anything to light up."

Svintsov exchanged looks with his men, grinned, pulled out a rumpled pack of Little Star cigarettes, withdrew two cigarettes with his crooked fingers, and handed one to Burly, saying: "There you go."

They lit up. Covering his cigarette with the palm of his hand, Svintsov puffed and glanced over at Burly, as if hesitating whether or not to ask him. "Listen, the thing is . . ." he said as if just curious, "you didn't happen to run into a corpse, did you?"

"A corpse?" echoed Burly, not overly surprised. "No, I don't think so. He run away?"

"Who?"

"The corpse."

Svintsov looked at Burly with narrowed eyes. "What the hell are you talking about? How could a corpse run away?"

"That's just what I was thinking too. We usually bury ours in the ground and they don't do any running. But this one . . . you asked me if I had run into any."

Svintsov paused to think. "Listen, the thing is," he began, uncertainly using the same phrase, "I've got something for you to do. But if you blab to anybody . . ." He brought his fist up to Burly's nose.

"What's with you!" Burly objected firmly. "Me tell anybody! I'd die first!"

"All right, look"—bringing his face closer to Burly's, Svintsov lowered his voice—"you remember that captain we had?"

"Yup, and so?"

"We're looking for him."

"What, was he resurrected?" Burly asked simply and again without any great surprise.

"What does resurrected have to do with it?" Svintsov frowned. "We're looking for his body. He's buried around here somewhere. Seen him or not?"

"I didn't see any bodies," said Burly. "But I did come across some bones. There's a field past the little hill near the village. Past the field there's a ditch and that's where the bones are, in the ditch."

"Human bones?" asked Svintsov, perking up.

"To tell you the truth, I don't know what kind they are, but they're there all right. When you climb up the hill you'll see the field. But I guess it's pretty wet over there now. Still, you won't drown. Not plowed too deep either. I plowed the autumn lands myself, that's right. Of course, it used to be people plowed a bit deeper when the land was their own. Now it all belongs to the kolkhoz. Now it doesn't matter how you plow, you get paid the same, like this." Burly turned and showed Svintsov his middle finger jabbing the air.

"What, you don't like the kolkhoz system?" Svintsov was all attention.

"Let's steer clear of politics," said Burly, avoiding a direct answer. "Far as the bones go, they're lying over in that ditch there, all pecked clean and smooth by the crows. You could take them right to a museum. Is that where you're taking them, a museum?"

"What?"

"The bones, of course."

"We really don't have any need for them," Svintsov said, remembering the secrecy of his mission.

"So then why did you ask?" said Burly in surprise.

"Just curious, that's all. And if you tell anybody we were interested in bones, we'll have your head, you understand?"

"Nothing too hard to understand there," confirmed Burly.

They let Burly go but chose not to retrieve the bones at once, they were too close to the village. They decided to wait in the forest until nightfall.

13

"Kapitolina, could you please work late today," said Major Figurin to his secretary. "There's an awful lot to do. We have to prepare for tomorrow. I'm going out for a short while. You stay here. If they call from the district, I'll be in the club. Have Svintsov wait for me when he comes back."

"Fine," said Kapa.

Preparations were underway for the solemn ceremony in the Railway Workers' House of Culture. On the stage Kuzma the carpenter was lining the coffin, which rested on two small stools, with red fabric. His work was being directed by Borisov, Secretary of the District Committee, Samodurov, the Chairman of the District Executive Committee, and Ermolkin the editor in chief.

A man with a notebook was strutting back and forth near the rear of the stage. He kept waving his arms and muttering under his breath and making notes with his stub of a pencil.

In one corner of the stage Gennady Shuteinikov, the artist, having nailed a sheet of Whatman paper to a piece of plywood, was finishing his portrait of Afanasy Milyaga, which he had copied, using the grid method, from a small passport photo.

"Uh-hm, uh-hm," said Figurin, taking a few steps back to compare the photo with the portrait. "Think it looks like him?" he asked the artist. "Somehow the portrait reminds me of someone else."

"Entirely possible," said the artist. "The passport photo's very small. And I usually draw Comrade Stalin's portrait for the holidays. And, you know, sometimes all by itself your hand just . . ."

"What do you mean, all by itself?" Figurin frowned. "This should direct the hand." He rapped a finger against his forehead. "So, please change the way he looks a little."

"All right, but I'm afraid he won't look much like himself."

"That's not important," said Figurin. "The important thing is that he doesn't look like the person he looks like now. You understand?"

"Yes, sure."

"I didn't know the captain personally, but I've heard that he loved life, loved to smile. So, put a smile on him."

"That might look odd," objected the artist timidly. "He is dead, you know."

"Of course he's dead. But he must remain alive in our memory. You understand me, alive," repeated Figurin, smiling sadly. He stepped back from the portrait but found his way blocked by the man with the notebook.

"Serafim Butilko," the man with the notebook introduced himself. "I write poetry and I publish it in the local paper, Ermolkin's." The poet pointed at the editor, who was fussing about the coffin.

"Pleased to meet you," said Figurin. "And what do you want?"

"I wanted to make your acquaintance . . . I've written a little something for tomorrow's sospik ceremony."

"Sospik?" asked Figurin curiously.

"Oh, that sospik of mine . . . I mean to say, so to speak," explained Butilko, a bit embarrassed.

"Ah, I see. If I understand you correctly, you've written a poem which you would like to recite tomorrow."

"Yes. Over the body of the sospik deceased."

"I don't know about reading it over his body. Better to say over his coffin. And you'd like to read it to me right now?"

"Yes, I would," agreed Butilko. "I'd like to get your opinion."

"All right, then," agreed Figurin. "If it's not too long . . ."

"It's quite short," Butilko assured him.

He took two steps back and struck his poetry-reciting pose. "Romantic, Chekist, Communist," he announced, and everyone who was bustling about the coffin turned around. Only Shuteinikov the artist kept on working.

Holding his notebook in his left hand and waving his right fist, Butilko began to bellow out his lines:

> Mist floated above the ravine.
> The air was transparent and pure.
> Afanasy Milyaga went out into battle
> a Romantic, a Chekist, a Communist.
>
> You went to fight for freedom,
> forsaking your family home;
> like a son of the working people
> you showed no mercy to the foe.
>
> Your eagle eye was crystal pure . . .
> Suddenly a bullet . . . bang, bang.
> The cry "Long live Stalin!"
> froze on your lips gone cold.
>
> You became an unfinished song,
> a shining example for others.

Can you feel how Iron Felix himself
bends down over your grave?

Serafim burst into tears while reading the final lines.

"All right," said Figurin. "In my opinion, there's nothing anti-Soviet in it. And, on the whole"—he made an indeterminate gesture with his hands—"it doesn't seem bad. What do you think?" he said to Borisov.

"A good poem," said Borisov. "It takes the right line, ours."

"But there was a little something out of place in the beginning," interrupted Ermolkin. "The mist was floating and at the same time what was the air like?"

"Transparent and pure," said Butilko, after a glance at his notebook.

"Something's wrong there. How can the air be transparent and pure when there's a mist?"

"The mist is over the ravine. In other places it's transparent and pure."

"Yes, the air can be like that," said Figurin authoritatively. "The ravine's down below and the mist is there, but a bit higher up . . . But, speaking personally, the end doesn't seem quite right. Iron Felix, that's good, graphic, but somehow I'd like it . . . I'd say a bit more optimistic."

"A bit more in a major key?" asked Butilko.

"That's it, a bit more in a major key," said Figurin, gladdened by the appropriate word. "And of course there in the beginning, and even more in the middle, where you write that the hero had perished, you need some sadness, can't do without that. But, at the same time, you can't let the poem as a whole cause any despondency, it should be a battle cry to new victories. You can say somehow that he perished but his exploits inspired others, and thousands of other fighters will rise to take his place."

"That's very good!" said Butilko with feeling. "Maybe something in this spirit.

Afanasy Milyaga has perished
but dadadeeda in battle
I, too, someday will lie down
for my native land.

How's that?"

"Closer, closer," said Figurin, waving his arms. "Something in that spirit, but get rid of that 'I'll lie down.' You've got one dead man in your poem already, that's enough. Maybe you can say, I'll take vengeance on your enemies."

"I'll take that into consideration," said Butilko.

"A very valuable observation," interjected Borisov.

"All right, then"—Figurin looked at his watch—"time for me to go. I remind you all—tomorrow, at twelve o'clock, everything must be calm and orderly. More people from the factories. And we must be able to hear who's saying what. If you hear anyone saying that Milyaga was not a hero, but just the other way around, make a note of it and inform one of our men, or even better, me personally, of their names. You'll be in charge," he said to Borisov, who nodded. "Two or three speeches here and two or three at the graveside. And you'll recite your poem. But I'll say it again, a little more optimism, so that afterward people will feel like living and struggling. Excuse me, comrades, I've got to hurry now."

14

Figurin left the club but did not head toward the Right Place but toward the House of the Artist. By now it was dark and drizzling. From time to time the major would wipe his face with the palm of his hand. He was in a good mood. Everything was going as planned. A few lines of the poem kept going around in his head:

but dadadeeda in battle
I, too, someday will lie down
for my native land.

A talent, thought Figurin of Butilko, a real talent. Though what does lie down for my native land mean? Where's he going to lie down and who with? And why does Iron Felix bend over the grave? Iron and bending? And is it right that he is bending over it? Shouldn't he always be straight as an arrow?

He should say something about it to Butilko, he can rewrite it. Perhaps, he, Figurin, had been too quick to say that the poem was not anti-Soviet, perhaps it was even 100 percent anti-Soviet. Strictly speaking, it was a matter of interpretation. In essence, every word written or just spoken aloud or, to go all the way, hatched in someone's brain, is anti-Soviet. This seemed an interesting thought to the major and he regretted not having his notebook, in which he usually jotted down his ideas.

In the House of the Artist he asked the old concierge behind the counter, who was knitting a sock, if there was anyone in room number 7. The old woman glanced at the board where the keys were hung and said: "Yes."

Figurin walked up to the second floor. Hearing some sort of noise from inside, he pressed his ear against the door.

"What, are we going to play silent here?" said a ringing voice. "It won't work! I can make a fish talk if I want to!"

Bending his knees, Figurin bent to the keyhole and what he saw startled even him. A plump woman wearing a green dress and heavy lipstick was sitting on a chair with its back to the table. Her hands were tied behind her. An adolescent wearing a white shirt was standing in front of her. He was holding a kerosene lamp, which he raised up to the woman's face.

—**213**—

"Citizen Investigator," implored the woman, "I'm telling you the truth. I don't know anything."

"Lies!" The boy cut her off mercilessly.

He shifted position, his back to the keyhole, his body blocking Figurin's view of the woman. Realizing that there wasn't a minute to lose, Figurin pushed open the door with his foot.

His appearance startled the boy, who recoiled from the woman; he stood confused, the lamp in his hand. The woman, too, was at a loss.

"What's going on here?" asked Figurin, shifting his gaze from the woman to the boy.

"Are you Major Figurin?" asked the woman.

"Yes," he said, not without pride. "I am Major Figurin."

"Klavdiya Vorobeva." The woman rose and introduced herself. "Sent by Colonel Luzhin to be at your disposal."

She still kept her hands behind her back.

"And the boy?" asked Figurin.

"My son Timosha," said Klavdiya.

"Your son?" said Figurin, surprised. "You have a strange relationship with your son."

"You heard everything?" She smiled.

"Not only that, I was watching."

"We were playing."

"Playing?" Figurin's brows rose.

"We play like that a lot," said Klavdiya. "What are you standing there for?" she shouted at her son. "Untie me!"

The boy set the lamp on the table and removed the scarf wound tightly around his mother's wrists.

"Fool! My hands were starting to get numb," she said, shaking them. "The point is," she explained, smiling to Figurin, "that Roman Gavrilovich promised to get Timosha into a special school, and in the meantime, I'm preparing him a bit myself."

"Aha," said Figurin. "An interesting system of child rearing. I am preparing my own son, too, but not quite so dramatically.

Good boy!" He thumped the boy's shoulder. "You a Young Communist?"

"I'm a Pioneer," said the boy, dropping his eyes.

"Good boy!" repeated Figurin. "You'll go far. Are you doing well in school?"

"Not well at all," said the mother, and her eyes grew sad. "Especially in arithmetic and Russian. He just can't get the hang of them. And he's growing up without a father. If his papa were here, he'd thrash him with his belt if he heard the way he talks, but he's not afraid of me. Go on, you parasite you!" Suddenly she grew excited. "I'll show you! You do badly in school, Roman Gavrilovich won't take you on anywhere."

"That's right, son," confirmed Figurin. "You absolutely must study and get only A's and B's. If you want to work with us, there's a lot you have to know. Mathematics, history, psychology, for example. That's not all! I saw you interrogating her. You stick the lamp in her face and it's: 'Come on, talk!' You shout, you stamp your feet. Now is that the right way? Try it without being so crude, try entering the soul of the prisoner so that he will realize the extent of his fall himself and repent sincerely."

"Yeah, sure, sincerely," said the boy doubtfully. "Enemies of the people, you know how stubborn they are."

"There's all kinds," said Figurin. "Stubborn included. And then there's the kind your lamp would only make more stubborn. So when you're dealing with a person, it's important to work on his pride, to exploit his love for his family or for vodka or for women. You like women?"

"What are you saying?" said Klavdiya. "He's still a child."

"Oh, right, I forgot. In any case, this isn't why I came here. Did Roman Gavrilovich explain your assignment to you?"

"Yes," said Klavdiya. "Tomorrow at the funeral I am to pretend to be Captain Milyaga's widow . . ."

"Yes, right," said Figurin. "The funeral is very important. Great political significance has been attached to it. People must understand that a remarkable man has perished at the hands of Chonkin the White's gang. It's one thing, you know, when you're just burying some soldier. He perished, he perished, and today many other people will perish at the front. But it's another thing when the coffin's there with the mother and the child beside it," he said, stroking Timosha's head. "Then, you see, a much stronger impression is made. So, tomorrow we'll place a little stool for you at the head of the coffin. Do you have a black dress? No? We'll get you one. Of course, there is no need to overdo the sobbing either, but it would still be good if your eyes were full of tears. Maybe you could crumble up some onions in your handkerchief?"

"For what?" said Klavdiya. "I know how to cry. When I used to act on amateur nights, I was always crying, it even surprised our director. Watch." She strained herself, her face turned red, and suddenly tears actually began streaming from her eyes.

"Wonderful!" said Figurin. "Very natural."

"But I don't know how to cry," said the boy.

"You don't have to. You're going to be our little man. You just have to stand beside your mother and comfort her, just as if it were your own father in the coffin."

15

After darkness had fallen Svintsov assembled his group at the edge of the forest. It was quiet and the rain had almost stopped. Dark figures in sopping-wet sweaters stood in front of Svintsov. He counted them by touching each one.

"All right, let's go," he ordered in a whisper, and took the lead.

They walked straight across the stubbly field, their feet sticking in the clayey soil. From time to time, Svintsov would look back and see that the others were following him Indian file, and making an effort not to fall behind.

"Sergeant," asked Khudyakov in a whisper, "all right to light up?"

"I'll light you up," said Svintsov, without turning around.

He kept on walking, gazing intently ahead, but he could not see anything except for the dim yellow stubble. Svintsov began to worry that they had already passed the spot Burly had told them about. He was considering turning his detachment around and combing the entire field, having his men walk side by side, when something crunched under his foot.

"Halt!" said Svintsov and bent down. "Seems to be it." He turned to his companions. "Everyone over here. Collect the bones and put them in the sack."

His companions surrounded Svintsov and formed a circle around something they could not see.

"Listen, Sergeant," said Khudyakov softly and with a tone of surprise, "these bones seem awful big."

Svintsov had noticed that himself. "That's none of your business," he muttered angrily. "Take the smaller ones."

But there turned out to be only a few smaller ones and it proved difficult to detach the large ones from the rest of the skeleton.

"Here's what you do," said Svintsov. "Break the big ones over your knee."

For a while the puffing of several strong men and the dry crunch of breaking bones could be heard through the sound of the rain. Having filled half the sack, weighing it in his hand, Svintsov ordered a halt to their work and then added a large oblong skull to what had already been collected.

16

It was getting on toward midnight. Kapitolina Goryachev was still on duty in the reception room, awaiting the return of her chief. All was calm. There had been two calls from the district. The first time they had asked how many sausages were left in the warehouse. Kapa had answered "Sixteen." The second time they wanted to know if the widow had arrived and what she had heard about the load. Kapa had answered that the widow and the orphan had registered at the kolkhoz and that the load was still being looked for. She was told, "When the load is found, inform the father-in-law."

Both conversations had been in code. In the first what was meant was how many cases remained whose investigation had not yet been concluded, and the second, had Klavdiya Vorobeva arrived and had Captain Milyaga's remains been found? Luzhin was the father-in-law.

A man pretending to be a woman called up and said he could give them valuable information concerning Hans, but he hung up when Kapa asked for his name.

There was nothing to do. Kapa drank some tea, got out her old tattered copy of Maupassant's stories, and grew so engrossed in her reading that she did not hear Major Figurin enter. She only looked up when she felt his bony hand on her shoulder. She was embarrassed and tried to put the book back in the drawer but the major grabbed it, looked at the cover, and read the author's name. "A good writer," he said. "He depicted the evils of the French society of his time accurately. But he did not fully understand the class nature of the contradictions he portrayed due to the limitations of his own world view and he could not offer people any way out of the situation. The solution lay only in the consolidation of all the progressive forces around the working class and this Maupassant never understood."

Having discussed the merits and shortcomings of Maupassant's creative work with Kapa, Figurin expressed concern at the long absence of Svintsov's group and asked her what news she had. Then he went off to his office to call the father-in-law.

Kapa was preparing to leave for home when Figurin appeared again and asked if she would like to keep him company over a glass of cognac. Embarrassed, Kapa answered that she had never tried cognac but that she had heard from knowledgeable people that it smelled like bedbugs.

"A common prejudice," objected Major Figurin. "Cognac is one of the best and healthiest drinks. It's made from the purest grape spirits and, as opposed to vodka, it contains no raw brandy. It strengthens the walls of the blood vessels and improves the functioning of the digestive tract. I, for example, thanks to cognac, have always had very good bowel movements," said the major and immediately smiled.

Perhaps Kapa found this piquant argument sufficiently convincing, for she went to Fedot Fedotovich's office, where he took a half-full bottle, two small metal wine glasses, and a lemon from his safe. He sliced the lemon into thin circles on a blank sheet of interrogation forms, using a small penknife shaped like a lady's shoe. He explained that it had been Nicholas II who first had the idea of nibbling on a piece of lemon while drinking cognac.

17

Events developed rapidly. After the fourth glass Kapa was sitting on Figurin's lap, while he, fumbling about under her skirt, was reciting his favorite poet and swaying back and forth:

> I do not regret, call out or weep.
> Everything will pass like the smoke
> from white apple trees. Seized by the gold of withering,
> I will be young no more . . .

"Oh yes, you will too!" breathed Kapa ardently, avidly.
"Undress!" commanded Figurin, trembling with impatience.
"What?" she said in surprise. "Completely?"

"Completely!" he said, and for some reason ran behind the wardrobe.

Shaken, she undressed hurriedly in the middle of the room. An intellectual, she thought, tossing her garters on the chair. What an improvement he was over the late Captain Milyaga, that dirty pig whom Kapa now recalled with disgust. That crude animal had never been interested in her physical beauty. That savage, he used to throw her down on the couch, not even letting her take off her boots.

Naked, Kapa waited with anticipation in the middle of the office, aware that she was covered with goose bumps, either from the cold or from passion. It was even becoming a bit awkward. The major was still puffing about behind the wardrobe. She could hear something tear and a brass button came rolling onto the floor with a ding.

Suddenly a triumphant cry!

"And here I am!" Like a kangaroo, the major bounded out from behind the wardrobe.

"Ach!" cried Kapa in fright, covering her face with her hands.

The major was completely naked, stripped of all signs of rank, though he was wearing a brightly polished crisscross gun belt on his flabby and rather hairy body, and his yellow holster containing his revolver slapped against his white thigh.

"What's that?" asked Kapa in a faint voice, tearing one hand away from her face.

"That?" Fedot Fedotovich blurted with embarrassment. "That's . . ." He tried to explain.

"No, not that," said Kapa hurriedly. "I mean the belt."

"I meant the belt too," said the major, even more embarrassed. "I always . . . I never . . . nowhere . . . without my weapon . . ." he panted, pushing her toward the couch.

Then came that storm which was even beyond the power of Maupassant's pen to describe. The couch and the major's belts squeaked, the ceiling swam, the chandeliers swayed, the walls caved in, and a desperate cry: "A-a-a-a-a-a!" pierced the thundering landslide.

It was only later that Kapa realized the cry had been hers.

Suddenly everything grew still, and a distant, delicate trumpet played taps.

18

"Most people don't understand the meaning of our work," said Major Figurin, absently drawing his little finger along Kapa's curls. "They're afraid of us, they hate us, they laugh at us on the sly, they fawn on us, but they do not understand. However"—he sprang from the couch, crossed his hands behind his back, and began pacing the room, reasoning aloud— "there is a meaning to our work and a very deep one." Kapa crawled into one corner of the couch and sat there with her legs crossed, covering herself with her hands above and below. The major, carried away by his thoughts, seemed to have entirely forgotten that he was not in the lecturer's usual attire. "Not only the greatest meaning but a humane one. Just imagine man without us. He could live without us, but how? Life would be boring. He wouldn't know what to do with himself, wouldn't know who needs him. He would eat, drink, answer the call of nature, go to work, quarrel with his wife, but all the while he'd have the feeling that he was a little person, that nobody had any use for him. Then we come. We tell him, You are surrounded by enemies. Look, somebody has tried to poison your well, somebody wants to blow up the train you were intending to take, someone wants to abduct your child. We say, Look both ways, your enemy is somewhere near you and he's not dozing either. We say that this is not a plain old enemy, not just some senile misanthrope, no. He's tied in with international capital, there are the mightiest of forces behind him. Now he becomes frightened, but at the same time he begins respecting himself. If such forces are constantly threatening his life, that means his life has colossal value. He becomes vigilant, he looks both ways, he sees enemies everywhere, spies, saboteurs, wreckers. His self-respect attains unbelievable proportions. Now, let's take one of our victims, let's say that Chonkin. Once upon a time he was a little man. He demanded nothing from life except a crust of bread, a roof over his head, and a woman by his side. Not that he was doing anything so bad either. All of a sudden it turns out that he's a deserter, and not only a deserter but a prince, and if he's a prince, that means he's connected to powerful forces and so, to his own surprise, from a small and empty creature he turns into a figure of international significance. He becomes the center of an enormous conspiracy, important people are interested in him, and you'll see what a metamorphosis he undergoes. We have declared him a prince and against his own will something majestic appears in his gaze, his bearing. And now he wouldn't change his current situation for his former one. No, no," said Figurin confidently, wagging his index finger above his head. "Well, naturally, certain troubles do threaten him because of being a prince, but had he remained the same old Chonkin, would his troubles have been any less? Hardly. All right, imagine that he's plain old Chonkin. He's taken to the front, where he gets slammed like a fly. I don't know, a stray bullet, a shell fragment knocks him down, a building collapses on him, he's drowned fording a river. In any case, his end would have no glory, it wouldn't even be noticed. But we're making somebody out of him, we're making him a prominent and significant person; and what's more, we too are filled with self-respect and it's good for all concerned. Now try and tell that Chonkin we made him a prince by mistake. Even try setting him free; he'll submit outwardly, naturally; he's used to submitting, but inwardly he'll be disappointed. Yes," cried Figurin, "he will be disappointed. Because . . ."

He never got to finish. The door burst open and Svintsov appeared in boots caked with mud to the knees, water running off his tarpaulin rain cape, a sopping-wet sack over his shoulder.

"Aha," said the major, "you're finally here."

He reached for his pocket watch, his hand sliding along his naked body. Figurin lowered his eyes, then looked over at Kapa, who, with an expression of horror on her face, was huddled on the couch; then he shifted his gaze to Svintsov's vacant face and, suddenly understanding, screamed: "Who permitted you to enter without knocking? Out of here!"

With a running start, he butted Svintsov in the stomach with his head. Knocking open the door, the enormous Svintsov flew out into the reception room and, his arms flailing, collapsed in a heap, his head under Kapa's desk.

The major shut the door immediately and yelled at Kapa: "Get dressed at once! Why aren't you in uniform!"

He ran behind the wardrobe and began hurriedly getting himself together.

Both of them now dressed, Kapa poured water from a decanter onto Svintsov, the major slapped his cheeks. Svintsov started coming around.

"There, there, Svintsov," the major said, almost tenderly. "I admit I did get a bit excited. Kapitolina Grigorevna and I were working, it got hot, we took off a few clothes and you, without knocking . . . Get up then, Svintsov, I think everything's all right now."

Groaning Svintsov rose and then sat back down, stretching his legs out in front of him, leaning against one leg of the desk. He grew dazed again, then looked guardedly at the major, at Kapa, and at the sack, which had fallen to one side.

"Well?" asked the major. "Better now? I can see that you are. And did you find what I sent you out for?"

"Over there," said Svintsov hoarsely, pointing with his chin. "In the sack."

"Over there?" The major looked at the sack with disbelief. "There's a corpse in there?" he said, cringing.

"Not a corpse but the . . ." said Svintsov.

"Remains?" prompted Figurin.

"Yes, the remains," agreed Svintsov. "The bones."

"I see, I see." The major bent over the sack, untying the cord. He pulled out a piece of bone with a knob at one end, looked at it, then over at Kapa, took out another bone, looked at it too with surprise, then grabbed the sack by the bottom and dumped everything out on the floor. The bones came rattling out and formed a small mound. The oblong skull came out by itself and rolled off to the side.

"Oh, mein Gott," cried Kapa, using a foreign expression for some reason, and closed her eyes.

The major picked up the skull and twirled it in his hands, feeling it with his long, thin fingers. "Svintsov," said Figurin severely, "what is this?"

"The head," said Svintsov, shrugging his shoulders. He seemed to be coming back around.

"It's not a head, it's a skull," corrected the major.

"All right, a skull," Svintsov agreed easily. "Six of one."

"And do you think this skull belongs to a human being?"

"It belongs to whoever found it," answered Svintsov evasively.

"Sergeant Svintsov!" Figurin raised his voice. "Why are you playing the fool? Do you mean to tell me that this is Captain Milyaga's skull?"

Svintsov had gradually returned to his senses, but he kept crinkling up his face to let Figurin know that he was not all there yet.

"Did you ever see him?" Svintsov asked a leading question.

"Who?"

"The captain, of course."

After exchanging glances with Kapa, the major confessed: "No, never."

"There you are. But Kapitolina, she saw him. She can tell

—**224**—

you, it looks like him. I won't speak for the rest, but the smile is his to a T."

Figurin looked over at Kapa again; she shrugged her shoulders uncertainly.

The major began thinking. Naturally Svintsov must be punished. But the funeral was scheduled for tomorrow, and if he punished Svintsov, where would he get other suitable remains? Or maybe they should bury Svintsov instead of Milyaga?

19

At the beginning of October the population of Krasnoye increased noticeably; evacuees from Leningrad province drove to Krasnoye or perhaps, more accurately, as the locals put it, were driven there. These were pitiful, unfortunate people, mostly old men, old women, and children, driven from their homes, who had spent a week and a half in cattle cars and had, as they told it, been bombed twice and then had spent three days in the open air on the railroad platform in Dolgov waiting to be assigned quarters.

When the newcomers were dispersed among the village's various huts, Aphrodite Gladishev, who had been assigned a small, dry, but haughty-looking old woman and her six-year-old grandson, began shouting to the entire village that she wasn't going to let anyone into her house, that the late Kuzma Matveyevich hadn't built the house and put his whole soul into it to let just anyone stay there and grow lice.

Perhaps no one would have paid the least attention to Aphrodite's wishes, the new tenants could be settled by force, but the old woman, having peeked in the hut, flew back out with bulging eyes and said she would have no part of such unsanitary conditions—especially since she wasn't alone but with a child, the son, by the way, of a political worker and a front-line soldier. And furthermore, she added, looking over at Aphrodite, it would be better to live in a pigsty than in a house like that. Naturally, the old woman had been struck by the odor which still lingered in the hut, though the jars which produced it had long since been removed.

Aphrodite, with her peculiar inconsistency, then flew into a fury and began arguing that there was no such odor in her house, that, on the contrary, it smelled as fresh as a pine forest. She argued fervidly, as if trying to entice the old woman back, but the old woman wouldn't even listen and requested that the chairman choose another place for her. The chairman turned to Nyura, who looked at the haughty old woman and her grandson, a nice, tow-haired little boy, and, without a moment's thought, said: "They can stay with me."

The old woman entered Nyura's apprehensively, took a good look and a good smell, then asked if there were any bedbugs in the house.

"There's a few," said Nyura, smiling bashfully. "What's life without bedbugs?"

"Does everyone here have bedbugs?"

"Sure," said Nyura. "Wherever there's people, there's bedbugs."

Resigned, the old woman began unpacking. Her luggage consisted of two large yellow suitcases with brass locks, and four bundles containing everything imaginable, including an enameled chamber pot for the child.

As compensation for the presence of bedbugs or perhaps for no reason at all, the old woman took over the main room and said that she and her grandson were going to sleep together in the bed where once Nyura had slept with Chonkin. Nyura was surprised but made no objection, saying only that she would take one pillow.

"And where are you going to sleep?" asked the old woman.

"I'll find someplace." Nyura smiled.

Seeing the value in Nyura's modesty, the old woman let down her guard and told her how hard the trip had been, no lights or train whistles allowed at night; the train made frequent stops but no one ever knew for how long, days or minutes, and afraid of being left behind, people relieved themselves through the moving train's open doors.

She told Nyura that her name was Olimpiada Petrovna, and the boy's was Vadik; her daughter was a nurse, and Vadik's father was a political instructor by the name of Yartsev (by the sort of coincidence which occurs only in novels and in life, this was the same Yartsev under whose tutelage Chonkin had learned the ABC's of political literacy not so very long before).

"And what's your name?" asked the old woman.

"Nyurka."

"What do you mean, Nyurka?" asked the old woman, not satisfied. "You call a goat Nyurka or a cat. Tell me your first name and patronymic."

And after that she began to call Nyura by her name and patronymic—Anna Alekseyevna.

At first Olimpiada Petrovna turned to Nyura with requests to borrow some salt, an onion, or one type of dish or another, but soon felt herself to be complete mistress of the house.

"Anna Alekseyevna," she said once, gazing sweetly at Borka the hog, who was lying under the table, "why don't you sell him. I'd give you a length of sateen for him. Will you sell him?"

"No," said Nyura.

"And you're not going to slaughter him?"

"No."

"A pity." Olimpiada Petrovna looked sympathetically at the hog, the way one looks at a man who has wasted his youth and not achieved what he was destined for.

After this she began waging a systematic campaign against Borka, expressing her indignation at keeping a hog in the same house as a child.

Vadik took a different attitude to Borka; he was always trying to scratch the hog behind the ear, which, of course, the old woman did not allow.

Olimpiada Petrovna asked Nyura nothing about her personal life until she noticed Chonkin's photograph pinned to the wall above the bench on which Nyura now slept.

"Is that your husband?" asked the old woman.

"He is," said Nyura without much confidence.

"At the front?"

"No," said Nyura. "In prison."

She said this simply, as if being in prison were an occupation as worthy as any other. But the old woman did not share that point of view.

"In prison?" she repeated. "And what for?"

"For nothing," said Nyura, just as simply.

Not replying, the old woman went off to her room, but returned shortly.

"Anna Alekseyevna," she said with a certain concealed defiance, "after all, they don't put people in prison for nothing."

"Is that right?" Nyura grew angry. "Here they do."

20

In the middle of the night Nyura was woken by a frightened whisper: "Anna Alekseyevna, Anna Alekseyevna!"

"Huh? What?" Nyura shook her head but just could not wake up.

"Do you hear that?" There was an apparition standing over her, Olimpiada Petrovna in a floor-length nightshirt.

"What?" asked Nyura.

"Shhh. Listen. Somebody's walking around out there."

"Where?"

"Outside."

Nyura lay listening with her eyes half closed. The clock on the wall hissed and clacked: *shhh-tock-shhh-tock-shhh-tock*.

"You hear that?"

"That's the clock," said Nyura.

"What does the clock have to do with it?" The old woman grew angry. "I'm telling you, it's outside."

Nyura raised herself on one elbow and looked out the window. It was raining, the wind was blowing, the branch of a fallen maple was knocking against the glass.

"It's the rain," said Nyura. "When it rains it always sounds like somebody's walking around outside."

"Anna Alekseyevna"—the old woman had now taken offense—"I am still in my right mind. And I'm telling you there's somebody walking around out there."

Nyura listened more closely. "Enough," she said to calm the old woman. "Who'd be walking around in rain like that?"

Still she got up and, bumping up against various objects, went out into the corridor barefoot, made her way to the outer door, and meant to open it just a crack, but the wind snatched it away and banged it against the wall. Nyura darted out onto the wet porch, slipped, and fell to one knee. The wind lifted up the hem of her shirt and spattered it with rain. Overcoming the resistance of the elements, Nyura closed the door, slid the wooden bolt, and took a look in the shed on her way back. Everything was peaceful and quiet there. The chickens were cackling sleepily in the dark, Borka the hog was snoring, and Beauty was sighing loudly.

Nyura went back inside. Olimpiada Petrovna was still standing in her doorway. "Well?" she asked in a whisper.

"Nothing there," said Nyura.

She rearranged her bed, lay down, and turned toward the wall.

Muttering to herself, the old woman went back to her room.

Holding her head with one hand, Nyura lay on her side and yawned convulsively, but sleep wouldn't come. Turning over on her back, she joined her hands on her stomach. Recently, she seemed to feel something there, some vague stirring within her, indistinct signs of new life.

Once, at her neighbor Gladishev's home she had seen a

picture of a fetus in some book, a hunched-up, horrible-looking creature with an excessively large head. Now she could clearly picture that mysterious balled-up creature, and she felt a tender pity for it. And though still nothing, nothing at all could be seen of it, she guarded this creature against every danger —she walked with her shoulders squared, and at the slightest sign of danger, she'd instinctively crisscross her hands over her belly.

She lay in bed listening intently to her body. A faint beam of light crept along the dark ceiling, then vanished. It sounded as if someone was running by and cursing right near the window. She started and wondered whether it had really happened or she'd been dreaming. The clock was still rustling and clacking, and the sound it made mixed in with the sound of the wind and the rain. Suddenly a car motor began roaring somewhere in back of the house. The sound grew louder and louder, then gradually began fading as the car drove away.

It's all right, thought Nyura, falling into oblivion, it's none of our business who's doing what out there.

As Nyura left home in the morning, she saw that the airplane was gone. The fence poles were strewn all around, there were boot prints all over the garden, and two deep ruts led to the road where they were lost among all the other ruts. Only the one wing which had been broken off by the 45-millimeter shell lay at the edge of the garden half sunk in the mud. You could see they'd been in a hurry and forgotten it.

Five or six women and Burly with them had run over to discuss the incident. They were all trying to figure out who could have done it. They recalled the Gypsy who had come, supposedly to price the wreck; he circled the plane, squeezed the undamaged wings, crawled into the cockpit, but in the end decided that even if you repaired that hunk of junk it couldn't take more than two people on board and he wanted to take his whole Gypsy camp in the air. It was plain the Gypsy had lost his desire for it. But then who?

Arriving at the scene of the incident, Volkov the bookkeeper (after Gladishev's disappearance he was considered one of the smartest people in the village) voiced the opinion that the theft was nothing less than the work of German Intelligence.

"What the hell do they need that for?" puzzled Burly. "It's all busted, you can't even fly it."

"They don't want it for flying," said Volkov. "They'll take it apart and send it to the CCB."

"To the what?" asked Burly.

"The Central Construction Bureau," explained Volkov. "They'll measure it with a compass, make sketches, then build thousands just like it."

"What do they need them for?" said Burly, puzzled. "Their planes are as good as ours."

"What a comparison!" The bookkeeper shook his head. "Theirs are expensive, you can't build a lot of them. But these, you take plywood and oilcloth, you cut them to size and glue them together. Then they choose a target and go flying at it in swarms like locusts. And though you turn a whole battery of ack-ack guns against them, you can knock down one, two, three, but you can't knock them all down."

"A battery all right, sure," agreed Burly, "but if you used fine shot . . ."

However, there had to be some reaction to this insolent theft, and in the absence of the chairman, Volkov the book-keeper called the district police and asked them to send over a squad and a bloodhound. They sent two policemen and a sheep dog named Taimir. They had Taimir sniff the remaining wing, then they let him out on a long leash; he set off at a run, lifted his leg up twice by the fence, then sat down in the middle of the garden, lifted his intelligent face in the air, and began howling sadly, as if to say that in this case even his skill was useless.

That evening, when Nyura was making her bed on the bench, Olimpiada Petrovna came in and with a look back at the door said that the theft of the airplane was of course no simple matter and Nyura should notify the Right Place. Nyura gave it some thought and agreed, not so much because of the airplane itself, but hoping that she could get in to see the new chief.

21

Apparently that was the first night of frost. The puddles stiffened into glass; fine snow fell and sharp gusts of wind blew it into drifts.

A great deal had changed in Dolgov during Nyura's absence. First to have changed was the social structure of the town due to the evacuation there of several important institutions, including a few scientific research institutes, two theaters, part of the Moscow Writers' Organization, and a documentary film studio. The level of cultural facilities had greatly increased. All in all, it was a perfect example of the historical progress which occurs when underdeveloped peoples are subdued by more civilized nations.

Along with the rise in the level of civilization and the influx of large numbers of people, who, though they were loyal to the system, were also lice-infested, a new delousing station was built in the town and the staff of Right People was significantly enlarged. The building with the offices of the State Hides and Skins Department, which had adjoined the Institution, was now taken over by it. Now both buildings were surrounded by a common fence by whose green gate stood a small structure serving as both a checkpoint and a waiting room, where there was a man on duty round the clock accepting oral and written statements from citizens.

That is, to go into details, there were clearly several people on duty (one man couldn't do it without any relief), but the people who had been there maintained that the people on duty resembled each other like twins; maybe you could tell them apart by their blood type or fingerprints, or maybe if you spent enough time with them you could finally tell them apart. But none of the witnesses questioned by this author ever spent time with them and none of them could tell them apart. So, the man described by the witnesses wore a gray civilian suit, was of middle age, medium height, a bit on the stocky side, with affable, mistrustful eyes. He offered Nyura a stool and took down her story about the theft. When Nyura asked if it was possible for her to see Chonkin or send him a parcel or at least a note, the civilian smiled, spread his arms wide, and said the first, the second, and the third request were all completely impossible at the moment because new circumstances, now being examined, had surfaced in Chonkin's case. What those circumstances were, the civilian could not say, but he promised: "When things are clearer, we'll call you in."

The civilian spread his arms wide apart again when Nyura asked if she could see the new chief. "Unfortunately, he's very busy right now."

22

Having left the Institution, Nyura headed for the market, where she hoped to acquire a pair of galoshes, even worn ones, as long as they were in one piece, or even the sort of sandals known as *chunis*. The present generation needs to be informed that in the long distant past *chuni* was the name for homemade galoshes, which sometimes had thick rubber soles cut from automobile tires that left a distinctive trail.

Nyura noticed a lone man by the newspaper stand combing his hair, looking at the stand as if it were a mirror. Nyura did not know that by combing his hair he was sending a signal to certain other people. Not imagining that anyone could be interested in her movements, Nyura set off for the market and six good-sized men and two women started behind her. Passing the Railway Workers' House of Culture, Nyura noticed some unusual excitement there. The area around the building was cordoned off by police and civilians wearing armbands marked PAB—Police Assistance Brigade. There was a throng of people around the House of Culture itself and a line of vehicles, a truck with its rear panel down and two military buses, whose headlights had been covered with slitted black-out lids. The sides of the truck were decorated with red cloth edged in black. In the back of the truck closer to the cab stood a tin-plated obelisk which narrowed at the top into a four-sided pyramid capped with a red star.

The people who had gathered in front of the main entrance streamed into the open doors, while others streamed back out, replacing their hats as they left. Some went on their way, others stayed to wait for the bearing out of the coffin, smoking and talking in subdued voices.

A bit to one side of everyone stood a group of the district's leaders, among them the cameraman, Marat Kukushkin, who had brought his camera to record the historic ceremony for posterity. Noticeable because of his great height and his casually unbuttoned coat was the children's writer Alexei Mukhin, well known for having been offered a position on a front-line newspaper and having flatly refused it; he wrote Stalin a letter saying that his potential death would be an irreplaceable loss "for our children who love reading." It was said that on the margins of Mukhin's letter Stalin wrote that a coward like that should be shot for the edification of children who love reading. That same day Mukhin spoke to a large audience in the Pioneers' Palace. He was standing at the rostrum reading one of his heroic poems sipping a little glass of water when he was yanked away by the legs. The children decided that the writer was performing a trick for them. One minute he's at the rostrum, then suddenly he disappears. First they didn't know what to do, then they started clapping. At that very moment two gorillas were dragging Mukhin out of the theater. He was taken to a fast, efficient troika, which sentenced him to a firing squad for dodging the defense of the motherland. Mukhin spent the night on death row. In the morning he was brought out to a paved courtyard where a special platoon shouldered their rifles. The platoon leader had already raised his hand when a luxurious limousine came wheeling into the courtyard. A well-fed and important-looking military man got out and handed Mukhin an official envelope sealed with wax. When Mukhin's almost uncontrollable hands finally managed to open the envelope, he found a small sheet of paper on which was written: *Just kidding. J. Stalin.* It all ended well. Mukhin the writer did not end up at the front, he remained alive, and it is said that till this very day he keeps the historical note at home framed under glass.*

Now Mukhin had appeared in Dolgov for Milyaga's funeral to represent the creative intelligentsia, and for lack of anything else to do, he was amusing the local satraps with frivolous anecdotes about a husband who returned from a business trip at the wrong time. His listeners smiled with restraint, trying at the same time to preserve an expression of official concern on their faces.

Major Figurin stepped lightly over to the group of leaders. He smiled at Mukhin, touched Borisov's sleeve and asked him why Revkin wasn't there.

"He didn't want to do us the honor," said Borisov, shrugging his shoulders.

A funereal melody wafted from the open doors.

Nyura squeezed her way in, and two of the inconspicuous men and the two women went in after her. The other four fanned out, taking up key positions on all the possible exit routes.

---

* Personally I don't believe one bit of this.

The benches had been removed from the packed auditorium. The nearer the stage, the thicker the crowd. It was stuffy and there was a smell of dying conifer needles; hidden in the pit, the military orchestra was softly playing Chopin.

23

Moving a bit forward and then on a diagonal, Nyura caught sight of the coffin covered in red cloth; by the head of the coffin on a small stool sat the inconsolable widow, all in black, and, beside her, a tall boy wearing short pants, a white shirt, and a red tie. From time to time the widow would wipe away her tears with her handkerchief, never taking her eyes from the lid of the coffin, as if she could see the beloved face through it.

A tall soldier with a black and red armband on his sleeve brought out the next change of the honor guard from the wings at precise intervals. The honor guard goose-stepped, legs high in the air, then each man would freeze in place as if suddenly paralyzed.

And above all this—above the coffin, the widow, the orphan, and the honor guard—towered an enormous portrait from which the deceased beamed a friendly smile to everyone who had come to attend his funeral.

"Holy smokes!" gasped Nyura, not believing her eyes. "He looks alive!"

"Right you are." An old man in a long raincoat whispered his agreement. "I knew the deceased well and I can confirm it—looks just like he's alive."

That was an error. In fact, the artist had not succeeded in capturing Captain Milyaga's likeness but such is the mysterious power of art that at times a distorted reflection of reality is so convincing that we will accept no other.

The further forward Nyura moved, the denser the crowd

became. Finally Nyura was wedged in tight. To her left an old woman in a black kerchief and to her right the same little man who had been petitioning for his straw.

Gazing at the stage, the old woman crossed herself, wept, and lamented half in a whisper. "What a shame, so young and left alone with a child!"

The straw-petitioner stood in silence. He had come figuring that in the natural unguarded atmosphere of a funeral it might be somehow possible to reach the officials unofficially with his petition and receive a correspondingly official decision; however, judging by the expression on his face, his hopes had clearly been to no avail.

"And the little one, the little one, an orphan now!" sobbed the old woman. "How will he live without his papa!"

Suddenly the music stopped. Several people filed onto the stage, hats in hand, and formed ranks in front of the coffin, where they stood as if waiting for a sadness suitable for the occasion to penetrate deeper into people's souls.

"Now they'll perform the service," Nyura explained to the old woman in the kerchief, and crossed herself.

Secretary Borisov took a step forward and lifted the hand which held his hat, as if calling everyone to silence, though everyone was already silent.

"Comrades," said Borisov, "I declare the funeral meeting open."

Then Borisov made a speech. He started with a short biography of the deceased, who, supposedly born into a simple worker's family, had known early in life the hunger, cold, and need typical of that time. Early in life he began to ponder the essence of social contradictions and early, too, he entered the struggle for freedom and happiness against the dark forces of reaction.

"An enemy bullet," continued Borisov, "cut short this lovely life in full flower. The fiery heart of a warrior, of a Party member, has ceased to beat. But we swear that we will respond to

Captain Milyaga's death by rallying closer around our Party and its great leader, Comrade Stalin."

"A good service; makes you feel sad." The old woman burst into tears.

A few tears escaped Nyura as well.

Samodurov repeated what Borisov had said almost word for word. Mukhin said that Milyaga, apart from everything else, was a friend, a considerate comrade, and a mentor to writers, as if all writers, before submitting their work for publication, would go to Milyaga, whose advice was precise and terse but always on the mark. Mukhin called on all writers from then on to give due consideration to the advice of the Right People.*

Serafim Butilko hiccuped and grinned, listening to Mukhin. He was hiccuping because he had drunk too much that morning (for courage) and he was grinning because Mukhin's words seemed too general and official. Butilko was imagining how he would take the stage, recite his poem, and amaze everyone that such a remarkable talent had sprung up in a place so far removed from the centers of culture.

So he took the stage, and after a moment of silence, he waved his fist and began to bellow.

> *Mist floated above the ravine.*
> *The air was transparent and pure.*
> *Afanasy Milyaga went out into battle,*
> *a Romantic, a Chekist, a Communist.*
>
> *You went to fight for freedom . . .*

Then Butilko stopped short and, nibbling his lips, began to look up at the ceiling. He had forgotten the rest and realized

---

* It is a known fact that by the time Mukhin arrived in Dolgov, Milyaga was no longer among the living. Therefore, one must assume that Mukhin (a writer, after all) had a generalized image of Milyaga in mind.

that stopping short like that was terrible, and the realization of how terrible it was made the words fly completely from his tipsy brain.

"You went to fight for freedom," repeated Butilko, glancing over at Borisov, who had a face of stone.

"You went to fight for freedom," Butilko repeated once more. Again he glanced over at Borisov, but then Figurin's face popped out from the wings.

"Forsaking your family home," prompted Figurin in a loud whisper.

Butilko's heart soared. "You went to fight for freedom," he continued confidently,

> Forsaking your family home,
> Like a son of the working people . . .

Then his memory balked again. He glanced over at Borisov. Borisov said nothing. Butilko was waiting for Figurin's head to pop out again. Figurin's head did not pop out again. Butilko began feverishly sorting through every possible variation. He thought that if he could remember the rhyme, it would help bring the whole line back. And, in fact, accompanying the rhymes coming to his aid came newly composed lines of poetry. "May his cup of life forever foam," said Butilko's mind. No, that wasn't good. "Protector of worried cows that roam . . ." No, that wasn't good either. Why cows? Why worried? "Saviors of sad widows alone."

Elbowing Butilko out of the way, Borisov announced: "The funeral meeting is closed."

He signaled the musicians, the musicians puffed out their cheeks, and again a funereal melody wafted through the auditorium.

The old woman in the black kerchief burst into tears, and Nyura burst into tears as well. She wasn't crying for Milyaga, nor was she thinking whether he had been a good man or not, but the coffin, the music, the solemn sorrow of the situation had so affected her that she was simply mourning for yet another human being departing this world.

24

Serafim Butilko had also burst into tears. As soon as he had walked away from the coffin, he had immediately remembered the ill-fated lines; he remembered the entire poem as if it had been written in large letters on an enormous screen in front of him. The awareness that now nothing could be done about it weighed on Butilko. If only he could recite it again from the beginning! If only Borisov would give him the floor again! He'd go out there, he'd read without a single pause, he'd read with real feeling. Everyone would sob. Butilko spun his head around and, seeing Figurin, who had just appeared from the wings, he laid his hands across his heart, his entire expression proof that he was not to blame, that he hadn't wanted it to happen like that. But Figurin did not accept this silent apology; he frowned and withdrew his eyes. The music came to a sudden halt. Borisov went out on stage again and asked that the hall be cleared so that those closest to the deceased could have the opportunity to say farewell to him in private.

People began leaving. In the meantime, the weather had cleared up; a cold wind was still blowing, but it was scattering the low-lying storm clouds and the sun had broken through a widening rent.

25

The people left the auditorium, the spies darting among them. Each suspicious person was accompanied by one or even two spies, like soccer guards. The spies who could not find anyone positively suspicious loitered in the crowd, going from one little group to another, listening in on the quiet conversations, sometimes even talking themselves, challenging the others to be frank.

The two Thinkers happened to be among those streaming back outside. They stood in silence, exchanging glances with each other as if conversing with their eyes.

"Well, what would you say about all this?" the First Thinker seemed to ask with his eyes.

"A colossal show," answered the Second with his gaze.

No disagreement there. They both remembered the rumors that Captain Milyaga had perished due to some idiotic error and they both knew rumors were much more reliable than official news (with the exception of those rumors which are unofficially spread by official institutions), and with an exchange of glances they came to the general conclusion that the ceremony had been conceived to distract attention from the situation at the front and the shortage of food. They exchanged glances again when they were approached by a spy (it was written all over his face) who asked them whose funeral it was.

The First Thinker was not taken aback and answered that they were burying a national hero, Captain Milyaga.

"But was he a good man?" asked the spy.

"Like crystal," answered the First Thinker firmly.

"What does that mean, like crystal?" The spy voiced his doubts. "Every person has some faults."

At that point the Second Thinker intervened, explaining that there are large faults, small faults, and completely insignificant faults.

"Absolutely true," corroborated the First Thinker. "And when a person has completely insignificant faults and enormous virtues, as, for example, the deceased, then those faults disappear entirely from view."

"In any case, it's not for us to judge," the Second Thinker said in support. Then he added that the untimely death of Captain Milyaga was an enormous loss for everyone. He did not, however, specify what everyone meant—everyone in the district, the province, the Soviet Union, or for all mankind?

"An enormous and irreplaceable loss," added the First Thinker, making his face sad and bowing his head as if in memory of the hero.

"However, I think, I believe," the Second Thinker continued, "our enemies have counted their chickens before they were hatched. Milyaga has perished, but new fighters will spring to his place."

"Hundreds of them," said the First quickly.

"Thousands," the Second corrected him.

The spy walked quietly away, in itself an admission of his defeat.

26

The doors were flung wide open, and out came the musicians —six soldiers and a fat woman in uniform, a triangular badge in her lapel. The woman was carrying a drum in front of her, which made her look enormously pregnant. The musicians stood before the crowd, faced the door, and got themselves ready. Marat Kukushkin the cameraman was now circling them.

Meanwhile, inside the club, the final preparations for the bearing out of the body were underway. Twice Figurin had run across the stage whispering instructions. Then he peeped out the door and made certain that the musicians were in place and that Kukushkin was ready to roll. He came back out on the stage.

"Comrades," announced Figurin, "prepare to bear out the body. Who will carry the coffin?"

"I will! I will!" Butilko came running over at top speed.

He wanted somehow to expiate his guilt. He pushed the slow-moving Ermolkin aside and stood in front of him. On one side was Samodurov, the Chairman of the District Executive

Committee, and Butilko on the other. The coffin was made of damp planks and heavy. But the weight did not bother Butilko, for now he felt like a great epic hero.

"That's right, that's right, comrades," commanded Figurin. "Raise it level. That side's a bit higher. That's it! Let's go!"

Butilko moved forward with everyone else. The doors were flung open. Music spurted into their ears, sun splashed their eyes. Squinting slightly, Butilko caught sight of the crowd, the band's instruments sparkling in the sun, the cameraman Marat Kukushkin, who was moving backward while turning the crank on his camera.

"For the newsreel *News of the Day*," surmised Butilko, assuming a dignified air. He imagined how the film would soon be on every screen in the Soviet Union and viewers in all corners of the country would be seeing him, Serafim Butilko, larger than life. And maybe . . . Butilko had heard, someone had told him that Stalin personally looked over everything that was to be screened. Maybe, viewing that film and puffing on his famous pipe, he would say: "And who is that nice-looking young man carrying . . . no, not that one, I said the nice-looking one, over there on the right." And he would point with his pipe stem at the screen.

That could really get the ball rolling! Butilko vividly pictured Stalin's assistants setting off at a run, all the telephones in government communication starting to ring, the identity of the nice-looking young man cleared up in no time. He arrives in Moscow traveling first-class. A luxury apartment with a swimming pool and parrots. A reception at the Kremlin. A friendly handshake from Comrade Stalin. A mass edition of his poem "The Ballad of Bread," the Stalin Prize, a leading position in the Writers' Union and . . .

He did not succeed in imagining what came after the "and." Distracted by his fantasies, his foot landed on empty air; instinctively he shoved the coffin away from him so as not to be crushed, and he went flying off the steps, his arms flailing.

Walking on the other side, Samodurov felt the coffin coming down on him and pushed it back with great force, while he, too, jumped off to the side. The others followed suit. Ermolkin was left holding the coffin. His eyes bulging with confusion, he stood on the bottom stair like a great hero from the old sagas, taking the whole weight of the coffin on himself. The coffin rocking on his shoulder was, at the same time, swinging back and forth like a compass needle; finally it went completely out of control, knocked Ermolkin off his feet, and headed for the ground. Pushing the coffin away from him, Ermolkin took a bad fall, his head struck a cobblestone, and losing consciousness, he heard someone's belated call: "Hold on! Hold on!"

27

There was a terrible cracking sound; one end of the coffin crashed to the pavement. The lid, held on by four nails, popped off and fell on Ermolkin, covering him up to his chin. Bones came rattling out of the coffin. The last to fly out was the oblong skull, striking a stone and shooting off to one side. Major Figurin started instinctively for the skull, wanting to grab it and hide it from the crowd, but he was not quick enough. A shabby dog sprang out from between a pair of legs, seized the skull in his teeth, and ran off with it. Perhaps he should have been left unmolested, but someone's efficient iron-shod boot landed squarely on the dog's back. With a pitiful howl the dog dropped its catch and disappeared.

People say that Marat Kukushkin did not think to stop photographing and kept mechanically turning the crank on his camera. They also say that Major Figurin later asked for the exposed film and watched it many times. Everything seemed to be going so well, even splendidly. The doors open solemnly. The front of the coffin appears. Then the faces of the two men bearing it, Butilko and Samodurov, larger than life. It was a silent film. There was no music. Still it felt as if you could hear music coming from somewhere beyond the frame. Butilko and Samodurov moved their legs carefully and ceremoniously. Butilko's face expressed appropriate sorrow, but even then you could see the self-satisfaction showing through the sorrow, as if he knew beforehand, the son-of-a-bitch, what was going to happen the next second and was gloating with malicious joy.

The irremediable always seems unbelievable. There was Butilko raising his right foot . . . "Stop the film! Stop!" Figurin would shout at that spot. He would stare deep in thought at the frozen frame as if he hoped that if he stopped the film there, then started it up again, everything would go right. Butilko's foot would come down on the first step, then his other foot would land on the second step . . . "Roll it," Figurin would order the projectionist, and again the same scene—the suddenly baffled face of Butilko, who the next second flies off the steps, his arms flailing.

28

The further it goes, the more horrible the story becomes.

The crowd became terribly excited and moved menacingly forward.

"Lord, Lord, Lord," mumbled the old woman in the black kerchief, who found herself in front of Nyura.

"It's a horse!" shouted a woman in a scandalized voice.

"It's a horse! A horse!" ran through the crowd.

People were buzzing. A police whistle rang out. Borisov's voice came through the noise: "Comrades, calm down! What do you mean a horse? That's a corpse!" he shouted, trying to palm Ermolkin off on the crowd.

As bad luck would have it, Ermolkin opened his eyes at that moment.

"They're burying a live man!" howled that same woman.

"What?" Those in back pressing forward wanted to know what was happening.

"They're burying a horse!"

"They're burying a live horse!"

The spies scattered through the crowd, pushing and shoving, having no other instructions. The crowd was highly excited. Finding himself in one group, the straw-petitioner, taking advantage of the pandemonium, decided to put forth his economic demands. "My straw!"

People yelled back at him! "Shut up, you chump, you bumpkin!"

Major Figurin thought they were yelling, "Free Chonkin!" Later on, this was to serve as the basis for his request that the local garrison be increased.

Meanwhile, the agitation of the masses had grown greater. Wishing to channel this element properly, Borisov hopped on the funeral truck and raised his right arm majestically. Just then a rotten tomato (from some generous soul) splattered on his right eye. (Later, in Figurin's report it was noted: *Individual acts of terror took place against the representatives of authority*.) Borisov felt the blow, and when he had unglued his eye he saw something red.

"They've killed me!" said Borisov softly, losing consciousness, his head falling toward the obelisk.

The tension mounted. Trying to control the situation, the authorities sent one of the military buses at the crowd, but apparently it conked out almost at once.

A resourceful spy saved the day. He jumped up on the steps of the bus. "Brothers!" he cried. "They're cashing in wheat coupons at the district store."

Jumping off the steps, he was the first to run off toward the store. At a loss, the crowd gasped and ran off after the spy.

Naturally there was no millet. The crowd kicked up a fuss, then quieted back down. Meanwhile, a new grave mound and a tin obelisk covered with artificial wreaths had appeared on the Square of Fallen Warriors. If one moved the wreaths aside, one could read:

Captain
Afanasy Petrovich Milyaga
(1903–1941)
perished heroically in battle with
the White Chonkin gang

People say that somewhat later on, having seized the Dolgov region, the Germans opened the grave and sent the skull to the museum of local lore, where it was kept under glass in the "Contemporary Period" section. There was also an explanatory plate with text in two languages:

Skull of the Soviet Commissar Milyaga

29

In the general turmoil one casualty went almost unnoticed . . .

Ermolkin was already on the ground unconscious by the time the coffin lid had flown off and struck him in the chest. Coming to, he saw that he was lying on his back on the cold cobblestones, his head surrounded by feet, and though he strained his memory, he could not remember why he was there or what had happened before.

There was uproar and racket all around him and a woman's shrill voice was screaming: "A horse! They're burying a horse!"

Something was pressing on his chest. He looked and saw that he was covered almost to his chin by the coffin lid wrapped in red cloth. A man pointed a finger at Ermolkin and said: "There's the corpse!" Then a shrill voice wailed that they were burying a live horse.

Ermolkin had nothing against being buried, but he was always on the lookout for errors of any sort.

"You're mistaken," he corrected them, smiling with dignity. "I am not a horse. I am Ermolkin, Boris Evgenevich."

Perhaps that's what he said, perhaps that's what he thought, perhaps he didn't say or think it and it just seemed to him that's what he said or thought.

From weakness his head rolled to the side and he noticed something white, something oblong, quite near him; it looked like a skull, yes, it was the skull of a horse; it had bared its teeth and was trying to bite Ermolkin's nose.

He didn't care about his nose, at that moment he didn't care about absolutely anything at all, he just wanted to understand why that skull was lying beside him. Then he recalled that someone was being buried, most likely him; he looked again at the white oblong object and realized that it was his own skull. That means I'm a horse, thought Ermolkin. That was strange. Strange and ridiculous. He worked as editor in chief of a newspaper, he occupied an important position, and no one had noticed that, in reality, he was just a horse, only a horse, an ordinary draft unit member of the horse population.

A shabby dog appeared before his eyes, bared its teeth, and then with a howl darted for his skull, which lay on the ground next to him. The dog dug its teeth into the skull and Ermolkin knew that now he was in for some terrific pain; he closed his eyes and his mind clouded over.

When he came to again, he saw an old man wearing a raggedy tank helmet bending over him.

"Young man," said the old man, "I wouldn't lie there if I were you. You could catch cold or be run over by a car or a horse."

He had met this valiant old tank man before, but he couldn't remember where or when. It must have been a long time ago. But not so very long ago people had been running around there, shouting, bustling about, burying someone, him, or some horse, yes, that was it, a horse, but he was that horse. The tank man was also saying something about a horse.

Well, he thought listlessly, if I am a horse and if they're burying me, then why does my chest hurt and my head ache, why am I thirsty and why do I see that tank man in front of me?

He guessed that the people in charge of the funeral had simply made a mistake and were burying an editor instead of a horse, but the horse or, more precisely, the gelding (someone had once called him a gelding, he remembered), was still alive by accident. And though everything was hurting him he felt joy, he realized that sometimes there were good mistakes, that it was better to be a live gelding than a dead editor in chief.

But what did that tank man want? What was he saying about a horse? He must have been sent to remedy the error . . .

Ermolkin decided to pretend to be a man. A Soviet man and a friend to Soviet tank men.

"But if suddenly," he sang aloud, smiling at the tank man, "your inveterate enemy should appear, he'll be beaten far and near . . ."

Then an old woman appeared beside the tank man in Ermolkin's field of vision. "Moishe," she said. "Leave him alone. Can't you see he's good and drunk."

Very well, thought Ermolkin, let them think I'm drunk. Horses don't get drunk. He raised himself on one elbow and continued his song, barely audibly but with genuine feeling.

> Then the drivers will press their starters.
> And through the forests, hills, and waters . . .

"I can see he's drunk," said the tank man, "but I'm afraid he'll catch cold and come down with pneumonia."

"Moishe," objected the old woman angrily, "you know full well that when these people have too much to drink they lie in puddles and ditches; doesn't matter, they're used to it and they never come down with pneumonia."

The main objective had been achieved: these people considered him a man. Now the important thing was for them to leave as fast as possible. Ermolkin closed his eyes and pretended to be sleeping. When he opened his eyes there was nobody there. He rose to his feet with great difficulty, a terrible weakness throughout his body, his legs trembling and sliding out from under him like a young colt's. And perhaps he was not in fact a gelding, but just a colt, maybe he was three and a half years old, people could taunt him, people could slaughter him, he had to find his mother, she would protect him, she would defend him. He started off, but it was hard to walk; his chest hurt, his head hurt, and he was very thirsty.

He saw a saddled horse by a fence. The horse was white, beautiful, and had kind human eyes. Hitched to a post, it was standing peacefully, but when it saw Ermolkin, it turned its face to him and, flaring its nostrils, began to neigh. "That's my mother!" Ermolkin realized.

"Mama," he said, and kneeling down, he began to cling to its udders. "Mama," he said again, sucking on one of the rough teats and smacking his puckered lips.

Feeling a familiar sensation in the area of her teats, the horse turned its head, perhaps expecting to see its own colt, but saw instead a two-legged creature, old and dirty and sick. The horse raised its rear leg, swung it disdainfully through the air, and its hoof struck Ermolkin square on the top of the head.

"Mama," muttered Ermolkin thickly, falling back to the ground and dying on the spot, this time for good.

30

That morning the Second Thinker had been taken ill. (He always came down with something at history's critical moments, when the struggle grew fiercer, or right before crucial meetings at which it would be necessary to stigmatize, subvert, or crush someone.) He was lying in his room, where he lived alone (he was a bachelor), and diligently sweating under his quilt when he heard a special signal at his door. The

Thinker got up, slipped on his galoshes, threw the quilt over his shoulders, and went to the door.

"What's wrong with you?" asked the First Thinker, appearing in the door. "Are you sick?"

The Second Thinker behaved very oddly. "As a matter of fact, it is I who should be asking you what's wrong with you." Stepping back, he pulled the quilt closer to him, revealing his ragged light-blue knit drawers.

"Aha." The First Thinker smiled slyly and winked. "Obviously it's my head you have in mind?"

"Yes, it is precisely your head I have in mind."

Having backed up to his bed, the Second Thinker lay down, pulled the quilt up to his chin, and closed his eyes. Opening them again, he saw the satisfied face of his friend.

"And just what do you think happened to my head?"

"I think that it has become oblong, like a cucumber, but maybe I'm just delirious."

"No more than anybody else," objected the First Thinker. "Maybe you'll think this is delirium too?" He handed the sick man a copy of the newspaper *Bolshevik Tempos*.

The sick man grabbed the newspaper greedily and slid his eyes from line to line, hoping to read something between them. In a report called "From the Soviet Information Bureau" he learned that our troops, employing a strategic maneuver, had abandoned Nikolaev and were waging local battles in the Velikiye Luki district. He read Serafim Butilko's fable "The Mad Mongrel" ("The German Dog, Mongrel No Tail," decided to make a *Drang nach Osten* and according to his plan Barbarossa he convened all the other mongrels . . ."). Finding nothing interesting in the local news, the ailing Thinker read on up to page 4, where he saw a black-edged funeral notice ". . . with profound sorrow we report the tragic death of the editor in . . ."

"What?" cried the sick man. "The editor in chief? Could they really have shot him?"

"No," his guest reassured him. "He just fell under a horse."

"Ah, ah," the Second Thinker said. But he sat up at once. "Listen, what does that mean—he just fell? Are you sure he just fell? Or perhaps"—he glanced over at the door and lowered his voice to a whisper—"or perhaps he was helped?"

"You think so?" said the First Thinker in surprise. "A very interesting idea. Strange, it never even entered my mind. But here's something more interesting."

"Where?" asked the sick man impatiently. "I don't see."

"Here," said his guest and stuck his finger on the headline of a large special article: THE INFLUENCE OF SOCIALIST CONDITIONS ON ANTHROPOLOGICAL TYPE.

Out of habit, the Second Thinker glanced down to the bottom of the article and read the author's name: K. Ushasty, Candidate in Biological Sciences.

31

A scholarly article, it put forth the idea that insofar as the October Revolution had not only changed the social conditions in our country but man's inner world as well—his relationship to work, to society—this must unfailingly lead to outward changes in his appearance, and just so, in time Soviet man will be as distinct from all other people as *Homo sapiens* is from Neanderthal man. Of course this change will not occur at once, but if, as Marxist dialectics teach us, gradual quantitative changes become qualitative leaps, then there is nothing surprising in the fact that among individuals distinguished by the consistency of their ideological convictions and the clarity of their world view, anthropological changes are already becoming noticeable, changes which are, naturally, first reflected in the structure of the skull. Numerous and authoritative analyses, maintained the author of the article, will demonstrate irrefutably that such changes are moving in the direction of an elongation of the skull as a result of the masticatory organ moving away from the thinking centers.

> Such changes [Ushasty wrote, developing his idea further] have been observed even by bourgeois scientists. Their leading scientists have noted that the long-headed people (dolichocephali) as a rule possess a stronger intellect than round-headed people (brachycephali),* but their narrow world view has not allowed these scientists (who themselves must be insufficiently long-headed) to rise to a true understanding of such phenomena. These scientists give precedence to racial distinctions, while our science, basing itself on the sole correct teaching of Marx-Engels-Lenin-Stalin, opposes a class approach to the social one.

The Second Thinker set the newspaper aside. "What is all that?" he asked in a weak voice.

"A new scientific discovery," said the First.

"It's absurd!" cried the Second Thinker.

"No more absurd than all the rest. Think for yourself. A traitor and a coward is declared a hero. They bury a horse in his place. Everyone's saying that the widow at the funeral was a fake, and the son too."

"In that case"—the Second Thinker grinned—"they should have brought a mare and a colt."

"It's no time for jokes," said the First Thinker sternly. "You don't understand. It's not all that simple. Why do you think they organized that whole business with the skull?"

"Bah." The Second Thinker waved his hand, falling back on his pillow. "They didn't care what they put in the coffin. They didn't know that drunken fool was going to stumble and drop it."

---

* This author's footnote is to ask that the latter not be confused with Bucephalus, Alexander the Great's horse.

"As always you are mistaken!" cried the First Thinker gleefully. "*They* never just happen to stumble. They did it on purpose."

"But for what?"

"That's the point. For what? Think about it yourself."

After a moment's strenuous thought the Second Thinker's face lit up. "I understand," he said happily. "Just as Caligula appointed his horse a consul, now they're . . ."

"Nonsense," interrupted the First Thinker. "If you're going to introduce historical analogies, the story of the Trojan horse is more appropriate here. This is quite another matter."

"What is it, then?" cried the Second impatiently.

"I think," said the First, "we will soon witness a revolution."

"A political one?" asked the Second Thinker in a whisper, with a glance at the door.

"Or a military one," answered the First, also in a whisper. "I think this is a plot against the mustached one and is being hatched by . . ."

"A longhead!" cried the Second Thinker, enraptured by his own quickness of wit.

"Shhh!" hissed the First, and he, too, glanced over at the door. "That's right," he whispered. "Precisely, a longhead."

"But who is he?" asked the Second, burning with impatience.

"But that's the greatest enigma," said the First sadly. "While you've been lying here, I've already spent some time in the library. I went through old newspaper files, I examined the portraits of all the members of their . . . what do they call it . . . politburo. I don't understand anything. They're all round-headed."

"But how about that"—the Second Thinker sat up in bed and crossed his legs—"what's his name . . . Kalinin?"

"Kalinin?" repeated the First. "No, wrong again. Besides, as usual you've got everything mixed up. His beard is long, not his head. I think it's going to be some complete unknown. Have you heard anything about Prince Golitsyn?"

"There's lots of Golitsyns," the Second Thinker answered evasively.

"Don't play the fool!" the First Thinker retorted angrily. "You know that I'm talking about the Golitsyn who's in prison here. Notice just how enigmatic that whole business is. Some Chonkin appears who seems to be completely alone, but they hurl an entire military unit against him. He proves difficult to arrest, and later it turns out that he's not Chonkin at all but Prince Golitsyn. Then there's the business with the long skull, and then this article. No, it's not all that simple."

"And what do you think?"

"I think that first of all you ought to put on this . . ." With those words the First Thinker pulled a wig out from inside his shirt and tossed it on the bed at his friend's feet. It was a remarkable wig, a masterpiece of its sort, with a quilted lining.

"That?" asked the Second Thinker, kicking the gift aside. "What is this?" He jumped up out of bed as if stung. "Never!" he shouted, brandishing his fists. "Mark my words, I'll never put that on."

"I said the same at first." The First Thinker grinned bitterly. "But afterward I thought, Better to have a long head than none at all. And you know, this just might be one of their usual campaigns. They'll round up all the roundheads, then they'll come to their senses when they see they can't function without them, and then you and I will perform a little trick." And with a conjurer's sweep of the hand he removed his own wig.

32

There is no record of how much more time and talk the First Thinker invested in trying to convince the Second that he was right, but by evening they both went out for their stroll (the Second Thinker had made a sudden recovery) along Post Office Cross Street (which, apparently, at that time had been renamed Milyaga Street but, as was learned later, only briefly). Hatless, they casually nodded their elongated heads to certain dumbfounded acquaintances.

They say that the First Thinker turned out to be completely right and there was a roundup of roundheads in Dolgov which lasted a few days. Certain people's heads seemed to elongate at once and those to whom this happened would say to their opponents in the heat of an argument: "I'm starting to think your head's awfully round."

I am not bothering to confirm any of this or deny it (of course I don't believe it personally), but the fact is that it certainly brought enormous trouble to Andrei Eremeyevich Revkin.

33

This is what happened to Revkin. He took Candidate Ushasty's scientific article as a personal attack on himself. He twirled back and forth in front of the mirror when Aglaya wasn't looking, measuring his skull from the occiput to the chin and from ear to ear, and these measurements proved depressing to him. Of course, he couldn't just elongate his head with the aid of a special wig, for people knew him as he was and he had no wish to lose his authority. However, realizing that power was slipping through his hands like sand, he decided on a most desperate step. He made it known that he would not tolerate such an abomination and sent Ushasty's article to the District Committee along with a memorandum calling the article pseudo-scientific and the work of a charlatan; he maintained that, of course, it had been inspired by the new chief of the Right People, who from the very beginning had behaved provocatively, had ignored the Party Organs, and had thereby set his Institution in opposition to the Party. Refuting the article's basic thesis, Revkin passed to a highly risky if not to say an insane objection in stating that, if the Marxist world view did in fact influence the structure of the skull, then Comrade Stalin would have the longest skull, for it was he who possessed the most consistent Marxist world view. "Meanwhile," maintained Revkin, "it is enough to look at any photograph of Comrade Stalin to convince oneself of the absurdity of K. Ushasty's arguments." Revkin proposed that Figurin be held answerable to the Party. He sent the memorandum to the Regional Committee, but he sent a copy still higher up, to the Central Committee. Not waiting for an answer, he decided to display his power on the spot. He wrote a brief note: *Comrade Figurin, you are required to drop by the District Committee at once to clear up certain matters.* He sent the note with his chauffeur, Motya. Waiting for the answer, Revkin was visibly nervous and could not concentrate on anything. Motya returned in forty minutes.

"Why so long?" Revkin flew at Motya.

Motya never managed an answer. Two tall young men in civilian clothes came in behind her, and one of them, after a smile, asked: "Where's your gun, chief?"

Most surprisingly, Revkin did not ask them for their papers and showed them at once the desk drawer containing his revolver.

Revkin went out to the reception room accompanied by the two young men.

"Anna Martinovna," he said to his secretary, "I'm obliged to be away for a short while. If they call from the barreling plant, tell them to hold the meeting without me."

"All right," said Anna Martinovna, glancing anxiously at Revkin. "And you'll . . . be back soon?"

Letting her know that the future did not depend on him (though she had already understood), Revkin looked over at one of the young men and asked politely: "What do you think, will we be done soon?"

But he just smiled and said: "Let's go, chief."

Major Figurin greeted his guest cordially.

"Very happy to see you, very happy," he mumbled, shaking Revkin's hand. "Meeting you has been on my mind for quite some time, but no sooner did I start to work here than everything began piling up on me. Chonkin, Milyaga . . . it got so involved that I couldn't even find time to present myself to you. But then your note arrived. And so I thought it might be more convenient for us to meet at my office than at yours."

Then he said that lately he'd found Revkin's behavior a bit disturbing. "I didn't mind very much," he said, "that you spoke out against poor Milyaga, after all he is a dead man, while you . . . you're not one yet yourself." Figurin smiled broadly. "You had personal accounts to settle with him?"

"I have no personal accounts with anyone," said Revkin sharply, "but Milyaga did not perish as a hero but as a traitor. I was a witness."

"Ach, Andrei Eremeyevich"—Figurin shook his head—"it's not for me to tell you that the only truths we need are the ones we can use. As to your indignation that the wrong skull ended up in the coffin, well, I know you saw how he died but you did not see his skull. Well, I agree it might have been the wrong skull, it might have been some other skull. Our boys were in a hurry, there was no time, there's a war on, they used what they found. Is it worth making a scandal over such a trifle?"

"It is," said Revkin angrily, "very much so. The whole district is talking about it."

"Pay less attention to rumors. All kinds of people talk, all kinds of people have skulls. In the end we can replace his skull with yours, everyone knows none of us have irreplaceable skulls."

Figurin smiled again and looked benevolently at Revkin.

"You don't agree with me? All right, then. Here's some paper for you to write on."

"For what?" asked Revkin.

"Write when and under what circumstances you took a course hostile to our government, who enlisted you, what you accomplished, what compensation you received, in what currency, and so forth and so on. Don't let your thoughts branch out too far, but you shouldn't omit the details either."

"Listen, you," said Revkin, "you should see a doctor immediately, you're a sick man, you're not all there."

"Yes, several people have already told me that," agreed Figurin sadly. "Doctors included. But where are they now? No, don't get the wrong idea, I'm not the touchy type, you can call me names, I don't care. But I do represent a certain organization well known to you and I don't recommend you insult it. That could only make your position, difficult as it is, worse. You will now be taken to a cell. There, in those peaceful surroundings, concentrate, think a while, and then we'll talk some more. And please don't display any unnecessary obstinacy, our people can be crude at times."

Revkin was taken to a cell and placed with criminals of various sorts, a painful wound to his pride.

35

That night Revkin became hysterical. He beat his head against the iron cell door and was not willing to heed the warden's warnings that making noise after lights-out was not allowed. Transferred to a punishment cell, Revkin got even worse and threatened to send a telegram to Comrade Stalin himself, but toward morning he grew calm and resigned.

That morning he asked to be brought to Figurin and there, in his presence, wrote, in his own hand, his deposition: *I made contact with the international forces of reaction,* he wrote, *in London. We held a few secret meetings attended by Trotsky, Chamberlain, and Gestapo Chief Himmler. At these meetings we discussed all manner of perfidious plans, subversion, sabotage, wrecking. To execute these plans, I, as Secretary of the District Committee, brought people hostile to the Soviet system into the Bureau of the District Committee and in the service of the world bourgeoisie, I directed their activities toward the breakdown of agriculture and the lowering of the living standard of the workers to a minimum in order to create dissatisfaction amid the population and, perhaps, even a rebellion. The latter aim, however, was not achieved.*

Penning this fantasy, Revkin hoped that the higher authorities would realize the absurdity of the accusations advanced by Figurin, but judging by the further course of events, this did not occur.

While reading the deposition, Figurin even praised Revkin: "You write very well. A rich imagination, a good style. You could make quite a decent writer."

To Revkin's surprise and secret joy, Figurin did not notice any contradictions in his deposition and dispatched a copy of the proceedings to the departments above him. Revkin awaited the results with impatience and even with a certain malicious joy. Later he was to learn that his deposition was accepted as satisfactory even "up top." Roman Gavrilovich Luzhin said Revkin's deposition was "monstrously interesting." Later, after some thought, Luzhin crossed out Chamberlain's name, pointing out that to mention a representative of Great Britain, an ally in the anti-Hitler coalition, was probably an error. Luzhin replaced Chamberlain's name with that of Chonkin. Revkin was supposed to have admitted Chonkin was the ringleader and, via Hans, connected with the German high command. Unexpectedly Revkin took offense. He had agreed to be considered a major criminal but refused to acknowledge himself the apprentice of any Chonkin. When they gave him a good beating, he grew contrary, angry, and started behaving provocatively. He denied his previous depositions. They reminded him that the Party had reared him, given him a free education, medicine, food, clothing, and shoes, but he displayed total ingratitude and wrote blasphemously: *Since 1924 I have been a member of a criminal organization called the Communist Party. I held a series of leadership positions, and along with the other members of this organization, I have inflicted maximal damage to our country and our people.*

Upon reading this statement, Major Figurin immediately dispatched Revkin for a psychiatric examination, where the physician, quite familiar with the major's medical doctrine, found:

The patient, Revkin, A. E., forty years old. Sent by Institution p/ya 1–BTS #86/312 for psychiatric examination.

PSYCHONEUROLOGIC EXAMINATION

Consciousness depressed to the point of stuporosity. Sense of smell is intact. Visual acuity and fields are intact, palpebral fissures $D = S$, extraocular muscles are intact, pupils are round, equal and react to light briskly, $D = S$, convergence and accommodation are normal.

Innervation of the facial muscles is intact, $D = S$, minimal deviation of the tongue to the left.

Swallowing, phonation, and articulation are intact, the palate and pharyngeal reflexes are intact, no involuntary movements of the mouth noted. Face is asymmetric $D < S$.

The gait is intact, synkineses are not present (Mingatsini-Barre test satisfactory). Patellar and Achilles' reflexes are hyperactive, $D = S$.

Romberg's sign is unstable. There are features of hemiballism, pseudobulbar disorder, pallidal and intention tremor, cataplexy and adiadochokineses.

Sensitivity to pain, temperature, and touch not impaired.

The patient is in a gloomy, depressed condition, uncommunicative, and responds to questions concerning his complaints with "My complaint is an illegal arrest." He answers other questions reluctantly, but then grows excited, jumps from his chair, shouts and demands to be left in peace. In some cases he still displays a desire for contact with the physician; he explains confusedly that in the past he held an important post ("I was in charge of an entire district"), "soldier of the party," "devoted to his people," "enjoyed high authority," and so forth. But then he imagines enemies and envious people arose at his place of work. They coveted his post and toward that end launched all sorts of intrigues against him, which ultimately brought him to prison. He maintains that before his arrest he had noticed that he was being followed. He says that during the investigation false testimony against him had been extorted from him by means of threats and physical violence. From time to time he weeps and threatens that this "will reach Stalin himself." He considers certain newspaper reports bearing no relation to him whatsoever to be directed against him personally. At times his ravings lose the resemblance of logic, he uses phrases about the advantage of the roundheads over the longheads, etc. Of the Soviet system he says he served it faithfully but that now he has grown disenchanted.

Diagnosis: The patient is suffering from a paranoid form of schizophrenia which has developed from a prolonged hatred for the Soviet system and is accompanied by delusions of grandeur and persecution. Prognosis doubtful. Symptomatic treatment. No contra-indications to his being kept under arrest.

Although Revkin had not turned out to be a Chonkin, he was still a rather important figure and it was ordered that he, too, be allotted a cell to himself. Unable to come up with anything better, the prison warden, Senior Lieutenant Kuryatnikov, placed the former secretary in the same cell with his cow, even though that meant that Revkin might steal a few mouthfuls of milk during the night.

36

Lavrenty Pavlovich Beria was sitting at his desk wearing an unbuttoned gabardine topcoat, boots, galoshes, and a gray hat pulled down over his eyes.

It was after one in the morning. He was ready to go home, but he didn't have the strength to get up. Holding his head in his hands, his eyes half closed, he was thinking about various sectors of the front. The situation was lousy, Stalin had spoken harshly to him that very night, reproaching Beria that his organization could not be doing any worse, that it was sluggish and not adapting to wartime conditions.

Moscow wouldn't have to be abandoned today or tomorrow, but the evacuation of the more important enterprises and institutions was being conducted in a disorganized, panicky fashion. There was a shortage of rolling stock. Often second-rate equipment was loaded, the most valuable left behind. Plenty of plant and factory managers were in a hurry not to save their plants and factories but themselves. The essential railroad and vehicle routes, the bridges and train stations, had still not been mined. Wild rumors were circulating in the city, and a significant part of the population was infected by a capitulatory mood; that is, to put it more simply, they were just waiting around for the Germans to arrive. Very little had been done to prepare special fighting units to remain behind and wage underground activities, demolition, diversion. Stalin had been most enraged by the report that in one of the now occupied provinces a secret organization was operating, facilitating the enemy's seizure of the province, and, what's more, Party members and even secret police workers were mixed up in the organization.

Stalin shouted at Beria and even spat in his face, but after a spell he cooled down and said, "Sorry, my nerves."

Nerves or no nerves, why spit in my face, Beria was thinking when his office door opened and a young colonel acting as a secretary approached him and laid a file bound with silk braid near the edge of his desk.

"What's that?" asked Beria without raising his eyes.

"The chief of counter-intelligence has requested you to familiarize yourself with this," said the secretary and left.

Clearly the file contained something of the highest importance if the chief of counter-intelligence and his secretary took it upon themselves to disturb a people's commissar at such a late hour.

Beria opened one eye, squinted over at the file, and noticed the name Golitsyn-Chonkin written very large; surprised, he opened his other eye and pulled the file over to him.

He undid the silk braid, spat on one finger, and began looking through the file: a letter concerning the deserter Chonkin signed "A resident of the village of Krasnoye"; an arrest warrant with a hole through its seal; the record of an interrogation; a personal data report; a report from Ramzai concerning a certain Hans; a report with the words "descended from the Princes Golitsyn" underlined three times in red pencil; a warrant for Hans's arrest; a record of the interrogation where Hans stated that Prince Golitsyn had disguised himself as a deserting private; another stack of various papers in which the prisoner was called Chonkin, the so-called Chonkin, White Chonkin, Chonkin-Golitsyn, and finally (someone had the idea of putting the right name in front), Golitsyn-Chonkin.

Beria pushed his hat back on his head, thought a minute, pressed a button, and summoned the chief of counter-intelligence, to whom he gave fifteen minutes to cross out the completely superfluous name of Chonkin in all the papers.

While this order was being executed, Beria did a few exercises, shaved, sprinkled on some eau de cologne, and drank a glass of strong tea.

37

Half an hour later, surrounded by a large retinue of colonels and generals, Beria appeared at a metro station which had no name. As soon as he appeared, a train emerged from the tunnel, its front car bearing the sign DEPOT. The train was almost an ordinary one, differing from others only in that its doors and windows were opaque.

The train stopped. The doors opened noisily and suddenly the platform was filled with armed men. Soldiers wearing helmets and waterproof capes poured from all the doors, ready to fire their submachine guns aimed at Beria and his retinue. Someone not in the know might well assume that a battle was about to commence on the spot. However, this was standard procedure when Beria went to see Stalin, who was, at that time, living in the metro.

Though standard, this procedure never failed to frighten Lavrenty Pavlovich. As always he moved back instinctively, stepping on the toes of the man behind him. But he regained his composure at once, snatched his yellow English briefcase from someone's hands, and stepped decisively forward toward the submachine guns trained on him.

Two men wearing helmets and waterproof capes, their hands empty, came out from behind the machine gunners. One saluted Lavrenty Pavlovich and said: "Your documents, please!"

Fumbling hastily in his pocket, Beria held out the small red book.

The soldier spent a long time examining the document and its bearer, his mistrustful glance moving back and forth from photograph to original. Then the document passed to the hands of the other soldier and he, too, compared the photograph and the original as if seeing both for the first time. Finally, the second soldier gave the little book back to the first, the first returned it to its owner, and, allowing him to pass, saluted again: "Please enter."

Beria entered the train, and took a seat in the corner, laying his briefcase on his lap, which made him look like a book-keeper on the way home from work. The men who had checked his documents sat across from him, and the submachine gunners took their places, two by each door. The doors closed, the train started moving. Beria glanced at his watch.

In secret documents the place where Stalin lived was called the underground dacha. Beria assumed the "dacha" was located at the next station, but he knew that in the interests of conspiracy they would try to pull the wool over his eyes and take him for a long ride on the circle line before delivering him to his destination.

No one said anything. All conversation between passengers and guards was strictly forbidden, in order to prevent any unnecessary contact.

38

They traveled forty-five minutes before arriving at their destination. The doors opened, but this time the submachine gunners stayed in the cars.

The two checkers again barred his path. The senior man again saluted and said: "Your documents, please!" and he said "Thank you!" again when returning them.

That, however, did not end the check. The personal guard of the person who lived in the metro station, consisting entirely of Beria's fellow Georgians, met him at the platform, aimed their submachine guns, and narrowed their eyes. Again "Your documents, please!", again "Thank you!"

Then, leading Beria to a special room, they requested that he undress to the waist to verify his identifying marks: a number of birthmarks and warts, a scar on his right ear, and a tattoo on his left forearm: "In life no happiness."

They peered in his briefcase and turned out his pockets, where they found nothing suspicious except for a small penknife shaped like a lady's shoe, which they ordered kept until his return.

The search ended with the same words "Thank you!" and the chief of the personal guard saluted.

While Lavrenty Pavlovich was getting dressed, a mischievous thought arose in his mind: How about checking the chief of the guard's performance of his unremitting labor? He looked over at the chief with a merry glance and then asked a seemingly completely innocent question, but which in fact could be the first step on the path toward informal relations.

"How are things, my friend?" asked Lavrenty Pavlovich intimately and in Georgian while buttoning his field jacket, his fingers now slightly chilled. At the same time he smiled and winked at the chief of the guard, as if saying, "Come on, we're all friends here, you can tell me about yourself, share your joys, your troubles." But the chief accepted neither the smile nor the intimate tone and seemed unaware of the words even as sounds. Pressing his lips together in silence, he waited patiently until Beria had dressed and only then did he say, in Russian, "Comrade Stalin is expecting you."

Allowing Lavrenty Pavlovich to pass on ahead, he pressed a button of a secret system which signaled that a new guest had arrived.

39

Stalin greeted his guest cordially at the threshold of his spacious office, which contained a globe and blinded windows, exactly like the office he had in the Kremlin. Some people who had been brought there in closed trains even thought they were in the Kremlin, having taken a secret, underground route.

"Hello, my friend," said Stalin, approaching Lavrenty with an outstretched hand.

"Hello, Koba!" answered Lavrenty Pavlovich in an exalted tone.

They walked up to each other, and Lavrenty Pavlovich, setting his briefcase on the floor, took the hand offered him in both of his.

"Hello again, my friend," said Stalin with feeling.

"Hello again, Koba!" responded the guest with even more feeling.

"And once more hello, my friend!" Stalin embraced his guest and kissed him firmly on the lips, tickling him with his mustache.

"Huh-uh-lo," Beria slipped into ecstasy.

"Come in, come in, my friend," said Stalin, thumping Beria on the back. "How was the ride? How're your wife and children? Well?"

"Well, thank God." Picking up his briefcase Beria followed Stalin into the depths of the office. "Along with me and our entire people, their only concern is that you be well."

"Sit down, my friend." Stalin pointed to the leather couch and walked back to his chair, opened a pack of Herzegovina Flora cigarettes, and, breaking them apart, began stuffing his pipe with the tobacco.

"You look upset about something," he said, gazing with concern at Beria, who was sitting on the couch holding his briefcase on his knees.

"Me?" Beria tossed up his head. "No, it's nothing, it's not important."

"But still?"

"Pay no attention." Beria lowered his eyes. "It's just nonsense. It shouldn't be any concern of yours. You have more important concerns."

"Of course," agreed Stalin. "I have a great many concerns. But how could I not be concerned about you. After all, you are my faithful comrade in arms and it hurts me to see you out of sorts. I very much want to know what's in your soul."

"Aiaiai!" Beria waved his arms. "They're only trifles, I don't have the right . . . Yes, you spotted it right off, I am a bit grieved, I'm a little grieved by your lack of trust in me, but that has no significance whatsoever."

"What does that mean, it has no significance?" Stalin frowned. "It would have great significance if it were true. But tell me, where do you see my lack of trust?"

"All right, then, I'll tell you, but it does make me feel awkward. I see a little distrust in the fact that your people bring me here in a closed train, then search me and force me to undress as if I were some kind of criminal. Naturally, I understand that war is cruel, a very high level of vigilance is needed, and your life is dearer than the apple of our eye, but all the same, such treatment, ever so slightly, just the least little bit, reduces my human dignity."

"Human dignity?" Surprised, Stalin puffed on his pipe and began pacing the room. "I understand you very well, Lavrenty. But judge for yourself, what can I do with my people? They love me so much. They're so afraid for me. It isn't only you they search, it's everybody."

"Yes, yes, yes, yes." Lavrenty nodded. "But still it seems to me, still I sometimes think that for you I'm, how should I put it, not just the same as everybody else."

"Yes, of course." His pipe between his teeth, Stalin sat down beside him, smacking his lips. "And you're not the same as everybody else. You're special to me. And I ought to trust you one hundred percent, even a little more. But sometimes, for some reason, I feel that of all the people who come here there's probably no one I should trust less than you."

Stalin took his pipe from his mouth, turned abruptly toward Lavrenty, and began looking at him without blinking, as if trying to read his thoughts. His master's gaze was very disturbing to Lavrenty, but he did not turn away or lower his eyes; on the contrary, he, too, stared unblinkingly back at Stalin through his pince-nez. And so they sat staring at each other without breaking eye contact like two boa constrictors. Stalin gave in first.

"Only the devil knows you," he said, turning aside, sighing. "I see through everybody, you're the only one I can't see through. Sometimes I think maybe he's an honest man, sometimes I think maybe he's a dog. Sometimes I think maybe he's made a deal with Hitler or Himmler to hand over Moscow and turn me over to them. Well?" Stalin turned to Beria again and stared at him. "Admit it, have you made a deal?"

"Me?" Tossing his briefcase to the side, Lavrenty Pavlovich fell to his knees, embraced Stalin's boot, pressed it to his heart, then pressed his cheek to it. "Koba," he said in reproach, "you can say that? Sure I'm a dog. A dog, yes. But what makes a dog different from a man? His devotion to his master. You can abuse me, but a devoted dog cannot take offense at his master and I don't take offense at you. And if you need me to gnaw and bite somebody, I'll gnaw him. I'll bite him. Just point him out and say, 'Sic him!' and I . . ."

Lavrenty Pavlovich got on all fours and bared his teeth.

"All right." Stalin was touched. A tear glistened on his cheek. He patted Lavrenty Pavlovich's now sweaty bald spot. "All right. I was just . . . I just wanted to check up on you a little. I'm not in a good mood, you know. I sit in here like a mole." Stalin rose and walked over to the globe. "And the Germans are already here. Here. Quite close. What do you think, we'll probably have to hand over Moscow."

"No," said Lavrenty, brushing off his knees. "We won't have to. Now we won't."

"Now we won't?" Stalin narrowed his eyes. "And what's happened that now we won't have to?"

"I'll show you something right this minute," said Lavrenty, unbuckling his briefcase and withdrawing the file bound with braided silk. "You know I would never have thought of disturbing you at such a late hour with minor matters." He brought over the file and laid it on the edge of Stalin's desk. "There," he said triumphantly, "the Prince Golitsyn case."

"Golitsyn?" said Stalin, surprised.

"Prince Golitsyn," repeated Beria, emphasizing the word "Prince." "An extremely far-flung conspiracy. My boys did a little work. They kept at it. Well, read it yourself. It's all there."

"I have no time for reading." Stalin took a sidelong glance at the file. "Give me a brief account."

"Fine. Very brief. Picture a completely unremarkable summer day not long before the start of the war. A Russian village in the middle of nowhere. All those Russian villages of theirs are in the middle of nowhere. The sun is shining, the birds are singing, the roses . . . No, not the roses . . . the potatoes are blooming, the butterflies"—Lavrenty mimicked the butterflies flying—". . . are flying. Then suddenly, something very big, not a butterfly, an airplane . . ."

Beria said nothing for a moment, allowing the picture to sink in.

"Listen, Lavrenty." Stalin frowned. "Don't tell me about the butterflies. I can get somebody else better than you to tell me about butterflies. Just get to the point."

"Fine," agreed Beria. "The point. Picture the city of Berlin, the Reichführer's chancellery, Hitler sitting in his office. He's thinking about his plan Barbarossa. He's preparing to attack the Soviet Union, but he realizes it's a dangerous business. Of course, Germany is a strong state, but the Soviet Union is stronger. He thinks: I've got cannons, tanks, and planes, but he (that is you) also has cannons, tanks, and planes. So I can't rely on force alone but on the shaky (that's his opinion, of course) internal situation. In his opinion the new system still hasn't taken a strong hold in Russia. The Russian people, raised in the tradition of autocracy, want the Tsar and the landowner, so the landowner will say to them: 'You plow here, you sow there, and when you gather the harvest, you give half to me and half you can keep yourself.' And so Hitler starts looking at our enemies who gave us the slip, former noblemen, former Tsarist lackeys, and he comes across Prince Golitsyn. Hitler needs the prince as a banner around which all the malcontents here can be rallied, united, and readied for battle against Soviet power. And so, not long before the war, that very Golitsyn, disguised as a simple Red Army soldier, arrives by plane at the village of Krasnoye, which is approximately here"—Beria poked the globe with one finger—"settles down with one of the local women, and begins spinning his spider web. His plan is simple and clear: wait until Hitler hurls his 190 divisions at us, prepare an uprising, then, at the proper moment, on a signal from Berlin, knife us in the back. In that way he hopes to deflect part of our forces from the front, smash them, and then . . ."

"Enough!" Stalin interrupted abruptly. "Enough. Where is he now, this prince?"

"Don't worry. He's in reliable hands," said Beria, making two fists.

Stalin laid his pipe down on his desk and, folding his hands behind his back, began pacing the room. "Golitsyn! Prince Golitsyn!" he muttered almost to himself.

Beria knew what he was doing. He knew that as never before Stalin needed someone on whom he could lay the blame for the failures at the beginning of the war.

"Yes," said Stalin after a moment's thought. "I always knew that one internal enemy was more dangerous than a hundred external enemies. I was always pointing out that the former exploiters and aristocrats would never reconcile themselves to their historical defeat. But obviously I'm too trusting, I couldn't even imagine that those people hated the new system so much, hated the new Russia so much, that they were prepared to act against it in an alliance with its worst enemy. Well, so, Lavrenty, our enemies hurl us a challenge, we'll accept it. We'll use that Golitsyn as an example to show our people what these capitalists and landowners are after. And we'll use the same example to show the capitalists and the landowners that our people love Soviet power and do not want them back. And with that same example we will show that raving Führer that he's counting in vain on those petty underlings, they won't be any help to him."

He picked up his pen and on the first sheet of the Prince Golitsyn file traced out in his small but legible handwriting:

Prince Golitsyn and his accomplices are to be given a public trial with full press coverage. I don't know about the others, but as for Prince Golitsyn, I don't think that the firing squad would be too severe a punishment under the laws of wartime.

J. Stalin

40

The old-timers remembered that the dogs howled something awful that night in the village. They howled, whimpered, barked, and darted around on their chains as if trying to warn their masters of something. Volkov the bookkeeper noticed Jack's behavior and even thought that something was amiss; a dog doesn't get that worked up over nothing. Volkov looked up at the sky; it was clear, there were stars but no moon. Invisible in the mist a droning airplane was drilling a hole through the sky, but the sputter of its motor sounded normal and peaceful. The bookkeeper wet his finger with spit and held it up, trying to determine the force and direction of the wind, but it had neither force nor direction. Volkov stood for a while smoking, took a leak under an apple tree, and then, before buttoning his fly, jumped up and down a few times.

Jack was still straining at his chain, barking, howling, even seeming to cry.

"There, there, don't you be bad," his master shouted, and gave him a boot in the face.

The dog began whimpering and squealing, then hid in his doghouse, where he resumed his howling.

Yes, thought Volkov, this has to mean something.

In the twenties, when serving in the Turkestan military district, Volkov happened to witness a strong earthquake. Then, too, the dogs had howled and carried on like that. But in the latitudes where the one-armed bookkeeper now lived nature behaved peacefully; trees knocked down by wind or the Typoa's insignificant little floods was the worst that ever happened.

Not knowing what to make of the animal's behavior, Volkov returned to his hut.

41

Borka the hog also seemed to sense the approach of something unusual. That evening he began to squeal and grunt at the door, and when Nyura let him in, it took him a long time to find himself a place; he raced around the room, hiding first under the stove, then under a bench.

That night Nyura had a hard time falling asleep. She kept thinking of Chonkin, her life; all sorts of nonsense had crept into her head.

Later she dreamed that she was walking with Chonkin through a field. He was holding her hand, asking if it was still far, and she answered, No, not far at all. They met Lieutenant Colonel Luzhin, wearing only underpants, and galoshes on his bare feet. He said: "So, Belyashova, I was just about to offer you this Chonkin in place of yours, maybe he'll suit you." Nyura looked at Chonkin, who winked at her as if to say, Go along with it because I'm really me. Nyura looked searchingly at him and couldn't figure out if he was the real Chonkin or a fake one. Then Lyubov Mikhailovna appeared, bringing Nyura three months' salary. Then they were seated at the table, Nyura and Chonkin and Luzhin and Lyubov Mikhailovna. Suddenly Olimpiada Petrovna came bursting in the room, shouting in an inhuman voice: "The light! The light! What a horrible light!"

Nyura woke up and it was not in her dream but in reality that her room was illuminated by a truly terrible, penetrating, unnatural light, and an unusually tall Olimpiada Petrovna was darting about the room shouting something. Nyura leapt from her bed, looked out the window, and then she, too, began shouting. The whole area was flooded with a piercing, dead, shadowless light, the river Tyopa was ablaze; an enormous flame swirled above it, for what seemed to be its whole length. The flame seemed to move from the river to the village; everything seemed about to catch on fire.

"What is it?" Nyura heard Olimpiada Petrovna whisper behind her.

"I don't know," said Nyura.

Then a long figure in white descended from the sky to the middle of the street. Its hands raised in the air, the figure kept moving its legs and jumping up and down as if performing some shamanistic dance. Suddenly it turned its white face to Nyura, its eyes gleaming horribly.

"Ai!" cried Nyura, recognizing Gladishev's corpse.

Then other figures in white appeared on the street. Thinking that it was the end of the world, people came running outside in their underwear. A crazed rooster, having no doubt decided that it had slept through daybreak, hopped up on the fence, flapped its wings, and began its piercing cry.

Meanwhile, the more level-headed people, having gotten hold of themselves, realized that the horrible, blinding light was coming from a semicircle of vehicles surrounding the village. How many were there—fifty, a hundred, a thousand? After the event, the accounts varied widely. The light made the river mist look like flame.

Later it was learned that this was an operation designed and brilliantly executed by the Right People; its leaders were rewarded and the operation was afterward frequently mentioned in various orders, instructions, and analyses of tactics. Three years later it was brilliantly repeated by Marshal Zhukov at the Kyustrin bridgehead and forever took its place in history.

People were only just regaining their composure when a truck bristling with what appeared to be gramophone speakers, only much larger, drove into the village.

"Attention!" shouted a deafening bark of a voice. "I am ordering all villagers to take what they need with them, no more than twenty kilograms per person, and assemble in front of the office to be loaded onto trucks. You have forty minutes to assemble. Those who are late will be brought by force. All measures including armed force will be used against anyone failing to comply. Attention!"

The vehicle moved slowly from one end of the village to the other and then back, barking out the order again and again.

42

The vehicles which had illuminated the operation regrouped with the others; a small column entered the village and lined up across from the office. Some of the vehicles kept their lights on. A new MK, waxed to a gleam, drove in with the column and stopped a bit off to one side. Its rear door opened and a man of average height wearing white felt boots stitched with strips of leather, a topcoat with a fur collar, a tall sheepskin hat, glasses, and white gloves slowly emerged. He stepped out onto the running board, put one foot on the ground, and then stayed in that position, one foot on the ground, the other on the running board, his right hand motionless on the half-open door. The man continued to stand in that position, moving neither forward nor back, as in a freeze frame.

From the sidelines he observed the action occurring in front of his eyes as if he had no direct relation to it. Yet it was he who was the chief organizer and leader of this operation, astonishing in its scale and intention. He stood alone, and no one in the nearby group of lesser officers ventured to approach him, but it would not have taken more than one move of his finger for any or all of them to come running to carry out his any command.

43

It was Luzhin.

He stood, he listened to the cries, the curses, the sobbing, and the howls of despair, but none of it touched the strings of his soul. His only concern was that the loading of the human cargo be carried out on schedule and, insofar as possible, with a minimum of fuss.

Old Olimpiada Petrovna was absolutely unable to accept the inevitability of it all. She kept darting over to the mass of guards surrounding the square.

"Comrades!" she would call out, pointing at Vadik. "This boy is the son of a Red Army political worker."

The guards turned their faces away. Catching hold of her shirt, Vadik cried, "Grandma!"

It all seemed like a dream to Nyura. Suddenly Gladishev, shoved by guards, appeared in front of her with Hercules in his arms. Nyura felt no surprise. It was plainly the Day of Judgment and the dead had arisen.

Later it was learned that Gladishev had staged his suicide. In fact, he had been hiding all that time in the cellar, which was why Aphrodite did not want any strangers quartered in her house. He came out only at night and to sleep with his wife. And now they had raked him out, alive and kicking, along with everybody else.

Later Nyura was unable to recall the order of events and how she found herself in a truck beside the Gladishev family. Her memory was all in bits and pieces.

The loading was finished; the guards closed the sides of the trucks and took their places on separate benches, their backs to the cab, facing their charges. The lead truck had already swung around in front of the office, Luzhin had already brought his left foot even with his right on the running board of his car when cries of "Stop! Stop!" were heard.

A scene, magnificent in its own way, was then revealed to the eyes of the departing villagers. Two hefty guards had seized Ilya Zhikin, the legless Civil War invalid, by the arms, and were rolling him down the street at a run on his platform and castors.

The lead truck stopped, and its tailgate was reopened.

"One–two. Up you go."

Without losing a stride the guards took the invalid under his arms and began swinging him back and forth, preparing to heave him up into the truck. Then the unforeseen occurred. Zhikin managed to tear his right arm free and while falling to paste the guard on his left in the eye. The guard groaned, brought his hands to his eye, and let go of Zhikin. At the same time the other guard managed to grab hold of Zhikin's right hand. Already in a state of free fall, Zhikin's abbreviated body gave a twitch and his homemade cart, to which he was strapped with belts, struck the other guard full force just below the knee. The guard collapsed as if he'd been shot and writhed with heart-rending howls in the dust. His comrade had both hands to his blackening eye. Zhikin himself lay motionless off to one side, his castors gleaming, like a wrecked car.

Two other brave lads raced toward Zhikin, but he came back to life and, grabbing one by the leg, tried to topple him too.

Now a whole gang of them went racing over. Crowding around Zhikin, they cursed and shouted; it was obvious they were hitting the rebel, working him over, but he did not cry out.

A murmur passed through the trucks. Someone shouted out, "Fascists!"

Roman Gavrilovich Luzhin realized that the scene now underway could make an unpleasant impression on the people in the trucks, and without saying a word, he clapped his hands. He didn't clap hard but the scene changed in an instant. The guards rushed from Zhikin like cockroaches. Only Zhikin and the guard he had struck with his cart remained on the ground.

"You!" said Luzhin to one of the officers, beckoning him with a lazy finger.

The officer ran over, saluted, standing at attention, hands at his sides.

"Him," said Luzhin, slowly moving his finger down a little and to the side.

"To be shot?" The officer stood even straighter.

"Released!" said Luzhin.

They set Zhikin back on his castors, gave him a little push, and not even bothering to express the least gratitude for that humane gesture, he rolled quickly down the street, pushing against the ground with arms loose and limber as a monkey's. He was soon gone in the dark.

When the column had formed, all headlights were extinguished at once. The trucks which had illuminated the operation then took their own place in the column in total darkness.

44

The same number of Krasnoyans arrived in Dolgov as had departed Krasnoye. On the way Grandpa Shapkin had quietly expired, which was balanced by Ninka Kurzov's giving birth to a boy whom she later named Nikodim in honor of his paternal grandfather. Burly, who was never the least bit serious no matter what the situation, suggested that, in view of the circumstances of its birth, it be called Enkayveedom.*

45

Chairman Golubev escaped the common lot because he was in the district town that night. The night before he had been summoned by Piotr Terentevich Khudobchenko, who was pleasant and friendly to him. Golubev learned from him that his personal case was being rescinded since it had been instigated against him by enemies of the people in an effort to assault the ranks of the Party. Khudobchenko wasted no time taking Golubev's Party card from his safe and telling his friend: "Here, take it. You held the right position in the harvest question and defended it like a Bolshevik, but next time, I don't recommend throwing your Party card on the table."

Overjoyed, Golubev got soused, spent the night in the Regional Committee's hotel, rose before dawn, and met the morning on the road.

As he drove he pondered the caprices of fate. The day before he'd been ready for anything his insolent behavior might have caused—if they didn't have him shot they'd at least put him behind bars—but then everything spun right around. Revkin and Chmikhalov were in jail and he was driving home with his Party card in his pocket.

He remembered his conversation with the prosecutor, who had said that sooner or later, no matter what, you'll turn out to be guilty, no matter what you've done.

They can punish me, thought the chairman, but you never know when or for what and so you might as well do what you think is right.

The morning air was fresh, the horse ran swiftly. The chair-

* NKVD—secret police under Stalin.—Trans.

man raised the collar of his sheepskin coat, tucked his hands in his pockets, and half dozed, not having slept enough in the hotel. The wheels hummed, the springs squeaked. Near the village the wagon began jolting noticeably. Golubev opened his eyes and saw that the road had been seriously damaged by two deep ruts, which could hardly have been caused even by one very heavy vehicle. The chairman was surprised, but he attached no significance to it, all kinds of things could happen, all kinds of people could drive past. Clearly it had been some sort of military column, but he couldn't see why it needed to pass down that road, which led away from the main highway and was in fact a dead end. Besides, there were so many things you couldn't understand in this life that he'd lost the habit of surprise. He seized the reins and brought the horse to the edge of the road so as not to turn over in a rut.

On the other side of the hillock, where the village came into view, he was met by Borka the hog, who was obviously awaiting Nyura's return. There was something surprising about the village, though Golubev couldn't say just exactly what; it looked the same yet there was something strange about it. It was only much later that he realized that it was the lack of smoke coming from any chimney. The closer he drew, the stranger things seemed. A constant mournful wail issued from the village: dogs howling and cattle lowing. Courtyard gates and the doors of most huts were wide open; on the road, rutted up by unknown vehicles, casual belongings lay scattered where they'd been dropped—a straw hat, a baby's vest, a jar of pickles. Golubev halted his horse by Nyura's hut and rapped at the window with his whip handle.

"Hey, anyone alive in there?" cried the chairman.

He shouted the same at Gladishev's window. There was no response there either.

The kolkhoz office was open as well. The chairman climbed up the steps; there were muddy boot prints all over the floor, which was littered with cigarette butts and a two-day-old copy of *Pravda*. Naturally, he made a dash for the safe, which, to all appearances, had not been touched. Its contents proved to be in place. Then the chairman left the office as it was and started for home. There was nobody in his house either. There were unwashed dishes on the table in the kitchen. The beds had not been made. Traces of hasty flight were visible everywhere. There were things thrown about the whole house. The trunk's lid was open. The kerosene lamp on the table was burning low. Neither his wife nor his children were there. Then he found a note from his oldest son, Grinka, on the floor: *Papa, they're taking us away.*

Ivan Timofeyevich sat down at the table, seized his head in his hands, and sank into thought. "What does 'they're taking us away' mean? Could it really mean everybody, the old people, the women, the children? It looked that way. But where and what for? And why such haste? An evacuation. But judging from the newspaper reports, if you could believe them even a little, the Germans were still too far away."

Golubev sat and thought, then with a sudden start he ran to the office and telephoned Borisov. Borisov was unable to give him any intelligible explanation but did advise Golubev to stick where he was and not budge.

Golubev returned home, made a bundle of his pillow and blanket, and carried them to his office, along with two buckets of home brew he found in Granny Dunya's deserted hut. There he locked himself in, drank some home brew, lit the stove, and drank some more; lying on the sofa, he would jump up, wave his arms in the air, then lie down again, then jump back up, his mind racing. Sometimes he thought to himself, but mostly out loud: How did such an idiotic life come about? Whose fault was it—the people's or the system's? But he could not ascertain the truth; on the one hand, people formed the system, but on the other, the system was composed of people.

The phone rang every now and again, and representatives of various organizations requested information about the delivery of milk and meat, about the requisitioning of supplementary horses for the army, the preparation of the seed fund; they asked about the livestock, farrows, the number of laying hens and the fodder supply.

"Everything's going according to plan," Golubev would answer and hang up.

They'd call back. "What do you mean according to plan, when this isn't being done and there's none of that and that's not happening?"

"All according to plan," Golubev would repeat and hang up.

He still hadn't finished the first pail when stubby and swollen-faced he was arrested for blocking deliveries and counter-revolutionary sabotage.

Trembling in the back of the Black Maria, Golubev recalled everything one of the villagers, Lyosha Zharov, had told him about how new prisoners were treated, and he began to feel queasy. He clearly imagined how, just for fun, the thieves would torment him with the tricks, the "election," the "parachute jump," that Zharov had told him about. No, no, no way could that be allowed. You had to show them who you were right off so such things would be out of the question. Better they just cut his throat. Then he remembered more of what Zharov had told him and prepared himself to enter a new life.

46

Life had been going on as usual in cell 34 of "Badge of Honor" Prison No. 1. Little had changed there since Chonkin had been taken away. They were still getting people up in the morning, still making them take out the honey pot, and still feeding them dishwater three times a day; well, maybe, it was now even a bit less nourishing than before. Professor Tsinubel had risen to a position of authority, having been appointed cell elder. Now he did not sleep by the honey pot but on one of the lower bunks.

A new day in prison had just begun and each man was spending it the best he could. Zapyataev and Tsinubel were playing chess with chessmen made from bread. Up on the bunks Cheishvili the Georgian was telling one of the newcomers his usual poetic tale of how he once lived with two singers. Then a terrible cry rang out and Pan Kalyuzhny dragged Bayonet struggling down from his bunk.

"You're going to steal? Steal?" repeated Pan Kalyuzhny, twisting Bayonet's ear, red enough as it was.

"Let go, you dead meat, you pigeon, you dog head," howled Bayonet, trying to struggle free.

"What's the matter?" Tsinubel said, looking up.

"He stole my lard," explained Pan Kalyuzhny. "I swapped my hat with the guard for a piece of lard and yesterday I hid it under my pillow and today I go to look for it and it's not there."

"Let him go!" said the professor sharply. "What kind of methods are those? Vasya, did you take his lard?"

"Come on, Professor, I didn't take it. I'll be a son-of-a-whore and rot in jail for a hundred years if I took it."

"Look, Vasya, we don't tolerate stealing in our collective here. Aren't you ashamed of yourself, Vasya? Why are you like that? After all, you weren't born under the old regime. You were born in a new society where the social basis for crime has been forever liquidated. And you're not in here for a hundred years. You'll be going free . . . Everything's still open to you . . . And where's your behavior going to get you?"

"Stop it, Professor! I should die, I didn't take that lousy lard. Ech, the rats"—he suddenly flared up—"you pigeons don't have a real leader. He'd steal you blind, you shits, he'd teach you to love freedom."

"Yes, Vasya," said the professor sadly, "clearly a lot of work is still needed to make a real man out of you."

"You, Professor, can go to . . ." He walked off to the corner, pulled down his pants, and sat down on the pot.

The conflict, however, somehow died out by itself. Reconciled to his loss, Kalyuzhny crept back up on his bunk. The professor and Zapyataev concentrated on their clumsy little chessmen. Sitting on the pot, Bayonet began to reflect on his life, which had not gone too well. He had been a pickpocket, just starting out. He was always getting caught. He was beaten up on tram cars and on trains; once they even threw him from a moving train onto the embankment. He was always dreaming that a real ringleader would turn up and take him under his wing. "Hand's off this kid, you shits," the leader would say. "He works for me."

Just then the door was flung open, revealing a heavyset, fierce-looking, bearded man in a sheepskin coat, with a hat pulled down over his eyes. It was Ivan Timofeyevich Golubev. All eyes were turned on him with what seemed to be open hostility. The two prisoners standing by the stool playing some strange game seemed especially frightening to him. Cutthroats! Ivan Timofeyevich shuddered inwardly. Now they'll start picking on me or just kill me. No, I've got to show them right off they've picked the wrong guy.

The door slammed shut behind him, the key ground in the lock. Golubev stayed in the doorway, face to face with the gang of cutthroats.

"What's wrong with you, you goddamn dead meat, don't you know the law?" he shouted right away to all of them, making his eyes ferocious while shivering from fear.

"What are you?" Bayonet raised his head, without moving from the pot. "A real crook or did you just steal to eat?"

"Out of my way, low life!" Without a moment's hesitation, Golubev kicked him in the butt with his boot. Bayonet went flying off the pot, almost knocking it over.

"What are you doing?" Bayonet began running in circles about the cell, holding up his pants with one hand, the other holding on to his injured backside.

"The towel! Where's the towel, you disgraceful sons-of-bitches?" The new prisoner was beside himself, his eyes bulging ferociously.

Bayonet was the first to realize what he meant. Still holding up his pants with one hand, he snatched a filthy towel hanging from the bunks and threw it to the ferocious newcomer. Golubev caught it in midair, flung it to his feet, and began wiping his boots on it.

"A leader!" gasped Bayonet. "I'll be damned, a real dyed-in-the-wool leader!" he cried out, excited, overjoyed. Finally, venturing to approach the newcomer, and looking him over from head to toe, he asked ingratiatingly, "What do they call you, papa?"

A bit thrown, Golubev was about to say his last name, first name, and patronymic, but then he remembered that thieves always had to have underworld nicknames. And having no time to think up anything better, he said: "They call me the Chairman!" and tossed the towel in the pot.

47

I envy future Chonkinologists. At some point the secret archives will be opened to them and by then technology will have achieved new heights. They'll lie on a sofa, press a button or several buttons, and there will flash before them on an ample color TV screen any interrogation record, any arrest warrant, or the decision resulting from the investigation. There it will be, food for an inquisitive mind! Take your fill of pleasure!

It's much harder for this author. They won't let me in the archives, they won't give me the old newspaper files. So, use what you've got.

What is there?

Well, here's an article from a Moscow newspaper. The name of the paper has been torn off, and the date is unknown. The article is entitled "A Titled Judas" and is signed by representatives of certain aristocratic families, which by some miracle had survived revolutionary justice.

It was with a sense of anger and indignation [the article said] that we learned of the black treachery of a certain Golitsyn, a former prince. We have to admit that in our time we did not all accept the Great October Socialist Revolution. Blinded by family and class prejudices, having lost our estates, some of us looked hostilely upon the agonies of the working class in our country. Many of us had to experience an agonizing spiritual crisis on the path to political maturity, to an understanding of the historical significance of the October Revolution and its leading force, the working class. But no matter what views we previously held, each of us, in this hour so ominous for the motherland, has realized that we are not only former noblemen and aristocrats, we are Russians, we must be with our own people in this hour, join ranks with them around the Bolsheviks' Communist Party and around the person of Comrade Stalin. What a complete scoundrel a person must be to resolve on such black treachery at a time so difficult for our motherland! Now, caught red-handed, this, pardon the expression, prince will cry crocodile tears and repent. Everyone knows that our system is the most humane in the world. But we have no forgiveness for treason and there is no place for traitors in our land, nor should there be.

48

Readers enjoying the confidence of the Right People can receive special passes and rummage through the old files. There they will no doubt find the uncompromising, angry, and high-minded speeches of Academician Petin and Vadim Shornikov the writer, notices written by the well-known cattle butcher Terenty Knish and the illustrious kolkhoznik Alevtina Myakisheva. Using the same exact expressions (she seemed to have written with her left hand), they heaped shame upon the traitor-prince.

They say that many well-known people responded to the newspaper's offer to give this turncoat the rebukes he deserved in print. It must be said that these well-known people responded in a completely disinterested fashion because no fees were paid them for these notices and articles. But it just so happened that not long after their articles appeared, one of them received the Stalin Prize for scientific achievement, another's novel was suddenly published (till then not a single publishing house had accepted it because it was so dull), one received a deferment from front-line duty, another a warrant for extra rations. One way or the other a grateful motherland, in the person of the Right People, took care of everyone.

But, as the saying goes, there's always one bad apple. There was talk that a certain well-known figure from a region whose name was not recorded permitted himself to doubt. He was a young but highly advanced scientist. For all his learning, he did not give due respect to the doctrine of our Leader and Teacher, which states that no one is indispensable. He thought there were no rules without exceptions, that, although in general no one was truly indispensable, he nevertheless, personally, was.

So the Moscow newspaper called this indispensable person one morning and politely inquired if he had read the above-mentioned letter from the former nobleman.

"Yes, yes," he confirmed, "just last night at dinner . . ."

"So, Yuri Sergeyevich [that apparently was his name], our readers would like to find out your opinion as well in this regard."

"But why my opinion actually?" declared Yuri Sergeyevich.

"You know I'm no noble. My mother was a laundress and my father . . ."

The polite voice interrupted to say that, for him to express indignation at treachery, it was not the least bit obligatory to be a nobleman. All Soviet people, so to speak, were expressing their attitude unambiguously. Academicians, writers, milkmaids . . .

It was awkward in the extreme for Yuri Sergeyevich to set himself in opposition to other Soviet people. "Of course, it's not at all that I wish to refuse," he said, "but you see, I'm not familiar with the case. I don't know anything about it."

"But you've read our newspaper."

"Yes, yes, of course, I read the paper, but to speak out in print against a person whose guilt, as far as I can see, has yet to be fully proved, and who has not yet been tried . . ."

"Well, too bad, then," said the newspaper worker and hung up.

Yuri Sergeyevich's mood was spoiled. He could not get down to work. I must have insulted that editor, he thought. Perhaps he's a good man and called me out of the goodness of his heart and I . . . Yes, but I just can't write about a person when I don't have the slightest idea . . .

That same day Yuri Sergeyevich was summoned to the secretary of the Party organization of which he was, as a non-Party man, not a member. The secretary seated him in a soft armchair and began to express his bewilderment that he did not wish to have his say in print in regard to the prince. "You are a Soviet man, aren't you?" the secretary asked him, looking him straight in the eye.

Yuri Sergeyevich ardently affirmed that, yes, he was a Soviet man.

"Personally, I believe you," said the secretary, letting him know that faith in him was now in short supply. "All the more reason I cannot understand why you are taking that prince's side. What do you have in common with him?"

"What was that?" The scientist was thrown for a loss. "Just why should I have anything in common with him?"

"So then how do you want your behavior interpreted? After all, at a moment when the entire public is speaking out decisively against the prince, you are trying to avoid doing so."

"I'm not avoiding it," said the scientist. "I'm completely ready. All I want is to acquaint myself with the facts of the case before I speak out."

"I don't understand," said the Party organizer, now a bit angry. "This isn't enough for you?" He showed him the newspaper clipping he had prepared beforehand. "Here, academicians, writers, leading workers, all writing. And you, you don't believe them?"

"I have no basis for not believing them, but before I speak out, I need to personally acquaint myself with the facts. You see, if someone asks me what it's all about, I wouldn't even know."

"All right, then," said the Party organizer. "Clearly we don't see eye to eye. I see that not only don't you trust the authors of those letters, you don't trust our Party press, which means you don't trust our Party. With views like those you'll go far."

The Party organizer must have had a crystal ball. Our scientist in no time had gone as far as Kolyma, in a prison train. He might have ended up in the national guard but his bronchial asthma and extreme nearsightedness did not permit him to expiate his guilt to the motherland in that fashion. In Kolyma he pushed a wheelbarrow, and for a while, he was in that capacity truly indispensable.

49

At the beginning of October 1941, Admiral Canaris received the following report from his personal agent:

In Dolgov the organs of the NKVD have uncovered a major conspiracy directed by a certain Ivan Golitsyn, a representative of one of the most aristocratic families of old Russia. As I have already reported, for a certain period prior to this, the so-called Chonkin gang had been operating in this district. Authoritative sources think that Chonkin and Golitsyn are one and the same.

The local authorities and the propaganda organs are trying to play down the scale of the conspiracy, but, judging by the measures taken, they are themselves treating this matter with the utmost seriousness.

The newspapers are full of multiple allusions, veiled threats, calls for vigilance, increased discipline, loyalty to the Soviet system, and invocations of mass patriotism.

Vociferous meetings are being held in the kolkhozes, state farms, local industrial enterprises, schools and kindergartens, with hysterical demands for reprisals against the rebels.

Judging by the rumors circulating among the population, a large portion of the region's territory has been hit by riots.

The authorities are taking urgent measures to liquidate the after-effects of the conspiracy. No less than two special NKVD motorized units have been brought into the city and a tank brigade has been stationed in a nearby forest. In the city there has been an epidemic of arrests among the ruling Party elite, beginning with the First Secretary of the District Committee of the Communist Party, Andrei Revkin.

Decisive measures have been taken to pacify the rebellious population. Thus, for example, the inhabitants of the village of Krasnoye, the site of Golitsyn-Chonkin's headquarters, have all been deported to Dolgov and quartered in the local elementary school, which has been surrounded by barbed wire and turned into a temporary prison (in addition to the already existing non-temporary one). According to rumors, everyone, except for children under twelve, is slated for the most severe punishment. (According to Soviet law, children over twelve are fully responsible to the law, on a par with adults.)

An airplane, of outmoded Soviet construction, with one wing missing, which belonged to the conspirators, is being exhibited to the public on one of the city's central squares.

To the best of my knowledge Prince Golitsyn is a representative of White émigré circles and of the exiled Tsarist family, operating on instructions from the German high command. If this is so, I am extremely surprised, dear Admiral, that Colonel Peckenbrock did not trouble to put me in contact with Golitsyn-Chonkin at the appropriate time, for, working in communication, we could have operated much more effectively.

Judging by newspaper reports, information drawn from the instructions issued to Party propaganda workers and other sources, the chief aims of the conspiracy were a wide-ranging uprising of the local population against the soviets (mainly exploiting dissatisfaction with the kolkhoz system), seizure of the territory, and the holding of it until the arrival of German troops.

The conspirators were close to their goal when a tragic misfortune befell them. However, I do not believe that all is yet lost. Moreover, I think that the district is in an extremely favorable situation for our troops to deal it a decisive blow. That situation is conditioned by the following factors:

1. The front line in the sector in question has been greatly weakened by the Soviets having to withdraw a portion of its troops to crush the rebellion.

2. Politically, the population is fully prepared for a change of rule.

3. A significant number of people with initiative, followers of Golitsyn now under arrest, can serve as a strong nucleus for the creation of institutions of self-rule, rear-line units, and local police departments. With their help, we can further develop and consolidate the successes achieved by our troops.

50

A theatrical presentation, *The Trial of Prince Golitsyn,* was being readied at the Dolgov Railway Workers' House of Culture. An open trial behind closed doors. Admission free, with a pass.

CHARACTERS AND ACTORS
Prince Golitsyn—Ivan Chonkin
State Prosecutor—Prosecutor Evpraksein
Chairman of the Court—Colonel Dobrenky
Members of the Court—Majors Tselikov and Dubinin
Court Secretary—an old, fat sergeant; no name
Defense Counsel—a member of the local Board of Attorneys
Pseudo-witnesses, pseudo-experts, pseudo-spectators,
and other pseudos anticipated as well

In the center of the spacious, well-lit stage stood a long table covered with red cloth, and three high-backed oak chairs. In the left corner of the stage, behind a wooden partition, Ivan Chonkin was sitting on a stool, playing the role of Prince Golitsyn. He was clearly unsuited for the role of a prince, not having changed in the least. Short, puny, lop-eared, wearing an old Red Army uniform, he was sitting with his legs spread apart and twisting his shorn, knobby head left and right. Nevertheless, there was a guard on either side of him. They, too, were so lop-eared and bowlegged that either of them could have replaced Chonkin or he either of them and no change would have been apparent.

Prosecutor Evpraksein, seated at a small table between Chonkin and the large table, had put on his glasses and was looking through the papers which lay in front of him.

On the other side of the stage, the court secretary and the counsel for the defense sat at equally small tables.

The defense counsel, a weak-sighted, hunched, shabby man

in a suit that had been turned (the buttons were now on the left), kept twisting his head like a rooster, his left ear touching the edge of the table; he was writing something with a flourish on sheets of paper torn from a notebook, his hand moving jerkily across the paper. He had obviously decided to play out his role in its full glory, to astonish the audience with his eloquence; playing the great courtroom lawyer, a sort of local Plevako; from time to time he would glance over at the prosecutor, his neck would twitch, and he seemed to wink as if to let his opponent know that he should reconcile himself beforehand to defeat. While the defense counsel was staring at the prosecutor, his hand slipped off the paper and he finished writing his sentence on the tabletop, another time it even went off the edge of the table.

Not fully understanding why he had been brought there, Chonkin kept turning his head and gazing curiously at the prosecutor, the defense counsel, the guards, and the audience, which was gazing curiously back at him.

The audience was disappointed. It had expected to see a prince, someone with a mustache and a big, ugly face, someone ferocious-looking in a Circassian fur coat with bandolier pockets, or in a White Guard uniform with spots from the torn-off epaulettes and crosses that had not yet faded away. But that was no prince in front of them; the devil only knew what that one was.

51

The directors were in the wings (just as they should be before a première): Major Figurin, Colonel Luzhin, and a dry little old man with a small, clipped, gray mustache wearing a shabby coat. Outwardly he looked like some, say, bathhouse attendant or hotel doorman, but he was neither a bathhouse attendant nor a hotel doorman; he was a general who had come from Moscow to observe the trial. His hands held behind his back, with the sort of quiet voice only high officials know how to employ, he was at that moment issuing final instructions to three actors who had not yet appeared on the stage—the chairman and the two members of the court.

Alexei Mukhin, the children's writer, was loitering just inside the wings. His assignment was to relate in print, graphically and intelligently not only for "our kids who love reading" but for adult readers as well, the story of the stern, unbiased, and just trial of a base traitor to the motherland.

Having concluded his instructions, the general looked over at Luzhin to see if everything was ready. Luzhin looked over at the major, the major nodded to Luzhin, Luzhin nodded to the general, the general nudged Colonel Dobrenky in the stomach and said, "All right, begin."

52

Three men came out onto the stage from the wings. The first, Chairman of the Assizes of the Military Tribunal, Colonel Dobrenky, was carrying a file. His face was puffy, his nose purplish, his eyes small. Behind him came two members of the court, two majors, a pair of scowlers, Tselikov and Dubinin.

SECRETARY (*solemnly springing to his feet*): All rise! Court is in session!
(*The chairs rumble as they are shoved back and everyone rises. The three take their places at the long table, the* CHAIRMAN *in the center, one member of the court on either side. The* CHAIRMAN *lays the file in front of him and unties the cord binding it.*)
SECRETARY: You may be seated.
CHAIRMAN (*after a short pause, now gazing at the audience*): We shall hear the case against Golitsyn, Ivan Vasilyevich, accused of betraying the motherland, counterrevolutionary sabotage, anti-Soviet agitation, and other crimes. The defendant

should now rise. (CHONKIN *remains seated, thinking someone else has been addressed.*) Defendant, I'm speaking to you. Rise!

CHONKIN (*poking his chest with a finger*): Me?

CHAIRMAN (*smiling*): Certainly not me. (*Sternly*) Rise. (CHONKIN *rises, holding on to the partition rail with both hands.*) The defendant will state his first name, patronymic, and last name.

CHONKIN: Mine?

(*Laughter in the court.*)

CHAIRMAN (*in anger*): This is not a circus here. This is a session of the Military Tribunal. I advise you not to play the fool and to answer all questions clearly. Your last name?

CHONKIN (*uncertainly*): Used to be Chonkin.

CHAIRMAN: And now?

CHONKIN (*after a moment's thought*): I don't know.

CHAIRMAN: What do you mean you don't know? During the preliminary investigation you stated that you were Prince Golitsyn, enemy of the people, henchman of White émigré circles and international capitalists. Do you confirm your testimony? (CHONKIN *does not reply.*) Defendant Golitsyn, do you have any objection to the composition of the board? No? Be seated! (*To the audience*) The court will now hear the bill of indictment.

53

Every performance is preceded by rehearsals. Perhaps that is the reason Chonkin turned out to be a poor actor, he'd been put through too much agony. Very important investigators had been sent from Moscow and had worked on him in shifts. They interrogated him for many days in a row, not allowing him to sleep or eat. The blinds had been drawn and the lamplight was a constant irritating yellow, and so he never knew when it was day or night and lost all sense of time.

The interrogators kept hammering away with the same

questions: Who had sent him? What was his assignment? Who were his contacts?

Seeing that none of his answers could satisfy them, Chonkin began to answer all questions with the same phrase: "Who's supposed to know, knows." In the course of the interrogation he aged and grew emaciated; sometimes he would drop off to sleep while being questioned, other times he would lose consciousness. They would slap his cheeks, douse him with water, set him up on his chair, and again begin asking him who, where, when, codes, passwords, and secret addresses. Then Chonkin, barely able to make his rough, dry tongue move, would repeat dully, nonsensically: "Who's supposed to know, knows." The investigator would say, "Very stubborn," and even the most imperturbable of them would fly into rages, shout, stamp their feet, use their fists, and even start spitting. One of them, at his wits' end, fell to his knees in front of Chonkin. "You damned tyrant, you, if you don't pity yourself, at least have pity on me. I'm a family man."

Chonkin's torments ended when Major Figurin took charge of the case again. Having examined the situation, Figurin had Chonkin fed and brought tea, treated him to long cigarettes, which made Chonkin sweetly dizzy, and spoke to him nicely, man to man: "Unfortunately, Vanya, not all our workers are saints. It's the work they do. Sometimes it makes you cruel without your knowing it. And besides, the people who end up here do not always evaluate things soberly, they don't always have a correct sense of what is demanded of them. Let's say we bring in a man and we say to him, 'You are our enemy.' He doesn't agree, he objects, 'No, I'm not.' But how could that be? If we arrest a man, naturally he hates us. And if, on top of that, he considers himself innocent, then he hates us twice as much, three times as much. And if he hates us, that means he's our enemy and that means he's guilty. And so, Vanya, that's why I personally consider innocent people our worst enemies."

Major Figurin had no desire to compose a long list of lies

and nonsense about Chonkin. "I am not an adherent of such methods. In my work I use facts not conjectures. So, you were sent to the village of Krasnoye by your commander, right?"

"Right."

"You were given a rifle, cartridges, put in an airplane, and dispatched to Krasnoye, right?"

"Right."

"And so that's what we'll write down. 'Upon receiving the assignment from my command I was issued a rifle and ammunition and air-routed to the village of Krasnoye. Correct?"

Chonkin shrugged his shoulders—it sounded correct.

"Let's keep going. You were left alone, just standing there was boring, you started looking around, you spotted Nyura, you helped her in the garden, you had a few drinks together, you spent the night, later on you got to know some of the other villagers, you talked with them about one thing and another. You were interested in their lives . . . I'm not mixing anything up?"

"No."

"All right, then, we'll make a note: 'Upon my arrival in the locale of my forthcoming activity, I conducted visual observation, formed connections, established contacts, entered into an unlawful relationship with Belyashova . . .'"

"Hey, hey!" Chonkin, smelling a rat, was alarmed. "What's this unlawful business? I didn't force her to, she agreed."

"I'm not saying anything of the sort," said the major. "What I have in mind is that you and she did not register a marriage. Is that true or not?"

"Oh, that." Now Chonkin understood. "Yuh, that's true."

No, realized Chonkin, it isn't true what they say, investigators aren't all the same. Major Figurin was better than the others because he didn't shout, stamp his feet, raise his hand to you, and ask idiotic questions; he wrote everything down like it was, though to tell the truth he did use some tricky words which had a kind of sinister sound to them. And as for what the major added on about the world bourgeoisie, émigré circles, former landowners, and capitalists, Chonkin knew educated people wrote about those kinds of things in the newspapers, talked about them at meetings, and his political instructor Yartsev was always saying them over and over again at political training.

The major behaved well with Chonkin and Chonkin behaved well with the major. On every sheet of paper given him he wrote out as neatly as could be *Chonkin*. That at least he could do right, and the major kept praising him: "Good work," he'd say. "Just fine." And then each time he would add the name Golitsyn in parentheses.

The play went as planned, following exactly the script prepared beforehand.

Summoned onto the stage, the expert witnesses examined the material evidence—a rifle model 1891/30 and the warrant for the arrest of the accused. Having read the results of the dactyloscopic, ballistic, and chemical analysis, they demonstrated irrefutably that the perforation in the warrant had been caused by a bullet fired from the rifle in question, which, at the moment it was fired, was being used by the accused.

The experts were succeeded by the witnesses, escorted into the courtroom by guards.

Witness Gladishev stated that the accused, from the very moment he had arrived in Krasnoye, had caused trouble; he had lived licentiously, abandoned his post, begun cohabiting with the postwoman Belyashova, conducted provocative conversations, allowed the destruction of a garden possessing inestimable scientific value, and resisted the authorities. The witness had been unaware that Prince Golitsyn was concealed behind the mask of Private Chonkin, but the defendant's behavior had caused him to suspect that he wasn't one of them, not a real Soviet person, especially since Red Army soldiers just could not act like that.

Revkin's testimony aroused special indignation in the audience. He admitted that while a member of a secret Trotskyist group he had seized the post of Secretary of the District Committee, that acting under the direct orders of the accused, he had systematically undertaken the destruction of the Party's cadres and done everything possible to disrupt ideological-political work among the population. With the aid of people he had positioned in key places, he artificially caused a constant slump in crop yields, a decrease in the productivity in cattle breeding, and pursued a course designed to impoverish the collective farm peasants in order to set them against the Soviet system.

Witness Hans Filippov, who had penetrated the NKVD on orders from German Intelligence, constituted the direct link between the accused and the high command of the Third Reich . . .

While Filippov was being examined, Major Figurin received a phone call and learned that the Chanters had finally arrived. The Chanters had been expected on the morning train, which had been detained en route, and it had not been clear whether or not it would arrive at all.

Postponing the pleadings, the summations, and the passing of sentence to the following day had been considered but had proved unnecessary.

The major reported the news to the general, who said: "Very good, go give them their instructions . . ."

Figurin found the group of young people sitting on the chairs along the wall in the corridor by his own reception room. An experienced eye could immediately detect that these young people were from the capital—they were a bit more free and easy than people usually were in institutions of that sort or institutions of any sort for that matter.

The group consisted of nine people—eight young men and one young woman, who wore a beret at a jaunty angle. A cheap cigarette dangled from her lips bright with lipstick. She was flirting with the young man sitting beside her. He had a beard, a small mustache, and hair long enough to get himself thrown in jail in those days.

"Hello, comrades." Figurin greeted them as he approached. The ragtag group responded discordantly.

Figurin inquired as to their leader. The young man with the beard and long hair rose and Figurin invited him into his office.

In the office the young man presented his papers and Figurin explained what was what, then phoned the director of the Railway Workers' House of Culture and ordered him to receive this newly arrived group of nine during the recess, to give them the opportunity to familiarize themselves with the auditorium and to cooperate with them in preparing their work positions.

54

The director, a small, fussy man, greeted the group respectfully, a note pad in his hands, his face expressing his readiness to render them any service.

After shaking hands with the director, the young man with the beard introduced himself as Fyodor Shilkin and, pointing to the others, said: "And those are my people."

The group fanned out through the auditorium, which had been cleared for the recess. Shilkin sat down in the front row, two others sat at a certain distance from each other in the fourth, one took the seventh row, two the tenth, the girl with the beret the thirteenth, and the last two took the sixteenth.

"All right." Shilkin rose and looked back at the auditorium. "Everyone in place? Good. Ready! Lyusa, stop smoking! Let's go! One and two!"

They all jumped to their feet, and to the director's great surprise (a real provincial, he had never seen anything like it before), they began clapping their hands and chanting in chorus:

Masha ate Sasha's kasha!
Masha ate Sasha's kasha!

They repeated this chant a few more times. Then, leaving his place, Shilkin moved about the auditorium, listening attentively to the chorus from each position. He waved his hands. "That's it, thanks, guys. Thanks to you too," he said to the director. "Of course the acoustics are nothing to rave about, but it doesn't matter, we'll manage. Please reserve those places for us."

"Yes, of course," said the director, dutifully making a note on his pad.

Their rehearsal done, the group headed off for the cafeteria to cash in their travel coupons.

55

In Moscow, Leningrad, and perhaps in other large cities where the theater thrives, there exists a special class of citizens known as fans. No theatrical performance of any distinction, be it opera, ballet, or drama, can manage without the collaboration of fans. They gain entry to every première, respond boisterously to well-delivered lines, applaud loudly, and shout "Bravo" or chant the names of their stage idols. There are fans who love everything and also those who favor one theatrical art over the others. They can be divided into Lemishists, Kozlovists, Kachalovists, Yablochkinists, Ulanovists, and so on, depending on which idol they are devoted to. Fyodor Shilkin was an Obukhovist. This does not mean that he paid no heed to other performers, no, as an objective connoisseur of opera, he recognized greatness in quite a few, but his heart belonged only to the mezzo-soprano Obukhova. Fedya was proud of not having missed a single opera or concert sung by his favorite in Moscow (at times he would even follow her on the road). He never failed to bring flowers to each performance, which, on his meager salary (Fedya held an insignificant position in an insignificant office), cost him dearly. He always wore the same old patched suit; sometimes he did without lunch and sometimes even without dinner, but he never failed to appear with a bouquet at Obukhova's every performance. The flowers were carefully chosen, but there were always roses, carnations, or, at the very least, dahlias.

Fedya would not shout or clap his hands during a performance or concert. He would sit decorously and wait for the performance to end. But, during the curtain calls, when the performers came out to take their bows, Fedya would be transformed. He would run right up to the stage, crouch like a beast of prey, then hurl his bouquet like a grenade to the feet of his favorite singer. Sometimes, Nadezhda Andreyevna would pick up his bouquet and gaze out into the hall, to see who deserved her roving smile. That was almost more than Fedya could bear.

"Bravo!" he would cry. "Bra-vo!" He would clap his hands and wriggle. "Bra-vo! Bra-vo!"

The people beside Fedya looked at him oddly, thinking him some sort of nut. But Fedya, red from his exertions, his eyes bulging, would twitch and chant her beloved name, "O-bu-khov-a! O-bu-khov-a!"

An electric field was created around him and people near him would gradually be carried away and begin chanting along with Fedya. Fedya himself admitted that, in those moments when he was running up to the stage, flinging the flowers and chanting, he experienced that superior delight a man can know from love or vodka.

Fedya's changeless and selfless devotion to art and to Obukhova personally were finally rewarded; Nadezhda Andreyevna noticed him and singled him out from among her admirers. The story spread how, one rainy night, leaving the theater after the performance through a crowd of patient fans, Obukhova ran her eyes along their delighted faces until she found Fedya's, and then, smiling to him alone, she said: "Fedya, be so kind as to fetch me a cab."

Entering the taxi with an armful of flowers, pushing away the fans pressing around her, Obukhova took a postcard with her picture and did not merely sign it as she usually did but printed distinctly: *To Fedya from Obukhova.*

Fedya framed the postcard, hung it in his room, and was always ready to tell all his neighbors, relatives, and friends for the thousandth time the story of her autograph, how he had been standing by the stage door, how Obukhova had come out, how her eyes had sought him out, how, with a smile, she had asked him (Fedya did a very accurate imitation of her intonation), "Fedya, be so kind as to fetch me a cab."

Fedya's career was interrupted in a most unexpected manner. He lived in those romantic days when the Right People were waging a ceaseless struggle for a bright future. Having destroyed the exploiter classes, having triumphed over the bourgeois parties, having finished forever (or for a good long time) with all forms of opposition, they began striking at smaller hostile groups—numismatists, philatelists, Baptists, Esperantists, and Solitarists. Finally the fans' turn came as well. One fine night, nearly all of them were dragged out of bed and taken off with no idea that their destination was the Lubyanka.

The fans vanished, Fedya among them. Just to be on the safe side, Fedya's mother tore up Obukhova's picture and flushed it down the toilet.

The theaters grew boring. No, naturally the life of the theater went on. People bought tickets and filled the halls, the actors came out on stage and played their parts, but the atmosphere wasn't right. A certain explosive quality was gone, a certain high elation; the audiences clapped listlessly, flowers seldom fell on the stage, no one mobbed the stars after the show, which even drove some of them to drink. Sadly Obukhova would tell her relatives, friends, and acquaintances of the days when she was hounded by fans, one of whom, the most devoted, had once fetched her a cab.

Suddenly a rumor flew through theatrical circles—Fedya was back. He had been seen in the Bolshoi Theater sitting in the second row. The people on stage were playing various roles—distinguished milkmaids, shepherds, swineherds, creators of new breeds of cattle, and specialists in livestock. The performance was entitled *The All-Union Conference of the Foremost Figures in Livestock*. They made speeches and, identifying with their roles, they promised to achieve unheard-of successes in the production of meat, milk, wool, eggs; as soon as possible, in all categories, they intended to overtake and surpass the most developed capitalist countries. (In the course of the conference, the Presidium received a telegram from one patriotic young mother who had just named her newborn twins Overtake and Surpass.)

When the conference was over and a resolution had been passed to send a letter of greeting to the Central Committee and to one certain comrade personally, and the toasts and ovations had begun, rhythmic cries could be heard in the hall, not loud and clear at first, but then growing mightier and mightier, until in a few seconds everyone was on his feet, chanting: "O-ver-take U.S.A.! O-ver-take U.S.A.!"

Thereafter the activity of Fedya and his group was approved by the higher spheres and the entire group was put on the staff of the Institution under the code name Chanters. The group proved absolutely indispensable. No conference, rally, or meeting of any significance could manage without the Chanters, and when the newspaper accounts noted in small print *Stormy applause. Everyone rose and applauded such and such*, this was the work of Fedya and his group.

Naturally, certain fans (those who had been spared by chance in the raid) held the Chanters in contempt, considering them betrayers of high art. Some of what they said reached

Fedya's ears, but he dismissed it with one wave of his hand, saying that true art serves the people directly and that he, Fedya, derived more aesthetic pleasure from Alevtina Mya-kishev's solemn promise to milk two tons of milk per year from every cow than from any aria elegantly performed by any celebrated songstress from the big city.

56

During the recess Pavel Trofimovich Evpraksein had lunched and taken his usual hundred and fifty grams of vodka to steady himself. He had been assigned the role of state prose-cutor (the military prosecutor who was supposed to play the part had been taken ill). He hadn't wanted to, but he had submitted. What could he do? He had a Party card in his pocket and a family at home.

The night before, on the other hand, having drunk a bit too much, he raised hell at home and even sketched out a resolu-tion: *The accusations made against the defendant are not sup-ported by the materials of the case. As a prosecutor I am lodging a protest and as a Communist I am leaving* . . . He wept, he beat his chest. "I won't be a bastard anymore . . ." He swore to turn in his Party card "like Vanka Golubev." In the morning, however, he got up in a different mood, burned what he had written the night before, cleaned his suit and shoes, then set out to discharge his duty.

During the morning session he had thought while reading his speech: So what. If I don't do it, somebody else will. It's curtains for him anyway, why should I go down with him? From time to time he would glance over at Chonkin, and a few times their eyes met. The defendant seemed to be looking hopefully at him and that worried Evpraksein. Don't you be waiting or hoping, he answered Chonkin's eyes in thought. You were ready to go under, so go under; you don't have to pull other people along with you. Maybe your life's not worth a kopeck to you, but I've got a family, kids, I have no intention of making them orphans, and when it comes right down to it, I'm not obliged to be any hero. This isn't my idea, they gave me orders, I'm carrying them out. Anyway, I don't know who you really are. If you're not a prince you shouldn't have signed everything they stuck in front of you. But since you did sign and since you did admit you're a prince, there's no reason to play dumb, so answer with dignity.

Chonkin continued to irritate Evpraksein by his appearance and his insolent behavior, especially when he tried to use his right to question the witness for his own personal ends. At the fateful phrase "The state prosecutor will now speak," the prosecutor rose, and to stall for time, began spreading the papers out in front of him; he felt his hands trembling, his knees shaking, and an unpleasant aftertaste in his mouth, which lately had been happening to him every time he did something his conscience opposed. Now that part of his brain which was governed by fear of the higher-ups was sending his organism orders of one sort, while another part was sending orders of another sort, and the cells or nucleic acids or some other such thing in there, not knowing which to obey, collided with each other, causing an abnormal heartbeat, a trembling of the extremities, and a repulsive taste in his mouth.

"Comrade Judges!" he said, without raising his eyes. Hearing the sound of his own voice helped restore him. "The prosecutor's role in the present case is extraordinarily complex and important. Before us is a person who has encroached"—the prosecutor swallowed—"on that which is most"—he spoke slowly as if hypnotized—"precious to each of us, our state, our motherland, our new life."

Now he felt better. The part of him ruled by fear of higher-ups had taken the upper hand, while the other part was on the defensive and retracting its orders.

"And although our investigative branch has conducted a most painstaking analysis of all the defendant's actions, fully exposed their roots, which fed the noxious tree of his crimes with poisonous sap . . ."

"Speaks well, doesn't he?" Luzhin ran over to the general in the wings.

"Not bad." The general nodded.

"O-o-o-o," stuttered Mukhin the writer.

"What?" said the general, surprised.

"Outstanding."

"Aha," said the general.

". . . The great October Socialist Revolution not only established a new political system, it also produced the most profound changes in the social structure of our society. Like a mighty, refreshing wind it raced throughout the vast expanses of our land and tossed out the landowners, capitalists, and other exploiters of the working class like so many slops. Supported by the party of Lenin and Stalin, our people set about the building of a new, free life . . ."

The prosecutor kept glancing more frequently at Chonkin, who sat, small and repulsive, turning his shorn and knobby head, no bigger than a fist, one way, then another. The defendant's repulsive appearance comforted the prosecutor and inspired him with a sense of confidence in his own righteousness.

Chonkin sighed and tried to listen to the prosecutor, but, exhausted by days and nights of interrogation, he could not concentrate on the achievements enumerated by Evpraksein: collectivization, industrialization, Dneprogress, Papanin, and Polina Osipenko . . .

". . . But, as our great leader Comrade Stalin teaches us, with the establishment of the dictatorship of the proletariat, the class struggle not only does not abate, it grows even more acute. The exploiter class, smashed and thrown overboard from the ship of history, will never reconcile themselves to their defeat. They"—the prosecutor pointed his finger straight at Chonkin—"have already attempted and are still refining their attempts aimed at the restoration of their obsolete order."

The prosecutor now seemed to have mastered both himself and his audience.

"The event which occurred in Krasnoye a few days before the outbreak of the war can serve as a striking example of Comrade Stalin's brilliant foresight. I will venture to remind you of precisely what did occur. One sunny summer day the inhabitants of Krasnoye became witnesses to an unprecedented event. Past the outskirts of the village, not far from the post-mistress Belyashova's house, an airplane with Soviet markings made a forced landing. The villagers, naturally, gathered at a run to have a look at this unparalleled wonder. Even Chairman Golubev, now unmasked as an enemy of the people, came to see it. Our people love our army and its airmen, Stalin's falcons, and naturally the people of Krasnoye treated the pilot with respect. It entered no one's mind, the chairman included, to check the supposed pilot's papers. However, displaying criminal gullibility, the chairman invited the pilot to his office and put an official telephone at his disposal, which the pilot used to effect immediate contact with his headquarters. Then, another aviational vehicle appeared above the village, bearing as its passenger of honor our defendant, on special assignment . . ."

At that point, overcome by sleep, Chonkin again found himself in Krasnoye, young, good-looking, and full of life. The sun was shining, the grasshoppers were chirping; he felt like eating, drinking, singing, smoking, answering nature's calls, and in the most varied ways breaking the regulations concerning guard and garrison duty. He broke them all, he chased after girls who drove by on a wagon, he shouted something to them and they shouted something back to him; then he approached Nyura, spoke to her, and she spoke to him, but some sort of loud, metallic voice kept interfering, speaking the devil's own nonsense: ". . . issued a weapon, ammunition, he entered into unlawful relations with Belyashova by air . . ."

Knowing that Nyura could vanish any second, Chonkin tried to enter into some of those unlawful relations with her right then and there. She wasn't against it, she played around with him, tickled him, and then, happy as could be, Chonkin broke into a smile.

But then that same metallic voice invaded his ear: "He then not only mocked the Marxist theory of the origin of man but is, at this very moment, laughing at Soviet justice."

"What insolence!" said someone, and Chonkin woke up.

He did not remember all at once where he was, who all the people were, and who that terrible man was, pointing a long finger at him.

Pausing until the audience's indignation at the defendant's behavior had subsided and until the defendant stopped fidgeting on his stool, the prosecutor took a sip from the glass of water in front of him and continued: "I, personally, Comrade Judges, am against hypocrisy in sexual matters. I will not condemn Belyashova for entering into intimate relations with a man she had just met for the first time in her life. In evaluating her frivolous behavior, one must take into account that she had encountered an obstinate foe . . ."

Chonkin was overcome with drowsiness again. His head kept bobbing, he fell off his stool, woke up, bugged out his eyes, fell back asleep, then woke up again. Dream and waking mingled, the prosecutor turned into a devil, then into a wood goblin, then into a bird, a frog, a scarecrow. The guards, the judges, and the spectators turned into monsters who would first be sitting in their places, then evaporate and reemerge gurgling in some sort of swamp, making horrible faces.

"Comrade Judges! On July 3, with enormous spiritual excitement, we all heard Comrade Stalin's historic speech on the radio. The residents of Krasnoye heard it, as did the defendant. He could not help but see what a profound impression the heartfelt, unforgettable words of our beloved leader made on these people. And—to eradicate that impression, he undertook a most cunning and, I would even say, a most original maneuver. He let Belyashova's cow into the garden belonging to the kolkhoznik Gladishev, the well-known Michurinite and breeder who, by the way, has also now been unmasked as an enemy of the people. In that manner the defendant killed two birds with one stone. First, with the aid of the cow, he destroyed Gladishev's scientific achievements, and second, he deflected the kolkhozniks' attention from the great national problems. With what goal did this criminal come to our parts and what did he wish to achieve?"

The prosecutor turned from a crocodile into a raven, which flew up onto a branch, cleaned its feathers, and cried out: "In order to understand the motives, the secret mechanism of this or any other crime, one question must first of all be answered: Whom does the crime serve? We can answer that question easily enough if we recall who this so-called Chonkin proved to be, to what class he belongs, and whose interests he represents."

The raven flew off the branch, turned back into the prosecutor, and took a sip of water from the glass.

"Our investigative organs have established that the cover of Private Chonkin concealed a sworn enemy of our way of life, a representative of the high court aristocracy, Prince Golitsyn. And just who are the Golitsyns? The founder of that family was once the Prince of Novgorod and Ladoga. Countless serf-owning landlords and reactionaries descended from him. As far back as 1607, one of the defendant's ancestors directed the suppression of a popular uprising. Another was three times a pretender to the Russian throne, the only serious rival to the founder of the Romanov dynasty, Tsar Mikhail. Over a span of three hundred years, the Princes Golitsyn occupied the most important positions in the Tsar's court. And so I pose this question: It is an accident that a representative of this particular family turned up in the village of Krasnoye on the eve of the war? And, to answer my own question, no, it was no accident. Marxist dialectics teach us that there is nothing accidental in nature. All phenomena occurring in the world are interrelated, flow from one another, and influence each other."

Dazzled by his own eloquence, the more the prosecutor said, the more he believed his own words, and he no longer saw an innocent victim in front of him but a sinister figure who held the invisible threads of a worldwide conspiracy in his hands.

"Utterly defeated, White Bandits of every stripe from Kerensky to Denikin did not settle down, they did not lose the hope of seeing their estates, plants, and factories returned to them. Supported by the international bourgeoisie, Hitler's Fascism, and Japanese militarism, nurturing plans to restore Tsarism, counting on the aid of hidden enemies of the people, entering into the underground of Trotskyists and the remnants of the kulak class, exploiting the dissatisfaction of all those Revkins and Golubevs, and exploiting as well the dissatisfaction of the individual shortcomings and difficulties which do exist here and there, they sent the defendant here as their emissary. As a representative of the higher rungs of the hierarchy of the nobility, he, more than anyone, had a stake in the restoration of Tsarism, and perhaps, he even"—the prosecutor gasped from a thought which had started to occur to him earlier, from a sudden intuition which frightened him but which he could not restrain—"and perhaps he even . . . he even desired to become Tsar himself!" the prosecutor cried out rapidly, shaking his fists and head, and then he sat down, stunned by his own discovery.

There was a roar in the auditorium like a wave dashing against the rocks.

The people backstage were drawn into the wings.

"What did he say?" asked the general in a whisper.

"He said that he"—Luzhin fearfully pointed a finger at Chonkin—"wanted to become the . . ."

"Tsssaaar," stuttered Mukhin from behind.

The only sound in the courtroom's dead silence was the sweat-covered defense counselor tearing the draft of his speech into little pieces. Everyone was looking at Chonkin, who, woken by the sudden silence, looked back at them, unable to fathom where he was, where all those devils had come from, and why they were quietly staring at him.

"Comrade Judges!"

Having recovered from his discovery, the prosecutor rose to continue his remarkable speech.

Meanwhile, the general had dashed off to the Right Place and sent a coded message "upstairs": *During the court examination Prosecutor Evpraksein has irrefutably established that defendant Golitsyn intended to declare himself Emperor Ivan VII.*

Traveling at the speed of light, the coded message reached Moscow, where it caused a new commotion. Generals and colonels began running like madmen up and down corridors. Comrade Lavrenty Beria was not in his office and was located in quite another part of Moscow, in some actress's bed.

The prosecutor had still not concluded his speech when a coded reply was received from Moscow: *I express my personal gratitude to Prosecutor Evpraksein. Lavrenty Beria.*

". . . The defendant and his foreign masters did not, in their filthy calculations, reckon on the fact that our people are dedicated to their system, their Party, and to the person of Comrade Stalin. They have no need of tsars, emperors, or frenzied führers. The defendant's actions found no support among the broad masses of the people. Our valiant Chekists, faithful to Dzerzhinsky's behests, stopped the pernicious activities of God's Anointed Sovereign in time, and his pitiful band of cohorts could not bring themselves to stand up alongside him.

Completely unmasked, he at first showed furious resistance to the special detachment sent to arrest him and then later to the regular units of the Red Army. Furiously resisting his fate, he cherished the hope, insane in his situation, of holding his beachhead no matter what, to hold out at any cost until Hitler's troops arrived.

"But it didn't work, ladies and gentlemen, it didn't work!" cried the prosecutor, turning to the judges. "And it never will."

Turning back into a devil, the prosecutor began enumerating the crimes committed by Chonkin: breaking guard-duty regulations, desertion, armed resistance, forcing people whose duty was to discharge official obligations to break those obligations, damaging a garden by criminal negligence, ill treatment of prisoners. He named the articles of the criminal code under which Chonkin, in wartime conditions and under aggravated circumstances, could be shot three or four times over . . .

"But," said the devil, waving his hoof, "this tangle of crimes, which would have sufficed to send an entire gang of bandits before a firing squad, was, for the defendant, only a prelude to his principal wrongdoing. Those wrongdoings have been provided for by the articles of the criminal code, which I consider necessary to quote in full."

The devil pulled his glasses down over his eyes, opened some black book, and began reading: "Article 58.2. An armed uprising or an invasion of armed bands with counterrevolutionary intent on Soviet territory, the seizure of power in the capital or in the provinces with the same intent and, in particular, with the intent of forcibly tearing any portion of territory away from the U.S.S.R. or any separate Soviet republic, or annulling treaties concluded by the Soviet Union with foreign governments, carries the highest measure of punishment, the firing squad, or being declared an enemy of the workers, with confiscation of property and deprivation of citizenship in both the Soviet republic and the U.S.S.R., and with banishment from the limits of the U.S.S.R. forever, with the assumption, under mitigating circumstances, of a reduction of a sentence to no less than three years' deprivation of liberty and the confiscation of all or a portion of property.

"Article 58.3. Dealings with a counterrevolutionary intent with a foreign state or its individual representatives and the abetting by whatever means of a foreign power which finds itself within the U.S.S.R. in a state of war, or warring against it by means of intervention or blockade, carries a penalty . . .

"Article 58.4. The rendering of any aid whatsoever to that portion of the international bourgeoisie which, not acknowledging the equality of the Communist system which has replaced the capitalist system, strives toward its overthrow . . . carries a penalty . . .

"Article 58.5. The disposing of any foreign state or any social group within it, by means of relations with its representatives, toward a declaration of war, armed intervention in the affairs of the U.S.S.R., or other hostile activities, in particular, blockades, seizures of state property of the U.S.S.R. or the Soviet republics, the breaking off of diplomatic relations, the breaking of agreements concluded with the U.S.S.R., and so on, carries a penalty of . . .

"Article 58.8. Committing acts of terrorism carries a penalty of . . .

"Article 58.10. Carries a penalty of . . ."

. . . Chonkin was walking along the bottom of a ravine beside a brook babbling over the rocks. He could hear some words amid the babbling . . .

". . . the aggregate of acts committed, taking into account the aggravated conditions of wartime . . ."

He bent down to the brook for a drink and saw a face. He thought it was his own reflection, but looking closer saw that it was the prosecutor's.

It was hard to hear and Chonkin plunged his head into the water, but it was not the prosecutor he saw but Nyura, who, now a water nymph, was beckoning him to her, batting her eyelashes and fins. She was saying something to him.

"What?" asked Chonkin.

"Dive," repeated Nyura. "Dive in."

He dove in. Nyura seemed close by, right in front of him. With sharp strokes he tried to swim nearer to her, but she went deeper and farther away from him. Nyura beckoned him on and he yielded, though he realized he wouldn't be able to make it back to the surface.

Ah, what's the difference, he said to himself, and opened his mouth wide.

The water gushed into his mouth and gurgled into his lungs, turning into air bubbles, and to his joy, Chonkin discovered that this water was as breathable as air, if not better, and now, reassured, he began swimming alongside Nyura like a fish.

"Good?" asked Nyura, tickling him lightly with her fin.

"Good!" he said, tickling her.

"And do you admit your guilt?"

"I do."

"And can you talk devil talk?"

"No," he admitted. "I can't."

"But I can." Nyura laughed, and making a mischievous face she began to mutter away in devil talk: "Communism, capitalism, Fascism, idealism, cataclysm, workers' movement, peace movement . . ."

"Bowel movement!" cried Chonkin, delighted that he, too, had remembered a devil word.

They both began laughing, plunging deeper, turning over and over. Chonkin kept shouting, "Bowel movement! Bowel movement!" and suddenly he saw that the water had divided into two streams. Nyura was in one stream, he in the other, and the distance between them was increasing fast. Chonkin's stream was bearing him toward a steep rock. Through the roar of the waterfall behind the rock he again heard:

". . . the highest measure of proletarian humanism . . . a firing squad . . . of all his property . . . no place on our earth . . ."

Falling off his stool, Chonkin managed to grab hold of the partition rail and slammed his foot against the floor. At that very moment the audience burst into applause and a long-haired devil with a little beard ran up to the stage, bulged out his eyes, and began howling: "Breath entrance! Breath entrance!"

Chonkin was amazed. What did "breath entrance" mean? Then he saw and heard that it was not only the devil with the little beard who was shouting but others as well, standing farther back in the hall. Then everyone in the auditorium jumped from their seats and began shouting: "Breath entrance! Breath entrance!" and only then did Chonkin realize that they were not shouting "Breath entrance" but "Death sentence."

57

Mukhin the writer dashed over to Pavel Trofimovich in the wings and began shaking his hand and stuttering: "Co-co-co-congratulations! Fir-fir-fir-first-rate!"

Major Figurin walked over and shook his hand in silence.

Colonel Luzhin walked over and smiled. "Your speech was monstrously interesting."

The general approached, neither offering his hand nor smiling but, in a squeaky voice, he said, "On behalf of Comrade Beria, I am to convey to you his personal gratitude."

Other people came over as well, shook Evpraksein's hand and spoke to him. Only one person, Colonel Dobrenky, quitting his judge's chair for a spell, was about to express his displeasure at Evprakscin's ad libbing, but learning that those ad libs had pleased Lavrenty Pavlovich Beria himself, he changed his position at once and he, too, offered his congratulations most energetically. The prosecutor accepted the congratulations, but he was gloomy, replied in monosyllables, and lighting one cigarette after another, listened with only one ear to the defense counselor, who was speaking after him.

"Comrade Judges!" he began with excitement, "a lawyer's duty consists of defending his client. Because of the nature of my profession I have had occasion to defend thieves, burglars, rapists, and murderers. And no matter how grave the crime of my client I always found mitigating circumstances of one sort or another for his actions. But, Comrade Judges, a Soviet lawyer is, first and foremost, a Soviet man. And as a Soviet man and a Communist, my present client's actions stir my profound indignation. Yes, I am a defense counselor," he said, raising his voice, "but when I see such a heinous criminal, I have an involuntary urge not to defend him but to defend our people, our country, and our state from him. And it is precisely with the aim of defending all our fighting men that I absolutely support the prosecutor's demand and believe that there is no punishment which could even begin to approach the defendant's appalling crimes."

58

The lawyer sat down. The assessors began moving their chairs, the audience began fidgeting in their seats, the prosecutor took a sip of water. Colonel Dobrenky, averting his face, blew his nose resoundingly and, folding his handkerchief in four, announced: "The court will now hear the defendant's final statement. The defendant will rise. What do you wish to say to the court?"

Chonkin rose, his hands grasping the upper edge of the partition. There was a great deal he wanted to say, but he could not say anything. Having little confidence in his mental abilities, he thought that the people who would now decide his fate were guided by something beyond his understanding.

Even before this he had never known which of his actions or inactions would cause what effects, why he was punished or why he was rewarded. In time he had come to a rather hopeless conclusion—no matter what you say, no matter what you do, this, that, or the other, it all turns against you in the end.

"Defendant," said Dobrenky warmly, "I will explain your rights to you. You can attempt to refute the prosecutor's conclusions, you can challenge certain accusations, you can say something in your own defense."

Chonkin said nothing. What could he say in his own defense? That he was still young and hadn't seen life yet, that he had not yet enjoyed enough food or water or freedom or lovemaking. He had no sense that he was a miracle unique in nature, that a whole world would die with him. Possessing a practical, unegotistical imagination, he knew for a fact that nothing around him would change with his disappearance. The sun would continue to rise and set, day would be followed by night, winter by summer; it would rain, grass would grow, cows would moo, goats would bleat, and people would ride horses, sleep with their women, guard airplanes, and, all in all, do what they were assigned to do. It would have been easier on him had he seen Nyura even just once in all that time. She would have told him her news and he would have learned that his seed had taken hold in her, had sprouted, and something tadpole-like had begun its cycle of mysterious development in order finally to become a human creature, maybe bowlegged, maybe lop-eared, but resembling Chonkin.

"Defendant," said the chairman, to make his presence known, "are you going to say anything or not?"

"Please forgive me," said Chonkin, barely moving his lips.

"Now look what he wants, us to forgive him," cried out a pseudo-human from the audience.

Another one, almost the same but a bit better, elbowed him in the belly and said loudly: "Shut up, dog meat."

These two unexpected outbursts seemed to destroy the

solemnity of the moment. All heads turned in the direction of the noise. The one who had shouted second was pale, regretting that, without wishing to, he had acted human.

"The court will adjourn to deliberate on the passing of sentence," announced Dobrenky, rising.

59

Han's dispatch had been received by Admiral Canaris on Tuesday. That same evening, at a regular meeting with the Führer centering on a discussion of Operation Typhoon (the plan to seize Moscow), Canaris reported on Hans's dispatch from Dolgov. Hitler took an unexpected interest.

"Who is he, this Russian?" asked Hitler.

"The Princes Golitsyn come from one of the most ancient branches of the nobility," explained Canaris.

"I realize that," interrupted Hitler. "I'm asking is this man yours?"

Canaris thought that Hitler was somehow displeased and he answered quickly that Golitsyn was not among his agents.

"A shame," said Hitler. He jumped up and began darting about his office. "Nevertheless, gentlemen, this is an excellent symptom. I don't believe anything of this sort has happened before."

True, nothing had. Counting on the might of his armed forces, Hitler had not foreseen that the Russian people would resist so stubbornly. He had been certain that Russians dreamed only of casting off the yoke of Communist slavery. He thought they would come out to welcome his troops with bread and salt. Like every dictator, Hitler was not only cruel, he was sentimental. While planning the extinction of various peoples, deep down he wanted those very people, Jews, Gypsies, Poles, Russians, to love him as their liberator. He could not understand why the Russians did not rise up against the Bolsheviks and why they did not come out to greet his troops.

"Gentlemen!" Stopping in the middle of the room, he raised one hand high, to let it be known that he was making a historic decision. "I think we ought to help this Russian. We don't have the right to leave him alone in his misfortune. And we"—he stretched his index finger out horizontally—"we will help him."

"But, my Führer, I repeat," said Canaris, "I don't know who he is. He's not listed among my agents."

"My Führer," interjected Himmler, who had not yet spoken, "there are other agencies at work in Russia besides Canaris's."

"You mean that this . . . what is his name? . . . Golitsyn . . . is your man?"

"I must check that out, my Führer." Himmler smiled benevolently.

Naturally Himmler did not think that the mythical prince was in his service, but seeing that the Führer was about to launch a new venture, he decided not to waste time climbing aboard. Canaris realized what was happening and so did Hitler, but, carried away by his new idea, he was glad of Himmler's indirect support.

"Remarkable!" Hitler kept repeating as he walked around the room, waving his arms. "Astonishing! Superb! Guderian! Where are our tanks now?" he shouted.

Colonel General Guderian rose, straightened his uniform, and glanced at his watch, as if waiting for the precise moment of which he spoke: "At the present moment, my Führer, my tanks are in the district of Kashira; having broken through the Russian cover detachment, they are now heading straight for Moscow."

"Turn them toward Dolgov!"

"What?" The word came flying from Guderian's mouth.

Brauchitsch's head jerked up. Colonel General Halder pulled in his head. Only Keitel continued to sit as imperturbably as before. Even Himmler looked over apprehensively at the Führer, but then immediately lowered his eyes.

"But, my Führer . . ." There were tears in Guderian's eyes. "It's only eight hundred kilometers to Moscow. My tanks can burst into the capital on the run."

"And your tanks will burst into Moscow on the run. But first let them take Dolgov and set that poor prince free. It would be truly ignoble to leave him there in trouble. As a Christian I could never forgive myself."

A terrible commotion arose. All the generals sprang to their feet and were shouting, interrupting, and shoving each other: "My Führer! My Führer! My Führer!"

"Silence!" Hitler slapped the palm of his hand against the table and then shook it in pain. "Silence, all of you! One at a time. What is it? Are you displeased?"

"My Führer." Field Marshal Bock spoke first. "In the current conditions, when our troops are so close to Moscow . . ."

"I understand that, Bock, and I'm telling you we can always take Moscow."

"But I think . . ." Brauchitsch approached him.

"Enough!" said Hitler irritably, whacking the table again. "The time for you to think was before I made my decision. Now your only obligation is to carry it out. Why are you all standing there? You are all dismissed."

Like schoolboys at recess the generals and the marshals dashed for the open doors, crowding together and almost knocking each other over. Only Hitler and Himmler remained in the room. Hitler was still darting about the office, waving his arms and shouting.

"Nothings! Zeroes! Gnats! 'I think.' Who are you to think! You've decked yourselves with medals and epaulettes and now you think you are really strategists, generals. But, in one second I could strip all that from you and you would be naked! Paltry, stupid old men with flabby bellies!"

Himmler was sitting in an easy chair observing his leader's hysterics with an easy smile.

"But, my Führer," he said, with that easy smile, "it's not

worth your while to get so angry with them. A dozen mediocre minds can never comprehend a single thought from a genius."

"Are you flattering me?" asked Hitler, turning quickly to him.

"Yes, my Führer," said Himmler, and they both burst into merry laughter.

60

They say that by October there was total panic in Moscow. No one knew what was happening at the front, no one was working, no one was obeying anyone. The situation at the train stations was beyond belief. People besieged the cattle cars and the suburban trains on the tracks; any direction was good as long as it was away from the city. People fled on cars, motorcycles, horses, bicycles; they went on foot, pushing their belongings in wheelbarrows. The metro was not working. Stores and banks were closed: you could just go in and take whatever you found. Works by Marx, Engels, Lenin, Stalin, and other such authors were piled by the rubbish heaps. Hungry dogs abandoned by their masters wandered among those volumes, sniffed them, and turned up their noses, yelping sadly.

Neither military patrols nor police were to be seen on the streets, the District Committees and the District Executive Committees were not functioning, there was no authority.

They say that the Germans could have taken the Russian capital that day with their bare hands.

Why didn't they?

The vast literature on this subject contains no few contradictions and, at times, some highly original opinions. Some consider weather conditions the cause, others oppose that view with the moral-political factor—mass heroism—which, of course, did exist. One occasionally even hears mention of the personal merits of one of the secondary characters in this present work. I have in mind here the man who lived in the metro. We won, they say, because he was with us.

To tell the truth, the author has spent long years following the skirmishes of historians with a grin of bitter irony. How many thousands of words have been spoken, how many forests cut down for paper, how many chips went flying in vain, when the truth was right there at hand?

No. I will not completely deny the merits of the man who lived in the metro. He did his part too—he smoked his pipe, he soiled his globe with a greasy finger, indicating where a division was to be hurled and the best way to annihilate the troops. But he wasn't with us. He was down in the metro, having left us to fend for ourselves up on top of the ground.

However, if one is to speak not just of common merits but of outstanding and decisive ones, then we now know that they belong to the principal hero of our modest tale who, in that fateful hour, diverted Guderian's tanks toward himself and thus saved the capital. So what if he was on the short side, lop-eared and a bit bowlegged? For if we examine everything conscientiously, and not in feverish haste, we will see that the man who lived in the metro was in no way better than Chonkin. That man was a meter and a half tall in his service cap, his face was pitted from smallpox, he had a withered hand, a forehead two inches wide, and crooked, yellow teeth. And in spite of those glaring weaknesses he has gone down in history and been portrayed in countless books either as a mountain eagle or as a perfect pig.

In concluding this present passage, we express the hope that now, when complete clarity has been shed on this complex historical problem, this old polemic among various schools and tendencies will, having lost all apparent reason for being, cease of its own accord.

Having fulfilled the mission entrusted him from above, the author will now modestly step aside.

61

General Drinov received an unexpected promotion. The army of shock troops, joined by Drinov's division, lost half its men and then broke out of the encirclement. The commander was arrested for failing to hold Kashira, and Drinov was assigned to his place. With the remains of that battered army he was supposed to hold the approaches to Moscow. Not an enviable position. The countryside was flat and devoid of all vegetation except grass. The new commander ordered his troops to dig in and wait for the Germans to appear. German tanks came the next morning. Drinov's army had four antitank guns—one was defective, one had no ammunition—and a 45-millimeter cannon, but no shells for it. It was futile to resist. But Drinov had received an order: "Not one step back," and he intended to carry it out. The tanks were advancing in line formation. One antitank gun yapped, then fell silent, struck by a German shell. The other one managed to put one German tank out of action, but that was the end of the ammunition. Then Drinov decided on a desperate step. He drew himself up to his full height and yelled: "For the motherland! For Stalin! Hurrah!" Brandishing his pistol, he began running straight for the tanks.

Carried away by his passion, the soldiers followed him, the distance between them and the tanks diminishing swiftly.

Then suddenly (the things that can happen) the tanks stopped. The huge, iron monsters stood without moving and, as if unsure what to do, swung the muzzles of their cannons back and forth.

Drinov's soldiers stopped as well, so confused that no one even thought of hitting the ground.

Suddenly, obviously having received a radio command, all the tanks simultaneously made a 180-degree turn and took to their heels.

Everyone was stunned.

"Good God, what's happening?" marveled an old Red Army man near Drinov, crossing himself, not believing his eyes.

"Ah, the rats, they turned yellow," shouted Drinov, and ran after them with his pistol.

When Alexander Krivovaty, a *Pravda* correspondent, learned of all this from eyewitnesses (he could not have seen it himself, for he preferred to describe heroics from a comfortable distance), he phoned in an urgent report to his paper.

The next morning, reading through the papers, Stalin came upon this article.

"What unmitigated nonsense!" he said, and ordered Malenkov to telephone the editorial offices and to have correspondent Krivovaty told on his behalf that he was lying and that he had better stop. Malenkov returned in a state of surprise and said: "Krivovaty swears that this time he did not pretty things up one iota, that it's all true." Malenkov called front headquarters and they, too, confirmed that it was all true: stopped by Drinov's army, Guderian's tank group had retreated and contact with them had been lost.

Stalin ordered that Major General Drinov be made a lieutenant general, recommended for the title of Hero of the Soviet Union, and brought to the "underground dacha" for a private conversation.

Needless to say, all three orders were executed at once.

62

Drinov did not arrive at the underground dacha alone but as part of a group of generals, all of them distinguished in one way or another.

They were taken to a closed metro car, and each of them was subjected to a body search in the guard room.

A small hitch occurred—a flat metal object emitting a ticking sound was found in the pocket of one general's tunic. When questioned about the purpose of the object, the general explained that it was a captured enemy cigarette case which opened only at certain timed intervals. The general wished to make a present of the case to Stalin, who, he had heard, had been smoking too much lately.

"Open it!" ordered the commander of the guard, a lean Georgian with two bars in his lapel.

"Unfortunately, that's impossible," explained the general, smiling. "That is precisely the principle on which it operates. The time of each opening is determined within the case itself."

The commander of the guard turned the case over in his hands and looked the general searchingly in the eye. "When is the mechanism due to work again?"

"In about fifteen minutes, I think," said the general uncertainly, with a glance at his watch. "I meant to time it so that at the exact moment the gift was presented to Comrade Sta . . ."

"So, at that very moment?" asked the commander of the guard, staring at the unfortunate general.

"Yes, I thought . . ."

"But why are you so upset?" interrupted the commander of the guard.

"I'm . . . I'm not upset," babbled the general, his voice completely crushed.

While this conversation was occurring, several guards dispersed about the room, their submachine guns held ready and aimed at the generals.

The commander of the guard walked over to the telephone, dialed a number, and, without removing his eyes from the suspect general, had a brief conversation with someone in Georgian.

"Bachevadze!" Hanging up, he addressed one of his subordinates and, again saying a few words in Georgian, handed him the cigarette case. The guard, seizing the case with one hand, and holding his submachine gun slung over his back with the other, left the room in a hurry. It grew quiet. The generals, instinctively separating themselves from their suspect colleague, stood in the middle of the guard room, huddling together like sheep. None of them said a word. One general, a short, fat man, was breathing heavily, and something could be heard wheezing and gurgling in his throat. The fat man was the first to give in to the tension and glanced at his watch. His comrades followed, lifting the sleeves of their tunics and glancing at their own watches.

"It'll be opening any minute now," the owner of the case said all of a sudden, but without much confidence in his voice, to the commander of the guard.

The commander did not reply and looked at his own watch again.

His subordinates stood near the walls, their feet planted apart and their weapons ready, though now the barrels were held a bit lower.

Encouraged, the owner of the case walked over to Drinov. "It'll open in a minute," he said to Drinov, who turned away.

Later, this foolish general would tell people that, even knowing the cigarette case was just that, a cigarette case and nothing else, he nevertheless experienced an inexplicable fear that the cigarette case, despite its very nature, might still explode.

The door opened, Bachevadze returned. In one hand he held the opened case, stuffed with Herzegovina Flora cigarettes. The commander of the guard took the case from him, turned it back and forth in his hand, laid it on the table. Then he announced to the generals that, accompanied by the duty officer, they could proceed on to Comrade Stalin.

"Now may I take the case?" asked its owner.

"Leave it for the time being," said the commander of the guard.

"But I wanted to give it to Comrade Stalin as a present."

The commander of the guard looked over at him and pronounced slowly: "Comrade Stalin does not like gifts like that."

The guests were escorted to a small room where they were asked to take off their topcoats and to line up according to height. As soon as they had done so, the lights went out, then came right back on. Dazzled, the generals saw before them a plain-looking little man in a soiled broadcloth uniform without any insignia of rank. The little man was sucking on a pipe that had gone out and, his faded mustache twitching, was running his tenacious, guarded gaze along the generals' faces. At first the generals were surprised; who could this be? and then they were struck by the sudden realization. Drinov, the first to size up the situation, roared out as if on review: "To our great military leader, Comrade Stalin, hurrah!"

"Hurrah! Hurrah! Hurrah!" roared the generals.

The greeting clearly pleased Stalin, especially since it had not been rehearsed. The leader loved sincere proofs of love. He smiled at Drinov and then at the group as a whole; then, clamping his pipe in his yellow teeth, he jokingly stuck his fingers in his ears to show how he might have been deafened; then he began to clap his hands. Of course the generals followed suit. Drinov, in ecstasy that Stalin had smiled directly at him, applauded frenziedly, like a little boy at a stadium. Stalin noticed this and again smiled at him alone. The clapping went on a good while. Then the master of the dacha cut it off, letting it be known that he considered their resounding applause a sufficient expression of their love for him personally, and, through his person, for the Party, the government, the people, the motherland, and every birch tree in its boundless expanse. Having halted the applause, Comrade Stalin walked in front of the formation and began thrusting his wrinkled hand toward each man to shake.

"So that's you!" he said, walking up to Drinov.

Out of fear Drinov overdid the handshake. The great leader grimaced in pain and cast a suspicious glance at Drinov. But he at once understood that the general had not done it with any terroristic motives but from a plentitude of feeling and, with a grin behind his mustache, Stalin said with a marked accent: "So there's still some strength left in our muscles, Comrade Drinov?"

"Yes, sir, Comrade Stalin!" said Drinov, not looking at his face.

"Yes, sir?" Stalin asked quickly, with a certain surprise. "What are you, Comrade Drinov, an admirer of Tsarist army expressions?"

"Absolutely not!" barked Drinov, then stopped short, blushed, and turned pale, sensing the end of his military career.

Stalin said nothing. He looked with silent curiosity at Drinov, watching his changing face.

"Why absolutely not?" Stalin said suddenly, and smiled again. "We don't have to renounce what was good in the Tsarist army. Maybe we ought to bring back certain of the good traditions from the old army. Do you agree with me?"

"Yes, sir!" responded Drinov, no longer the least apprehensive.

Drinov's behavior and outward appearance so pleased Stalin that he asked him to remain after the general reception to have a talk with him alone. They spoke of the overall situation on the different fronts and the situation in the sector controlled by Drinov's army. Drinov answered every question in military fashion, brief and precise. Stalin asked him about his background and Drinov said that he was from a simple peasant family.

"So, you're a peasant by birth?"

"Yes, sir, by birth," answered Drinov.

Further discussion revealed that Drinov's grandfather had been one of Prince Golitsyn's serfs.

"How about that!" marveled Stalin. "By the way, we recently unmasked one of your former masters." The thought of the Prince Golitsyn case improved Stalin's mood. "Tell me, Comrade Drinov, would you like to become one of Prince Golitsyn's serfs again?"

"What are you saying, Comrade Stalin," objected the general, then grew confused, thinking that it was perhaps in this sense that the great teacher wanted to return to the old traditions (in that case Drinov would naturally want to become one of Prince Golitsyn's serfs again). But Stalin had a different thought in mind and was again pleased by Drinov's answer.

"Right, Comrade Drinov," said Stalin. "But now certain princes think that the Russian people dream only of ending up as their serfs again. I suppose, from the political point of view, we ought to raise one ordinary man dedicated to our system and our Party because we, after all, have opened the way to the future for him. And among simple people I think there are quite a few true heroes who would not begrudge their lives to make our nation stronger. Isn't that so, Comrade Drinov?"

Drinov was quick to agree. Then Stalin asked him to name one simple soldier, preferably of peasant stock, who could serve as an example of selfless service, of true heroism, to the motherland.

"I know one like that, Comrade Stalin."

It must be said that Chonkin's courage had been much to Drinov's liking. It made Drinov uncomfortable that he had not shown sufficient firmness and had turned the soldier over to the Right People. He wanted to tell Stalin about Chonkin, but still he had his doubts.

"So who is it, then?" asked Stalin. "I see something's bothering you."

"Yes, sir, there is, Comrade Stalin."

"So just what is it?"

Here goes nothing, thought Drinov. "Here's the thing, Comrade Stalin, there's this soldier, Chonkin, Ivan . . ."

"Chonkin, Ivan?" repeated Stalin. "Very good. A simple Russian name. And so what has this Ivan Chonkin done?"

Drinov told him everything. Chonkin was at his post, his unit was sent to the front, and in the pandemonium Chonkin was forgotten. He was frequently told that he could quit his post, but he could not and did not want to break the regulations. He stood guard without being relieved many days in a row. He ran out of rations but he stayed at his post. He ran out of rolling tobacco but he stayed at his post. His boots wore through. Still he stayed at his post. Once his post was attacked by an armed detachment consisting of seven men, and Chonkin took all of them prisoner.

"One man took seven armed men prisoner?" Stalin was thunderstruck.

"Hold on a second, Comrade Stalin," said Drinov, rather boldly. "Listen to what happened next. A regiment was hurled in to aid the detachment. Chonkin was asked to surrender but he refused, accepted battle, and fought to his last bullet."

"To his last bullet," Stalin repeated pensively and wiped away a brimming tear with the palm of his hand. "He was killed, of course?"

"No, Comrade Stalin, he only suffered a concussion."

"He was taken prisoner?" Stalin frowned.

"Absolutely not, Comrade Stalin. You see, the point is that it wasn't a German regiment."

"Then whose was it?" asked Stalin in surprise.

"Mine," said Drinov, risking all.

"What? Yours?"

Drinov related the details. Stalin loved the story; he kept laughing and slapping his thighs. He found especially funny the part about the reconnaissance team seizing a prisoner who subsequently turned out to be a Soviet captain (Drinov omitted mentioning that Captain Milyaga was executed and why). Laughing till he cried, Stalin's mood grew so expansive that he even invited Drinov to join him for dinner.

"Chonkin." He kept trying out variations on this favorite new name of his. "Private Chonkin. Soldier Chonkin. By the way, soldier sounds much better than Red Army man or fighter. Comrade Drinov, where do you think his name comes from? Could it be from the word 'CHON'?"*

"You're asking me?" answered Drinov, not knowing which hand to use for the knife and which for the fork, and afraid of doing it wrong.

"Eat whatever way's best for you," said Stalin, pouring his guest a glass of vodka from a moisture-beaded decanter. "No, I don't think it's from the word 'CHON.' I think it has a more ancient origin. Comrade Drinov, let's drink to the health of a simple Russian soldier Ivan Chonkin."

63

His coat crumpled under him, Chonkin was curled up on a bunk waiting for his sentence to be executed, abandoning himself to unhappy thoughts. Could it have even entered his mind that at that very moment Stalin himself was rising to drink his health?

Having dismissed Drinov, Stalin set to work on current business; in turn he saw four people's commissars and two factory directors. He spoke to the front commander by phone, discussed the construction of a new airplane, issued instructions concerning the evacuation of a major machine-building plant, scrutinized the details of a plan for the creation of partisan units, signed lists for honors and executions, dictated a telegram to Churchill, and it was only at four in the morning, after a glass of kefir, that he got into bed. Drifting off to sleep, he remembered General Drinov's story and again began to think about Chonkin with warmth and love.

"Chonkin! Chonkin!" he murmured, falling off to sleep, smacking his lips, savoring the name.

* CHON—acronym for Special Assignment Troops, whose function was to suppress peasant uprisings.—Trans.

Then he dreamed about Chonkin. In the dream Chonkin was enormously tall, like the hero of a Russian epic poem, with long blond hair and a clear gaze in his light-blue eyes. Brandishing a club, Chonkin was smashing all his enemies while Hitler himself, the coward, was running around on all fours, looking like a nasty dog in a political cartoon.

The same evening Stalin met with Drinov, Hitler received a telephone message that Guderian's tank group had forced a crossing on the river Tyopa and had begun Operation Golitsyn.

Hitler went to bed in excellent spirits. He dreamed of Prince Golitsyn, an enormously tall epic hero with long blond hair and a clear gaze in his light-blue eyes. He was riding a white horse, carrying a white banner fastened to the long shaft of his lance. The prince was followed by a vast army of long-bearded peasants wearing bast sandals and peasant coats belted with rope. Raising their right arms, the peasants exulted and cried: "Heil Hitler!"

64

The evening after the trial, the end of the case was celebrated in the District Committee dining room. The local leaders and their wives and members of the assizes attended. The general, Luzhin, and Figurin were also invited, but did not deign to appear.

Colonel Dobrenky chaired the festivities as he had the trial, but, of course, the hero of the evening was Pavel Trofimovich Evpraksein. Everyone knew whose personal gratitude he had received; everyone congratulated him, asked about his health, his wife and children. Borisov's wife, Manka, sat beside Evpraksein, made eyes at him, and rubbed her knee against his. After each toast, she bent over to Evpraksein and pressed her full bosom against him, which would have excited anyone except for a complete dunce.

But she did not excite Evpraksein (though he was no dunce;

who knows, that part of his life had always been a total mystery). In any case, Manka's appeals met with no response this time, and Manka, as well as the other women there that evening, decided that the prosecutor had simply lost his head over the good fortune which had descended upon him or, perhaps, worse still, had grown conceited.

But, of course, it was not a matter of his growing conceited; he was gloomy right from the start, and he would rise mechanically when they drank to Stalin, to victory, whatever. He drank a lot, took very little food with his vodka, and in his mind's eyes, saw nothing but the small red-eared man whose numbed lips were barely able to move enough to say: "Please forgive me."

The gramophone was playing "On the Hills of Manchuria" and Colonel Dobrenky sang: "Oh, you, Galya, Galya so young." Then they sang "Khaz Bulat the Bold," "The Little Box," and one other song. Manka Borisov exerted herself more than the rest and screeched till she had tears in her eyes. Then they danced to the gramophone while the prosecutor sat in his place, drank, stared at some point in space, and saw nothing before him except for Chonkin moving his lips: "Please forgive me!"

Afterwards no one could recall exactly when and how the prosecutor left. His wife, Azalia Mitrofanovna, stated that when he arrived home in the middle of the night she noticed nothing unusual about him. Of course, his coat was unbuttoned, he had lost a few buttons along the way, a strap had been torn off, his right side was covered in chalk, and his right cheek was scratched, but none of those were firsts. But, if the truth be told, he did act a little oddly. He did not rant and holler; on the contrary, he made an effort to be quiet, he removed his boots and foot cloths in the front hall, walked barefoot to his desk, turned on his lamp, and sat down to write. Whenever he was drunk he wrote letters and statements of some sort, but he usually hollered and beat his breast and threatened to do something right then and there, but this time he did not say a word. Once he raised his head and Aza glimpsed a tear running down his cheek. She began to grow worried and was about to ask what was wrong, but did not, afraid to rouse the beast in him.

He continued writing, and as was later discovered, these were variations on a single thought: *I request that Chonkin's trial be considered invalid* (crossed out) *Please consider my speech invalid* (crossed out) . . .

He kept writing and crossing out, balling up the papers and tossing them under his desk, but finally he grew tired and let his head fall onto his arms. Calmer now, Aza dozed off. She thought she had only slept a short while, but when she woke up Pavel Trofimovich was no longer in the house.

Had Aza discovered the gun missing right away, she could still have rushed outside and even perhaps have averted the catastrophe (though that, of course, was unlikely), but it did not even enter her mind, as she later explained, that he would harm himself.

While she was lying in bed with her eyes open, thinking where her husband might have taken himself to, he was standing by the communal toilet with his loaded shotgun. It was dark and freezing cold. The wind had started blowing, grains of snow were falling from among the scattered stars. Everything had started to turn white.

"This is it!" the prosecutor kept repeating to himself. "Now this is really it!"

His decision was firm. He thought of what was to come without fear, calmly; nothing could stop him. He took his time.

He had read or heard somewhere that just before his death a person recalls his whole life from beginning to end, especially his childhood. He tried to remember something of his childhood, but nothing came to him except that he had been a fat and clumsy boy and that his nickname had been kielbasa in the Railway Institute, where he had been educated. He dimly recalled the years of his youth, when he, taller and thinner, wore a leather jacket, carried a Nagant revolver, arrested speculators, broke into the apartments of the bourgeoisie, and was a member of the armed groups who spearheaded the campaigns against the kulaks and others less memorable. He remembered the people he had either sent to prison or to the firing squad, and now it seemed that they all looked like Chonkin and were all moving their numbed lips asking to be forgiven.

But he had been acting in the name of the Revolution, he allowed no one to be forgiven, he allowed no weakness, demanding ever more sacrifices for the bright future which was always just a step or two away.

He forgave no one, he never weakened, he was always sacrificing someone, though never himself; he had lost all humanity, but still they kept saying, More, more. In time, he began to notice that he was not so much acting from a sense of duty, and not at all from any higher considerations, as simply from the fear of being accused of criminal spinelessness, that is, of being insufficiently cruel. So he strove to be sufficiently cruel and, just to be on the safe side, did more than he needed to. But his conscience kept gnawing away at him from within. He tried to drown it in vodka, but that didn't work. His life became pure torture and no court could have sentenced him to a worse punishment.

Resting his chin on the barrel of the gun, the prosecutor thought a while, muttered something, then shrieked, his face wet with tears.

All right, then, he said to himself. Enough! You failed as a human being, but to live like a crawling reptile, a worm, a cockroach, no, thank you.

To carry out his plan, he first needed to remove his boots. Just as he began, a heart-rending cough was heard from the outhouse, a door squeaked, and someone came out, lighting his way with matches.

"Who's there?" the man asked in a frightened voice.

The prosecutor did not reply. The person came closer and Pavel Trofimovich recognized his neighbor, Kurdyumov, the military commissar. He was in his boots and underwear, an overcoat flung over his shoulders.

"Trofimovich?" Kurdyumov said in surprise. "What are you standing out here for? You on a spree?"

"Yes, that's right," the prosecutor answered gloomily.

"With a shotgun?"

"Yes, that's right."

"Hmm, all right." The prosecutor's behavior seemed odd to Kurdyumov. "Weather's been unseasonably cold lately," he said, chewing on his lip. "Last year, I remember, I was still running around in my field shirt on Revolution Day, and now you shiver with your topcoat on, right?" Kurdyumov yawned, his mouth wide open.

The prosecutor did not reply. He stood leaning on his shotgun, looking past Kurdyumov. A cold tear detached itself from his chin and rolled down into his collar.

"But I still don't understand," said Kurdyumov, "why people don't realize the necessity of civilized behavior in communal places. There's plenty of holes in the bathroom, but they go and make their little piles in front of the door so that if you don't light your way with matches you'll step in some excrement. Trofimovich, as the prosecutor you ought to post an announcement that anybody who maliciously craps except where they're supposed to will be criminally liable. Eh, Trofimovich? Aren't I right?"

"Go to . . ." said the prosecutor through his teeth.

"What?" Kurdyumov had not understood.

"Go to hell, you bastard!" repeated Evpraksein distinctly.

"Aha," said Kurdyumov, and hunching his shoulders, he began moving away quickly. "Hey!" he shouted from somewhere in the dark. "You ought to get rid of that gun. You shouldn't go around with a gun at night!"

But the prosecutor could no longer hear him.

It's time! he said to himself. Enough! Enough! he repeated, resting his left boot tip on the back of his right boot. I enjoyed life, I had some good times, thank you and goodbye.

It took some effort to push off his boot; then, hopping on one foot, he unwound his foot cloth and tossed it aside. The wind snatched it up and bore it whirling away.

"There," he said, relieved, "and now it's quite simple."

Leaning on the barrel, he raised his right foot and inserted his big toe into the trigger guard. All that remained was to move that toe, only just move that toe, and everything would be settled instantly, once and for all. Surprisingly, he felt no fear, he was completely calm.

"All right, then," he said and, covering the muzzle with his chin, he tried to make his toe move, but nothing happened. The prosecutor did not realize immediately that his own toe was refusing to obey him.

"What nonsense," he muttered, and once again tried to make his toe move, and once again the toe would not obey. That was strange and surprising. He decided to move his entire leg, but his leg, bent at the knee, did not budge.

What's going on here? he thought, almost in a panic. Am I really such a coward, such a rag of a man that I cannot do what I want? But I'm ready, I'm not afraid, I'm completely calm.

"Ah!" he called out, as if he were chopping wood, and thrusting his shoulder forward, he made another effort of the will to make his leg move, but it remained motionless. His entire anatomy was revolting, refusing to carry out the orders sent it by the brain.

His inner efforts had made him warm and quickened his breathing. He decided to catch his breath, summon new strength, and lull the body's vigilance.

Now, he promised himself, now everything will be all right.

I just have to take myself in hand. I really am not afraid, not afraid at all, I'm ready. Nothing so terrible about death. Death is no calamity. Death is just nothing, emptiness.

He became aware that he was shivering, and his thoughts took a different turn. But what about other people? he thought. They're no better than me. They steal, they kill, they lie, they betray their closest friends, renounce their wives, children, and parents, and live out their lives without suffering one bit and die peacefully in their own beds. I'm still young and full of life, I could still do something. Why should I get the death penalty after all I've suffered? I want to live, I want to live! It doesn't matter how—like a bastard, a crook, a crawling reptile, a worm, a cockroach, just to live!

Then he knew fear as never before, he felt his entire body shake, and his foot, still in position, give an involuntary twitch. His big toe just managed to catch hold of the trigger.

"I don't want to!" he cried out hoarsely into space, trying to withdraw his big toe.

At that moment he lost his balance, his full weight came down on the trigger, and at the same time he covered the muzzle with his hands as if trying to hold back his death.

The fiery sphere blazed against his hands, pierced them, then jabbed resiliently through his chin. There was a dull cracking sound and a lilac-colored light began to shine and spread everywhere.

Pavel Trofimovich felt better than he had ever felt before. He felt that he was becoming a pool of water that was spreading, spreading, spreading, vanishing in the sand . . .

65

By the time people came running to the scene, everything had already been cordoned off by police and plainclothesmen. The prosecutor, his face disfigured, had toppled onto his back. His arms and legs were spread apart, the gun had rolled off to one side. There was a boot on one foot, the other was bare. Azalia Mitrofanovna stood beside him and, nibbling her lips, looked off to one side. Two policemen were measuring something with a long tape measure, another was taking photographs with a magnesium flash, the chief physician of the district hospital, Raisa Semenovna Gurvich, her notebook on the hood of the police car, was jotting down her conclusions by the light of a pocket flashlight. Major Figurin, wearing a new, tightly belted topcoat, stood with his legs planted apart, his hands crossed behind his back.

A fat police lieutenant elbowed his way over to Figurin. "Here," he said, handing him a piece of paper. "This was lying on his desk."

Figurin brought the paper up to his eyes, shining his flashlight on it.

"Drunken ravings," he said after scanning the paper, and then he put it in his pocket.

That paper was never seen again and its precise contents have remained a mystery. However, it was subsequently learned from Azalia Mitrofanovna that the suicide note consisted of a single sentence: *Please consider my life invalid.*

Thus, stupidly and ingloriously, did Prosecutor Evpraksein end his life, he, who, perhaps, had been born to do some good and who perhaps wished people well but did them harm. But, as the saying goes, he neither lived nor let live. Of course it is a pity that it all turned out the way it did. You may say, Why pity him, he was a prosecutor. Of course he was, no one's arguing that, but they all don't shoot themselves either.

66

Returning to his office in the Institution, Major Figurin spent considerable time on this affair. Colonel Dobrenky called him. He himself called Luzhin, who had left immediately after the trial. Then the new editor of the newspaper, Lifshits, arrived and asked to be seen in spite of the lateness of the hour. Lifshits wanted advice as to whether or not to run an obituary in tomorrow's paper and, if so, should it read "untimely demise" or "tragic death"?

"Tragedy?" said Figurin gloomily. "He died like a coward. He deserted at the most critical moment. Write something like this: 'He ended his life by suicide while in a state of deep depression caused by chronic alcoholism.'"

Figurin got practically no sleep that night. After Lifshits left he conducted a strategy conference.

It was going to be a tough day—execution of Chonkin's sentence and a separate trial for the remaining accomplices. It was decided to try the accomplices all together without a prosecutor, and to sentence them to an indeterminate period of exile in a remote region of Siberia.

The stationmaster had been summoned to the meeting and was ordered to prepare a special train during the night. The stationmaster swore that he didn't have a single car available.

"And you need an entire train!" he cried. "You're kidding me! Where am I supposed to get it?"

He was told, "Get it wherever you want. If the train is not ready by twelve hundred hours tomorrow, you'll be lying on the platform with a hole in your head."

The commander of the local garrison was summoned and ordered to bring all available military units to a state of battle readiness in case of any disorders and provocations, and to beef up the military patrols.

It was after three when Figurin returned home exhausted. To his sleepy wife's anxious question, why was he so late, he responded monosyllabically: Work.

He set his alarm for eight, undressed, and got into bed, having first placed his revolver under his pillow.

67

The alarm clock proved unnecessary. Some noise woke him and he saw Margarita, her face crumpled from sleep, her hair tangled, sitting on the edge of the bed, looking fearfully out the window.

"What's wrong with you?" he asked in surprise.

A distant explosion rattled their windowpanes.

"You hear that?" Margarita asked in a whisper.

"I hear it," he said, stretching. "Why are you so upset?"

Another explosion rattled the panes.

"Firing practice," explained Fedot Fedotovich.

"Are you sure?" she asked doubtfully.

"Absolutely," he assured her. "The Germans are still a long way off."

He rose, did a brief set of exercises, sponged himself with cold water, had a quick breakfast, then left for work.

He heard a few more distant explosions on his way. An old woman walking toward him kept crossing herself. Ignorance, thought Figurin, continuing on his way. He noticed nothing strange in the streets, but later he remembered that the streets might have been unusually empty for that hour.

Upon arriving at work, he was surprised not to find Kapa, his secretary, in the reception room. The drawers had been pulled out of the two desks, the wardrobe and the safe were open, there were papers strewn about the floor, some stamped SECRET and some even TOP SECRET. Figurin ran into his own office and gasped—his desk drawers and safe were also open, and his papers were strewn over the floor. It took only one glance to see there was not much left. Only on his desk everything was in its usual neat order: the little jars with the colored pencils, the marble inkwell, the marble paperweight, the desk calendar, the telephone book, the file marked CURRENT CASES and, on top of that file, two sheets of paper with typed text. These were secret phone messages obviously received during the night. The first read:

> In connection with the unexpected German breakthrough in your sector of the front and the possible seizure of Dolgov and surrounding area, and in accordance with instructions from the highest agencies, the sentence of Enemy of the People Golitsyn is to be carried out immediately. His accomplices to be dealt with as circumstances permit.
>
> *Luzhin*

The second message read:

> The Supreme Commander in Chief has ordered that Private Chonkin be brought immediately to Moscow, to be presented with a governmental award. I am charging you with the execution of this order.
>
> *Luzhin*

Both were marked with the time they had been received: 6:04. With no idea what any of it meant, Figurin shook his head. Then he spotted a third sheet of paper. In large, even, calligraphic print, the following was written:

> *Dearest Idiot Idiotovich!*
> I hereby report that I am leaving your office, having taken papers which I hope to put in good hands. With great pleasure I recall working together with cretins like yourself and your predecessors. True, the work was easy and pleasant. You must not be angry at me. After all, basically we were doing the same sort of work.
>   You would be wrong to think me a traitor to the motherland. I have never betrayed my motherland, Great Germany.
>
> *Kapitolina Goryachev*
> *(Code name "Hans")*
> P.S. I have a real name, too, but, alas, I cannot reveal it for the time being.

68

"What are these stupid jokes?" said Figurin. "Stupid jokes. Stupid jokes! Stupid jokes!" he shouted, jumping up and down and shaking his fists. Suddenly he ran out to the reception room and shouted: "Anybody here?"

There was no answer.

"Anybody here?" he shouted out in the corridor, and without waiting for an answer, he grabbed his pistol and started shooting at the ceiling.

The door opened and in came Svintsov, astonished. Figurin stopped shooting and asked Svintsov where everybody was.

"Everybody's taken off," said Svintsov, gazing at Figurin's pistol, which was issuing a slow, fine stream of smoke.

"What do you mean, taken off?"

"I mean they ran away," explained Svintsov.

"Where to?" said Figurin, realizing the question sounded foolish. "What's happening in the school, do you know?"

"The commander of the escort called. He says he's removing the guard and leaving. He says he's freeing all the prisoners."

"Freeing them?" Figurin's brows rose. "Whose decision was that?"

Svintsov shrugged his shoulders.

"All right, then," said Figurin, a bit calmer now. "Go back there and wait. I'll need you."

Figurin went back to his office and lifted the receiver.

"Comrade Figurin?" said the operator. "Can you tell me what's happening?"

"What is happening?" said Figurin. "Far as I can tell nothing's happening. Connect me with Borisov."

Borisov proved to be neither at home nor at work. Figurin called Dobrenky at the House of the Kolkhozniks, but he was not at his post either.

"Connect me with provincial headquarters," ordered Figurin.

The operator at provincial headquarters answered.

"Give me Luzhin!" ordered Figurin abruptly.

"Luzhin who?" she asked.

"*The* Luzhin."

"Ah, that Luzhin." The operator laughed. "One moment."

Why is she laughing? thought Figurin. They still must not know anything over there.

No one came to the phone for a long time and Figurin began clicking the button impatiently. He was about to give up when a voice said something very strange.

"*Stellvertreter des Militär-Kommandeurs, Oberleutnant Meier am apparat,*" the voice repeated.

Figurin set the phone down and thought a minute. Then he grabbed the receiver again and nervously clicked the button, but now there was no answer at all.

A few minutes later he went into the recreation room and found Svintsov sleeping blissfully on a bare wooden cot, his fist under his head.

Nerves of steel, thought Figurin with envy.

He shook Svintsov awake and ordered him to get ready to go.

"Go where?" asked Svintsov.

"Prison."

"Prison? Me?" asked Svintsov.

"Just listen." Figurin grinned. "You go to the prison, you get what's his name, Golitsyn or Chonkin or whoever the hell he is, if he's still there and leave town with him."

"And go where?"

"Anywhere east. On foot or with whatever you can find. Then somewhere along the way you . . . You know what I mean . . . while attempting to escape, understand?"

"You don't need a big brain for that," answered Svintsov. "That's simple enough."

"All right, then," said Figurin. "When you reach our people, you tell them that Major Figurin, loyal to his **duty** . . .

that's it, loyal to his duty . . . remained behind to destroy secret documents so they would not fall into enemy hands. Then I'll try to get out of here. But if I can't, I won't be taken alive. Understood?"

"Understood." Svintsov nodded.

"All right, Svintsov, let's say goodbye." Figurin walked over to Svintsov, put his arms around him, and kissed him three times. Svintsov stood at attention, turned his face away, and grimaced.

69

The road rose gently uphill. On either side was a lifeless expanse, something between steppe and desert, without bushes, a blade of grass, a grain of sand, a single stone: in the center of that smooth, unique expanse was a white, dusty road, endless, edgeless, which to all appearances went from one nowhere to another.

Chonkin tried to think but he could not remember how he happened to be on that road, how long he had been walking it, and why up the road and not down it. Either way he had no idea of what lay in store for him.

He was barefoot except for his puttees, which kept unwinding and crawling away like snakes: he thought about wrapping them back up, but one glance showed him it would be pointless; like two mourning bands fringing the road, the puttees trailed off into infinity.

Deciding to rid himself altogether of his puttees, he bent over and began unwinding them from the top, but there was no end of them from the top; they fell coiled into the dust and crawled wriggling away.

"Hey, you, get up!" he was told.

Chonkin raised his head and saw that he was still on the same road but it was no longer deserted; traveling in his direction was an endless column of silent wayfarers who looked like prisoners of war. He straightened up and started walking with them.

"Hello!" said one of them beside him.

Chonkin looked over and saw an actual devil with horns, a tail, and fur thick with dust. Looking closer, Chonkin saw it was Samushkin, his old nemesis from the army.

"Going far?" inquired Samushkin without, it seemed, any special interest.

"No place special," said Chonkin.

"Perhaps you'd like to join us?"

"Where are you going?"

"To hell, of course, where else?"

"Oh, sure," said Chonkin. "That's what I always wanted, to be cooked in a frying pan."

"You fool!" Samushkin shook his horns indignantly. "That's just slander put out by our enemies. Why should we fry sinners, our own people? Of course, if we got hold of a righteous man, we'd fry him good, but you're no righteous man. For example, how many lives have you taken?"

"Me?" Chonkin looked at him in astonishment. "Me, a murderer?"

"No? Not even one man? In your whole life?"

"Not even one."

"Is that so!" muttered Samushkin. "But of course you stole, right?"

"Happened once," admitted Chonkin. "There was this sack of millet in the kolkhoz . . ."

"Stealing from the kolkhoz doesn't count. So tell me," said Samushkin hopefully, "did you ever sleep with married women?"

"No," said Chonkin, after a moment's thought. "Never had occasion to."

"Then you're a fool," said Samushkin, vanishing.

All the people and the road vanished with him.

Suddenly he saw Colonel Dobrenky and the assessors sitting before him on high-backed chairs at a large table covered with a white tablecloth.

"And who is this one?" asked Dobrenky sternly.

One of the assessors looked into a thick book and said: "God's servant Ivan Chonkin. He has come as sentenced by the military tri . . ."

"I know, I know," interrupted Dobrenky, smiling. "Well, Ivan, God's servant, tell me what you've brought here with you, what good did you do in the life granted you?"

"None," said Chonkin, after sorting through the memories of his life.

"That can't be," said Dobrenky. "You didn't live in the world to no purpose, you must have done some good. You must have helped somebody some time, lent a hand, pulled somebody out of the water or from a fire, or given someone the shirt off your back?"

Chonkin thought. He didn't recall anything about fire or water, and as for his shirt, who would have even wanted it?

"No," he said with a sigh, "nothing like that happened."

"All right. But since you did nothing, that's one good thing in itself. Besides, as a person unjustly sentenced, you can have everything you lacked or desired greatly in life. What do you want?"

"Nothing," said Chonkin.

"What do you mean, nothing? Every person wants something. Perhaps it's fame you want?"

"No."

"Power over other people?"

"No."

"Then what? Perhaps just to live it up? To have lots of money, women, vodka?"

"No."

"Then perhaps a quiet family life? Perhaps to live with Nyura?"

"No." Chonkin shook his head. "I don't want anything."

At that moment thunder rumbled and he woke up.

At first he could not fathom where he was and what was happening, but then he realized he was in his cell, alive, a fact which grieved him enormously.

Desires had awoken in his now rested body. He felt like sleeping a little more, taking a leak, having a bite to eat, scratching his shoulder blade and, what was most unpleasant in his situation, he felt like living.

It thundered again outside, shaking him in his bed; he moved his head and through his tears he saw the lamplight swaying above the edge of the upper bunks.

It thundered again and again; cursing fiercely, his boots pounding, someone ran past in the corridor.

Then came a series of explosions, as if someone were outside smashing the walls with a heavy hammer. Chonkin realized that it was cannon fire, and not that far away either. He didn't wonder who was shooting, at whom or why, but for some reason, he felt those cannons promised him salvation.

But then he started worrying that a shell would land on the prison and bury him alive. However, the firing ceased abruptly and the cell grew quiet.

Wiping away his tears, he let himself down from his bunk, walked over to the door, and listened intently. It was quiet in the corridor, no voices, no footsteps, no rattling of keys.

Having taken a leak in the pot, Chonkin was about to return to his bunk, but then changed his mind and began wandering around the cell. For the first time he was able to examine it in detail, he hadn't been up to it before. Now he saw that all the cell's walls were speckled with graffiti—curses, threats, sayings, verses, declarations of love, regrets for wasted years. To the right of the door a laconic inscription had been scratched into the wall with something sharp, probably a nail: *Inspector Maslov was here.*

There was all sorts of nonsense as well—a column of figures, a very simple drawing easy to understand, senseless curses, a recipe complete with all ingredients from mutton to salt and spices, the phrase "Lived sinning, died grinning," more curses, followed by a line that ran over to the next wall in the bold handwriting of that same Inspector Maslov: *And yet it turns!* (what, why, and where were not indicated).

Going from wall to wall, Chonkin read everything written on them and then he, too, felt like leaving something in the same spirit, something edifying for posterity. He knocked a small piece of wood off a bunk and walked over to the wall. But the wall was already so thickly covered with writing that all he could have done was squeeze a few words in edgewise. Then he had a brainstorm. He dragged the pot over to the wall, stood on the edge of it, so that he could write above all the rest. And, since he had risen above all the others, he should write something extraordinary, something so . . . But nothing of that sort came into his head, and risking falling over, pot and all, he wrote a single word: *Chonkin.* It was just his last name, but still, it was above all the others. Satisfied, he hopped down from the pot, walked back toward the bunks, glanced up, and was dumbfounded. His name was high, a good inch higher than anything else, but still higher, on the very ceiling, another name had been written in a semicircle. A certain Kuzyakov or Puzyakov, not desiring to vanish without a trace, had scribbled his name in shit, which had petrified in time. Of course that it was written in shit was not surprising (zeks will use anything to write), what was surprising was that it was on the ceiling; how did he get himself up there, he was a man, after all, not a fly. Chonkin racked his brains and eyeballed the distance every which way but, even mentally, he could not reach that Kuzyakov or Puzyakov. You couldn't stretch that far from the bunks and, from the floor, even putting one pot on top of another, the ceiling was still out of reach. It was plain that this Kuzyakov or Puzyakov had had a strong desire that at least the new generation of zeks remember the brief fact that a man with that unlovely name had lived in this world.

A key gnashed in the lock snapping Chonkin from his idle thoughts. The door opened and Svintsov appeared in the doorway, heavily armed. There was a Nagant revolver in a canvas holster at his side and he was holding a rifle in his hands.

"Out!" said Svintsov to Chonkin with a jerk of his head.

The firing squad, thought Chonkin, sensing doom, but just in case, he asked, "Can I take my coat?"

He reasoned that if there was to be a firing squad he would not be allowed to take his coat. Why riddle a good coat for no good reason?

"Take it," said Svintsov.

He also took his knapsack. If they weren't going to shoot him, it might come in handy.

There was a wagon hitched to an undersized bay waiting in the prison yard. The wagon had been strewn with hay. Svintsov prodded the hay, plunging his rifle in and out, then nodded to Chonkin: "Climb up!"

Chonkin obeyed, found himself a spot toward the back, then sat down cross-legged, like an Asian.

Svintsov took a seat on the box, fidgeted a bit trying to find a more comfortable position, undid the reins, and flicked the horse. The horse winced and then started walking lazily. The wagon began squeaking, the wheels clattered on the cobblestones and rolled out to the street through the unguarded gate.

In no time they had ridden out of town.

After the third village a dismal yellow steppe began, walled off in the distance by a faded forest.

"Hey, you!" Svintsov turned around. "Not chilly back there?"

"No," said Chonkin, "it's fine." He was sitting hunched over, his hands pulled up into his sleeves.

"Take a little run, it'll warm you up," suggested Svintsov.

"Don't feel like it."

"What do you mean? Look how cold you are, even your nose's turned blue. Run a little, I'm telling you. Otherwise you'll be dead as a doornail by the time we get where we're going."

Chonkin wanted to ask where it was they were going but said nothing. Svintsov, trying to draw him in by his own example, jumped to the ground and started running beside the wagon, slapping his sides.

"Oh, that's good, that's really great!" he exclaimed. "You can feel the blood start circulating right away. Oh, that's good."

But Chonkin did not reply, he didn't even look at Svintsov, who, realizing the futility of his efforts, hopped back onto the wagon on the run, puffing and panting angrily.

They were already approaching the forest when a familiar sound reached Chonkin's ear. At first he paid no attention, but then he bestirred himself and stood, gazing upward, turning his head. He saw a small dot on the distant horizon. The dot was making the sound. An airplane! gasped Chonkin inwardly. But he at once reined himself in, remembering how he had once mistaken a mosquito for an airplane. Now he believed neither his eyes nor his forebodings. He closed his eyes. But the sound continued . . .

Chonkin opened his eyes and saw a real airplane; there could no longer be any doubt.

"An airplane!" cried Chonkin, poking Svintsov in the back with his fist.

"It's an airplane, so what?" said Svintsov. "You never saw one before?"

"You dope!" shouted Chonkin. "What's wrong with that stupid head of yours! It's for me, don't you know!"

"Oh, sure." Svintsov grinned in disbelief.

"I'll show you. Hey, hey!" Chonkin sprang to his feet, tore off his field cap, and began waving it, inviting the pilot to come closer. "Hey, you!" he shouted, jumping up and down in the jolting wagon, not concerned about falling out. "Over here! Here I am, it's me here!"

As if in response to Chonkin's appeal, the plane swung sharply and reduced its altitude.

"Come on!" cried Chonkin, waving his field cap. "Land! Land on the road!"

In Chonkin's mind everything seemed to happen disjointedly. First he saw the road pucker, like when you skip small stones across the water. Then he heard the machine guns firing. The plane banked sharply upward with a terrible howl right over Chonkin's head, and it was then that he had a clear view of the black crosses on the wings. Chonkin did not have time to be surprised, because just then the horse lurched into a dash. Losing his balance, Chonkin fell off the wagon.

He lay on the ground a while thinking he had been killed. The airplane passed over him again. Chonkin bunched himself up. He felt too huge, too huge a spot on the dusty road. He realized that he should hide, even if it was just behind the roadside bushes, but he did not have the strength. Finally, he rose and saw the plane above him for a third time. Clearly the pilot had not expected Chonkin to get up. He fired a burst but it was too late, the bullets puckered the road far ahead.

"So there!" shouted Chonkin, jumping to his feet, twirling a finger by the side of his head. "You screwball!"

No doubt this hurt the pilot's pride. But, by the time he had executed a battle turn, Chonkin was already dashing full speed for the safety of the nearby forest. The roar of the motor approached again. The wings with their crosses flashed overhead, but this time the pilot could not spot Chonkin. Taking no chances, he fired a last pointless burst through the treetops.

70

Waiting until it was clear that the plane would not return, Chonkin tore himself from the pine tree and moved on. He walked straight ahead, not knowing where he was going or what his purpose was, for the first time ever having consciously violated his responsibilities as a soldier and a prisoner, evading fate for the first time as well.

Passing through a bog and thorny bushes, he arrived at a small clearing. A large rotten tree whose branches had been chopped off lay in the middle of the clearing.

Chonkin looked around. Everything was peaceful and quiet. An undaunted woodpecker was pecking at the crown of a half-withered pine and somewhere a cuckoo was singing in autumnal melancholy.

Chonkin sat down on the trunk of the rotted tree, rewound one puttee, and started on the other. Suddenly the bushes started rustling and crackling.

A bear! thought Chonkin, fear-struck, and boot in hand, he sprang to his feet.

The bushes parted and Svintsov appeared in the clearing, his cheek cut, holding his rifle and Chonkin's empty knapsack. He approached Chonkin glowering. Retreating behind a tree, Chonkin tossed his puttee aside to free his hand, then switched his boot from his left hand to his right. A boot is no grenade, of course, and not much of a weapon against a rifle, but if you hit a man square in the head . . .

"Here, take it!" said Svintsov, tossing Chonkin the rifle as if they were doing a drill.

Chonkin succeeded in dropping the boot and grabbing hold of the rifle, though not without hurting his thumb.

"Take this too!" The empty knapsack landed lightly at his feet.

Svintsov sat down on the tree, and touching the scratch on

his cheek with a crooked finger, he offered a brief explanation of his behavior.

"I made up my mind to escape from them." Then, with a crooked grin, he added, "I'm fed up."

It was somehow strange, miraculous, too much to understand. Thinking about what had just happened, Chonkin retrieved his puttee and sat down a little way from Svintsov. One end was quite wet but the other was all right. He wrung out the wet end, then began to swaddle his foot with the dry end.

"You'll give us away," said Svintsov, twisting his nose.

"What?" said Chonkin.

"Wind them faster, you hear, otherwise they'll be sniffing us out here."

"Aha," said Chonkin and, taking Svintsov seriously, began to hurry.

The puttee wound, he put on his boot and regarded it with a critical eye—it wouldn't last much longer.

Svintsov pulled out his cigarettes and offered one to Chonkin, who accepted it cautiously, still fearing some dirty trick.

They lit up.

"Well," said Svintsov, after a moment's silence, "should we go on together or split up?"

"Where can we go?" said Chonkin sadly.

"Where?" repeated Svintsov. "We can wander the forests. We'll go in deep, build ourselves a lean-to out of hay and live free like wild animals. What do you think of that?" Svintsov tossed back his head. "We've got guns, we've got ammo, we can shoot game, we'll dry mushrooms and berries, we can make stewed fruit. You like stewed fruit?"

"Stewed fruit?" Chonkin looked over at Svintsov as if he were mad. "What next?" he turned his head. "Stewed fruit, he says, for stewed fruit you need sugar."

"Sugar gives you toothaches," retorted Svintsov with a grin. "And of course we've got to stock up on salt and tobacco, matches too. No problem. We can trek over to Krasnoye and have a look around. If all's quiet, you can run over to Nyura's and get what we'll need for a start. So you'll have a little fun with her, after all. I don't advise you to stay there though. They'll grab you. Agreed?"

Chonkin hadn't given it any thought yet, but to be with Nyura, if only for a short while, was something he truly desired.

Evening was falling when they arrived at Krasnoye.

Leaving the rifle with Svintsov, Chonkin walked from the forest carrying his empty knapsack. Going part of the way along the banks of the Tyopa, he then climbed up to a spot where a few isolated barns stood. He hid behind them for quite some time, but he couldn't see a damn thing from there.

He ran down to Nyura's hut and knocked on the door. It was locked. He was about to start looking for the key under the floorboards when he heard distant voices. Peering into the twilight, he saw that the villagers had again gathered by the office and there was a dust-covered vehicle parked in the road.

Not another meeting, thought Chonkin and, driven by dangerous curiosity, he moved first to the fence, then to Gladishev's hut, and, then, in a quick bound, to the car and from there to the office.

The people were standing packed closely together. Chonkin rose on tiptoe, thrusting his chin forward. His mouth fell open.

On the office porch a tall, thin German in a black uniform and glasses was waving his arms and shouting: "Peasants! The victorious German army has come to your aid and has liberated you forever from Bolshevik rule. You won't be robbed by Jews and commissars anymore. The German high command hopes that you will welcome your liberators with gratitude and voluntarily surrender your surplus food supplies to our representatives."

Legs planted far apart, wearing his broad-brimmed straw

hat, Kuzma Gladishev was standing out in front of everyone.

"That's right!" he kept repeating at the proper moments, clapping his hands.

Chonkin backed away to the car and then, unseen by anyone, quickly left the village.